PENGUIN CLASSICS

THE MARQUISE OF O—

AND OTHER STORIES

HEINRICH VON KLEIST, born in 1777, came of an old Prussian military family but disliked military life and resigned his commission in 1799 to devote himself to studious pursuits. He turned to creative writing after undergoing an intellectual and personal crisis in 1801, and during the next ten years produced some of the most remarkable plays in German literature (notably the comedies *Amphitryon* and *Der zerbrochene Krug*, the tragedy *Penthesilea* and the problem drama *Prinz Friedrich von Homburg*) as well as eight masterly short stories and various minor writings.

Kleist had an unstable and almost schizophrenic personality; he was intensely ambitious yet unsure of his gifts. His works reflect his passionately uncompromising nature and his periodic fits of wild enthusiasm and morose melancholia. Episodes of great lyrical beauty alternate with scenes of the most frenzied brutality, and the highly emotional style predominating in his plays is often replaced in the stories by one of clinical detachment. Kleist committed suicide in 1811.

DAVID LUKE was born in 1921 and is an Emeritus Student (Emeritus Fellow) of Christ Church, Oxford, where he was Tutor in German until 1988. He has published articles and essays on German literature, and various prose and verse translations, including Stifter's *Limestone and Other Stories*, *Selected Tales* by the brothers Grimm, *Death in Venice and Other Stories* by Thomas Mann, and Goethe's *Selected Verse*, Parts One and Two of *Faust*, a volume of his erotic poetry, *Iphigenia in Tauris* and *Hermann and Dorothea*. His translation of *Faust* Part One was awarded the European Poetry Translation Prize in 1989.

NIGEL REEVES was born in 1939 and graduated at Worcester College, Oxford, in 1963, taking his D.Phil. in 1970. He was an Alexander von Humboldt Fellow at the University of Tübingen and from 1975 to 1990 was Professor of German at the University of Surrey. Since 1990 he has been Professor of German at Aston University and was Head of the Department of Languages and European Studies from 1990 to 1996. He has translated stories by Kleist and Keller for the *Penguin Book of German Stories* and has published monographs on Heinrich Heine and Friedrich Schiller.

HEINRICH VON KLEIST

The Marquise of O—

AND OTHER STORIES

Translated with an Introduction by
DAVID LUKE AND NIGEL REEVES

PENGUIN BOOKS

PENGUIN BOOKS

Published by the Penguin Group
Penguin Books Ltd, 80 Strand, London WC2R ORL, England
Penguin Group (USA) Inc., 375 Hudson Street, New York, New York 10014, USA
Penguin Books Australia Ltd, 250 Camberwell Road, Camberwell, Victoria 3124, Australia
Penguin Books Canada Ltd, 10 Alcorn Avenue, Toronto, Ontario, Canada M4V 3B2
Penguin Books India (P) Ltd, 11 Community Centre, Panchsheel Park, New Delhi – 110 017, India
Penguin Books (NZ) Ltd, Cnr Rosedale and Airborne Roads, Albany, Auckland, New Zealand
Penguin Books (South Africa) (Pty) Ltd, 24 Sturdee Avenue, Rosebank 2196, South Africa

Penguin Books Ltd, Registered Offices: 80 Strand, London WC2R ORL, England

www.penguin.com

This translation first published 1978
Reprinted with a new Chronology and Further Reading 2004

33

Translation and Introduction copyright © David Luke and Nigel Reeves, 1978
Chronology and Further Reading copyright © David Deißner, 2004
All rights reserved

Printed in England by Clays Ltd, St Ives plc
Filmset in Linotype Pilgrim

ISBN-13: 978-0-140-44359-2

www.greenpenguin.co.uk

Penguin Books is committed to a sustainable future
for our business, our readers and our planet.
The book in your hands is made from paper
certified by the Forest Stewardship Council.

Contents

Introduction

IN the spring of 1799 the 21-year-old Heinrich von Kleist wrote to his half-sister Ulrike that he found it 'incomprehensible how a human being can live without a plan for his life (*Lebensplan*); the sense of security with which I employ my present time and the calm with which I look to the future make me profoundly aware of just what inestimable happiness my life-plan assures me'. But fear evidently lay behind this confidence, and indeed behind the very notion of a 'life-plan', for he continued: 'Existing without a life-plan, without any firm purpose, constantly wavering between uncertain desires, constantly at variance with my duties, the plaything of chance, a puppet on the strings of fate – such an unworthy situation seems so contemptible to me and would make me so wretched that death would be preferable by far.' Less than thirteen years later Kleist wrote to Ulrike that there was no remedy for him on earth, and within hours of his completing this letter two shots rang out from beside the Wannsee near Berlin. In a suicide pact for which he had long sought a willing partner Kleist had first shot dead Henriette Vogel, a 31-year-old woman suffering from incurable cancer, and had then blown out his own brains. During those thirteen years Kleist had written plays and stories of a kind quite unprecedented in German literature. The special interest of his best work, its peculiar inner tension, lies in its negative expression of the ideals of the Enlightenment at the very point of their collapse as he personally experienced it. A typical intellectual product of the late eighteenth century, Kleist had started from certain unquestioned assumptions: that life can be planned, that its random element can be eliminated, that happiness can

7

be achieved and assured if we go about it the right way, that man is educable and society perfectible, that the world is rationally ordered and that all things in principle can, and in due course will, be completely understood and explained. His creative writings expressed the state of mind that follows upon the loss of every article of this faith. They radically called in question the idealistic humanism which still inspired the mature works of Goethe and Schiller, the representative masterpieces of Weimar Classicism. Among his contemporaries Kleist met with little or no positive response. Goethe took a patronizing interest in him for a time, then snubbed and dropped him, writing him off as a pathological case, quite failing to recognize his genius and evidently sensing in him a threat to his own precariously-won Olympian balance. And yet it is precisely Kleist's vulnerability and disequilibrium, his desperate challenge to established values and beliefs, that carry him further than Goethe or Schiller across the gap between the eighteenth century and our own age.

Bernd Heinrich Wilhelm von Kleist was born in Frankfurt an der Oder on 18 October 1777, the son of Joachim Friedrich von Kleist, a captain in the Prussian army, and his second wife Juliane Ulrike. The family belongs to the ancient nobility (*Uradel*) and has innumerable ramifications. Heinrich's father died when he was only eleven, and his mother, though eighteen years younger than her husband, when he was fifteen. He was educated privately in Berlin by a Protestant minister and entered army service shortly before his mother's death. This was a natural step since the family was, and continued to be, renowned in Prussian military circles. He soon experienced action during the Rhineland campaign against the armies of revolutionary France. But his heart lay elsewhere: he loved music, was a talented clarinettist, and studied mathematics with enthusiasm. Convinced that the maximization of his personal happiness was not only possible but his duty as a rational man, and that this goal could not be reached under the oppressive and dehumanizing discipline of the Prussian army, he resigned his commission in 1799 and embarked on what was to be a planless, uncertain, unstable life, never achieving a career or even holding a firm post, estranged from all but a very few members of his family, travelling restlessly about a Europe racked by the Napoleonic Wars. For a time he studied physics, mathematics, history and Latin at the University of Frankfurt an der Oder. In 1800, on little more than an impulse, he entered into a 'suitable' conventional engagement with the daughter of the local garrison commandant, Wilhelmine von Zenge, but set off the same year on a journey through Leipzig and Dresden, ending in Würzburg where he underwent some kind of unspecified medical or surgical treatment which would make him, as he enigmatically wrote to her, 'worthy' of his fiancée. (This obscure episode has never been clarified; in any case Kleist later broke off the engagement to Wilhelmine with callous abruptness, and a certain amount of mystery surrounds his sexual life in general.) A further attempt to settle down in state service, this time in a civilian capacity, lasted only a few months. Early in 1801 the conflict between his basic psychological instability and his frenzied longing for security broke out in the form of a crucial intellectual experience. The rationalistic and optimistic beliefs which he had imbibed from Wieland and other fashionable writers reflecting the spirit of the European and German Enlightenment were shattered by his reading of Kant. 'Lately,' he wrote to Wilhelmine in March 1801, 'I became acquainted with the recent so-called Kantian philosophy.' What exactly he had read is not certain, but it was the Kantian epistemological theory that seems above all to have disturbed him. Kant had demarcated the limits of human knowledge not in order to undermine confidence in man's rational faculty or strengthen the case for atheism: on the contrary he had intended to clarify the true foundations for religious belief, to show what was properly beyond empirical exploration and therefore a matter of faith, not of knowledge. But Kant's distinction between the unknowability of things in themselves as *noumena* and our cognitive operations with things as they appear (*phenomena*) seemed to Kleist to make a mockery of the ideal of self-cultivation, of man's progress towards the complete possession of truth. If Kant was right, then appearance and reality, Kleist thought, were for ever confounded, nothing was predictable, there was no ascertainable single right answer or right way; human nature, our own selves, were a riddle, everything that had seemed straightforward became ambiguous and baffling. To Wilhelmine he wrote: '... we cannot determine whether what we call truth really is truth, or merely seems so to us'; and to Ulrike: 'The thought that here on earth we know nothing of the truth, absolutely nothing ... has shaken me in the very sanctuary of my soul – my *only* purpose, my *supreme* purpose has collapsed; I have none left.' Yet it was precisely this breakdown of all his hopes, this very personal crisis of intellectual despair, that turned him into a creative writer.

In the years that followed Kleist travelled through Germany, lived for a while in Switzerland where he entertained Rousseauistic ideas of settling down on the land as a simple peasant, and even tried to join the French army in the hope of being killed during Napoleon's planned invasion of England. Meanwhile his first play, *The Schroffenstein Family*, a grotesque tragedy of errors thematically indebted to *Romeo and Juliet*, had appeared anonymously in February 1803, and he had begun work on *The Broken Pitcher*, one of the few really successful German comedies. In 1803 he also wrote at least part of a grandly conceived second tragedy, *Robert Guiscard*, but burned the manuscript in a fit of discouragement. In 1805 a second attempt to join the Prussian civil service failed after a few months of preparatory studies. In January 1807 he was arrested by the French on suspicion of being a spy when trying to enter occupied Berlin without a passport, and spent nearly six months in a French prison. Here he wrote much of one of his finest works, the tragedy *Penthesilea* – stark, strange and ecstatic, breaking utterly with the established classicistic conception of Greek serenity and balance, and recapturing instead the Dionysian savagery of Euripides' *Bacchae* which in part inspired this play. In Kleist's version of the story of the tragic passion of the warrior Amazon queen for Achilles, love is shown to be ambiguously allied with hatred, a relentless elemental drive in which tenderness and the lust to destroy and devour are profoundly fused.

During his imprisonment Kleist's friend Rühle von Lilienstern had found a publisher for his comedy or tragi-comedy *Amphitryon*, perhaps the subtlest of all the many dramatic treatments of this ancient tale, partly based on Molière's version but reducing the latter, by comparison, to the level of elegant and unimportant farce. Then, upon his return from France, as if from the dead, his first completed short story, *The Earthquake in Chile*, appeared in a periodical under the title of *Jerónimo and Josefa*. In Dresden Kleist now founded a journal of his own in collaboration with the philosopher Adam Müller: they called it *Phoebus* and published in it *The Broken Pitcher*, *The Marquise of O—*, excerpts from *Penthesilea* and part of *Michael Kohlhaas*. But the venture was a financial failure and ended in a bitter quarrel between the two editors. Nor was the performance of *The Broken Pitcher* at the Weimar court theatre, under Goethe's auspices, any more successful: Goethe's production of it was a travesty and precipitated his final breach with Kleist. In 1809 it seemed possible that at least the disastrous political situation would improve and that Austria would be able to stem the tide of Napoleonic conquest. Since the crushing defeat of Prussia at Jena in 1806, Kleist had increasingly turned to fanatical patriotic fervour as a source of literary inspiration and for a sense of purpose in life;

he wrote a number of political poems and tracts and notably, in 1808, *The Battle with Hermann* (*Die Hermannsschlacht*), a gruesome dramatic celebration of the Teutonic chieftain's victory over the Roman legions in A.D. 9. But in July 1809 Austria was decisively defeated at Wagram; after visiting the scene of part of the campaign Kleist fled to the safety of Prague, where he fell seriously ill. After his recovery he returned to Berlin, and 1810 was perhaps the year of his greatest recognition as a writer during his lifetime. *Kätchen of Heilbronn*, a play designed to gratify the current popular taste for Gothick romance and chivalry, was performed in Vienna, and the first volume of his collected stories appeared, containing *Michael Kohlhaas*, *The Marquise of O—* and *The Earthquake in Chile*. At the same time Kleist became founder-editor of one of Germany's first daily newspapers, the *Berliner Abendblätter*, which began very promisingly in October and in which he published two more of his stories, *The Beggarwoman of Locarno* and *St Cecilia*. These, together with *The Betrothal in Santo Domingo* (which had already been printed in another periodical), *The Foundling* and *The Duel*, then made up the second volume of collected stories which followed in 1811.

But Kleist's relatively good fortune did not last. The initial popularity of the *Abendblätter* had been due much less to his own literary contributions than to articles on current affairs and above all, of course, to the sensational crime reports which during the first weeks were supplied to Kleist by the city chief of police. The government was embarrassed by some of the political comments and ordered strict censorship of the paper; its sales declined sharply and it closed down in March 1811, leaving Kleist in desperate financial straits. The small unofficial pension he had enjoyed from Queen Luise had ceased with her death, his own private means were long since exhausted, and his applications to rejoin the civil service or the army met, not surprisingly, with a cool reception. His most mature and balanced, yet still deeply enigmatic play, *Prince Friedrich of Homburg*, was completed in September 1811 and dedicated to Princess Amalie Marie Anne, wife of Prince William of Prussia, the King's brother. But this work, though thoroughly patriotic in sentiment, found no favour with the royal family. Kleist's psychological realism, already shockingly manifested in *Penthesilea*, had led him to include in it a scene in which the young hero, unlike any proper hero, Prussian officer or gentleman, collapses into elemental panic at the prospect of his imminent execution and begs for his life at any price, like Claudio in Shakespeare's *Measure for Measure*. This breach of convention was found intolerable and the play was not published until ten years after Kleist's death, which followed soon after. The suicide pact with Henriette Vogel was executed on 22 November 1811, and on 28 December *The Times* carried the following report:

The attention of the people of Berlin has lately been very much occupied by the tragical adventure of M. Kleist, the celebrated Prussian poet, and Madame Vogel. The reports which were at first circulated with regard to the cause of this unfortunate affair, have been strongly contradicted by the family of the lady; and it has been particularly denied that love was in any respect the cause of it. Madame Vogel, it is said, had suffered long under an incurable disorder; her physicians had declared her death inevitable; she herself formed a resolution to put a period to her existence. M. Kleist, the poet, and a friend of her family, had also long determined to kill himself. These two unhappy beings having confidentially communicated to each other their horrible resolution, resolved to carry it into effect at the same time. They repaired to the Inn at Wilhelmstadt, between Berlin and Potsdam, on the border of the *Sacred Lake* [sic]. For one night and one day they were preparing themselves for death, by putting up prayers, singing, *drinking a number of bottles of wine and rum*, and last of all by taking about sixteen cups of coffee. They wrote a letter to M. Vogel, to announce to him the resolution they had taken, and to beg him to come as speedily as possible, for the purpose of seeing their remains interred. The letter was sent to Berlin by express. This done, they repaired to the banks of the *Sacred Lake*, where they sat down opposite each other. M. Kleist took a loaded pistol, and shot Madame Vogel through the heart, who fell back dead; he then re-loaded the pistol, and shot himself through the head. Soon after M. Vogel arrived, and found them both dead. The public are far from admiring, or even of approving, this act of insanity. An apology for this suicide, by M. Peghuilhen, Counsellor at War, has excited unanimously indignation among all who have the principles either of religion or morality ...

The eight canonical stories, those published in the two-volume book edition of 1810–11, vary in length from the two or three pages of *The Beggarwoman of Locarno* to *Michael Kohlhaas*, which has the dimensions of a short novel. Kleist also filled up the pages of the *Berliner Abendblätter* with some miscellaneous anecdotes of lesser importance; in addition there is some reason to believe that he did in fact write a full-length novel (as he states in a letter of July 1811) though this has never come to light. It may have been destroyed by Kleist himself, or suppressed by his family with other revealing personal papers which were rumoured to be still secretly extant in this century but were finally lost during the Second World War. The present edition of the stories departs slightly from Kleist's own arrangement of them in the book edition, since it aims to approximate to the chronological order of their composition, or partial composition, so far as this is known. As we have noted, most of them first appeared in one or another short-lived periodical, exceptions being *The Foundling* and *The Duel* which were published in the book edition for the first time. the text of *St Cecilia or The Power of Music* in the same volume is an extended and improved version of the original story which had come out earlier. The preliminary fragment of *Michael Kohlhaas*, probably conceived in 1805, and printed in the November 1808 number of *Phoebus*, ran to only a quarter of its final length. Apart from this more complicated case there seems to be no good reason for assigning to any of the stories a date of composition in whole or in part significantly earlier than that of their first publication. On this basis, the first (or first completed) stories were *The Earthquake in Chile* and *The Marquise of O——*. The former was probably written in 1806 or early in 1807, appearing in September of that year in Cotta's *Morgenblatt*; the latter, on which Kleist was probably working during his imprisonment in France, appeared in *Phoebus* in February 1808.

These two stories make an interesting stylistic contrast, although they might both be said to deal with a basically similar theme which is also that of the other stories and of most of the plays. Virtually all his important work reveals Kleist's epistemological obsession, his preoccupation with the tragic or potentially tragic deceptiveness of appearances in the world and in human nature. He constantly presents situations and characters which are disturbingly paradoxical and intractable to rational analysis; they point towards the 'absurdity' of life, as Albert Camus was to call it nearly a century and a half later, and it is therefore not surprising that in his treatment of them he can range between the tragic and the comic modes.

The Earthquake in Chile, in some ways the most remarkable of all the stories, is starkly tragic and raises, by implication at least, the deepest theological and existential questions, leaving them of course unanswered. It is constructed with consummate artistry and also serves as a particularly good example of the laconic self-effacement which is Kleist's typical stance as a narrator. In general his method is to abstain from comment on the events he chronicles, and indeed from almost any kind of explicit communication with the reader; where value-judgements occur in the course of the narrative they can usually be seen to be incidental and relative, arising from a kind of momentary dramatic identification with the particular character in an immediate situation, rather than representing the author-narrator's overall viewpoint. Kleist here simply puts before us a sequence of events, based on the historical fact of an earthquake which destroyed Santiago on 13 May 1647; he had some knowledge of the details of this disaster, though it is not clear from what source. But uppermost in his mind must have been the famous earthquake of 1755 which not only shattered Lisbon but severely shook the optimistic theodicy of the Enlightenment. His story about the Chilean earthquake offers no explanation of why it has occurred, or rather it suggests a number of different possible explanations which cancel each other out. We are left with the impression that the author is no better placed to interpret his story to us than the reader or even the characters themselves. This 'deadpan' narrative effect is one of the factors that give Kleist's work a more modern flavour than that of most of his contemporaries, and has led to its being compared with that of Kafka, who, it is known, greatly admired his stories.

Strictly speaking, Kleist does not maintain a wholly neutral attitude in his story of Jerónimo and Josefa but seems to invite our sympathy for the lovers and compassion for their fate. The paradoxes nevertheless remain. A young girl, forced into a convent against her will, cannot renounce her lover, becomes pregnant by him, and eventually collapses in labour pains on the steps of the cathedral during a solemn festival. She is condemned to death for fornication and sacrilege, and an enormous crowd makes elaborate preparations, in a spirit of sanctimonious vindictiveness, to watch her execution. A matter of minutes before what they describe as divine justice can take its course, Josefa's life is spared by the earthquake, which at the same time kills thousands of other innocent people. The earthquake also saves her imprisoned lover Jerónimo only seconds before he is about to hang himself in despair, shattering the walls of his prison and terrifying him into a renewed desire for mere physical survival. It destroys both the just and the unjust, those who like the Abbess have been merciful to the young couple and those who have condemned them. The common disaster brings out in human nature both the best – heroic courage and self-sacrifice, mutual help and compassion, and the worst – the frenzied search for a scapegoat and the religious zeal that serves as a pretext for sickening cruelty. In the central section of the story the lovers are reunited, along with other survivors, in the countryside outside the stricken city, and in this idyllic interlude, the eye of the storm as it were, hope temporarily revives – the fabric of corrupt civilization has collapsed and what Rousseau regarded as the natural goodness of mankind has apparently been restored. But in the conclusion, with dreadful irony, Jerónimo and Josefa perish after all: returning to the only church in the city left standing to give thanks to God for their deliverance, they hear their sin denounced from the pulpit and are then recognized and lynched by a fanatical mob, only their child surviving when the wrong baby has been savagely killed instead. If the earthquake has been an 'act of God', then human reason can make very little of God's deeds, unless on the hypothesis that he is an omnipotent and highly sophisticated devil. In two letters written in 1806 Kleist expresses the hope that, contrary to evidence, the world is not governed by an evil spirit, but simply by one who is not understood. At least *The Earthquake in Chile* renders impossible any theodicy to which the concepts of mystery and paradox are not central. The world as experienced here by human beings is theologically ambiguous, as is the world of real life; in this sense the story is radically truthful. It is no accident that it presents the church and the clergy in so unfavourable a light; at this level of questioning, the answers offered by conventional and institutional religion cannot avail.

The Marquise of O— operates in a very different literary

vein. The mystery with which it deals is domestic and psychological rather than cosmic. In it Kleist refers to what he was fond of calling *die gebrechliche Einrichtung der Welt*, the faulty or imperfect or unstable structure or ordering of the world, the flaw in the scheme of things : but here he modulates this concept in a non-tragic direction. *Gebrechlich* strictly means 'fragile', which the earth's crust in *The Earthquake in Chile* literally is. In the *Marquise of O—*, the phrase *gebrechliche Einrichtung der Welt* occurs at the end, when the world's 'inherent imperfection' is invoked as a reason for the conciliatory conclusion of the story (p. 113); but at another crucial point (p. 93) a significant variant of the idea is offered : the heroine thinks of the 'order of the world' as not only 'inexplicable' (*unerklärlich*) but also 'great and sacred' (*gross und heilig*), and we are told that she 'wholly submits' to it, intellectually at least. She has still to learn the full facts of her particular situation, and to face her own feelings; when this more personal acceptance is in due course achieved the story reaches its foreseeably happy ending. It would be a mistake to take either the story or its ending too solemnly : as in the case of *Amphitryon*, Kleist's treatment hovers ambiguously between the serious and the comic. The contemporary setting of *The Marquise of O—* and the relative realism of its numerous and extensive dialogues (especially those in direct speech – an untypical feature) are consistent with an at least partly humorous intention; the style is pitched in an altogether lower key than that of most of the other stories. Although it must be conceded that the Marquise has in a certain sense been raped and that rape is not an unserious matter, it is worth noting that at no point is she threatened with anything more grave than a certain amount of social scandal and at worst a breach with her aristocratic family, of whom she is in any case financially independent. The basic idea – and here again *Amphitryon* is a parallel – has a long, ribald ancestry. Like that of rape by impersonation (Jupiter–Amphitryon–

Alcmene) the theme of a woman made pregnant without her knowledge (while asleep or drunk or in a swoon) has wide currency in world literature and occurs for example in the following anecdote from Montaigne's essay *Of Drunkennesse* (here quoted in Florio's translation):

A widdow Country-woman, reputed very chaste and honest, suspecting herself to be with childe, told her neighbours, that had she a husband, she should verily thinke she were with childe. But the occasion of this suspition encreasing more and more, and perceiving herselfe so big-bellied, that she could no longer conceale it, she resolved to make the Parish-priest acquainted with it, whom she entreated to publish in the Church, that whosoever hee were, that was guilty of the fact, and would avow it, she would freely forgive him, and if he were so pleased, take him to her husband. A certaine swaine or hyne-boy of hers, emboldned by this proclamation, declared, how that having one holliday found her well-tippled with wine, and so sound asleep by the chimnie side, lying so fit, and ready for him, that without awaking her he had the full use of her body. Whom she accepted for her husband, and both live together at this day.

Kleist may well have read this pleasing little tale in France where he probably wrote *The Marquise of O—*; he himself claimed (in a note appended to the table of contents in the periodical where it first appeared) that his story was founded on fact, on events which he had fictionally transposed 'from the north to the south', i.e. to Italy, presumably from Germany. What matters, however, is that Kleist as narrator of course knows from the outset who is responsible for this virtuous young widow's condition *intéressante*, and that from an early point in the story he allows the reader to share this knowledge. Like several of his works (*The Duel* among the stories and *The Broken Pitcher* and *Amphitryon* among the plays), *The Marquise of O—* has something of the character of a detective-story, a 'who-dunnit', thus betokening yet again his preoccupation with the problem of truth. All

these four works revolve entirely around the seeming misconduct of a virtuous young woman. *The Broken Pitcher*
is scarcely more than a straightforward farce in which the
accidental breaking of a valuable ornamental jug is ingeni-
ously made to symbolize the suspected loss of a simple
young girl's virginity, and the fat rogue of a village judge
is involved in the ludicrous situation of trying a case in
which he knows he is himself the culprit. *Amphitryon* ends
satisfactorily with the vindication of the heroine's moral
if not technical innocence (of which the audience is of
course aware all along) and her husband's acquiescence in
the prospect of becoming the putative father of Hercules
as his reward for having unwittingly conceded the *jus
primae noctis* to Jupiter; but Kleist also emphasizes
Alcmene's confusion and anguish and subtly exploits the
theme's serious potential. His procedure in *The Marquise
of O—* is essentially similar. What has happened? During
the storming by Russian forces of a citadel commanded by
the heroine's father, she has fallen into the hands of some
ruffianly enemy troops who attempt to rape her; she is
rescued from them by the young Russian officer Count F—,
but he himself, in the heat of battle, yields to the sudden
temptation offered by her fainting-fit. Kleist at first withholds this last fact from the reader by teasingly inserting a
dash into the middle of a sentence, but we are almost at once
supplied with two clues to it: the Count's unexplained
embarrassment when asked to identify the would-be perpetrators of the outrage, and secondly his cry, as he falls
apparently mortally wounded in another battle, of 'Giulietta, this bullet avenges you' – using what we are told is
the Marquise's first name. The narrative presently refers to
her unaccountable symptoms of early pregnancy, and then
immediately to F—'s extraordinary first visit to her family's
house, when with inexplicable insistence he urged her to
marry him at once: inexplicable, that is, to the Marquise
and her relatives, but the reader by now at the latest shares

the Count's and the narrator's knowledge of the true facts. If the slowness of everyone else to grasp them, and the extraordinary consternation and fuss that follow their eventual disclosure, seem excessive to the present-day reader, he must bear in mind the standards and prejudices of North German aristocratic families such as Kleist's own – the code by which what this gentleman has done to this lady is not only unspeakable but literally unthinkable. What is not wholly clear is whether, and if so to what extent, Kleist consciously intended to put the melodramatic behaviour of Giulietta and her family in an ironic, parodistic light. If he did not, then the story does not really come off as a work of art; if he did, then it has a subtlety comparable with that of *Amphitryon*. In either case, however, it is a text of considerable psychological interest. One curious feature is Kleist's depiction of the extreme rage of the father at his daughter's supposed fall from virtue, and the more or less explicitly incestuous element in the scene of their reconciliation. The motif of a father's jealous and protective love for his daughter and her passionate devotion to him, brought into currency by Rousseau's *La Nouvelle Héloïse*, was in Kleist's time a literary topos in German drama (cf. Lessing's *Emilia Galotti*, Lenz's *The Soldiers*, H. L. Wagner's *The Infanticide*, Schiller's *Luise Miller*; post-Kleistian parallels are Hebbel's *Maria Magdalena* and Hauptmann's *Rosa Berndt*). In *The Marquise of O—* Kleist accentuates this commonplace theme, parodistically perhaps, to a point verging on the grotesque. Then there is Giulietta's dramatic polarization of her lover or assailant into 'angel' and 'devil'; this too might be dismissed as a literary cliché, but it seems to be something more. Giulietta's whole relationship to the Count is an enigma to her, which she can only gradually resolve. The Count himself is enigmatic, with a dark and irrational streak in his nature. He rescues Giulietta from his troops, only to use her himself a moment later as a prize of war – we are reminded of the paradoxical association of

love and violence in *Penthesilea*. Above all, Count F—
carries with him, as we learn in what is certainly the oddest
passage in the story (p. 82), a memory of having once as a
child, on a perverse impulse, hurled mud at a beautiful white
swan, an act of 'defilement' which he unconsciously identi-
fies with his violation of the chaste Giulietta. Emotionally
disturbed as he was, Kleist clearly had some strangely
modern insights into erotic psychology; in the final scene of
Penthesilea he had even unwittingly anticipated, by a certain choice of metaphor, Freud's theory that slips of the
tongue can express repudiated unconscious drives. Needless
to say, *The Marquise of O*— was no less incomprehensible
than *Penthesilea* to his contemporaries, who found both
works deeply shocking and offensive to good taste, or at best
ludicrous.

Michael Kohlhaas is not only by far the longest story in
the collection but also probably the best known or at least
the most discussed. As already mentioned, about one quarter
of it was first published in November 1808 in *Phoebus*; it is
not clear when that fragment was written. The story in its
general outline was founded on fact: Kleist's chief source
seems to have been an excerpt from an earlier chronicle
published in 1731 which tells how in the middle of the sixteenth century a horse-dealer named Hans (not Michael)
Kohlhaas from Kohlhaasenbrück, a village near Berlin and
just on the Brandenburg side of the frontier with Saxony,
had two of his horses wrongfully detained and ill-treated
while travelling to Dresden; how his legal action for damages
failed owing to corrupt intervention; how he then took the
law into his own hands, hired an armed band and, bent on
vengeance, pursued the Junker von Tronka, burning down
his castle and also part of Wittenberg; and how this private
war grew in scale despite an attempt by Martin Luther to
reason with Kohlhaas and persuade him to desist. The
chronicle also mentions *inter alia* the political complications, the involvement of the Elector of Brandenburg and

the eventual execution of Kohlhaas in Berlin on the Monday after Palm Sunday. The main events of the *Phoebus* fragment may be summarized as follows: Michael Kohlhaas is a prosperous and honourable man with a strongly developed sense of justice and fair dealing. It is this very passion for justice that will turn him (Kleist states this characteristic central paradox in his first paragraph) 'into a robber and a murderer', and make him 'one of the most honourable as well as one of the most terrible men of his age'. Kleist keeps to the outline of his source, but makes Kohlhaas's grievance the more poignant by having his wife, Lisbeth, die from an injury sustained when she is warded off by a bodyguard as she vainly tries to present to the Elector personally her husband's petition, hitherto suppressed by corrupt courtiers. Lisbeth's intervention is Kohlhaas's last step within the bounds of legality; he has already mortgaged his property to raise money for his resort to violence. Immediately after he has buried his wife, he assembles the first of his followers and rides off to attack Tronka Castle. The *Phoebus* fragment of 1808 breaks off at this point (page 138 of our text). The remainder was not written, or at least not finished, until the summer of 1810. In these further seventy-five pages Kleist greatly complicates the material. If he had followed the story's natural line of development and adhered more closely to his main source, he would have narrated only the following events: Kohlhaas and his men storm Tronka Castle and destroy it, but the Junker Wenzel himself manages to escape to Wittenberg. Kohlhaas now begins to issue proclamations of an increasingly paranoid character, declaring himself to be the representative of the Archangel Michael and to have formed a new 'world government', calling upon all good Christians to support his just cause against Tronka, and demanding that the latter be handed over to him for chastisement. The pay he offers, together with the prospect of further gain from plunder, naturally attracts an increasing number of followers. He sets fire to

Wittenberg three times, defeating or evading the ever more formidable military expeditions sent against him, and also attacks Leipzig, to which he thinks the Junker has been taken, although he is in fact still in Wittenberg under heavy guard. At this point Luther intervenes with a public proclamation addressed to Kohlhaas, condemning his course of action. The horse-dealer, who deeply reveres Luther, returns secretly to Wittenberg and presents himself to the theologian. Society, he argues, has set him outside the law by refusing him the law's protection; he is therefore justified and compelled to use force. His quarrel with the Junker has already cost him his wife and it is too late to stop now. Luther, as his spiritual father, urges him (as his dying wife had done) to forgive his enemy, and when Kohlhaas remains obdurate on this point, refuses him absolution. He consents, however, to negotiate on his behalf with the Elector of Saxony who, it appears, has improperly been kept in ignorance of Kohlhaas's justified legal claims. When Kohlhaas has left, Luther writes to the Elector, pointing out that the horse-dealer has in fact been wronged and virtually outlawed, and that in view of the increasingly strong public feeling on his side there is danger of a general revolt. He advises the Elector not to treat him as a rebel but to allow his case to be reopened in Dresden, granting him for this purpose a safe-conduct to the Saxon capital and an amnesty in respect of his deeds of violence. The Elector discusses this now extremely embarrassing situation with his advisers, who include Wenzel von Tronka's cousins, Hinz and Kunz, both high officials at the court, and eventually decides to issue a proclamation to Kohlhaas in the sense advised by Luther. On reading it, Kohlhaas disbands all his men in accordance with the Elector's stipulation, proceeds to Dresden and reopens his case against Junker Wenzel, applying to the court as before for his punishment, for damages and for restitution of all losses, including restoration of the horses to their former healthy condition. The Junker is released from Wittenberg and received in Dresden by his cousins, who are furious with him for making their family a laughing-stock. To make matters worse, it turns out after some investigation that the two horses are still alive but in so neglected a state that they have already been handed over to a knacker, who is ordered to bring them to Dresden. Hearing that the emaciated animals are on public display in the market square, Wenzel and Kunz von Tronka hasten to the scene; Kohlhaas is summoned to identify the horses as his, but the Tronka servants refuse to touch creatures in such a disgraceful condition and a riot breaks out. This grotesque incident turns public sentiment against the horse-dealer, and he is now willing to settle out of court for a simple payment of compensation. But chance, or rather the natural entropy of events in a corrupt human world, again operates against him, for a number of his officially dispersed followers led by a certain brutal and unscrupulous Johann Nagelschmidt (who is mentioned in Kleist's source) have started to plunder the countryside under cover of Kohlhaas's name and cause. Kohlhaas at once publicly dissociates himself from Nagelschmidt, but the Tronka family see their advantage : the amnesty is in danger of collapsing, time is on their side, and they begin to prolong the case by vexatious special pleadings. Kohlhaas notices that the number of lansquenets set to guard his house have increased and realizes that he has in effect been made a prisoner. To test this – for it is clear by now that he is obsessed by a desire to unmask official hypocrisy and politic dissimulation – he attempts to leave on a social visit but is prevented by a series of transparent pretexts. Nagelschmidt now writes to him suggesting that he should resume command of the band, and offering to engineer his escape. Unknown to Kohlhaas, this letter has been intercepted and read by the authorities. Since he now despairs of the amnesty and the whole affair, and intends to abandon his claims and emigrate, he writes back accepting Nagelschmidt's offer and thus falls into the trap which the Tronka party have persuaded the Elector to lay for him. His letter to Nagelschmidt is published in order to discredit him, he is put on trial for conspiracy, makes no defence and is condemned to death by burning and quartering. He has, however, a friend at the Electoral court in Berlin, who has now at last succeeded in bringing the whole inside story of the affair to the notice of the Elector of Brandenburg. The latter intervenes; he dismisses the corrupt official who, as a relative of the Tronka family, had prevented Kohlhaas's previous submissions from reaching him, and motivated partly by a desire to show his political strength as a potential ally of Poland, which is threatening Saxony with war, he makes the following demands: Kohlhaas, as a Brandenburg citizen, is to be transferred immediately to Berlin, where a Saxon attorney may present the case against him for his acts of violence in Saxony on which he will be tried according to Brandenburg law; and a Brandenburg attorney is to be allowed to come to Dresden to ensure that the Saxon court deals properly with Kohlhaas's own case against Wenzel von Tronka. The Saxon Elector reluctantly agrees to the extradition of the horse-dealer but decides to appeal to the Holy Roman Emperor, who is not bound by any Saxon amnesty whether broken or unbroken; the Emperor is petitioned to send a representative to Berlin who will prosecute Kohlhaas for breach of the Imperial peace. All this is done, and the Berlin court duly pronounces sentence of death by beheading on Kohlhaas. He accepts this with equanimity on hearing that his claims against Tronka are also to be met in full. At the place of execution he finds the Elector of Brandenburg waiting, together with the Imperial prosecutor and other officials; his two fine black horses, the mistreatment of which set the whole terrible train of events in motion and which run through the tale as a sort of *leitmotiv*, are presented to him fully restored to health; the Junker, he is informed, has been sentenced in Dresden to two years' imprisonment. He declares himself fully satisfied and ready in his turn to make reparation to the Emperor for having taken the law into his own hands. Thereupon he is beheaded; both sides have made their point.

This, at least, is the story as Kleist might have completed it : the story of an individual grievance developing, with fascinating and dreadful realism, through ever-increasing complexities until it becomes a major affair of state and is then brought to a paradoxical but impressively logical resolution. It is thought that the Kohlhaas chronicle was originally suggested to Kleist as the theme for a drama; it has obvious theatrical potential, and this was in fact well exploited recently by James Saunders in his brilliant stage adaptation of the story under the title *Hans Kohlhaas*, which was produced at the Questors Theatre in London in 1972 and also broadcast as a radio play (it has also been produced in Germany). Mr Saunders used the sequence of events outlined above, with no essential alteration, merely filling out some of the details and accommodating the present-day taste for Brechtian distancing effects. The result had great force and unity. Unfortunately, however, Kleist was not content to finish *Michael Kohlhaas* on those lines, but introduced a bizarre and fantastic sub-plot which seriously damages the artistic structure of an already long and complex narrative. This added material, which Mr Saunders wisely omitted, contains the episode of the gypsy-woman and her mysterious prophecy about the fate of the ruling dynasty of Saxony, which she writes on a piece of paper and gives to Kohlhaas as a kind of talisman which he can use to bargain for his life with the Saxon Elector. The latter learns at the time of the horse-dealer's extradition to Brandenburg that it is he who is in possession of this fateful secret, and desperately tries every means to have him rescued or pardoned or somehow to retrieve from him the piece of paper which Kohlhaas carries with him everywhere; but Kohlhaas goes to his death rather than surrender it. The

Elector, as he sees it, has cheated him by solemnly promising him an amnesty and then violating it in connection with the Nagelschmidt affair. Warned by the gypsy-woman, who also turns out inexplicably to be a kind of *Doppelgängerin* of his dead wife, that the Elector intends to recover the paper from his body after his execution and that for this purpose he will be standing incognito beside the scaffold, he removes it from around his neck just before putting his head on the block, tantalizingly reads it to himself in full view of the man whom he knows to be the Saxon Elector, and then swallows it so that it is lost for ever.

There are several artistic objections to this digressive subplot. For one thing, Kohlhaas's final action destroys the sense of reconciliation at the close. Despite having at last, on Luther's authority, received absolution and taken the sacrament, he dies gratifying a thirst for revenge, like Piachi in *The Foundling*. Moreover, the fact that the old gypsy-woman has furnished him with this last and only weapon of vengeance against the Elector, and generally added fuel to his vindictiveness, makes nonsense of the supposed identification of her with his deceased wife who had died begging him to forgive his enemies. It might be argued that Kleist intends all along to stress the obsessive, irrational element in Kohlhaas's nature and to suggest, especially in the final scene, a psychologically realistic obscurity in the distinction between justice and vengeance – an illustration in advance, as it were, of the truth of Nietzsche's punning aphorism to the effect that *ich bin gerecht* (I am just) really means *ich bin gerächt* (I am avenged). On the other hand it seems that Kleist was certainly motivated by an artistically extraneous desire to discredit Saxony. As we have seen, he had at about the time of completing *Michael Kohlhaas* become a fervent spokesman of the patriotic campaign of hatred against Napoleon. A few years earlier Saxony had joined the Confederation of the Rhine, the group of German states allied to France and enjoying Napoleonic protection; this had been in 1806, not long after the disastrous defeat of Prussia at Jena. Accordingly, in *The Battle with Hermann*, the King (as he now was) of Saxony had under a transparent allegorical disguise been represented as a traitor to the German cause. In 1810, filled with hopes of a Prussian resurgence, Kleist found it appropriate to invent in *Michael Kohlhaas* the notion of a prophecy foretelling the fall of Saxony and the future prosperity of Brandenburg–Prussia; he could thus underline the latter's historic mission and greatness, which he was to celebrate again in *Prince Friedrich of Homburg*.

His reasons for adding the gypsy episode may also have included a literary intention, misguided in this case, of deliberately creating mystery. *Michael Kohlhaas* has the dramatic urgency of the best of Kleist's other stories, but none of their economy of means. Its ever increasing and ever more confusing complications suggest that the narrator wishes to lose both himself and the reader in an impenetrable world, in a maze of detail and coincidence. The mystifying affair of the old woman was to have been, perhaps, the culmination of this process, raising it to a supernatural level. Not only the Holy Roman Emperor, but God himself, or Fate, is brought into play. Whereas, for example, *The Earthquake in Chile* implicitly raises theological questions and, as will be seen, certain other stories (*The Beggarwoman of Locarno*, *St Cecilia*, *The Foundling*) introduce or suggest a dimension of the more-than-natural, they all do so with great subtlety and tact. In *Michael Kohlhaas* the 'real' and the 'fantastic' are not compellingly fused but clumsily mixed. Close inspection of the episode of the gypsy's prophecy shows it to have been cobbled on to the rest of the text with considerable carelessness. As already mentioned, the *Phoebus* fragment stops precisely at the point where Kohlhaas, after his wife's funeral, rides off to attack Tronka Castle. In the book version he accidentally meets the Elector of Saxony while he is being escorted to Berlin and, not recognizing him, tells how he acquired the mysterious piece of paper kept in a lead locket which he has worn round his neck ever since. It was, he says, on the very day after his wife had been buried, and while he was on his way with armed followers to Tronka Castle, that he encountered simultaneously the Electors of Saxony and of Brandenburg, who were conferring in Jüterbock. He goes on to relate how, in the evening, the two princes had mingled with the crowd in friendly conversation, and how he, having paused at an inn with his men, stood idly watching them speak to the old gypsy-woman, in an incident roughly following the pattern of the meeting of Macbeth and Banquo with the three witches. Brandenburg frivolously asks the woman to make a prophecy about himself and receives an auspicious answer; Saxony does the same but the woman, instead of replying, writes her answer on a piece of paper and hands it to Kohlhaas. All this happens in public, in circumstances in which the horse-dealer, although not near enough to the two Electors to hear their conversation with the gypsy, obviously has easy access to them, and they are after all the ultimate judges in his dispute with the Tronka family. He gives in his account, however, no explanation of why he did not at least attempt to petition them for justice, nor does he even mention that it occurred to him to do so. It seems that he merely stood looking on, even exchanging a genial remark with the gypsy-woman when she approached him, as if the death of his wife and the events leading up to it had never happened. Thus the sub-plot, at its point of juncture with the main line of the Kohlhaas story, involves a gross improbability of behaviour on the part of Kohlhaas himself. This reinforces the reader's impression that the whole thing is an artistically unfortunate afterthought; a further explanation may be that Kleist wanted to appeal to the popular taste, at this peak period of German Roman- ticism, for folkloristic, fairytale-like material. He had done the same thing in *Kätchen of Heilbronn* which for that very reason, although arguably the weakest of his plays, was the only one to be produced with some degree of success in his lifetime. But Kleist was 'romantic' and irrationalistic in too profound a sense to have needed to make such concessions to literary convention.

If the weighty realism of *Michael Kohlhaas* is stylistically and structurally marred by an ill-considered excursion into the region of the fantastic and the uncanny, this is not to say that in certain other works he did not cross or approach its frontier with greater success. *The Beggarwoman of Locarno* is a case in point. We may note in this connection the peculiar nature of convincingly uncanny or eerie effects in literature. They are borderline effects, depending for their force on what is not said rather than what is said, on suggestion, insinuation and reserve rather than on whimsical elaboration. They require realism and rationality as their background and starting-point, precisely because they consist in the confounding of reason. But reason and realism must be there to be confounded. This point was made by Freud in one of his most interesting papers, *The Uncanny* (*Das Unheimliche*, 1919). Using as his chief example a story (*The Sandman*) by Kleist's near-contemporary E. T. A. Hoffmann, he attempts to interpret psychologically that type of experience or situation which we commonly describe as 'uncanny' and the literary effect that corresponds to it. Essentially, as he shows, an uncanny phenomenon is something quite 'impossible' which intrudes into the 'real' world of common sense: the recrudescence (or apparent recrudescence) of a primitive magical world which the adult rational consciousness has taught itself to repudiate. It is in this sense impossible, for instance, that the dead should still be alive, that one and the same person or thing should simultaneously be in two different places or should both exist and not exist. Thus, the strictly uncanny effect cannot be achieved in a work of literature which is wholly fantastic, such as a straightforward fairy-story; there must be a realistic background or frame of reference, the norms of which are at one point inexplicably breached by the re-emergence into it of the impossible, repudiated world. It follows that the ghost-story is the uncanny story *par excellence*. *The Beggarwoman of Locarno* is a ghost-story, a miniature masterpiece of the uncanny genre, wholly succeeding in the area in which *Michael Kohlhaas* has failed, and surpassing anything that had been or was to be achieved by Hoffmann or any of the other writers commonly classified as Romantics, not excepting *The Sandman*, which is itself an outstanding exception. If *Michael Kohlhaas* achieves dramatic effect by sheer cumulative power and urgent flow, *The Beggarwoman of Locarno* does so by brilliant concentration and organization. In one of his most penetrating essays in literary analysis, Emil Staiger has shown that this brief story is an integrated microcosm of interacting functional parts, an intellectual whole exactly similar in principle to one of Kleist's long complex sentences with its multiplicity of subordinated, functionally interrelated elements. As at the level of grammatical structure, so at that of narrative composition, the organizing mind of the dramatist is reflected: what goes before prepares what is to come, what comes recalls what has gone before. Unobtrusively, without recourse to any conventional devices of atmospheric description, tension and suspense are generated, an explosive climax carefully prepared. Details are included for the significance they later take on: at the beginning of the story, for example, when the Marquis roughly tells the old beggarwoman to spare him the sight of her by crossing the room to lie down again behind the stove, the direction in which she is to move across the room is mentioned, implying apparently no more than an irritable gesture of the Marquis's hand; and this, as we later discover, is the very direction in which her ghost will move, night after night, from one corner of the room to the other. But not only the mind of the dramatist is betokened by this story – it is also the Kleistian mind which incessantly seeks, like Kohlhaas, to impose a rational pattern on a world which in reality moves by a different dynamic. In this particular case the eeriness is increased by the fact that the Marquis, when he becomes aware of the haunting, nevertheless does not seem to remember the comparatively trivial incident of his inhospitable behaviour to the old woman who is now avenging herself so strangely. He does not identify the audible but invisible ghost, and his rational intellect, despite mounting evidence, refuses to acknowledge its incomprehensible reality. The climax comes when, at his third and final attempt to establish the truth, he is accompanied by his dog, a creature whose perceptions are not limited by human rational consciousness. As Staiger points out, Kleist highlights this dramatic turning-point by dropping the hypotactic sentence-structure and also by moving into the historic-present tense (this stylistic device cannot be satisfactorily reproduced in English). The dog, as soon as it hears the ghost, also sees it, and backs away from it in obvious terror, across the room, towards the corner in which the woman had died. The Marquis, though panic-stricken, still remains uncomprehending, but his reason gives way and he destroys both the house and himself. He is following the remorseless logic of an obsession, falling victim to a world which in an unaccountable way refuses to forget what his conscious mind refuses to remember. On this analysis there seems to be not only a particular subtlety in Kleist's art, but also an especially close correlation between his art and his self-destructive psychological make-up.

In *St Cecilia*, as in *The Beggarwoman of Locarno*, his management of the 'uncanny' element is again very much more skilful than in *Michael Kohlhaas*. The irruption of the inexplicable into an otherwise explicable world is here again very far from seeming to be a mere whimsical and stylistically alien digression: instead, it is once more the precise centre and appalling *pointe* of the whole tale. *St*

Cecilia or The Power of Music (to give it its full title) is described by the author as 'a legend': it tells of a miracle supposedly performed by St Cecilia, the patron saint of music and also of a Catholic convent which existed (in the story, though apparently not in historical fact) in Aachen in the sixteenth century. The convent is threatened with destruction by a mob of Protestant iconoclasts; the riot is planned to start during the solemn Mass on the day of Corpus Christi, and the ringleaders are four brothers who with numerous followers have mingled with the congregation at the service which the Abbess, despite knowledge of the danger, insists on holding. An ancient and impressive setting of the Mass by an unknown Italian composer is performed in circumstances which turn out later to have been very mysterious. The performance unexpectedly strikes the four brothers into a state of strange religious madness: they begin fervently crossing and prostrating themselves, their companions are dumbfounded and the riot does not take place. The condition and behaviour of the young men compel the civil authorities to consign them to the lunatic asylum in Aachen where they remain for the rest of their lives; they spend their days gazing with rapt attention at a crucifix and never uttering a word. But at midnight they start to their feet and for one hour precisely they chant 'in a hideous voice' something that resembles the setting they have heard of the *Gloria in excelsis* from the Mass. Their performance is, however, less like singing than like the howling of wild animals or of damned souls in hell; the impression of those who witness it is that the brothers are diabolically possessed, and Kleist's depiction certainly hints that they have been reduced to a state of automatism, when they rise 'with a simultaneous movement' as midnight strikes. Kleist seems, moreover, to be quite well aware that the condition of the four young men could be regarded merely as a psychological phenomenon and that religious madness of one sort or another is a clinically attested fact.

He is known to have been interested in psychopathology and to have visited madhouses to look at their inmates. It is highly probable that in his conception of this particular story he had been influenced by an account written by the poet Matthias Claudius of four patients at an institution in Hamburg: these were, Claudius reports, four brothers who spent most of their time in silence, except that whenever the bell was tolled to signify that someone in the asylum had died, they would sing part of a dirge and had thus come to be known as the 'death cocks' (*Totenhähne*). Since this account resembles the St Cecilia story in several particulars there can be little doubt that Kleist was acquainted with it, and in general with the fact that compulsive singing is a feature of the religious madness syndrome, evidently related to glossolalia or echolalia. But he also appears to have known that such 'singing' can in some cases be weird, cacophonous and terrifying. The report by Claudius was doubtless a source for his story, but an even more curious and striking parallel case occurred in England at the end of January 1973 and was widely reported in the press. The following extracts are from the *Daily Telegraph* of 2 February 1973:

Two young men and a woman, members of an American-based religious cult which encourages its followers to put themselves into a hypnotic trance, were in the psychiatric unit of Great Yarmouth hospital last night.

They were taken from a house in Stafford Road after neighbours, frightened by continuous wailing and chanting for three days, called in police and local church leaders ...

The Rev. Stanley Miller ... identified the chanting as a perverted form of glossolalia – a term for 'speaking in tongues', the mind having no control of what is said ... It was the continuous chanting of one phrase, 'Baby Jesus', which frightened neighbours in the terrace ...

Mr Miller added that when he saw the two women and three men in the house on Wednesday night they were in such an advanced state of trance as to be possessed by the devil. 'Their eyes were closed and what they were doing was manifestly evil. The chanting was spine-chilling' ...

The Times reported a neighbour as saying: 'The chanting was something I never want to hear again. It was spine-chilling and could be heard fifty yards from the house.' Similarly, the chanting of the four brothers in Kleist's tale, when they begin it after their return from the church, wakes the neighbours who rush to the inn in horror to see what is going on.

In *St Cecilia* Kleist is taking us two ways into the realm of the uncanny: first there is the phenomenon of the madness itself, the psychotic manifestation in which, as Freud would say, the repudiated or repressed material re-emerges or returns to the supposedly rational surface of life. But secondly – and this appears to be the point that Kleist particularly wanted to emphasize – this sudden and seemingly pathological conversion of four anti-Catholic militants takes place in circumstances that cannot be wholly accounted for without supposing some sort of supernatural intervention. Only one of the nuns in the convent knows how to play and conduct the mysterious Italian Mass which, on the Abbess's instructions, is to be performed. This particular nun, Sister Antonia, is on the morning of the festival lying mortally sick in her cell; nevertheless, she appears at the last moment, seats herself at the organ and conducts the music with triumphant and devastating effect. But witnesses later testify that Sister Antonia had never left her cell or even regained consciousness, dying the same evening. The conclusion seems to be that St Cecilia herself has impersonated Sister Antonia in order to save her convent and punish the 'blasphemers'.

In the elaborated extension of the story for the book version, Kleist arranges the events in a manner that seems specifically designed to highlight the mysterious central occurrence, namely the direct intervention of the saint. The final version begins with two paragraphs of narration which

take the reader only as far as the moment during the Corpus
Christi Mass when, contrary to expectation, the sacred
music proceeds without interruption. This narrative then
breaks off, ending merely with a reference to the convent's
further half-century of prosperity until its secularization
at the end of the Thirty Years War. The third paragraph
takes up the tale six years after that Corpus Christi Day,
introducing a new character who is not mentioned in the
original version, and whose introduction increases the
story's dramatic poignancy : the mother of the four young
men, having heard no news of them for all these years,
comes to Aachen to make inquiries and to her horror discovers them in the madhouse, oblivious to everything but
their strange monotonous life of religious contemplation
and repetitive cacophonous chanting. She is told nothing
about the connection between their madness and the intended iconoclastic riot, which has long been forgotten by
most of Aachen. This omission of the explanatory connection creates a dramatic suspense which in the long fourth
paragraph Kleist proceeds to resolve, using the device of
retrospective ('flashback') narration. The mother visits a
further new character, the cloth-merchant Veit Gotthelf, a
former friend of the brothers, and his account takes us back
to the point at which the second paragraph ended. During
the Mass on Corpus Christi Day six years before, he and
the other would-be iconoclasts had been awaiting the signal
to disrupt the service, which one of the brothers was to
have given. But no signal was given : instead, the brothers
had suddenly bowed their heads as the music began and
sunk to their knees in an attitude of the utmost devotion.
After the service their followers had dispersed in bewilderment; later, having vainly waited for the brothers, Veit
Gotthelf and some friends went back to the convent church
and there found them still kneeling in prayer. Then follows
the vivid description of their strange and terrifying
behaviour at the inn that night and their eventual consign-

ment to the asylum. But Veit Gotthelf's narrative still leaves one link missing: what is the explanation of the immediate and astonishing effect of the liturgical music on the four young disbelievers? The process of detection is not yet complete, Kleist's story is still circling around its own central mystery, namely the apparent celestial intervention. The disclosure of this is reserved deliberately until the penultimate fifth paragraph, in which the mother hears a second flashback account from the Abbess herself. This tells of the inexplicable double location of Sister Antonia, and of the official recognition of the whole occurrence as a miracle; the Abbess states in conclusion that she has only just received a letter from the Pope confirming this recognition. Having stopped just short of the central point three times we thus finally reach it and Kleist adds: 'here this legends ends'. The double title *St Cecilia or The Power of Music* seems deliberately to leave open the question of whether the sudden conversion of the brothers is to be explained in terms of supernatural intervention or merely of psychopathology; the final narrative of the Abbess, with its evidence of Sister Antonia's incapacitation, seems to decide in favour of the former hypothesis; on the other hand, by the designation 'legend', the narrator seems to disclaim responsibility for the truth of what the Abbess states. Thus an ambiguous balance is achieved. Again, the 'miracle' is described with characteristic paradox as 'both terrible and glorious' – as in *The Earthquake in Chile*, the divine action has a double aspect. The wrath of God or of St Cecilia smites the brothers into a state in some ways resembling demonic possession, though in other ways it is a state of contentment, and we are told that they eventually die a peaceful death after once more howling the *Gloria in excelsis*.

One other detail seems relevant in this context. Ever since the day on which it saved the convent, the score of the anonymous Italian setting of the Mass has been kept in the

Abbess's room. The mother of the four converts looks at it when she is there, and is told that this was the music performed on the fateful morning; she then notices with a feeling of dread that it happens to be standing open at the *Gloria*. The sentence describing her reaction suggests an association between music, cryptography, magic spells and 'terrible spirits': 'She gazed at the unknown magical signs, with which some terrible spirit seemed to be marking out its mysterious sphere ...' The theme of the sinister and fatal fascination of music was one that also attracted E. T. A. Hoffmann, and it was to be given its fullest elaboration by another of Kleist's twentieth-century admirers, Thomas Mann, in his novel about the composer whose art symbolizes the black magic of Dr Faustus.

The Betrothal in Santo Domingo to some extent resembles *The Earthquake in Chile*: both are stories about the tragic fate of two young lovers whose relationship is set against a background of disaster and violent social upheaval. Unlike Jerónimo and Josefa, however, Gustav and Toni perish not, in the last resort, because of external circumstances and the wickedness of other people, but because of a flaw in their own relationship. The essential theme here is not the cruelty of man to man (though, as usual, Kleist well illustrates this), nor even the unaccountable operations of God or nature or fate, but – as in *The Duel* and at least three of the plays – that of love being put on trial. The lover is confronted with an ambiguity of appearances, with ambiguous behaviour on the part of his beloved, which in the present case misleads him into a fatal misunderstanding, with tragic results. As in *The Duel* Kleist seems to construct the whole rather complicated story deliberately round this point, which becomes explicit in the girl's dying words, 'You should not have mistrusted me'. He subtly uses the archetypal symbolic equation of black with evil and white with good to reinforce the ambiguity which leads to this mistrust. The circumstances of the tragedy are based on actual historical fact, namely the war between the French settlers on the island of Santo Domingo (Haiti) and their former negro slaves, emancipated by a decree of the National Convention in 1794. The blacks have turned with murderous savagery on their white oppressors, and in 1803 the French have fallen back on Port-au-Prince where they are making a last stand against the advancing negro army led by General Dessalines. Into this situation Kleist inserts his fictitious story of Toni, the daughter of a mulatto woman and a white man, who lives with her mother on a plantation occupied by a band of negroes under the leadership of the brutal and ferocious Congo Hoango. He and his men have murdered the former white owners of the property and are now taking part in the campaign to exterminate all Europeans left on the island. If any white man seeks refuge in the house during his absence, Babekan and Toni are under Hoango's orders to detain him with feigned hospitality until the negroes return and kill him. Toni is for this purpose cast in the role of the sexually attractive decoy, to which she is well suited since as a quadroon or 'mestiza' she has almost white skin. The young Swiss officer Gustav von der Ried, whom she and Babekan receive as a fugitive, is with good reason suspicious of their motives, and in particular the behaviour of Toni presents itself to him in an ambiguous light. As if to underline and polarize this ambiguity, already symbolized by Toni's complexion, Kleist makes him in the course of the evening's conversation tell two contrasting stories, one about a treacherous and vindictive negress who ensnared a white man and deliberately infected him with yellow fever, and the other about a virtuous and loving European girl to whom he had become engaged while living in France at the time of the Revolution, and who had sacrificed her life on the guillotine in order to save his. Toni is moved to tears by this second story, which he tells her while she is alone with him in his bedroom acting on her mother's guileful instructions. She falls into his arms and he seduces her, partly on an impulse of genuine emotion and partly in order to win her love and thus increase the chances of safety for himself and his friends who are hiding in the woods nearby. Toni now for the first time truly loves a white man in whose murder she is supposed to be assisting; intent on saving the stranger, who has promised to take her back to Europe and marry her, she has to play a double role and allay the suspicions of her mother and of Congo Hoango, who returns unexpectedly in the middle of the night. She takes the only action open to her in these circumstances and ties her sleeping lover to his bed with a length of rope, pretending to Hoango that she has deceived and trapped the white man. Her ruse succeeds in that she gains time to run secretly to meet Gustav's companions and lead them back to the house to rescue him. But by the time they have successfully overpowered the blacks she has still had no chance to explain to her lover the real reason for her actions, and before she can do so he shoots her in rage and despair at her supposed treachery. In judging her motives he has had nothing to go by but the tangible evidence of his senses: to grasp something so intangible as the reality of her love, the real distinction between what she seems to be and what she is, would have required of him an act of intuition and faith which, at the moment of crisis, he cannot achieve. On discovering his mistake he kills himself also.

Unlike Goethe and Schiller in this as in other ways, Kleist seems to have had an interestingly pronounced sense of evil, which would be evident if *The Foundling* were the only thing he had written. This story again takes us into the realm of the uncanny and confronts us, seemingly, with the operation of some kind of malign magic, and certainly with the existence of terrifying, elemental psychological possibilities. The well-ordered and (apart from one rather strange and sad feature of his present second marriage) apparently happy existence of the rich Roman merchant

Piachi is invaded, accidentally it seems, by a fateful agent of destruction. Out of a plague-stricken city to which his business takes him, there emerges the orphaned foundling boy Nicolo, and Piachi's impulse of kindness towards him leads gradually to his own total ruin, beginning with the death of his own young son Paolo from the plague. Nicolo takes Paolo's place, is adopted and educated by Piachi, made a partner in his business, and becomes not only his heir but also the owner by deed of gift of almost all his property, including his house. For the events that ensue, Kleist is known to have had at least two literary sources. One is again Molière. The relationship between Piachi and his adopted son Nicolo is a tragic version of the story of Orgon and his bigoted and hypocritical protégé Tartuffe. (Nicolo, too, is described as bigoted, and frequents the corrupt clergy of Rome.) In both cases, when the protégé is finally unmasked in the act of trying to seduce his benefactor's wife and the latter orders him out of the house, he turns the tables by declaring that the house is now legally his and that it is for the husband to leave it. Kleist combines this with other motifs, one of which he took from the late Latin collection of tales attributed to Hyginus: the widowed Laodamia has a life-sized wax image made of her dead husband Protesilaus, places it in a kind of sanctuary in her bedroom and secretly worships it. As she is doing so one morning a servant looks through a chink in the door, sees her apparently embracing and kissing a man, and reports to her father that she has taken a lover.

Kleist's version of this idea gives it a morbid and eerie flavour. As we have already mentioned, there is something not quite normal about Piachi's marriage to his young second wife Elvira. It is for some reason childless (the boy Paolo was the son of Piachi's first marriage) and Elvira's emotions are romantically fixated on a young Genoese nobleman who, twelve years earlier, had saved her from a burning house when she was a child and had died of an injury incurred during the rescue. Elvira still adores his memory, grieves inconsolably when anything reminds her of him, and secretly keeps a life-size portrait of him in a screened alcove in her bedroom. This private cult is known only to Piachi, until Nicolo eventually discovers it. He already bears malice against his young adoptive mother for her disapproval of his immoral way of life, which has also put him out of favour with Piachi; and when by chance he looks through Elvira's keyhole and sees her apparently kneeling at the feet of a lover, he relishes the prospect of being able to denounce this sham paragon of virtue. When he searches Elvira's bedroom in her absence, however, he discovers his error.

It is at this point that Kleist's very characteristic variation on the Hyginus story begins. Three further motifs are introduced, all of them associated with the realm of the sinister and the occult. First, that of the *Doppelgänger*: Nicolo discovers that the figure in the portrait exactly resembles himself. Secondly, while idly toying one day with the six letters of a child's alphabet that compose his name, he finds that it is an anagram of the name 'Colino' which he has heard Elvira murmur to the portrait. In traditional magical lore, anagrams and similar verbal devices have since antiquity played a well-recognized part, as have also such divinatory procedures as throwing down letters of the alphabet at random; this in fact happens in Ira Levin's macabre novel about satanism in present-day New York, *Rosemary's Baby* (1967), in which the heroine discovers by throwing down some letters that the name of her neighbour Roman Castavet is an anagram of the name of a well-known diabolist, Stevan Marcato. The third and crucial additional motif is that of the 'uncanny' mingling or confusion of the inanimate with the animate, the dead with the living, the portrait with the model. (There are many parallels to this idea, both before and after Kleist; Hoffmann, for instance, was attracted by the theme of automata, which he uses notably in *The Sandman*.) The impersonation by the evil Nicolo of his polar opposite, the virtuous and noble Colino, is in fact the central *pointe* and dramatic climax of this *Novelle*. Kleist skilfully prepares it and builds up to it, just as he does to the central incident with the dog in *The Beggar-woman of Locarno*. Nicolo discovers his affinity with the portrait and the connexion between the names; he remembers that Elvira fainted when, after a masked ball, by coincidence she saw him wearing the same costume as the Genoese knight of the portrait; and he notes how disturbed she becomes when he deliberately confronts her with the six letters rearranged to form the name 'Colino'. He also discovers Colino's identity and the mystery of his adoptive mother's perpetual infatuation with a dead man. The impersonation scene itself, in which he exploits all these discoveries, has a dramatic force not unlike that of the crucial confrontation in Oscar Wilde's story, *The Picture of Dorian Gray*, between the beautiful but profoundly corrupted Dorian and his *alter ego* or real self, the mysterious life-sized portrait which, hidden in an attic, has aged and grown foul, while he as the world knows him has retained the innocent youthfulness painted long ago by a man who saw him with the vision of a lover. (It may be noted that at the very beginning of *The Foundling* Nicolo is described as beautiful in a way that is 'strangely statuesque' – *eigentümlich starr*, literally 'rigid', a phrase suggesting some kind of portrait or mask.)

The remainder of Kleist's story simply works out the logical consequences of this scene, the remorseless conclusion of a world turned mad and satanic : the death of the horrified Elvira after her secret fantasy has become a ghostly reality, the dreadful murder of Nicolo by Piachi, the transformation of this kindly old man into an obsessed avenger literally craving for Hell where, like Dante's Ugolino, he may eternally torment this emissary of nothingness who has taken everything from him – his son, his property, his wife, his life, and his soul. We never discover who 'Nicolo' is, nor by what sinister coincidence or for what other reason he is the double of 'Colino' and is called by an inversion, as it were, of his name. The polarity which can lie within one and the same character, that of Kohlhaas, for instance, or of the angel-devil Count F—, is here externalized into two persons, each the opposite of the other. This 'good–evil' version of the *Doppelgänger* theme is also used by Hoffmann in his novel *The Devil's Elixir*; R. L. Stevenson's *Dr Jekyll and Mr Hyde* is a later variant of it, and numerous others could no doubt be found.

In the last story, *The Duel*, as in the first, *The Earthquake in Chile*, God himself acts ambiguously. *The Duel* has a medieval setting and is based partly on a chronicle by Froissart and partly on an episode from Cervantes' romance *Persiles y Sigismunda*. What seems to have interested Kleist was the idea he found in his source material that the procedure of trial by ordeal (here ordeal by single combat), which according to medieval belief was the ultimate and infallible method of discovering the truth when ordinary evidence could not establish it, might at times yield a misleading, seemingly incorrect answer. This theme, as incorporated in the apparent defeat of the heroine's champion by Jakob Rotbart, is accordingly the dramatic *pointe* of *The Duel*, just as Toni's binding up her sleeping lover is that of *The Betrothal in Santo Domingo*, the behaviour of the dog that of *The Beggarwoman of Locarno*, the portrait scene that of *The Foundling*, and the unearthly performance of the Mass that of *St Cecilia*. It has been objected that Kleist over-complicates the structure of *The Duel* by making the involved preliminary story of the murder of Duke Wilhelm, which was not in his sources, precede the main story of Littegarde and her champion Friedrich von Trota; but he must have felt this to be artistically necessary if the central enigma were to be convincingly and pointedly set up. The essential situation, as in *The Broken Pitcher*, *Amphitryon*, and *The Marquise of O—*, is that of the apparently chaste woman suspected of unchastity on the basis of seemingly damning evidence. The case against Littegarde would be weakened if Count Rotbart were obviously a scoundrel, but he is regarded as an honourable man by many and it is only because he is on trial for his life on a charge of murder that, as an alibi, he can seem justified in making (with a due show of gentlemanly reluctance) his disclosure that the night on which the murder was committed had been spent by him in Littegarde's bedroom. Moreover, just as in *Amphitryon* Alcmene is bafflingly confronted with a golden diadem which must appear to be a love-gift from someone other than her husband, the Count is able to produce a ring which he declares Littegarde had given him on that night. (It may also be noted that both Littegarde and the Marquise of O— are widows, which of course makes their alleged misconduct more difficult to disprove.) But in Littegarde's case there are not only worldly presumptions and specific evidence against her: proof seems to become absolute at the point where her champion, having appealed to the irrefutable judgement of God, is apparently defeated by her supposed paramour. Not surprisingly, she here undergoes a kind of mental crisis and ceases to believe even in her own innocence. Nowhere in Kleist's work is the discrepancy between reality and appearance so sharply polarized. Littegarde's despairing confession to Friedrich von Trota in the prison scene puts Trota to the ultimate test of the lover's faith in his beloved, a subtle personal parallel to the public trial by ordeal he has undergone already. At first, overwhelmed by the monstrous contradiction between what he unquestioningly believed to be true and what now presents itself as true, that faith momentarily collapses and he faints, as the Marquise fainted when the midwife declared her to be pregnant, or Elvira when 'Colino' confronted her. But he recovers, and passes the test in which Gustav von der Ried had failed. He utters the words which sum up Kleist's whole conviction of the limitations of rationalism, urging Littegarde to hold fast at all costs to her inner intuitive feeling that she is innocent, notwithstanding all the indications to the contrary and notwithstanding even the apparently contrary divine pronouncement. This point of crisis and positive faith having been reached, Kleist (or God) can proceed to the vindication of Littegarde on the basis of evidence: the mystery is not an irrational one at all; the narrator has the key to it all the time, as in *The Marquise of O—*, and therefore, like that story, *The Duel* does not end tragically. The difference between the two stories is that in *The Duel* the solution is not shared all along with the reader, to whom the narrative therefore presents itself with tension and tragic potential. Unlike Count F—, even Rotbart himself does not know the real explanation of what has happened, and nor does anyone else until the very end when it is discovered accidentally – or rather (in terms of the story's medieval Christian frame of reference) revealed by God in his own time. On the night of the murder the Count has in fact been received at Auerstein Castle, but not by Littegarde as he fondly imagines; her maid-in-waiting, an abandoned mistress of Rotbart, has deceived the latter by impersonating Littegarde, in whom she knows him to be interested, has stolen her lady's ring and given it to him, taking him in the darkness of the night to a sumptuous bedroom in a deserted wing of the castle. And in fact Rotbart has nevertheless been responsible for the murder of Duke Wilhelm, having employed a henchman to shoot him down; but in stating that he was with Littegarde on the night in question he has been in good faith. The real and paradoxical outcome of the duel therefore turns out to be entirely appropriate: Trota recovers from his seemingly mortal wound, while Rotbart dies slowly and horribly from his slight scratch, which has turned gangrenous. Informed of the maid Rosalie's spiteful deception of him, he makes as he dies a public confession which at the last moment saves the lovers from being burnt at the stake for blasphemy, and the Emperor orders a modification of the statute about trial by ordeal: a clause is to be inserted indicating that this procedure will reveal the truth immediately 'if it be God's will'. If it is not his will, then presumably he will reveal it later. But does Kleist here imply that this later revelation will always, as in the case of Friedrich and Littegarde, be in time to prevent a miscarriage of temporal justice? Perhaps not; but if not, then ironically enough the whole ordeal procedure ceases to be reliable, and the conclusion of *The Duel* cannot be said to be unequivocally optimistic. In the last resort the inscrutability of God's ways must be accepted; he cannot be magically compelled to answer questions. At best (as Kleist had suggested in 1806) the world is governed by a being who is 'not understood'; and the presumptuous claim to understand him can be raised by those who are guided by nothing more than their own cruel passions, with the terrible consequences which *The Earthquake in Chile* makes manifest.

The world of all these stories is an unpredictable one, a world of dislocated causality on which inexplicable factors intrude and in which sanity is poised on the brink of destruction. They are the work of a rationalist tormented by his loss of faith in Reason and desperately searching for certainty, for an order which is not *'gebrechlich'*. In Kleist's life this search could only fail; the only imposable order was that of his art, an order of words, the strange patterns of his three or four dramatic masterpieces, the electrifying articulated structures of his narrative prose. The qualities of the latter which have made it the subject of much intensive stylistic scrutiny are of course the very qualities to which a translator cannot hope to do justice. He must merely seek to achieve a compromise that will suggest something of the simultaneous complexity and elegance of the original, while respecting the limits to which English syntax can reasonably be pushed. We have felt that a new attempt was justified: Martin Greenberg's version (New York, 1960; Faber and Faber 1963; now out of print) was marred by too many errors of comprehension and taste, which we have tried to avoid, while remaining in good measure indebted to its frequent felicities.

Nigel Reeves and David Luke collaborated on the Introduction and on the translation of *Michael Kohlhaas*; the other seven stories were translated by David Luke.

The Earthquake in Chile

In Santiago, the capital of the kingdom of Chile, at the moment of the great earthquake of 1647 in which many thousands lost their lives, a young Spaniard called Jerónimo Rugera was standing beside one of the pillars in the prison to which he had been committed on a criminal charge, and was about to hang himself. A year or so previously Don Enrico Asterón, one of the richest noblemen of the city, had turned him out of his house where he had been employed as a tutor, for being on too intimate a footing with Asterón's only daughter, Doña Josefa. She herself was sternly warned, but owing to the malicious vigilance of her proud brother she was discovered nevertheless in a secret rendezvous with Jerónimo, and this so aroused her old father's indignation that he forced her to enter the Carmelite convent of Our Lady of the Mountain.

A happy chance had enabled her lover to resume the liaison in this very place, and one quiet night the convent garden became the scene of his joy's consummation. On the day of Corpus Christi, the solemn procession of the nuns, with the novices following them, was just beginning when, as the bells pealed out, the unhappy Josefa collapsed on the cathedral steps in the pangs of childbirth.

This incident caused an extraordinary public stir; without any regard for her condition the young sinner was at once imprisoned, and her confinement was scarcely over when by the Archbishop's command she was put on trial with the utmost rigour. The scandal was talked of in the city with so much anger and the whole convent in which it had taken place was criticized on all sides with such harshness that neither the intercession of the Asterón family, nor even the wishes of the Abbess herself, who had conceived an affection for the young girl on account of her otherwise irreproachable conduct, could mitigate the strict penalty to which she was subject by conventual law. All that could be done was that the Viceroy commuted her sentence from death at the stake to death by beheading, a decision which greatly outraged the matrons and virgins of Santiago.

In the streets through which the culprit was to be led to her execution the windows were rented, the roofs of the houses were partly dismantled, and the pious daughters of the city invited their female friends to witness with them, in sisterly companionship, this spectacle about to be offered to divine vengeance.

Jerónimo, who in the meantime had also been imprisoned, went almost out of his mind when he was informed of this appalling turn of events. In vain he pondered plans of rescue: wherever the wings of his most reckless imaginings carried him, bolts and walls were in his way; when he attempted to file through the window bars this was discovered, and merely led to his being locked up still more strictly. He fell on his knees before an image of the Holy Mother of God and prayed to her with infinite fervour, convinced that she alone could save them now.

Yet the fearful day came, and with it an inward certainty of the utter hopelessness of his position. The bells that accompanied Josefa's passage to the place of execution began to toll, and despair overcame him. Hating his life, he resolved to put an end to it by means of a length of rope which by chance had been left in his cell. He was standing by one of the walls under a pillar, as already related, holding the rope that would release him from this miserable world, and was in the very act of fastening it to an iron bracket attached to the cornice, when suddenly, with a crash as if the very firmament had shattered, the greater part of the city collapsed, burying every living thing beneath its ruins. Jerónimo Rugera stood rigid with horror; and as if every thought had been obliterated from his mind, he now clung to the pillar on which he had wanted to die. and tried to stop himself falling. The ground was heaving under his feet, great cracks appeared in the walls all round him, the whole edifice toppled towards the street and would have crashed down into it had not its slow fall been met by that of the house opposite, and only the arch thus formed by chance prevented its complete destruction. Trembling, his hair on end, his knees nearly giving way, Jerónimo slid down the steeply sloping floor to the gap that had been torn through the front wall of his prison as the two buildings collided.

He was scarcely outside when a second tremor completely demolished the already subsiding street. Panic-stricken, with no idea of how to save himself from this general doom, he ran on over wreckage and fallen timber towards one of the nearest city gates, while death assailed him from all directions. Here another house caved in, scattering its debris far and wide and driving him into a side street; here flames, flashing through clouds of smoke, were licking out of every gable and chased him in terror into another; here the Mapocho river, overflowing its banks, rolled roaring towards him and forced him into a third. Here lay a heap of corpses, there a voice still moaned under the rubble, here people were screaming on burning house-tops, there men and animals were struggling in the floodwater, here a brave rescuer tried to help and there stood another man, pale as death, speechlessly extending his trembling hands to heaven. When Jerónimo had reached the gate and climbed a hill beyond it, he fell down at the top in a dead faint.

He had probably lain there quite unconscious for about a quarter of an hour when he finally recovered his senses and half raised himself up, his back turned to the city. He felt his forehead and his chest, not knowing what to make of his condition, and an unspeakable feeling of bliss came over him as a westerly breeze from the sea fanned his returning life and his eyes wandered in all directions over the fertile surroundings of Santiago. Only the sight of crowds of distraught people everywhere troubled him; he did not understand what could have brought them and him to this place, and only when he turned and saw the city levelled to the ground behind him did he remember the terrifying moments he had just experienced. He bowed his forehead to the very ground as he thanked God for his miraculous escape; and as if this one appalling memory, stamping itself on his mind, had erased all others, he wept with rapture to find that the blessing of life, in all its wealth and variety, was still his to enjoy.

But a moment later, noticing a ring on his finger, he suddenly also remembered Josefa, and with her his prison, the bells he had there heard tolling, and the moment that had preceded its collapse. Deep sorrow again filled his heart; he began to regret his prayer and to think with horror of the Being who rules above the clouds. He mixed with the people who, busy salvaging their possessions, were pouring out of all the city gates, and ventured a few diffident inquiries about Asterón's daughter and whether the sentence against her had been carried out; but there was no one who could give him detailed information. A woman carrying an enormous load of household goods on her shoulders, bent almost to the ground and with two small children clinging to her breast, said as she passed, as if she herself had witnessed it, that Josefa had been beheaded. Jerónimo turned away from her; and since he himself, on calculating the time, felt no doubt that the execution had taken place, he sat down in a lonely wood and abandoned himself entirely to his grief. He wished that the destructive fury of nature might unleash itself on him once more. He could not understand why he had escaped the death which his afflicted soul desired, when in those very moments, on all sides, it had of its own accord been offering him deliverance. He firmly resolved not to flinch if even now the oak trees should be uprooted and their crests come crashing down upon him. Presently, when he had finishing weeping and in the midst of his hottest tears hope had come to him again, he stood up and began exploring the whole area. He visited every hill-top on which people had gathered; on every road along which fugitives were still streaming, he went to meet them; wherever he caught sight of a woman's dress fluttering in the wind, there with trembling feet he hastened : but never was the wearer his beloved Josefa. The sun was going down, and his hopes with it, when he reached the edge of a cliff and from there could look down into a wide valley to which only a few people had come. Not sure what to do, he passed quickly among the different groups and was about to turn back again when suddenly, beside a stream that flowed through the ravine, he noticed a young woman busy washing a child in its waters. And at this sight his heart leapt up : eager with expectation he ran down over the rocks, and with a cry of 'Oh, holy Mother of God!' he recognized Josefa as on hearing his approach she shyly looked round. With what ecstasy they embraced, the unhappy pair, saved by a divine miracle!

On her way to her death, Josefa had already nearly reached the place of execution when suddenly the buildings had begun crashing down and scattered in all directions the procession that was leading her to the block. Her first terrified steps carried her towards the nearest gate of the town; but almost at once, regaining her presence of mind, she turned round and rushed back to the convent where she had left her helpless little son. She found the whole building already in flames, and the Abbess, who during those minutes which were to have been her last had promised to take care of her baby, was at the entrance crying out for help to rescue him. Josefa, undeterred by the smoke billowing towards her, dashed into the convent, which was already collapsing all round her and, as if protected by all the angels in heaven, emerged again uninjured at its gate, carrying her child. She was just about to embrace the Abbess when the latter, who had clasped her hands in blessing over her, was ignominiously struck dead by a falling gable, together with nearly all her nuns. Josefa retreated trembling at this dreadful sight; she hastily closed the Abbess's eyes and fled, utterly terrified, to bring to safety her beloved boy whom heaven had restored to her again.

She had taken only a few steps when she found before her the mangled body of the Archbishop, which had just been dragged from under the wreckage of the cathedral. The Viceroy's palace had collapsed, the law court in which sentence had been passed on her was in flames, and in the place where her father's house had stood there was now a seething lake from which reddish vapours were rising. Josefa summoned up all her strength to sustain her, hardening herself against all these distressing sights, and walked on bravely from street to street with her recaptured treasure. She was already near the gate when she saw the prison in which Jerónimo had languished: it too was in ruins. She reeled at this sight and nearly fell down in a swoon at the street corner, but at that very moment a building, its foundations loosened by the tremors, crashed down behind her and drove her on, fortified again by terror. She kissed her child, dashed the tears from her eyes, and no longer heeding the horrors that surrounded her reached the gate. When she found herself in open country she soon realized that not everyone who had been inside a demolished building had necessarily been crushed beneath it.

At the next crossroads she paused and waited, wondering whether the person who, after her little Felipe, was dearest to her in the world, might yet appear. But since he did not come and more and more people thronged past, she continued on her way, and turned round again, and waited again; then turned aside, shedding many tears, into a dark pine-shaded valley to pray for his (as she believed) departed soul; and here in this valley she found him, her lover, and with him such joy that the valley might have been the Garden of Eden.

All this, in a voice filled with emotion, she now told Jerónimo, and when she had finished, gave him the boy to kiss. Jerónimo, with all the inexpressible delight of fatherhood, took him and hugged him, and, when his unfamiliar face made the little one cry, kept caressing him till he was silent. In the meantime the loveliest of nights had fallen, wonderfully mild and fragrant, silvery and still, a night such as only a poet might dream of. Everywhere along the banks of the stream, in the glittering moonlight, people had settled and were preparing soft beds of moss and foliage on which to rest after so harrowing a day. And since these poor victims of the disaster were still lamenting, one the loss of his house, another that of his wife and child, and a third that of everything he had possessed, Jerónimo and Josefa slipped away into a denser part of the wood, not wanting to give offence to anyone by the secret exultation of their own hearts. They found a splendid pomegranate tree, its outspread branches heavy with scented fruit, and high on its crest the nightingale piped its voluptuous song. Here, with Jerónimo leaning against its trunk and covering them with his cloak, they sat down to rest, Josefa on his lap and Felipe on hers. The tree's shadow with its scattered points of light passed over them, and the moon was already fading in the glow of dawn before they slept. For there was no end to what they had to talk about, the convent garden, their prisons, and what they had suffered for each other's sake; and it moved them greatly to think how much misery had had to afflict the world in order to bring about their happiness.

They decided that as soon as the tremors had ceased they would go to La Concepción, for Josefa had an intimate friend there, and with a small sum of money she hoped to borrow from her they would be able to embark there for Spain, where Jerónimo's relatives on his mother's side lived; there they could be happy for the rest of their days. Upon this thought, amid many kisses, they fell asleep.

When they woke, the sun was already well up in the sky, and they noticed not far from them several families busy making themselves some breakfast at a fire. Jerónimo was just wondering how he too could get some food for his child and its mother when a well-dressed young man, carrying an infant, approached Josefa and asked her politely whether she would be willing to feed at her breast for a while this poor little creature, whose mother was lying injured over there among the trees. Josefa was thrown into some embarrassment when she recognized him as an acquaintance; but when, misinterpreting her confusion, he continued : 'It will only be for a few minutes, Doña Josefa, and this child has not been fed since the time of the disaster which overtook us all,' she said, 'I had – a different reason for not replying, Don Fernando; in a terrible time like this no one can refuse to share whatever they may have.' So saying she took the little stranger, handing her own child to its father, and put it to her breast. Don Fernando was most grateful for this kindness and asked her to come with him to his own party, where breakfast was just being prepared at the fire. Josefa answered that she would accept the invitation with pleasure and, since Jerónimo also made no objection, she accompanied Don Fernando to his family, where his two sisters-in-law, whom she knew to be young ladies of excellent character, received her most warmly and affectionately.

Doña Elvira, Don Fernando's wife, was lying on the ground with her feet seriously injured, and when she saw her sickly little boy at Josefa's breast she drew the latter down towards her and kissed her lovingly. Don Pedro, Elvira's father, who was wounded in the shoulder, also nodded to her in the most friendly manner.

In the minds of Jerónimo and Josefa strange thoughts began to stir. When they found themselves treated with so much familiarity and kindness they did not know what to think of the recent past: of the place of execution, the prison and the bells; or had all these been merely a dream? It seemed that in everyone's mind, after the terrible blow that had so shaken them all, there was a spirit of reconciliation. Their memories seemed not to reach back beyond the disaster. Only Doña Isabel, who had been invited by a friend to witness yesterday's spectacle but had declined the invitation, let her gaze rest pensively from time to time upon Josefa; but always her mind, having strayed only a little from the present, was snatched back into it as she heard the report of some new and ghastly misfortune.

There were stories of how, immediately after the first main tremors, women all over the city had given birth to children in the sight of all the men; of how monks, crucifix in hand, had rushed hither and thither crying out that the end of the world had come; how on the Viceroy's orders a guard had tried to clear the people out of a church, only to be told that there was no longer any Viceroy of Chile; how in the worst moments of the disaster the Viceroy had been obliged to have gallows erected to deter looters, and how one innocent man, escaping through a burning house by the back door, had been over-hastily arrested by the owner and strung up on the spot.

Doña Elvira, whose injuries Josefa was busily tending, had taken the opportunity at a moment when these very tales were being most excitedly exchanged to ask her how, on that terrible day, she herself had fared. And when Josefa, her heart filled with anxiety, outlined to her some of the main features of her story, she had the joy of seeing the lady's eyes fill with tears; Doña Elvira clasped her hand and pressed it, and with a gesture bade her say no more. Josefa felt as if she were in the land of the blessed. She had a feeling, which she could not suppress, that the preceding day, despite all the misery it had brought upon the world, had been a mercy such as heaven had never yet bestowed on her. And indeed, in the midst of this horrifying time in which all the earthly possessions of men were perishing and all nature was in danger of being engulfed, the human spirit itself seemed to unfold like the fairest of flowers. In the fields, as far as the eye could see, men and women of every social station could be seen lying side by side, princes and beggars, ladies and peasant women, government officials and day labourers, friars and nuns: pitying one another, helping one another, gladly sharing anything they had saved to keep themselves alive, as if the general disaster had united all its survivors into a single family.

Instead of the usual trivial tea-table gossip about the ways of the world, everyone was now telling stories of extraordinary heroic deeds. Persons hitherto held to be of little consequence in society had shown a Roman greatness of character; there were countless instances of fearlessness, of magnanimous contempt for danger, of self-denial and superhuman self-sacrifice, of life unhesitatingly cast away as if it were the most trifling of possessions and could be recovered a moment later. Indeed, since there was no one who on that day had not experienced some touching kindness or had not himself performed some generous action, the sorrow in every heart was mingled with so much sweetness and delight that Josefa felt it would be hard to say whether the sum of general well-being had not increased on the one hand by as much as it had diminished on the other.

When they had both finished silently pondering these matters, Jerónimo took Josefa's arm and in a state of inexpressible happiness walked up and down with her under the shady boughs of the pomegranate trees. He told her that, the public mood being now as it was and the old order of things having undergone such an upheaval, he was abandoning his intention of embarking for Europe; that since the Viceroy had always been favourably disposed towards his cause, he would venture a personal appeal to him, if he should still be alive; and that he thus hoped to be able – and he kissed her as he said so – to remain with her in Chile. Josefa replied that similar thoughts had occurred to her; that she too did not doubt that if her father were still alive he would be ready to forgive her; but that instead of the personal approach he had suggested she thought it would be more prudent to go to La Concepción and address a written petition to the Viceroy from there; there they would in any case be within reach of the port, and after all, if their negotiations should achieve the desired result, they could easily return to Santiago. After brief reflection Jerónimo expressed his approval of this wise precaution; they strolled a little further along the avenues of trees, thinking with happy anticipation of their future, and then rejoined the company.

Meanwhile the afternoon had come, and since the tremors had abated, the fears of the wandering refugees had no sooner been somewhat calmed than the news spread that in the Dominican church, the only one the earthquake had spared, a solemn Mass would be read by the Prior of the monastery himself, who would implore heaven to prevent further disasters. Everywhere people were already setting out and streaming towards the city. Someone in Don Fernando's party raised the question of whether they too should not participate in this solemnity and join the general procession. Doña Isabel, with some embarrassment, recalled the terrible misfortune the church had suffered on the previous day; she pointed out that such services of thanksgiving would certainly be repeated and that then, with the danger less fresh in their minds, they would be able to respond more gladly and more easily to the mood of thankfulness. Josefa, rising at once enthusiastically to her feet, declared that she had never felt a stronger impulse to cast herself down before her Maker than at this very time, when His incomprehensible and sublime power was being made so evident. Doña Elvira emphatically endorsed Josefa's opinion. She insisted that they should hear the Mass and called upon Don Fernando to lead the party, whereupon all of them rose from their seats, including Doña Isabel. But the latter, in making the various small preparations for her departure, seemed to do so tardily and with her heart beating fast; and on being asked what was wrong with her she replied that she had an unhappy foreboding, though she could not tell of what. Doña Elvira calmed her and suggested that she should remain behind with her and her sick father. Josefa said: 'In that case, Doña Isabel, perhaps you will relieve me of this little darling, who, as you can see, has found his way to me again.' 'Gladly,' replied Doña Isabel, and reached out to take the baby; but when the latter wailed piteously at this infringement of his rights and would not consent to it on any terms, Josefa said with a smile that she would keep him and kissed him till he was quiet again. Then Don Fernando, who was charmed by the dignity and grace of her bearing, offered her his arm; Jerónimo, carrying little Felipe, escorted Doña Constanza; the others who had joined the party followed behind, and in this order they set off towards the city.

They had scarcely walked fifty paces when Doña Isabel, who had been having an animated private discussion with Doña Elvira, was heard to call out: 'Don Fernando!' And she ran forward to catch them up, evidently in some agitation. Don Fernando stopped and turned round, waiting for her without letting go of Josefa's arm; but when she remained standing some distance away as if waiting for him to come and meet her, he asked her what she wanted. At this Doña Isabel approached them, though evidently with reluctance, and murmured some words in his ear in such a way that Josefa could not hear them. 'Well?' asked Don Fernando, 'and what harm can come of that?' Doña Isabel, looking quite distraught, continued to whisper sharply in his ear. Don Fernando flushed with irritation and replied: 'That will do! Tell Doña Elvira that there is no need for concern.' So saying, he continued to escort Josefa on their way.

When they arrived at the Dominican church the organ greeted them with splendid music, and an immense crowd was surging inside. The throng extended far beyond the portals into the square in front of the church, and inside it small boys had climbed up the walls and were perched against the frames of paintings, with their caps clutched expectantly in their hands. All the candelabra were blazing with light, the pillars cast mysterious shadows in the gathering dusk, the great rose window of stained glass at the far end of the church burned like the very evening sun that gleamed upon it, and now that the organ was silent, stillness reigned in the whole assembly as if everyone there had been struck dumb. Never did such a flame of zeal rise to heaven from a Christian cathedral as on that day from the Dominican church at Santiago, and no hearts nourished it with a warmer fervour than those of Jerónimo and Josefa.

The service began with a sermon delivered from the pulpit by one of the oldest canons, vested in ceremonial robes. Raising his trembling hands high up to heaven, with the wide folds of his surplice flowing around them, he began at once to give praise and glory and thanks that there should still be, in this part of the world that was crumbling to ruins, men and women able to raise up their faltering voices to God; he described how, at the will of the Almighty, an event had taken place that must scarcely be less terrible than the Last Judgement; and when, nevertheless, pointing to a crack in the wall of the cathedral, he called yesterday's earthquake a mere foretaste of that day of doom, a shudder ran through the whole congregation. From this point his flood of priestly eloquence bore him on to the subject of the city's moral depravity : he castigated it for abominations such as Sodom and Gomorrah had not known, and ascribed it only to God's infinite forbearance that Santiago had not been totally obliterated from the face of the earth.

But what a piercing dagger-stroke it was to the hearts of our two unhappy friends, rent as they were already by the preacher's words, when he took occasion to dwell in detail on the outrage that had been perpetrated in the garden of the Carmelite convent! He condemned as impious the indulgence with which it had been treated by society, and even digressed, with copious imprecations, to mention the two sinners themselves by name and to consign their souls to all the princes of hell. Doña Constanza, plucking Jerónimo by the arm, called out: 'Don Fernando!' but the latter replied as emphatically and at the same time as surreptitiously as possible, 'Do not say a word, Doña; do not so much as move your eyes, but pretend that you are about to faint, and then we shall leave the church.' But before Doña Constanza had even executed this ingenious stratagem for their escape, a voice, loudly interrupting the canon's sermon, cried out: 'Citizens of Santiago, here stand those two godless sinners! Keep clear, keep well away from them!' And as a wide circle of people backed away in horror, a second terror-stricken voice asked: 'Where?' A third man replied: 'Here!' and filled with brutal fervour he seized Josefa by the hair and would have dragged her to the ground together with Don Fernando's child, if the latter had not supported her. 'Are you mad?' cried the young man, putting his arm round Josefa. 'I am Don Fernando Ormez, the son of the Commandant of this city, whom you all know.' 'Don Fernando Ormez?' exclaimed someone who now came and stood right in front of him; he was a cobbler who had worked for Josefa and knew her at least as well as he knew her tiny feet. 'Who is this child's father?' he demanded, turning with shameless insolence to Asterón's daughter. Don Fernando turned pale at this question. By turns he glanced furtively at Jerónimo and scanned the congregation, to see if there was anyone who knew him. Under the constraint of this appalling situation Josefa cried out: 'This is not my child, Master Pedrillo, as you think'; and looking at Don Fernando in unspeakable anguish of mind she added, 'This young gentleman is Don Fernando Ormez, the son of the Commandant of this city, whom you all know!' The cobbler asked: 'Citizens, which of you knows this young man?' And several of the by-standers repeated: 'Who knows Jerónimo Rugera? Let him step forward!' Now it so happened that at this very moment little Juan, frightened by the uproar, began struggling in Josefa's arms and reaching out towards Don Fernando. At once a voice yelled: 'He is the father!' and another, 'He is Jerónimo Rugera!' and a third, 'These are the blasphemers!' And the whole assembly of Christians in that temple of Jesus raised a cry of 'Stone them! Stone them!' At this Jerónimo now cried out: 'Stop! You monsters! If you are looking for Jerónimo Rugera, he is here! Set free that man, who is innocent!'

The furious mob, confused by Jerónimo's words, hesitated; several hands released Don Fernando; and when at that moment a naval officer of high rank approached hurriedly and, pushing his way through the crowd, asked: 'Don Fernando Ormez! What has happened to you?', the latter, now quite free, replied with truly heroic presence of mind, 'Why, look, Don Alonzo, what murderous villains these are! I should have been a dead man if this worthy gentleman had not calmed the raging crowd by pretending to be Jerónimo Rugera. Be so kind as to take him into protective custody, and this young lady as well; and as for this scoundrel,' he added, seizing Master Pedrillo, 'arrest him, for it was he who started the whole commotion!' The cobbler shouted: 'Don Alonzo Onoreja, I ask you on your conscience, is this girl not Josefa Asterón?' And when Don Alonzo, who knew Josefa well, hesitated before answering, and several people, stung to new fury by this, cried out: 'It is her! it is her! Kill her!', Josefa placed both little Felipe, whom Jerónimo had hitherto been carrying, and little Juan in Don Fernando's arms, and said, 'Go, Don Fernando, save your two children and leave us to our fate!'

Don Fernando took both children and said he would sooner perish that allow any member of his party to suffer harm. He requested the naval officer to lend him his sword, offered his arm to Josefa, and told the couple behind them to follow him. And since in these circumstances the people made way for them with an adequate show of respect, they did indeed reach the door of the church, and thought themselves saved. But they had hardly entered the equally crowded forecourt when a voice from among the frenzied mob that had pursued them cried out: 'Citizens, this is Jerónimo Rugera, for I am his own father!' And the speaker, raising a cudgel, struck Jerónimo a colossal blow that felled him to the ground at Doña Constanza's side. 'Jesus! Holy Mother of God!' screamed Doña Constanza, fleeing to her brother-in-law's side; but immediately there was a cry of 'Convent whore!' and a second blow from another direction struck her down lifeless beside Jerónimo. 'Monsters!' cried an unidentified bystander, 'that was Doña Constanza Xares!' 'Why did they lie to us?' retorted the cobbler. 'Find the right one, and kill her!' Don Fernando, seeing Doña Constanza lying dead beside him, was maddened with rage; drawing and brandishing his sword, he aimed so furious a blow at the fanatical murderer who had instigated these horrors that it would have split him in half if the man had not dodged aside. But as he could not overpower the surging mass that pressed in on him, Josefa cried out: 'Farewell, Don Fernando. Here I am, murder me, you bloodthirsty tigers!' and voluntarily threw herself into their midst, to put an end to the fighting. Master Pedrillo struck her dead with his club. Then, drenched with her blood, he shrieked: 'Send her bastard to hell after her!' and pressed forward again, his lust for slaughter not yet sated.

Don Fernando, filled with superhuman heroism, was now standing with his back to the church; on his left arm he held the children, in his right hand his sword, and with every blow he struck one of his attackers down, his blade flashing like lightning; a lion could not have defended itself better. Seven of the butchers lay dead in front of him, and the prince of the satanic rabble was himself wounded. But Master Pedrillo would not give up until he had seized one of the infants by its legs, dragged it from Don Fernando's grasp, and after whirling it round in the air above his head, dashed it against the edge of one of the pillars of the church. After this, silence fell and the whole crowd dispersed. When Don Fernando saw his little Juan lying at his feet with his brains oozing out, he raised his eyes to heaven in inexpressible anguish.

The naval officer now rejoined him, tried to comfort him and assured him that although his own inaction during this terrible incident had been for various reasons justified, he now keenly regretted it; but Don Fernando said that there was no cause for reproaching him, and only asked him now to help remove the bodies. Night was falling, and in the darkness they were all carried to Don Alonzo's house; Don Fernando followed, with little Felipe still in his arms and his bitter tears raining down on the child's face. He also spent the night with Don Alonzo, and for some time refrained, by means of pretexts and fictions, from acquainting his wife with the full extent of the calamity; firstly because she was ill, and also because he did not know how she would judge his own conduct in the episode. But before long, accidentally learning from a visitor everything that had happened, this excellent lady quietly wept out her maternal grief, and one morning, with the trace of a tear glistening in her eye, threw her arms round her husband's neck and kissed him. Don Fernando and Doña Elvira then adopted the little stranger as their own son; and when Don Fernando compared Felipe with Juan and the ways in which he had acquired the two of them, it almost seemed to him that he had reason to feel glad.

The Marquise of O—

(Based on a true incident, the setting of which has
been transposed from the north to the south)

IN M—, an important town in northern Italy, the widowed
Marquise of O—, a lady of unblemished reputation and the
mother of several well-brought-up children, inserted the
following announcement in the newspapers : that she had,
without knowledge of the cause, come to find herself in a
certain situation; that she would like the father of the child
she was expecting to disclose his identity to her; and that
she was resolved, out of consideration for her family, to
marry him. The lady who, under the constraint of unalter-
able circumstances, had with such boldness taken so strange
a step and thus exposed herself to the derision of society,
was the daughter of Colonel G—, the Commandant of the
citadel at M—. About three years earlier her husband, the
Marquis of O—, to whom she was most deeply and tenderly
attached, had lost his life in the course of a journey to Paris
on family business. At the request of her excellent mother
she had, after his death, left the country estate at V—
where she had lived hitherto, and had returned with her
two children to the house of her father the Commandant.
Here she had for the next few years lived a very secluded
life, devoted to art and reading, the education of her children
and the care of her parents, until the — War suddenly
filled the neighbourhood with the armed forces of almost
all the powerful European states, including those of Russia.
Colonel G—, who had orders to defend the citadel, told his
wife and daughter to withdraw either to the latter's country
estate or to that of his son, which was near V—. But before
the ladies had even concluded their deliberations, weighing
up the hardships to which they would be subject in the
fortress against the horrors to which they would be exposed

in the open country, the Russian troops were already besieging the citadel and calling upon it to surrender. The Colonel announced to his family that he would now simply act as if they were not present, and answered the Russians with bullets and grenades. The enemy replied by shelling the citadel. They set fire to the magazine, occupied an outwork, and when after a further call to surrender the Commandant still hesitated to do so, an attack was mounted during the night and the fortress taken by storm.

Just as the Russian troops, covered by heavy artillery fire, were forcing their way into the castle, the left wing of the Commandant's residence was set ablaze and the women were forced to leave. The Colonel's wife, hurrying after her daughter who was fleeing downstairs with her children, called out to her that they should all stay together and take refuge in the cellars below; but at that very moment a grenade exploding inside the house threw everything into complete confusion. The Marquise found herself, with her two children, in the outer precincts of the castle where fierce fighting was already in progress and shots flashed through the darkness, driving her back again into the burning building, panic-stricken and with no idea where to turn. Here, just as she was trying to escape through the back door, she had the misfortune to encounter a troop of enemy riflemen, who as soon as they saw her suddenly fell silent, slung their guns over their shoulders and, with obscene gestures, seized her and carried her off. In vain she screamed for help to her terrified women, who went fleeing back through the gate, as the dreadful rabble tugged her hither and thither, fighting among themselves. Dragging her into the innermost courtyard they began to assault her in the most shameful way, and she was just about to sink to the ground when a Russian officer, hearing her piercing screams, appeared on the scene and with furious blows of his sword drove the dogs back from the prey for which they lusted. To the Marquise he seemed an angel sent from heaven. He smashed the hilt of his sword into the face of one of the murderous brutes, who still had his arms round her slender waist, and the man reeled back with blood pouring from his mouth; he then addressed the lady politely in French, offered her his arm and led her into the other wing of the palace which the flames had not yet reached and where, having already been stricken speechless by her ordeal, she now collapsed in a dead faint. Then – the officer instructed the Marquise's frightened servants, who presently arrived, to send for a doctor; he assured them that she would soon recover, replaced his hat and returned to the fighting.

In a short time the fortress had been completely taken by the enemy; the Commandant, who had only continued to defend it because he had not been offered amnesty, was withdrawing to the main gate with dwindling strength when the Russian officer, his face very flushed, came out through it and called on him to surrender. The Commandant replied that this demand was all that he had been waiting for, handed over his sword, and asked permission to go into the castle and look for his family. The Russian officer, who to judge by the part he was playing seemed to be one of the leaders of the attack, gave him leave to do so, accompanied by a guard; he then rather hastily took command of a detachment, put an end to the fighting at all points where the issue still seemed to be in doubt, and rapidly garrisoned all the strong points of the citadel. Shortly after this he returned to the scene of action, gave orders for the extinction of the fire which was beginning to spread furiously, and joined in this work himself with heroic exertion when his orders were not carried out with sufficient zeal. At one moment he was climbing about among burning gables with a hose in his hand, directing the jet of water at the flame; the next moment, while his Asiatic compatriots stood appalled, he would be right inside the arsenals rolling out powder kegs and live grenades. Meanwhile the Commandant had entered the house and learned with utter conster-

nation of the misadventure which had befallen his daughter.
The Marquise, who without medical assistance had already
completely recovered from her fainting fit, as the Russian
officer had predicted, was so overjoyed to see all her family
alive and well that she stayed in bed only in deference to
their excessive solicitude, assuring her father that all she
wanted was to be allowed to get up and thank her rescuer.
She had already been told that he was Count F—,
Lieutenant-Colonel of the – Rifle Corps and Knight of an
Order of Merit and of various others. She asked her father
to request him most urgently not to leave the citadel without paying them a short call in the residential quarters. The
Commandant, approving his daughter's feelings, did indeed
return immediately to the fortifications and found the Count
hurrying to and fro, busy with a multitude of military tasks;
there being no better opportunity to do so, he spoke to
him on the ramparts where he was reviewing his injured
and disorganized soldiery. Here he conveyed his grateful
daughter's message, and Count F— assured him that he was
only waiting for a moment's respite from his business to
come and pay her his respects. He was in the act of inquiring about the lady's health when several officers came up
with reports which snatched him back again into the turmoil of war. At daybreak the general in command of the
Russian forces arrived and inspected the citadel. He com-
plimented the Commandant, expressed his regret that the
latter's courage had not been better matched by good fortune, and granted him permission, on his word of honour,
to go to whatever place he chose. The Commandant thanked
him warmly, and declared that the past twenty-four hours
had given him much reason to be grateful to the Russians
in general and in particular to young Count F—, Lieutenant-
Colonel of the — Rifle Corps. The general asked what had
happened, and when he was told of the criminal assault on
the Commandant's daughter, his indignation knew no
bounds. He called Count F— forward by name and, after a

brief speech commending him for his gallant behaviour, which caused the Count to blush scarlet, he declared that he would have the perpetrators of this shameful outrage shot for disgracing the name of the Tsar, and ordered the Count to identify them. Count F— replied in some confusion that he was not able to report their names, since the faint glimmer of the lamps in the castle courtyard had made it impossible for him to recognize their faces. The general, who had heard that at the time in question the castle had been on fire, expressed surprise at this, remarking that after all persons known to one could be recognized in the darkness by their voices; the Count could only shrug his shoulders in embarrassment, and the general directed him to investigate the affair with the utmost urgency and rigour. At this moment someone pressed forward through the assembled troops and reported that one of the miscreants wounded by Count F— had collapsed in the corridor, and had been dragged by the Commandant's servants to a cell in which he was still being held prisoner. The general immediately had him brought under guard to his presence, where he was summarily interrogated; the prisoner named his accomplices and the whole rabble, five in number, were then shot. Having dealt with this matter, the general ordered the withdrawal of his troops from the citadel, leaving only a small garrison to occupy it; the officers quickly returned to the various units under their command; amid the confusion of the general dispersal the Count approached the Commandant and said how very sorry he was that in the circumstances he could do no more than send his respectful compliments to the Marquise; and in less than an hour the whole fortress was again empty of Russian troops.

The family were now considering how they might find a future opportunity of expressing their gratitude to the Count in some way, when they were appalled to learn that on the very day of his departure from the fortress he had lost his life in an encounter with enemy troops. The messenger who brought this news to M— had himself seen him, with a mortal bullet-wound in the chest, being carried to P—, where according to a reliable report he had died just as his bearers were about to set him down. The Commandant, going in person to the post-house to find out further details of what had happened, merely learnt in addition that on the battlefield, at the moment of being hit, he had cried out 'Giulietta! This bullet avenges you!', whereupon his lips had been sealed forever. The Marquise was inconsolable at having missed the opportunity of throwing herself at his feet. She reproached herself bitterly that when he had refused, presumably for reasons of modesty, to come and see her in the castle, she had not gone to him herself; she grieved for the unfortunate lady, bearing the same name as herself, whom he had remembered at the very moment of his death, and made vain efforts to discover her whereabouts in order to tell her of this unhappy and moving event; and several months passed before she herself could forget him.

It was now necessary for the Commandant and his family to move out of the citadel and let the Russian commander take up residence there. They first considered settling on the Colonel's estate, of which the Marquise was very fond; but since her father did not like living in the country, the family took a house in the town and furnished it suitably as a permanent home. They now reverted entirely to their former way of life. The Marquise resumed the long-interrupted education of her children, taking up where she had left off, and for her leisure hours she again brought out her easel and her books. But whereas she had previously been the very paragon of good health, she now began to be afflicted by repeated indispositions, which would make her unfit for company for weeks at a time. She suffered from nausea, giddiness and fainting fits, and was at a loss to account for her strange condition. One morning, when the family were sitting at tea and her father had left the room for a moment, the Marquise, emerging from a long reverie, said to her mother: 'If any woman were to tell me that she had felt just as I did a moment ago when I picked up this teacup, I should say to myself that she must be with child.' The Commandant's wife said she did not understand, and the Marquise repeated her statement, saying that she had just experienced a sensation exactly similar to those she had had a few years ago when she had been expecting her second daughter. Her mother remarked with a laugh that she would no doubt be giving birth to the god of Fantasy. The Marquise replied in an equally jesting tone that at any rate Morpheus, or one of his attendant dreams, must be the father. But the Colonel returned to the room and the conversation was broken off, and since a few days later the Marquise felt quite herself again, the whole subject was forgotten.

Shortly after this, at a time when the Commandant's son, who was a forestry official, also happened to be at home, a footman entered and to the family's absolute consternation announced Count F—. 'Count F—!' exclaimed the father and his daughter simultaneously; and amazement made them all speechless. The footman assured them that he had seen and heard aright, and that the Count was already standing waiting in the anteroom. The Commandant himself leapt to his feet to open the door to him, and he entered the room, his face a little pale, but looking as beautiful as a young god. When the initial scene of incomprehension and astonishment was over, with the parents objecting that surely he was dead and the Count assuring them that he was alive, he turned to their daughter with a gaze betokening much emotion, and his first words to her were to ask her how she was. The Marquise assured him that she was very well, and only wished to know how he, for his part, had come to life again. The Count, however, would not be diverted, and answered that she could not be telling him the truth: to judge by her complexion, he said, she seemed strangely fatigued, and unless he was very much mistaken

she was unwell, and suffering from some indisposition. The
Marquise, touched by the sincerity with which he spoke,
answered that as a matter of fact this fatigue could, since
he insisted, be interpreted as the aftermath of an ailment
from which she had suffered a few weeks ago, but that she
had no reason to fear that it would be of any consequence.
At this he appeared overjoyed, exclaiming: 'Neither have I!'
– and then asked her if she would be willing to marry him.
The Marquise did not know what to think of this unusual
behaviour. Blushing deeply, she looked at her mother, and
the latter stared in embarrassment at her son and her husband; meanwhile the Count approached the Marquise and,
taking her hand as if to kiss it, asked again whether she
had understood his question. The Commandant asked him
if he would not be seated, and placed a chair for him, courteously but rather solemnly. The Commandant's wife said:
'Count, we shall certainly go on thinking you are a ghost,
until you have explained to us how you rose again from
the grave in which you were laid at P—.' The Count, letting
go of the young lady's hand, sat down and said that circumstances compelled him to be very brief. He told them that he
had been carried to P— mortally wounded in the chest; that
there he had despaired of his life for several months; that
during this time his every thought had been devoted to the
Marquise; that her presence in his mind had caused him an
intermingling of delight and pain that was indescribable;
that after his recovery he had finally rejoined the army;
that he had there been quite unable to set his mind at rest;
that he had several times taken up his pen to relieve the
agitation of his heart by writing to the Colonel and the
Marquise; that he had been suddenly sent to Naples with
dispatches; that he did not know whether from there he
might not be ordered to go on to Constantinople; that he
would perhaps even have to go to St Petersburg; that in the
meantime there was a compelling need in his soul, a certain
matter which he had to settle if he was to go on living; that

as he was passing through M— he had been unable to resist the impulse to take a few steps towards the fulfilment of this purpose; in short, that he deeply desired the happiness of the Marquise's hand in marriage, and that he most respectfully, fervently and urgently begged them to be so kind as to give him their answer on this point. The Commandant, after a long pause, replied that he of course felt greatly honoured by this proposal, if it was meant seriously, as he had no doubt it was. But on the death of her husband, the Marquis of O—, his daughter had resolved not to embark on any second marriage. Since, however, the Count had not long ago put her under so great an obligation, it was not impossible that her decision might thereby be altered in accordance with his wishes; but that for the present he would beg him on her behalf to allow her some little time in which to think the matter over quietly. The Count assured him that these kind words did indeed satisfy all his hopes; that they would in other circumstances even completely content him; that he was very well aware of the great impropriety of finding them insufficient; but that pressing circumstances, which he was not in a position to particularize further, made it extremely desirable that he should have a more definite reply; that the horses that were to take him to Naples were already harnessed to his carriage; and that if there was anything in this house that spoke in his favour – here he glanced at the Marquise – then he would most earnestly implore them not to let him depart without kindly making some declaration to that effect. The Colonel, rather disconcerted by his behaviour, answered that the gratitude the Marquise felt for him certainly justified him in entertaining considerable hopes, but not so great as these; in taking a step on which the happiness of her whole life depended she would not proceed without due circumspection. It was indispensable that his daughter, before committing herself, should have the pleasure of his closer acquaintance. He invited him to return to M— after com-

pleting his journey and his business as ordered, and to stay
for a time in the family's house as their guest. If his daughter
then came to feel that she could hope to find happiness with
him – but not until then – he, her father, would be delighted
to hear that she had given him a definite answer. The Count,
his face reddening, said that during his whole journey here
he had predicted to himself that this would be the outcome
of his impatient desire; that the distress into which it plunged
him was nevertheless extreme; that in view of the unfavourable impression which he knew must be created by the part
he was at present being forced to play, closer acquaintance
could not fail to be advantageous to him; that he felt he
could answer for his reputation, if indeed it was felt necessary to take into account this most dubious of all attributes;
that the one ignoble action he had committed in his life was
unknown to the world and that he was already taking steps
to make amends for it; that, in short, he was a man of
honour, and begged them to accept his assurance that this
assurance was the truth. The Commandant, smiling slightly,
but without irony, replied that he endorsed all these statements. He had, he said, never yet made the acquaintance
of any young man who had in so short a time displayed so
many admirable qualities of character. He was almost sure
that a short period of further consideration would dispel the
indecision that still prevailed; but before the matter had
been discussed both with his own son and with the Count's
family, he could give no other answer than the one he had
already given. To this the Count rejoined that his parents
were both dead and he was his own master; his uncle was
General K—, whose consent to the marriage he was prepared
to guarantee. He added that he possessed a substantial
fortune, and was prepared to settle in Italy. The Commandant made him a courteous bow, but repeated that his
own wishes were as he had just stated, and requested that
this subject should now be dropped until after the Count's
journey. The latter, after a short pause in which he showed

every sign of a great agitation, remarked, turning to the young lady's mother, that he had done his utmost to avoid being sent on this mission; that he had taken the most decisive possible steps to this end, venturing to approach the Commander-in-Chief as well as his uncle General K—; but that they had thought that this journey would dispel a state of melancholy in which his illness had left him, whereas instead it was now plunging him into utter wretchedness. The family were nonplussed by this statement. The Count, wiping his brow, added that if there were any hope that to do so would bring him nearer to the goal of his wishes, he would try postponing his journey for a day or perhaps even for a little longer. So saying he looked in turn at the Commandant, the Marquise, and her mother. The Commandant cast his eyes down in vexation and did not answer him. His wife said: 'Go, go, my dear Count, make your journey to Naples; on your way back give us for some time the pleasure of your company, and the rest will see to itself.' The Count sat for a moment, seeming to ponder what he should do. Then, rising and setting aside his chair, he said that since the hopes with which he had entered this house had admittedly been over-precipitate and since the family very understandably insisted on closer acquaintance, he would return his dispatches to headquarters at Z— for delivery by someone else, and accept their kind offer of hospitality in this house for a few weeks. So saying he paused for a moment, standing by the wall with his chair in his hand, and looked at the Commandant. The latter replied that he would be extremely sorry if the Count were to get himself into possibly very serious trouble as a result of the passion which he seemed to have conceived for his daughter; that he himself, however, presumably knew best what his duties were; that he should therefore send off his dispatches and move into the rooms which were at his disposal. The Count was seen to change colour on hearing this; he then kissed his hostess's hand respectfully, bowed to the others, and withdrew.

When he had left the room, the family was at a loss to know what to make of this scene. The Marquise's mother said she could hardly believe it possible that having set out for Naples with dispatches he would send them back to Z— merely because on his way through M— he had failed, in a conversation lasting five minutes, to extract a promise of marriage from a lady with whom he was totally unacquainted. Her son pointed out that for such frivolous behaviour he would at the very least be arrested and confined to barracks. 'And cashiered as well!' added the Commandant. But, he went on, there was in fact no such danger. The Count had merely been firing a warning salvo, and would surely think again before actually sending back the dispatches. His wife, hearing of the danger to which the young man would be exposing himself by sending them off, expressed the liveliest anxiety that he might in fact do so. She thought that his headstrong nature, obstinately bent on one single purpose, would be capable of precisely such an act. She most urgently entreated her son to go after the Count at once and dissuade him from so fatal a step. Her son replied that if he did so it would have exactly the opposite effect, and merely confirm the Count's hopes of winning the day by his intended stratagem. The Marquise was of the same opinion, though she predicted that if her brother did not take this action it was quite certain that the dispatches would be returned, since the Count would prefer to risk the consequences rather than expose his honour to any aspersion. All were agreed that his behaviour was extraordinary, and that he seemed to be accustomed to taking ladies' hearts, like fortresses, by storm. At this point the Commandant noticed that the Count's carriage was standing by his front door with the horses harnessed and ready. He called his family to the window to look, and asked one of the servants who now entered whether the Count was still in the house. The servant replied that he was downstairs in the servants' quarters, attended by an adjutant, writing letters and sealing up packages. The Commandant, concealing his dismay, hurried downstairs with his son and, seeing the Count busy at work on a table that did not well befit him, asked whether he would not rather make use of his own apartments, and whether there was not anything else they could do to meet his requirements. The Count, continuing to write with great rapidity, replied that he was deeply obliged, but that he had now finished his business; as he sealed the letter he also asked what time it was; he then handed over the entire portfolio to the adjutant and wished him a safe journey. The Commandant, scarcely believing his eyes, said as the adjutant left the house: 'Count, unless your reasons are extremely weighty –' 'They are absolutely compelling!' said the Count, interrupting him. He accompanied the adjutant to the carriage and opened the door for him. The Commandant persisted: 'In that case I would at least send the dispatches –' 'Impossible!' answered the Count, helping the adjutant into his seat. 'The dispatches would carry no authority in Naples without me. I did think of that too. Drive on!' 'And your uncle's letters, sir?' called the adjutant, leaning out of the carriage door. 'They will reach me in M—,' replied the Count. 'Drive on!' said the adjutant, and the carriage sped on its way.

Count F— then turned to the Commandant and asked him if he would be kind enough to have him shown to his room. 'It will be an honour for me to show you to it at once,' answered the bewildered Colonel. He called to his servants and to the Count's servants, telling them to look after the latter's luggage; he then conducted him to the apartments in his house which were set aside for guests and there rather stiffly took his leave of him. The Count changed his clothes, left the house to report his presence to the military governor, and was not seen in the house for the whole of the rest of that day, only returning just before dinner.

In the meantime the family were in considerable dismay. The Commandant's son described how categorical the Count's replies had been when his father had attempted to reason with him; his action, he thought, was to all appearances deliberate and considered; what on earth, he wondered, could be the motive of this post-haste wooing? The Commandant said that the whole thing was beyond his comprehension, and forbade the family to mention the subject again in his presence. His wife kept on looking out of the window as if she expected the Count to return, express regret for his hasty action, and take steps to reverse it. Eventually, when it grew dark, she joined her daughter who was sitting at a table absorbed in some work and evidently intent on avoiding conversation. As the Commandant paced up and down, she asked her in an undertone whether she had any idea of how this matter would end. The Marquise, with a diffident glance towards the Commandant, replied that if only her father could have prevailed on him to go to Naples, everything would have been all right. 'To Naples!' exclaimed her father, who had overheard this remark. 'Ought I to have sent for a priest? Or should I have had him arrested, locked up and sent to Naples under guard?' 'No,' answered his daughter, 'but emphatic remonstrances can be effective.' And she rather crossly looked down at her work again. Finally, towards nightfall, the Count reappeared. The family fully expected that, after the first exchange of courtesies, discussion of the point in question would be reopened, and they would then join in unanimously imploring him to retract, if it were still possible, the bold step he had taken. But a suitable moment for this exhortation was awaited in vain throughout dinner. Sedulously avoiding anything that might have led on to that particular topic, he conversed with the Commandant about the war and with his son, the forester, about hunting. When he mentioned the engagement at P— in the course of which he had been wounded, the Marquise's mother elicited from him an account of his illness, asking him how he had fared at so tiny a place and whether he had been provided there with all proper comforts. In answer he told them various interesting details relevant to his passion for the Marquise: how during his illness she had been constantly present to him, sitting at his bedside; how in the feverish delirium brought on by his wound he had kept confusing his visions of her with the sight of a swan, which, as a boy, he had watched on his uncle's estate; that he had been particularly moved by one memory, of an occasion on which he had once thrown some mud at this swan, whereupon it had silently dived under the surface and re-emerged, washed clean by the water; that she had always seemed to be swimming about on a fiery surface and that he had called out to her 'Tinka!', which had been the swan's name, but that he had not been able to lure her towards him. For she had preferred merely to glide about, arching her neck and thrusting out her breast. Suddenly, blushing scarlet, he declared that he loved her more than he could say; then looked down again at his plate and fell silent. At last it was time to rise from the table; and when the Count, after a further brief conversation with the Marquise's mother, bowed to the company and retired again to his room, they were all once more left standing there not knowing what to think. The Commandant was of the opinion that they must simply let things take their course. The Count, in acting as he did, was no doubt relying on his relatives without whose intervention on his behalf he must certainly face dishonourable discharge. The Marquise's mother asked her what she felt about him, and whether she could not perhaps bring herself to give him some indication or other that might avert an unfortunate outcome. Her daughter replied: 'My dear mother, that is impossible! I am sorry that my gratitude is being put to so severe a test. But I did decide not to marry again; I do not like to chance my happiness a second time, and certainly not with such ill-considered haste.' Her brother observed that if such was her firm intention, then a declaration to *that* effect could also help the Count, and that it looked rather as if they would have to give him *some* definite answer, one way or the other. The Colonel's wife replied that since the young man had so many outstanding qualities to recommend him, and had declared himself ready to settle in Italy, she thought that his offer deserved some consideration and that the Marquise should reflect carefully before deciding. Her son, sitting down beside his sister, asked her whether she found the Count personally attractive. The Marquise, with some embarrassment, answered that she found him both attractive and unattractive, and that she was willing to be guided by what the others felt. Her mother said: 'When he comes back from Naples, and if between now and then we were to make inquiries which did not reveal anything that ran contrary to the general impression you have formed of him, then what answer would you give him if he were to repeat his proposal?' 'In that case,' replied the Marquise, 'I – since his wishes do seem to be so pressing' – she faltered at this point and her eyes shone – 'I would consent to them for the sake of the obligation under which he has placed me.' Her mother, who had always hoped that her daughter would re-marry, had difficulty in concealing her delight at this declaration, and sat considering to what advantage it might be turned. Her son, getting up again in some uneasiness, said that if the Marquise were even remotely considering a possibility of one day bestowing her hand in marriage on the Count, some step in this direction must now immediately be taken if the consequences of his reckless course of action were to be forestalled. His mother agreed, remarking that after all they could be taking no very great risk, since the young man had displayed so many excellent qualities on the night of the Russian assault on the fortress that there was every reason to assume him to be a person of consistently good character. The Marquise cast down her eyes with an air of considerable agitation. 'After all,' continued her mother, taking her by the hand, 'one could perhaps intimate to him that until he returns from Naples you undertake not to enter into any other engagement.' The Marquise said: 'Dearest mother, *that* undertaking I can give him; but I fear it will not satisfy him and only compromise us.' 'Let me take care of that!' replied her mother, much elated; she looked round for her husband and seemed about to rise to her feet. 'Lorenzo!' she asked, 'What do you think?' The Commandant, who had heard this whole discussion, went on standing by the window, looking down into the street, and said nothing. The Marquise's brother declared that, on the strength of this noncommittal assurance from her, he would now personally guarantee to get the Count out of the house. 'Well then, do so! do so! Do so, all of you!' exclaimed his father, turning round. 'That makes twice already I must surrender to this Russian!' At this his wife sprang to her feet, kissed him and their daughter, and asked, with an eagerness which made her husband smile, how they were to set about conveying this intimation without delay to the Count. At her son's suggestion it was decided to send a footman to his room requesting him to be so kind, if he were not already undressed, as to rejoin the family for a moment. The Count sent back word that he would at once have the honour to appear, and scarcely had this message been brought when he himself, joy winging his step, followed it into the room and sank to his knees, with deep emotion, at the Marquise's feet. The Commandant was about to speak, but Count F—, standing up, declared that he already knew enough. He kissed the Colonel's hand and that of his wife, embraced the Marquise's brother, and merely asked if they would do him the favour of helping him to find a coach immediately. The Marquise, though visibly touched by this scene, nevertheless managed to say: 'I need not fear, Count, that rash hopes will mislead —' 'By no means, by no means!' replied the Count. 'I will hold you to nothing, if the outcome of such inquiries as you may make about me is in any way adverse to the feeling which has just recalled me to your presence.' At this the Commandant heartily embraced him, the Marquise's brother at once offered him his own travelling-carriage, a groom was dispatched in haste to the post-station to order horses at a premium rate, and there was more pleasure at this departure than has ever been shown at a guest's arrival. The Count said that he hoped to overtake his dispatches in B—, whence he now proposed to set out for Naples by a shorter route than the one through M—; in Naples he would do his utmost to get himself released from the further mission to Constantinople; in the last resort he was resolved to report himself as sick, and could therefore assure them that unless prevented by unavoidable circumstances he would without fail be back in M— within four to six weeks. At this point his groom reported that the carriage was harnessed and everything ready for his departure. The Count picked up his hat, went up to the Marquise and took her hand. 'Well, Giulietta,' he said, 'this sets my mind partly at rest.' Laying his hand in hers he added, 'Yet it was my dearest wish that before I left we should be married.' 'Married!' exclaimed the whole family. 'Married,' repeated the Count, kissing the Marquise's hand, and when she asked him whether he had taken leave of his senses he assured her that a day would come when she would understand what he meant. The family was on the point of losing patience with him, but he at once most warmly took his leave of them all, asked them to take no further notice of his last remark, and departed.

Several weeks passed, during which the family, with very mixed feelings, awaited the outcome of this strange affair. The Commandant received a courteous letter from General K—, the Count's uncle; the Count himself wrote from Naples; inquiries about him were put in hand and quite favourable reports received; in brief, the engagement was already regarded as virtually definitive – when the Marquise's indispositions recurred, more acutely than ever before. She noticed an incomprehensible change in her figure.

She confided with complete frankness in her mother, telling her that she did not know what to make of her condition. Her mother, learning of these strange symptoms, became extremely concerned about her daughter's health and insisted that she should consult a doctor. The Marquise, hoping that her natural good health would reassert itself, resisted this advice; she suffered severely for several more days without following it, until constantly repeated sensations of the most unusual kind threw her into a state of acute anxiety. She sent for a doctor who enjoyed the confidence of her father; at a time when her mother happened to be out of the house she invited him to sit down on the divan, and after an introductory remark or two jestingly told him what condition she believed herself to be in. The doctor gave her a searching look; he then carefully examined her, and after doing so was silent for a little; finally he answered with a very grave expression that the Marquise had judged correctly how things were. When the lady inquired what exactly he meant he explained himself unequivocally, adding with a smile which he could not suppress that she was perfectly well and needed no doctor, whereupon the Marquise rang the bell and with a very severe sidelong glance requested him to leave her. She murmured to herself in an undertone, as if it were beneath her dignity to address him, that she did not feel inclined to joke with him about such matters. The doctor, offended, replied that he could only wish she had always been as much in earnest as she was now; so saying, he picked up his hat and stick and made as if to take his leave. The Marquise assured him that she would inform her father of his insulting remarks. The doctor answered that he would swear to his statement in any court of law; with that he opened the door, bowed, and was about to leave the room. As he paused to pick up a glove he had dropped, the Marquise exclaimed: 'But doctor, how is what you say possible?' The doctor replied that she would presumably not expect him to explain the facts of life to her; he then bowed again and withdrew.

The Marquise stood as if thunderstruck. Recovering herself, she was on the point of going straight to her father; but the strangely serious manner of this man by whom she felt so insulted numbed her in every limb. She threw herself down on the divan in the greatest agitation. Mistrustful of herself, she cast her mind back over every moment of the past year, and when she thought of those through which she had just passed it seemed to her that she must be going crazy. At last her mother appeared, and in answer to her shocked inquiry as to why she was so distressed, the Marquise informed her of what the doctor had just said. Her mother declared him to be a shameless and contemptible wretch, and emboldened her in her resolution to report this insult to her father. The Marquise assured her that the doctor had been completely in earnest and seemed quite determined to repeat his insane assertion to her father's face. Did she then, asked her mother in some alarm, believe there was any possibility of her being in such a condition? 'I would sooner believe that graves can be made fertile,' answered the Marquise, 'and that new births can quicken in the womb of the dead!' 'Why then, you dear strange girl,' said her mother, hugging her warmly, 'what can be worrying you? If your conscience clears you, what can a doctor's verdict matter, or indeed the verdict of a whole panel of doctors? This particular one may be mistaken, or he may be malicious, but why need that concern you at all? Nevertheless it is proper that we should tell your father about it.' 'Oh, God!' said the Marquise, starting convulsively, 'how can I set my mind at rest? Do not my own feelings speak against me, those inner sensations I know only too well? If I knew that another woman was feeling as I do, would I not myself come to the conclusion that that was indeed how things stood with her?' 'But this is terrible!' exclaimed her mother. 'Malicious! mistaken!' continued the Marquise. 'What reasons can that man, whom until today we have always respected, what reasons can he have for insulting me so frivolously and basely? Why should he do so, when I have never said anything to offend him? When I received him here with complete trust, fully expecting to be bound to him in gratitude? When he came to me sincerely and honestly intending, as was evident from his very first words, to help me rather than to cause me far worse pain than I was already suffering? And if on the other hand,' she went on, while her mother gazed at her steadily, 'I were forced to choose between the two possibilities and preferred to suppose that he had made a mistake, is it in the least possible that a doctor, even one of quite mediocre skill, should be mistaken in such a case?' Her mother replied, a little ironically : 'And yet, of course, it must necessarily have been one or the other.' 'Yes, dearest mother!' answered the Marquise, kissing her hand but with an air of offended dignity and blushing scarlet, 'it must indeed, although the circumstances are so extraordinary that I may be permitted to doubt it. And since it seems that I must give you an assurance, I swear now that my conscience is as clear as that of my own children's; no less clear, my beloved and respected mother, than your own. Nevertheless, I ask you to have a midwife called in to see me, in order that I may convince myself of what is the case and then, whatever it may be, set my mind at rest.' 'A midwife!' exclaimed the Commandant's wife indignantly, 'a clear conscience, and a midwife!' And speech failed her. 'A midwife, my dearest mother,' repeated the Marquise, falling on her knees before her, 'and let her come at once, if I am not to go out of my mind.' 'Oh, by all means,' replied her mother. 'But the confinement, if you please, will not take place in my house.' And with these words she rose and would have left the room. Her daughter, following her with outspread arms, fell right down on her face and clasped her knees. 'If the irreproachable life I have led,' she cried, with anguish lending her eloquence, 'a life modelled on yours, gives me any claim at all to your respect, if there is in your heart any maternal feeling for me at all, even if only for so long as my guilt is not yet proved and clear as day, then do not abandon me at this terrible moment!' 'But what is upsetting you?' asked her mother. 'Is it nothing more than the doctor's verdict? Nothing more than your inner sensations?' 'Nothing more, dear mother,' replied the Marquise, laying her hand on her breast. 'Nothing, Giulietta?' continued her mother. 'Think carefully. If you have committed a fault, though that would grieve me indescribably, it would be forgivable and in the end I should have to forgive it; but if, in order to avoid censure from your mother, you were to invent a fable about the overturning of the whole order of nature, and dared to reiterate blasphemous vows in order to persuade me of its truth, knowing that my heart is all too eager to believe you, then that would be shameful; I could never feel the same about you again.' 'May the doors of salvation one day be as open to me as my soul is now open to you!' cried the Marquise. 'I have concealed nothing from you, mother.' This declaration, uttered with passionate solemnity, moved her mother deeply. 'Oh God!' she cried, 'my dear, dear child! How touchingly you speak!' And she lifted her up and kissed her and pressed her to her heart. 'Then what in the name of all the world are you afraid of? Come, you are quite ill,' she added, trying to lead her towards a bed. But the Marquise, weeping copiously, assured her that she was quite well and that there was nothing wrong with her, apart from her extraordinary and incomprehensible condition. 'Condition!' exclaimed her mother again, 'what condition? If your recollection of the past is so clear, what mad apprehension has possessed you? Can one not be deceived by such internal sensations, when they are still only obscurely stirring?' 'No! no!' said the Marquise, 'they are not deceiving me! And if you will have the midwife called, then you will hear that this terrible, annihilating thing is true.' 'Come, my darling,' said the Commandant's wife, who was beginning to fear for her daughter's reason. 'Come with me; you must go to bed. What was it you thought the

doctor said to you? Why, your cheeks are burning hot!
You're trembling in every limb! Now, what was it the
doctor told you?' And no longer believing that the scene
of which she had been told had really happened at all, she
took her daughter by the arm and tried to draw her away.
Then the Marquise, smiling through her tears, said: 'My
dear, excellent mother! I am in full possession of my senses.
The doctor told me that I am expecting a child. Send for
the midwife; and as soon as she tells me that it is not true
I shall regain my composure.' 'Very well, very well!' replied
her mother, concealing her apprehension. 'She shall come at
once; if that is what you want, she shall come and laugh
her head off at you and tell you what a silly girl you are to
imagine such things.' And so saying she rang the bell and
immediately sent one of her servants to call the midwife.

When the latter arrived the Marquise was still lying with
her mother's arms around her and her breast heaving in
agitation. The Commandant's wife told the woman of the
strange notion by which her daughter was afflicted: that
her ladyship swore her behaviour had been entirely virtuous
but that nevertheless, deluded by some mysterious sensation or other, she considered it necessary to submit her
condition to the scrutiny of a woman with professional
knowledge. The midwife, as she carried out her investigation, spoke of warm-blooded youth and the wiles of the
world; having finished her task she remarked that she had
come across such cases before; young widows who found
themselves in her ladyship's situation always believed
themselves to have been living on desert islands; but that
there was no cause for alarm, and her ladyship could rest
assured that the gay corsair who had come ashore in the
dark would come to light in due course. On hearing these
words, the Marquise fainted. Her mother was still sufficiently moved by natural affection to bring her back to her
senses with the midwife's assistance, but as soon as she
revived, maternal indignation proved stronger. 'Giulietta!'

she cried in anguish, 'will you confess to me, will you tell me who the father is?' And she still seemed disposed towards a reconciliation. But when the Marquise replied that she would go mad, her mother rose from the couch and said: 'Go from my sight, you are contemptible! I curse the day I bore you!' and left the room.

The Marquise, now nearly swooning again, drew the midwife down in front of her and laid her head against her breast, trembling violently. With a faltering voice she asked her what the ways of nature were, and whether such a thing as an unwitting conception was possible. The woman smiled, loosened her kerchief and said that that would, she was sure, not be the case with her ladyship. 'No, no,' answered the Marquise, 'I conceived knowingly, I am merely curious in a general way whether such a phenomenon exists in the realm of nature.' The midwife replied that with the exception of the Blessed Virgin it had never yet happened to any woman on earth. The Marquise trembled more violently than ever. She felt as if she might go into labour at any minute, and clung to the midwife in convulsive fear, begging her not to leave her. The woman calmed her apprehension, assuring her that the confinement was still a long way off; she also informed her of the ways and means by which it was possible in such cases to avoid the gossip of the world, and said she was sure everything would turn out nicely. But these consoling remarks merely pierced the unhappy lady to the very heart; composing herself with an effort she declared that she felt better, and requested her attendant to leave her.

The midwife was scarcely out of the room when a footman brought the Marquise a written message from her mother, who expressed herself as follows: 'In view of the circumstances which have come to light, Colonel G— desires you to leave his house. He sends you herewith the papers concerning your estate and hopes that God will spare him the unhappiness of ever seeing you again.' But the letter was wet with tears, and in one corner, half effaced, stood the word 'dictated'. Tears of grief started from the Marquise's eyes. Weeping bitterly at the thought of the error into which her excellent parents had fallen and the injustice into which it had misled them, she went to her mother's apartments, but was told that her mother was with the Commandant. Hardly able to walk, she made her way to her father's rooms. Finding the door locked she sank down outside it, and in a heartrending voice called upon all the saints to witness her innocence. She had been lying there for perhaps a few minutes when her brother emerged, his face flushed with anger, and said that as she already knew, the Commandant did not wish to see her. The Marquise, sobbing distractedly, exclaimed: 'Dearest brother!', and pushing her way into the room she cried: 'My beloved father!' She held out her arms towards the Commandant, but no sooner did he see her than he turned his back on her and hurried into his bedroom. As she tried to follow him he shouted 'Begone!' and tried to slam the door; but when she cried out imploringly and prevented him from doing so he suddenly desisted and letting the Marquise into the room, strode across to the far side of it with his back still turned to her. She had just thrown herself at his feet and tremblingly clasped his knees when a pistol which he had seized went off just as he was snatching it down from the wall, and a shot crashed into the ceiling. 'Oh, God preserve me!' exclaimed the Marquise, rising from her knees as pale as death, and fled from her father's apartment. Reaching her own, she gave orders that her carriage should be made ready at once, sat down in utter exhaustion, hastily dressed her children, and told the servants to pack her belongings. She was just holding her youngest child between her knees, wrapping one more garment round it, and everything was ready for their departure in the carriage, when her brother entered and demanded, on the Commandant's orders, that she should leave the children behind and hand them over to him. 'These children!' she exclaimed, rising to her feet. 'Tell your inhuman father that he can come here and shoot me dead, but he shall not take my children from me!' And armed with all the pride of innocence she snatched up her children, carried them with her to the coach, her brother not daring to stop her, and drove off.

This splendid effort of will gave her back her self-confidence, and as if with her own hands she raised herself right out of the depths into which fate had cast her. The turmoil and anguish of her heart ceased when she found herself on the open road with her beloved prize, the children; she covered them with kisses, reflecting with great satisfaction what a victory she had won over her brother by the sheer force of her clear conscience. Her reason was strong enough to withstand her strange situation without giving way, and she submitted herself wholly to the great, sacred and inexplicable order of the world. She saw that it would be impossible to convince her family of her innocence, realized that she must accept this fact for the sake of her own survival, and only a few days after her arrival at V— her grief had been replaced by a heroic resolve to arm herself with pride and let the world do its worst. She decided to withdraw altogether into her own life, to devote herself zealously and exclusively to the education of her two children, and to care with full maternal love for the third which God had now given her. Since her beautiful country house had fallen rather into disrepair owing to her long absence, she made arrangements for its restoration, to be completed in a few weeks' time, as soon as her confinement was over; she sat in the summer-house knitting little caps and socks for little feet, and thinking about what use she might most conveniently make of various rooms, which of them for instance she would fill with books and in which of them her easel might be most suitably placed. And thus, even before the date of Count F—'s expected return from Naples, she was quite reconciled to a life of perpetual cloistered seclusion. Her porter was ordered to admit no visitors to the house. The only thing she found intolerable was the thought that the little creature she had conceived in the utmost innocence and purity and whose origin, precisely because it was more mysterious, also seemed to her more divine than that of other men, was destined to bear a stigma of disgrace in good society. An unusual expedient for discovering the father had occurred to her: an expedient which, when she first thought of it, so startled her that she let fall her knitting. For whole nights on end, restless and sleepless, she turned it over and over in her mind, trying to get used to an idea the very nature of which offended her innermost feelings. She still felt the greatest repugnance at the thought of entering into any relationship with the person who had tricked her in such a fashion; for she most rightly concluded that he must after all irredeemably belong to the very scum of mankind, and that whatever position of society one might imagine him to occupy, his origin could only be from its lowest, vilest dregs. But with her sense of her own independence growing ever stronger, and reflecting as she did that a precious stone retains its value whatever its setting may be, she took heart one morning, as she felt the stirring of the new life inside her, and gave instructions for the insertion in the M— news-sheets of the extraordinary announcement quoted to the reader at the beginning of this story.

Meanwhile Count F—, detained in Naples by unavoidable duties, had written for the second time to the Marquise urging her to consider that unusual circumstances might arise which would make it desirable for her to abide by the tacit undertaking she had given him. As soon as he had succeeded in declining his further official journey to Constantinople, and as soon as his other business permitted, he at once left Naples and duly arrived in M— only a few days later than the date on which he had said he would do so. The Commandant received him with an air of embarrassment, said that he was about to leave the house on urgent business, and asked his son to entertain the Count in the meantime. The latter took him to his room and, after greeting him briefly, asked him whether he already knew about what had happened in the Commandant's house during his absence. The Count, turning pale for a moment, answered that he did not. The Marquise's brother thereupon informed him of the disgrace which his sister had brought upon the family, and narrated the events with which our readers are already acquainted. The Count struck his forehead with his hand and exclaimed, quite forgetting himself: 'Why were so many obstacles put in my way! If the marriage had taken place, we should have been spared all this shame and unhappiness!' The Commandant's son, staring at him wide-eyed, asked him whether he was so crazy as to want to be married to so contemptible a person. The Count replied that she was worth more than the whole of the world which despised her; that he for his part absolutely believed her declaration of innocence; and that he would go that very day to V— and renew his offer to her. So saying he at once picked up his hat and left, after bidding farewell to the Commandant's son, who concluded that he must have taken leave of his senses.

Taking a horse he galloped out to V—. When he had dismounted at the gate and was about to enter the forecourt, the porter told him that her ladyship was not at home to anyone. The Count inquired whether these instructions, issued presumably to keep away strangers, also applied to a friend of the family, to which the man answered that he was not aware of any exceptions to them; and he then almost at once inquired, in a rather dubious manner, whether the gentleman were not perhaps Count F—? The Count, after glancing at him sharply, answered that he was not; then turning to his servant, but speaking loudly enough for the other man to hear, he said that in these circumstances he would lodge at an inn and announce himself to her ladyship in writing. But as soon as he was out of the porter's sight he turned a corner and slipped quietly round the wall of an extensive garden which lay behind the house. By a door which he found unlocked he entered the garden, walked through it along the paths, and was just about to ascend the terrace to the rear of the house when in an arbour at one side of it he caught sight of the Marquise, her figure charmingly and mysteriously altered, sitting busily working at a little table. He approached her in such a manner that she could not notice him until he was standing at the entrance to the arbour, three short steps from her feet. 'Count F—!' she exclaimed as she looked up, blushing scarlet with surprise. The Count smiled, and remained standing motionless in the entrance for some moments; then, with a show of affection sufficiently modest not to alarm her, he sat down at her side, and before she could make up her mind what to do in so strange a situation, he put his arm gently and lovingly around her waist. 'But Count, how is this possible, where have you —' began the Marquise, and then shyly cast down her eyes. 'From M—,' said the Count, pressing her very gently to him. 'I found a back door open and came through it into your garden; I felt sure you would forgive me for doing so.' 'But when you were in M— did they not tell you — ?' she asked, still motionless in his arms. 'Everything, dearest lady,' replied the Count. 'But fully convinced of your innocence —' 'What!' cried the Marquise, rising to her feet and trying to free herself from him, 'and despite that you come here?' 'Despite the world,' he went on, holding her fast, 'and despite your family, and even despite your present enchanting appearance' — at which words he ardently kissed her breast. 'Go away!' she exclaimed, but he continued: '— as convinced, Giulietta, as if I were omniscient, as if my own soul were living in your body.' The Marquise cried: 'Let me go!' 'I have come,' he concluded, still without releasing her, 'to repeat my proposal and to receive, if you will accept it,

the bliss of paradise from your hand.' 'Let me go immediately!' she cried, 'I order you to let me go!', and freeing
herself forcibly from his embrace she started away from
him. 'Darling! adorable creature!' he whispered, rising
to his feet again and following her. 'You heard me!' cried
the Marquise, turning and evading him. 'One secret, whispered word!' said the Count, hastily snatching at her
smooth arm as it slipped from him. 'I *do not want to hear*
anything,' she retorted, violently pushing him back; then
she fled up on to the terrace and disappeared.

He was already half-way up to her, determined at all
costs to get a hearing, when the door was slammed in his
face, and in front of his hurrying steps he heard the bolt
rattle as with distraught vehemence she pushed it home. He
stood for a moment undecided what to do in this situation,
considering whether he should climb in through a side
window which was standing open, and pursue his purpose
until he had achieved it; but although it was in every sense
difficult for him to desist, it did now seem necessary to do so,
and bitterly vexed with himself for letting her slip from
his arms, he retreated from the terrace, left the garden,
and went to find his horse. He felt that his attempt to pour
out his heart to her in person had failed forever, and rode
slowly back to M—, thinking over the wording of a letter
which he now felt condemned to write. That evening, as
he was dining in a public place, very much out of humour,
he met the Marquise's brother, who at once asked him
whether he had successfully made his proposal in V—.
The Count answered curtly that he had not, and felt very
much inclined to dismiss his interlocutor with some bitter
phrase; but for the sake of politeness he presently added
that he had decided to write the lady a letter, which would
soon clarify the issue. The Commandant's son said he
noticed with regret that the Count's passion for his sister
was driving him quite out of his mind. He must, however,
assure the Count that she was already on her way to making

a different choice; so saying he rang for the latest newspapers and gave the Count the sheet in which was inserted his sister's advertisement appealing to the father of her child. The Count flushed suddenly as he read it; conflicting emotions rushed through him. The Marquise's brother asked him if he did not think that she would find the person she was looking for. 'Undoubtedly!' answered the Count, with his whole mind intent on the paper, greedily devouring the meaning of the announcement. Then, after folding it up and stepping over to the window for a moment, he said: 'Now everything is all right! Now I know what to do!' He then turned round, and after courteously asking the Commandant's son whether they would soon meet again, he took his leave of him and departed, quite reconciled to his lot.

Meanwhile some very animated scenes had taken place at the Commandant's house. His wife was in a state of extreme vexation at her husband's destructive vehemence and at her own weakness in allowing him to overrule her objections to his tyrannical banishment of their daughter. When she heard the pistol shot in his bedroom and saw her daughter rushing out of it she had fainted away; she had, to be sure, soon recovered herself, but all the Commandant did when she came to her senses was to apologize for causing her this unnecessary alarm, and throw the discharged pistol down on to a table. Later, when it was proposed to claim custody of their daughter's children, she timorously ventured to declare that they had no right to take such a step; in a voice still weak from her recent swoon, she touchingly implored him to avoid violent scenes in the house; but the Commandant, not answering her, had merely turned foaming with rage to his son and ordered him: 'Go to her! and bring them back here!' When Count F—'s second letter arrived, the Commandant had ordered that it should be sent out to the Marquise at V—; the messenger afterwards reported that she had simply laid it on one side and dismissed him. Her mother, to whom so much in this whole affair was incomprehensible, more particularly her daughter's inclination to get married again and to someone totally indifferent to her, tried vainly to initiate a discussion of this point. Each time she did so the Commandant requested her to be silent, in a manner more like an order than a request; on one such occasion he removed from the wall a portrait of his daughter that was still hanging there, declaring that he wished to expunge her completely from his memory; he no longer, he said, had a daughter. Then the Marquise's strange advertisement was published. The Commandant had handed the paper containing it to his wife, who read it with absolute amazement and went with it to her husband's rooms, where she found him working at a table, and asked him what on earth he thought of it. The Commandant continuing to write, said: 'Oh, she is innocent!' 'What!' exclaimed his wife, astonished beyond measure, 'innocent?' 'She did it in her sleep,' said the Commandant, without looking up. 'In her sleep!' replied his wife. 'And you are telling me that such a monstrous occurrence –' 'Silly woman!' exclaimed the Commandant, pushing his papers together and leaving the room.

On the next day on which news was published the Commandant's wife, seated with her husband at breakfast, was handed a news-sheet which had just arrived not yet dry from the printers, and in it she read the following answer: 'If the Marquise of O— will be present at 11 o'clock on the morning of the 3rd of — in the house of her father Colonel G—, the man whom she wishes to trace will there cast himself at her feet.'

The Colonel's wife became speechless before she had even read halfway through this extraordinary insertion; she glanced at the end, and handed the sheet to the Commandant. The latter read it through three times, as if he could not believe his own eyes. 'Now tell me, in heaven's name, Lorenzo,' cried his wife, 'what do you make of that?' 'Why, the infamous woman!' replied the Commandant, rising from the table, 'the sanctimonious hypocrite! The shamelessness of a bitch coupled with the cunning of a fox and multiplied tenfold are as nothing to hers! So sweet a face! Such eyes, as innocent as a cherub!' And nothing could calm his distress. 'But if it is a trick,' asked his wife, 'what on earth can be her purpose?' 'Her purpose?' retorted the Colonel. 'She is determined to force us to accept her contemptible pretence. She and that man have already learnt by heart the cock-and-bull story they will tell us when the two of them appear here on the third at eleven in the morning. And I shall be expected to say : "My dear little daughter, I did not know that, who could have thought such a thing, forgive me, receive my blessing, and let us be friends again." But I have a bullet ready for the man who steps across my threshold on the third! Or perhaps it would be more suitable to have him thrown out of the house by the servants.' His wife, after a further perusal of the announcement in the paper, said that if she was to believe one of two incomprehensible things, then she found it more credible that some extraordinary quirk of fate had occurred than that a daughter who had always been so virtuous should now behave so basely. But before she had even finished speaking, her husband was already shouting : 'Be so good as to hold your tongue! I cannot bear,' he added, leaving the room, 'even to hear this hateful matter mentioned.'

A few days later the Commandant received a letter from the Marquise referring to the second announcement, and most respectfully and touchingly begging him, since she had been deprived of the privilege of setting foot in his house, to be so kind as to send whoever presented himself there on the morning of the third out to her estate at V—. Her mother happened to be present when the Commandant received this letter, and she noticed by the expression on his face that his feelings had become confused; for if the whole thing was indeed a trick, what motive was he to impute to her now, since she seemed to be making no sort of claim to his forgiveness? Emboldened by this, she accordingly proposed a plan which her heart, troubled by doubts as it was, had for some time been harbouring. As her husband still stared expressionlessly at the paper, she said that she had an idea. Would he allow her to go for one or two days out to V—? She undertook to devise a situation in which the Marquise, if she really knew the man who had answered her advertisement as if he were a stranger, would undoubtedly betray herself, even if she was the world's most sophisticated deceiver. The Commandant, with sudden violence, tore his daughter's letter to shreds, and replied to his wife that, as she well knew, he wished to have nothing whatever to do with its writer, and absolutely forbade her mother to enter into any communication with her. He sealed up the torn pieces in an envelope, wrote the Marquise's address on it, and returned it to the messenger as his answer. His wife, inwardly exasperated by this headstrong obstinacy which would destroy any possibility they had of clearing the matter up, now decided to carry out her plan against her husband's will. On the very next morning, while the Commandant was still in bed, she took one of his grooms and drove with him out to V—. When she reached the gate of her daughter's country house, the porter told her that his orders were to admit no one to her ladyship's presence. The Commandant's wife replied that she knew of these orders, but that he was nevertheless to go and announce the wife of Colonel G—. To this the man answered that it would be useless to do so, since his mistress was receiving no one, and there were no exceptions. The Commandant's wife answered that she would be received by his mistress, as she was her mother; would he therefore be good enough to do his errand without further delay. But scarcely had the man, still predicting that this mission would be fruitless, entered the house than the Marquise was seen to emerge from it and come in haste to the gate, where she fell on her knees before her mother's carriage. The latter, assisted by her groom, stepped down from it, and in some emotion raised her daughter from the ground. The Marquise, quite overwhelmed by her feelings, bowed low over her mother's hand to kiss it; then, shedding frequent tears, she very respectfully conducted her through the rooms of her house and seated her on a divan. 'My dearest mother!' she exclaimed, still standing in front of her and drying her eyes, 'to what happy chance do I owe the inexpressible pleasure of your visit?' Her mother, taking her affectionately by the hand, said that she must tell her she had simply come to ask her forgiveness for the hard-hearted way in which she had been expelled from her parents' house. 'Forgiveness!' cried the Marquise, and tried to kiss her hand. But her mother, withdrawing her hand, continued: 'For not only did the recently published answer to – your advertisement convince myself and your father of your innocence, but I have also to tell you that the man in question, to our great delight and surprise, has already presented himself at our house yesterday.' '*Who* has already –?' asked the Marquise, sitting down beside her mother, '*what* man in question has presented himself –?' And her face was tense with expectation. Her mother answered: 'The man who wrote that reply, he himself in person, the man to whom your appeal was directed.' 'Well, then,' said the Marquise, with her breast heaving in agitation, 'who is he?' And she repeated: 'Who is he?' 'That,' replied her mother, 'is what I should like you to guess. For just imagine: yesterday, as we were sitting at tea, and in the act of reading that extraordinary newspaper announcement, a man with whom we are quite intimately acquainted rushed into the room with gestures of despair and threw himself down at your father's feet, and presently at mine as well. We had no idea what to make of this and asked him to explain himself. So he said that his conscience was giving him no peace, it was he who had so shamefully deceived our daughter; he could not but know how his crime was judged, and if retribution was to be exacted from him for it, he had come to submit himself to that retribution.' 'But who? who? who?' asked the Marquise. 'As I told you,' continued her mother, 'an otherwise well-brought-up young man whom we should never have considered capable of so base an act. But my dear daughter, you must not be alarmed to hear that he is of humble station, and quite lacks all the qualifications that a husband of yours might otherwise be expected to have.' 'Nevertheless, my most excellent mother,' said the Marquise, 'he cannot be wholly unworthy, since he came and threw himself at your feet before throwing himself at mine. But who? who? please tell me *who*!' 'Well,' replied her mother, 'it was Leopardo, the groom from Tyrol whom your father recently engaged, and whom as you may have noticed I have already brought with me to present to you as your fiancé.' 'Leopardo, the groom!' cried the Marquise, pressing her hand to her forehead with an expression of despair. 'Why are you startled?' asked her mother. 'Have you reasons for doubting it?' 'How? where? when?' asked the Marquise in confusion. 'That,' answered her mother, 'is something he wishes to confess only to you. Shame and love, he told us, made it impossible for him to communicate these facts to anyone except yourself. But if you like we will open the anteroom, where he is waiting with a beating heart for the outcome, and then I shall leave you together, and you will see whether you can elicit his secret from him.' 'Oh, God in heaven!' cried the Marquise: 'it did once happen that I had fallen asleep in the mid-day heat, on my divan, and when I woke up I saw him walking away from it!' Her face grew scarlet with shame and she covered it with her little hands. But at this point her mother fell to her knees before her. 'Oh, Giulietta!' she exclaimed, throwing her arms round her, 'oh, my dear excellent girl! And how contemptible of me!' And she buried her face in her daughter's lap. The Marquise gasped in consternation: 'What is the matter, mother?'

'For let me tell you now,' continued her mother, 'that nothing of what I have been saying to you is true; you are purer than an angel, you radiate such innocence that my corrupted soul could not believe in it, and I could not convince myself of it without descending to this shameful trick.' 'My dearest mother!' cried the Marquise, full of happy emotion, and stooped down to her, trying to raise her to her feet. But her mother said: 'No, I shall not move from your feet, you splendid, heavenly creature, until you tell me that you can forgive the baseness of my behaviour.' 'Am I to forgive you!' exclaimed her daughter. 'Please rise, I do implore you –' 'You heard me,' said the Commandant's wife. 'I want to know whether you can still love me, whether you can still respect me as sincerely as ever?' 'My adored mother!' cried the Marquise, now kneeling before her as well, 'my heart has never lost any of its respect and love for you. Under such extraordinary circumstances, how was it possible for anyone to trust me? How glad I am that you are convinced that I have done nothing wrong!' 'Well, my dearest child,' said her mother, standing up with her daughter's assistance, 'now I shall love and cherish you. You shall have your confinement in my house; and I shall treat you with no less tenderness and respect than if we had reason to expect your baby to be a young prince. I shall never desert you now as long as I live. I defy the whole world; I want no greater honour than your shame – if only you will love me again, and forget the hard-hearted way in which I rejected you!' The Marquise tried to comfort her with endless caresses and assurances, but evening fell and midnight struck before she had succeeded. Next day, when the old lady had recovered a little from her emotion, which had made her feverish during the night, the mother, daughter and grandchildren drove back in triumph, as it were, to M—. Their journey was a very happy one, and they joked about the groom Leopardo as he sat in front of them driving the carriage: the Marquise's mother said she noticed how her daughter blushed every time she looked at his broad shoulders, and the Marquise, reacting half with a sigh and half with a smile, answered: 'I wonder after all who the man will be who turns up at our house on the morning of the third!' Then, the nearer they got to M—, the more serious their mood became again, in anticipation of the crucial scenes that still awaited them. As soon as they had arrived at the house, the Commandant's wife, concealing her plans, showed her daughter back to her old rooms, and told her to make herself comfortable; then, saying that she would soon be back, she slipped away. An hour later she returned with her face very flushed. 'Why, what a doubting Thomas!' she said, though she seemed secretly delighted, 'what a doubting Thomas! Didn't I need a whole hour by the clock to convince him! But now he's sitting there weeping.' 'Who?' asked the Marquise. 'He himself,' answered her mother. 'Who else but the person with the most cause for it!' 'Surely not my father?' exclaimed the Marquise. 'Weeping like a child,' replied her mother. 'If I had not had to wipe the tears out of my own eyes, I should have burst out laughing as soon as I got outside the door.' 'And all this on my account?' asked her daughter, rising to her feet, 'and you expect me to stay here and —?' 'You shall not budge!' said her mother. 'Why did he dictate that letter to me! *He* shall come here to *you*, or *I* shall have no more to do with him as long as I live.' 'My dearest mother —' pleaded the Marquise, but her mother interrupted her. 'I'll not give way! Why did he reach for that pistol?' 'But I implore you —' 'You *shall* not go to him,' replied the Commandant's wife, forcing her daughter to sit down again, 'and if he does not come by this evening, I shall leave the house with you tomorrow.' The Marquise said that this would be a hard and unfair way to act, but her mother answered (for she could already hear sobs approaching from a distance): 'You need not worry; here he is already!' 'Where?' asked her daughter, and sat listening. 'Is there someone there at the door, quite convulsed with –?' 'Of course!' replied the Commandant's wife; 'he wants us to open it for him.' 'Let me go!' cried the Marquise, leaping from her chair. But her mother answered: 'Giulietta, if you love me, stay where you are!' – and at that very moment the Commandant entered the room, holding his handkerchief to his face. His wife placed herself directly between him and her daughter and turned her back on him. 'My dearest father!' cried the Marquise, stretching out her arms towards him. 'You shall not budge, I tell you!' said her mother. The Commandant stood there in the room, weeping. 'He is to apologize to you,' continued his wife. 'Why has he such a violent temper, and why is he so obstinate? I love him but I love you too; I respect him, but I respect you too. And if I must choose, then you are a finer person than him, and I shall stay with you.' The Commandant was standing bent almost double and weeping so loudly that the walls re-echoed. 'Oh, my God, but –' exclaimed the Marquise, suddenly giving up the struggle with her mother, and taking out her handkerchief to let her own tears flow. Her mother said: 'It's just that he can't speak!' and moved a little to one side. At this the Marquise rose, embraced her father, and begged him to calm himself. She too was weeping profusely. She asked him if he would not sit down, and tried to draw him on to a chair; she pushed one up for him to sit on; but he made no answer, he could not be induced to move, nor even sit down, but merely stood there with his face bowed low over the ground, and wept. The Marquise, holding him upright, half turned to her mother and said she thought he would make himself ill; her mother too seemed on the point of losing her composure, for he was going almost into convulsions. But when he had finally seated himself, yielding to the repeated pleas of his daughter, and the latter, ceaselessly caressing him, had sunk down at his feet, his wife returned to her point, declared that it served him right, and that now he would no doubt come to his senses; whereupon she departed and left the two of them in the room.

As soon as she was outside the door she wiped away her own tears, wondering whether the violent emotional upheaval she had caused him might not after all be dangerous, and whether it would be advisable to have a doctor called. She went to the kitchen and cooked for his dinner all the most nourishing and comforting dishes she could devise; she prepared and warmed his bed, intending to put him into it as soon as, hand in hand with his daughter, he reappeared. But when the dinner table was already laid and there was still no sign of him, she crept back to the Marquise's room to find out what on earth was going on. Putting her ear gently against the door and listening, she caught the last echo of some softly murmured words, spoken, as it seemed to her, by the Marquise; and looking through the keyhole she noticed that her daughter was even sitting on the Commandant's lap, a thing he had never before permitted. And when finally she opened the door she saw a sight that made her heart leap with joy: her daughter, with her head thrown right back and her eyes tightly shut, was lying quietly in her father's arms, while the latter, with tears glistening in his wide-open eyes, sat in the armchair, pressing long, ardent, avid kisses on to her mouth, just like a lover! His daughter said nothing, he said nothing; he sat with his face bowed over her, as if she were the first girl he had ever loved; he sat there holding her mouth near his and kissing her. Her mother felt quite transported with delight; standing unseen behind his chair, she hesitated to interrupt this blissful scene of reconciliation which had brought such joy back to her house. Finally, she approached her husband, and just as he was again stroking and kissing his daughter's mouth in indescribable ecstasy, she leaned round the side of the chair and looked at him. When the Commandant saw her he at once lowered his eyes again with a cross expression and was about to say something; but she exclaimed: 'Oh, what a face to make!' And then she in her turn smoothed it out with kisses, and talked jestingly until the atmosphere of emotion was dispelled. She asked them both to come and have dinner, and as she led the way they walked along like a pair of betrothed lovers; at table the Commandant seemed very happy, though he still sobbed from time to time, ate and spoke little, gazed down at his plate, and caressed his daughter's hand.

The question now was, who in the world would turn up at eleven o'clock on the following morning, for the next day to dawn would be the dreaded third. The Marquise's father and mother, as well as her brother who had arrived to share in the general reconciliation, were decidedly in favour of marriage, if the person should be at least tolerably acceptable; everything within the realm of possibility would be done to ensure her happiness. If, on the other hand, the circumstances of the person in question should turn out to be such that even with the help of her family they would still fall too far short of the Marquise's own, then her parents were opposed to her marrying him; they were resolved in that case to let her live with them as before and to adopt the child as theirs. It seemed, however, to be the Marquise's wish to keep her promise in any case, provided the person were not a complete scoundrel, and thus at all costs to provide the child with a father. On the eve of the assignation her mother raised the question of how the visitor was to be received. The Commandant was of the opinion that the most suitable procedure would be, when eleven o'clock came, to leave the Marquise by herself. The latter however insisted that both her parents, and her brother as well, should be present, since she did not want to share any secrets with the expected person. She also thought that this would be his own wish, which in his answer he had seemed to express by suggesting her father's house as the place for the meeting; and she added that she must confess to having been greatly pleased by this answer for that very reason. Her mother thought that under this arrangement the roles played by her husband and son would be most unseemly; she begged her daughter to consent to the two men being absent, but agreed to meet her wishes to the extent of being present herself when the person arrived. After the Marquise had thought it over for a little this last proposal was finally adopted. The night was then passed in a state of suspense and expectancy, and now the morning of the dreaded third had come. As the clock struck eleven both women were sitting in the reception room, festively attired as for a betrothal; their hearts were beating so hard that one could have heard them if the noises of daytime had ceased. The eleventh stroke of the clock was still reverberating when Leopardo entered, the groom whom the Commandant had hired from Tyrol. At the sight of him the women turned pale. 'I am to announce Count F—, my lady,' he said, 'his carriage is at the door.' 'Count F—!' they exclaimed simultaneously, thrown from one kind of consternation into another. The Marquise cried: 'Shut the doors! We are not at home to him!' She rose at once to lock the door of the room herself, and was in the act of thrusting out the groom as he stood in her way, when the Count entered, in exactly the same uniform, with the same decorations and weapons, as he had worn and carried on the day of the storming of the fortress. The Marquise felt she would sink into the ground from sheer confusion; she snatched up a handkerchief she had left lying on her chair and was about to rush off into a neighbouring room, when her mother, seizing her by the hand, exclaimed: 'Giulietta –!', and her thoughts seemed to stifle any further words. She stared straight at the Count, and repeated, drawing her daughter towards her: 'Why, Giulietta, whom have we been expecting –?' The Marquise, turning suddenly, cried: 'Well? You surely cannot mean him –?' She fixed on the Count such a look that it seemed to flash like a thunderbolt, and her face went deathly pale. He had gone down on one knee before her; his right hand was on his heart, his head meekly bowed, and there he remained, blushing scarlet and with downcast eyes, saying nothing. 'Who else?' exclaimed her mother, her voice almost failing. 'Who else but him? How stupid we have been –!' The Marquise stood over him, rigidly erect, and said: 'Mother, I shall go mad!' 'Foolish girl,' replied her mother, and she drew her towards her and whispered something into her ear. The Marquise turned away and collapsed on to the sofa with both hands pressed against her face. Her mother cried: 'Poor wretched girl! What is the matter with you? What has happened that can have taken you by surprise?' The Count did not move, but knelt on beside the Commandant's wife, and taking the outermost hem of her dress in his hand he kissed it. 'Dear, gracious, noble lady!' he whispered, and a tear rolled down his cheek. 'Stand up, Count,' she answered, 'stand up! Comfort my daughter; then we shall all be reconciled, and all will be forgiven and forgotten.' The Count rose to his feet, still shedding tears. He again knelt down in front of the Marquise, gently took her hand as if it were made of gold and the warmth of his own might tarnish it. But she, standing up, cried: 'Go away! go away! go away! I was prepared to meet a vicious man, but not – not a devil!' And so saying she moved away from him as if he were a person infected with the plague, threw open the door of the room and said: 'Call my father!' 'Giulietta!' cried her mother in astonishment. The Marquise stared at them each in turn with annihilating rage; her breast heaved, her face was aflame; no Fury's gaze could be more terrifying. The Commandant and his son arrived. 'Father,' said the Marquise, as they were in the act of entering the room, 'I cannot marry this man!' And dipping her hand into a vessel of holy water that was fastened to the door, she scattered it lavishly over her father, mother and brother, and fled.

The Commandant, disconcerted by this strange occurrence, asked what had happened, and turned pale when he noticed that Count F— was in the room at this decisive moment. His wife took the Count by the hand and said:

'Do not ask; this young man sincerely repents all that has happened; give him your blessing, give it, give it – and all will still turn out for the best.' The Count stood there utterly mortified. The Commandant laid his hand on his head; his eyelids twitched, his lips were as white as chalk. 'May the curse of heaven be averted from your head!' he exclaimed. 'When are you intending to get married?' 'To-morrow,' answered the Marquise's mother on the Count's behalf, for the latter was unable to utter a word. 'To-morrow or today, whichever you like; I am sure no time will be too soon for my lord the Count, who has shown such admirable zeal to make amends for his wrongdoing.' 'Then I shall have the pleasure of seeing you tomorrow at eleven o'clock at the Church of St Augustine!' said the Commandant; whereupon he bowed to him, asked his wife and son to accompany him to his daughter's room, and left the Count to himself.

The family made vain efforts to discover from the Marquise the reason for her strange behaviour; she was lying in an acutely feverish condition, refused absolutely to listen to any talk of getting married, and asked them to leave her alone. When they inquired why she had suddenly changed her mind and what made the Count more repugnant to her than any other suitor, she gave her father a blank wide-eyed stare and made no answer. Her mother asked whether she had forgotten that she was herself a mother; to which she replied that in the present case she was bound to consider her own interests before those of the child, and calling on all the angels and saints as witnesses she reasserted her refusal to marry. Her father, to whom it seemed obvious that she was in a hysterical state of mind, declared that she must keep her word; he then left her, and put in hand all the arrangements for the wedding after an appropriate written exchange with the Count. He submitted to him a marriage contract by which he would renounce all con-jugal rights while at the same time binding himself to fulfil any duties that might be imposed upon him. The document came back wet with tears, bearing the Count's signature. When the Commandant handed it the next morning to the Marquise she had somewhat recovered her composure. Still sitting in her bed, she read the paper through several times, folded it up thoughtfully, opened it again and re-read it; then she declared that she would come to the Church of St Augustine at eleven o'clock. She rose, dressed without saying a word, got into the carriage with her parents and brother when the hour struck, and drove off to the appointed meeting-place.

The Count was not permitted to join the family until they reached the entrance to the church. During the ceremony the Marquise stared rigidly at the painting behind the altar and did not vouchsafe even a fleeting glance at the man with whom she was exchanging rings. When the marriage service ended, the Count offered her his arm; but as soon as they reached the church door again the Countess took her leave of him with a bow; her father inquired whether he would occasionally have the honour of seeing him in his daughter's apartments; whereupon the Count muttered something unintelligible, raising his hat to the company, and disappeared. He moved into a residence in M— and spent several months there without ever once setting foot in the Commandant's house, where the Countess continued to live. It was only owing to his delicate, dignified, and wholly exemplary behaviour on all occasions on which he came into any contact at all with the family, that when in due course the Countess was delivered of an infant son he was invited to the christening. The Countess, still confined and sitting in her bed under richly embroidered coverlets, saw him only for an instant when he presented himself and greeted her from a respectful distance. Among the other presents with which the guests had welcomed the newcomer, he threw on to his son's cradle two documents; after his departure one of these turned out to be a deed of gift

of 20,000 roubles to the boy, and the other a will making
the boy's mother, in the event of the Count's death, heiress
to his entire fortune. From that day on the Commandant's
wife saw to it that he was frequently invited; the house was
open to him and soon not an evening passed without his
paying the family a visit. His instinct told him that, in
consideration of the imperfection inherent in the order of
the world, he had been forgiven by all of them, and he
therefore began a second wooing of the Countess, his wife;
when a year had passed he won from her a second consent,
and they even celebrated a second wedding, happier than
the first, after which the whole family moved out to the
estate at V—. A whole series of young Russians now
followed the first, and during one happy hour the Count
asked his wife why, on that terrible third day of the month,
when she had seemed willing to receive the most vicious of
debauchees, she had fled from him as if from a devil. Throwing her arms round his neck, she answered that she would
not have seen a devil in him then if she had not seen an
angel in him at their first meeting.

Michael Kohlhaas

(From an old chronicle)

ABOUT the middle of the sixteenth century there lived beside the banks of the River Havel a horse-dealer called Michael Kohlhaas, the son of a schoolmaster, who was one of the most honourable as well as one of the most terrible men of his age. Until his thirtieth year this extraordinary man could have been considered a paragon of civil virtues. In a village that still bears his name he owned a farm where he peacefully earned a living by his trade; his wife bore him children whom he brought up in the fear of God to be hard-working and honest; he had not one neighbour who was not indebted to his generosity or his fair-mindedness; in short, the world would have had cause to revere his memory, had he not pursued one of his virtues to excess. But his sense of justice made him a robber and a murderer.

One day he was riding out of Brandenburg with a string of young horses, all of them well nourished and with glossy coats. He was just considering how he would invest the profit he hoped to make from them at the markets – partly, as a wise businessman does, to yield fresh profit, but also partly for present enjoyment – when he reached the Elbe and, close to a magnificent castle on Saxon soil, encountered a toll-gate that he had never seen on this road before. Just as it was beginning to pour with rain he stopped his horses and called to the keeper, who soon poked a sullen face out of the window. The horse-dealer told him to open the barrier. 'What's happened here?' he asked when the toll-gate keeper finally emerged from the house. 'State privilege, conferred on Junker Wenzel von Tronka,' said the latter, opening the lock. 'I see,' said Kohlhaas, 'the Junker is called Wenzel, is he?' and stared at the castle, whose gleaming turrets looked out across the fields. 'So the old master is dead?' 'Died of an apoplexy,' replied the keeper, as he raised the barrier. 'Hm! A pity!' rejoined Kohlhaas. 'A fine old gentleman, who enjoyed people coming and going and assisted trade and traffic whenever he could. Once he had a road paved because a mare of mine broke her leg out there where the highway leads into the village. Well now! How much do I owe you?' he asked, and laboriously fished the small change demanded by the toll-keeper out of the pocket of his coat, which was flapping in the wind. 'Yes, old man,' he added as the latter muttered at him to hurry, and cursed the weather, 'it would have been better for me and for you if the tree for that pole had never been felled'; and thereupon he gave him the money and made to ride off. But hardly had he passed beneath the barrier when a fresh voice cried out from the tower behind him: 'Stop there, horse-dealer!' and he saw the castle warden slam a window to and come hurrying down towards him. 'Well, what's going on here?' Kohlhaas asked himself as he brought the horses to a halt. The warden, still fastening a waistcoat across his capacious body, came up and, bracing himself against the wind and rain, demanded the horse-dealer's permit. 'My permit?' asked Kohlhaas and added, a little disconcerted, that so far as he knew he did not possess one, but that if the warden would kindly explain what on earth such a thing was he just might possibly have one with him. The warden, looking askance at him, replied that without a state permit a dealer bringing horses could not be allowed across the border. The horse-dealer assured him that he had crossed the border seventeen times in his life without such a document; that he was accurately informed about all the state regulations affecting his trade; that there must have been a mistake, on which would they be so good as to reflect, and that since he still had a long way to go that day, he did not wish to be detained here pointlessly any longer. But the warden retorted that he would not slip through for the eighteenth time, that the regulation had only recently been made for precisely that reason, and that he must either purchase a passport on the spot or return whence he came. The horse-dealer, who was beginning to be angered by these illegal and extortionate demands, reflected for a moment, got off his horse, gave it to a stable-boy and said that he would speak to Junker von Tronka personally about the matter. With that he walked to the castle, the warden followed him muttering about niggardly cut-purses who could do with an occasional bleeding, and they entered the hall, looking each other up and down. As chance would have it, the Junker was carousing with some friends and an anecdote had just set off a tremendous roar of laughter among them when Kohlhaas came up to make his complaint. The Junker asked him what he wanted; the knights fell silent when they saw the stranger; but hardly had Kohlhaas begun to state his request concerning the horses when the whole company exclaimed 'Horses? Where are they?', and rushed to the window to look at them. Seeing what magnificent specimens they were they hastened, at the Junker's suggestion, down into the courtyard. The rain had stopped; the warden, the steward and the grooms gathered round behind them, and they all inspected the animals. One praised the sorrel with the blaze, another liked the chestnut, a third stroked the piebald with the tawny patches, and they all agreed that the horses were like stags and none finer had been reared in the entire country. Kohlhaas replied good-humouredly that the horses were no finer than the gentlemen who would ride them, and offered them for sale. The Junker, who was very attracted by the sorrel stallion, inquired what price he was asking, and the steward tried to persuade him to buy a pair of blacks, which he thought he could use on the estate as they had too few horses; but when the horse-dealer named his price the gentlemen thought it too high, and the Junker said that if that was how he rated his horses he would have to go and find King Arthur and the Round Table. Kohlhaas noticed the warden and the steward whispering together and throwing knowing glances at the blacks, and prompted by an obscure foreboding he did his utmost to get rid of the horses to them. He told the Junker: 'My lord, I bought the blacks six months ago for twenty-five gold florins; give me thirty and they are yours.' Two knights, standing near the Junker, said quite audibly that the horses were certainly worth that much, but the Junker declared that, while he might spend some money on the sorrel, he would not take the blacks, and began to turn away. At this, Kohlhaas said that he might be able to do a deal with him the next time he was passing through with his animals, took leave of the Junker and caught hold of his horse's bridle as if to ride off. At that moment the warden stepped forward from the company and said he had been told that he was not allowed to travel without a permit. Kohlhaas turned round and asked the Junker whether this regulation, which would ruin his whole business, was in fact correct? Moving away, the Junker answered, with a look of embarrassment: 'Yes, Kohlhaas, you will have to get a permit. Have a word with the warden and go on your way.' Kohlhaas assured him that it was in no way his intention to evade any laws affecting the exportation of horses, promised that when passing through Dresden he would have the permit made out at the Chancellery and asked that, as he had known nothing at all of this requirement, he might travel on just this once. 'Oh, well,' said the Junker, as the wind began to get up again and whistled between his spindly legs, 'let the poor wretch go. Come!' he said to his friends, turned round and was about to go back into the castle. The warden, looking at the Junker, said that Kohlhaas would at least have to leave something behind as surety that he would get the permit. The Junker stopped again in the castle gateway. Kohlhaas asked how much he would have to deposit in money or in goods on account of the blacks. The steward muttered into his beard that he might just as well leave the blacks themselves. 'Of course,' said the warden, 'that is the most practical solution; once he has bought the permit he can come and collect them whenever he likes.' Taken aback by such an unconscionable demand, Kohlhaas pointed out to the Junker, who was wrapping the tails of his jerkin round his freezing body, that he wanted to sell the blacks. But at that very moment a gust of wind drove a great sheet of rain and hail through the gateway, and to put an end to the matter the Junker shouted : 'If he refuses to leave the horses, throw him back over the toll-gate', and went in. Seeing clearly that he would have to yield to force, the horse-dealer decided that he had no choice but to do as they demanded; he unharnessed the blacks, and led them to a stable which the warden pointed out to him. He left a groom behind with them, provided him with some money, bade him take good care of the blacks until his return, and with the remainder of the horses continued his journey to Leipzig where he intended to visit the fair; it occurred to him that perhaps, after all, such a regulation might have been issued in Saxony on account of the expansion in horse-rearing.

Once he had reached Dresden, where he owned a house and some stables on the outskirts from which he carried on his trade at the smaller markets in the principality, he went to the Chancellery where he discovered from the officials, some of whom he knew, what his original feeling had already told him : the story about the permit was a mere fabrication. At his request and none too willingly, they furnished him with a written certificate of its ground-lessness and Kohlhaas smiled at the skinny Junker's joke, though he did not quite see what the purpose of it could have been. A few weeks later, with the string of horses he had brought with him sold to his satisfaction, he returned to Tronka Castle with no more bitterness in his heart than one might feel at the general sorry state of the world. The warden, to whom he showed the certificate, made no further comment, and when the horse-dealer asked if he could now have his horses back, told him just to go down and fetch them. But no sooner had Kohlhaas crossed the court-yard than to his unpleasant surprise he heard that his groom had been beaten and thrown out only a few days after being left behind at the castle, allegedly for insolent behaviour. Kohlhaas asked the stable-boy who told him this news what his man had done and who had looked after his horses in the meantime, but the boy replied that he did not know, and coming to the stable where they were, he opened it for the horse-dealer, whose heart was already alive with misgivings. But to his utter consternation he now beheld, instead of his two glossy, well-nourished blacks, a pair of scrawny, worn-out nags, their bones pro-truding like pegs you could have hung things on, their manes and coats matted together from lack of care and grooming – the very epitome of misery in the animal kingdom! Kohlhaas, to whom the beasts feebly whinnied a greeting, asked in extreme indignation what had hap-pened to his horses. The stable-boy, standing beside him, answered that nothing particular had happened to them, and that they had been given their proper feed, but that as it had been harvest-time and there had not been enough draught animals, they had been used a little in the fields. Kohlhaas cursed this shameful, premeditated outrage, but suppressed his fury which he knew would be futile, and as he had no choice, was just preparing to leave this robbers' den with his horses when the warden, hearing high words, came over and asked what was going on. 'What's going on?' retorted Kohlhaas. 'Who gave Junker von Tronka and his men permission to take the horses I left behind here and use them for field work? Was that,' he added, 'a humane thing to do?' He tried to rouse the exhausted beasts with a flick of his riding-switch and pointed out that they did not move. Staring at him haughtily for a few moments, the warden exclaimed: 'What a churlish fellow! A lout like you ought to thank his lucky stars that the animals are still alive!' He asked who was supposed to have looked after them when the groom had absconded, and whether it was not right that the horses should work for the fodder they had been given; and finally he said that Kohlhaas had better cause no trouble here or he would call the dogs and get peace restored in the yard that way. The horse-dealer's heart pounded against his doublet. He felt a strong impulse to hurl this pot-bellied villain into the mud and stamp on his copper-coloured face. But his sense of justice, which was as fine as a gold-balance, still wavered; the judge within his own heart could not decide whether his opponent was guilty; and as he walked over to the horses, stifling his imprecations, and combed out their manes, he asked in a subdued voice, silently weighing up the circumstances, what offence the groom had committed to be expelled from the castle. The warden retorted: 'The rogue behaved insubordinately in the stable-yard. He refused to accept a necessary change of stabling and demanded that the horses of two young gentlemen who were visiting Tronka Castle should stay out on the open road all night just for the sake of his nags.' Kohlhaas would gladly have sacrificed the whole value of the horses to have had the groom at hand and to be able to compare his statement with the statement of this loud-mouthed castle warden. He was still standing combing out the blacks' matted manes, and reflecting what was to be done in his situation, when the scene was suddenly transformed and Junker Wenzel von Tronka galloped into the castle yard with a troop of knights, attendants and hounds, fresh from hare-coursing. When he asked what had happened the warden immediately spoke up, and while the dogs, sighting the stranger, uttered bloodcurdling howls from one side and the knights shouted at them to be quiet from the other, he gave the Junker a most maliciously distorted account of how the horse-dealer was making all this stir just because his blacks had been used a little. Laughing scornfully, he said that Kohlhaas refused to recognize the horses as his own. Kohlhaas exclaimed: 'Those are *not* my horses, my lord; those are not the *horses* that were worth thirty gold florins! I want my healthy, well-nourished horses back!' The Junker dismounted, blenching for an instant, and said: 'If the damned fool won't take his horses back, let him leave them here. Come, Günter! Hans! Come!' he shouted again, as he and his friends were still in the doorway; and then he vanished into the house. Kohlhaas said that he would rather have the knacker come and take the horses to the flaying-yard than return with them to his stables at Kohlhaasenbrück in their present condition. Taking no more notice of the nags, he left them standing where they were, mounted his bay, vowed that he would see to it that justice was done him, and rode off.

He was already galloping down the road towards Dresden when his mind turned to the groom and the charge made against him at the castle. He slowed down to a walk, and before he had gone another mile turned his horse round in the direction of Kohlhaasenbrück, intending to ask the groom some preliminary questions, a course which seemed both prudent and fair. For despite the insults he had suffered, experience had already given him a realistic sense of the imperfection inherent in the order of the world, and this feeling inclined him to accept the loss of the horses as a just consequence, should the groom indeed be in some part guilty as the castle warden claimed. At the same time another equally praiseworthy feeling began to take ever deeper root in him as he rode along and heard, wherever he stopped, of the daily injustices committed at Tronka Castle against travellers: a feeling that if the whole affair had been deliberately preconceived, as it certainly appeared to have been, it was now his duty to the world at large to exert all his powers in securing redress for the wrongs already perpetrated and protection for his fellow citizens against such wrongs in the future.

Upon his return to Kohlhaasenbrück he embraced his

devoted wife, Lisbeth, kissed his children, who were jumping for joy round his knees, and immediately inquired about Herse, the head groom, and whether anything had been heard of him. 'Ah, dearest Michael,' said Lisbeth, 'poor Herse! Why, about a fortnight ago the wretch arrived here, most piteously beaten and so badly injured that he couldn't breathe properly. We put him to bed, where he kept vomiting blood, and, after repeatedly questioning him, we were told a story which none of us can understand. Apparently he was left behind by you at Tronka Castle with some horses that were not allowed free passage; he was then most shamefully ill-treated and forced to leave the castle, and it was impossible for him to bring the horses with him.' 'I see,' said Kohlhaas, taking off his coat. 'Has he recovered yet?' 'More or less,' replied Lisbeth, 'but he is still spitting up blood. I wanted to send another groom straight away to Tronka Castle to look after the horses until your return, for Herse has always been truthful and loyal to us, and indeed more so than anyone else. I had no reason to doubt his statement, for which there was so much evidence, nor to imagine that he might have lost the horses in any other manner. But he implored me not to ask anyone to show his face in that den of robbers, and told me that I should abandon the animals unless I wanted to sacrifice a man's life for them.' 'I suppose he is still in bed?' said Kohlhaas, untying his kerchief. 'He has been up and about on the farm for a few days now,' she replied, and added: 'You will soon see that all this is true and that the affair is another of the crimes they have been committing lately against strangers at Tronka Castle.' 'I shall have to investigate first,' answered Kohlhaas. 'Call him to me, Lisbeth, if he is up!' With these words he sat down in his armchair, and his wife, very pleased at his composure, went and fetched the groom.

'What did you do at Tronka Castle?' asked Kohlhaas, when Lisbeth brought him into the room, 'I'm not alto-

gether satisfied with your conduct.' For a few moments the
groom, whose pallid face flushed blotchy red at these words,
remained silent. Then he answered: 'You are right there,
master! I had with me by God's providence a slow-match
which would have set fire to that robbers' den they drove
me out of, but I threw it into the Elbe because I heard a
child crying indoors and thought to myself: let God's lightning burn it down – I'll not do it!' Moved by his words,
Kohlhaas asked: 'But what did you do to get turned out
of Tronka Castle?' Herse replied: 'It was a dirty trick,
sir,' and wiped the sweat from his brow. 'But what has
happened has happened. I didn't want the horses to be
ruined through working in the fields, and said that they
were still young and had never drawn anything.' Kohlhaas,
trying to conceal his confusion, replied that this was not
quite the truth since they had been harnessed up for a
little at the beginning of the previous spring. 'You were a
sort of guest at the castle,' he continued, 'and you could
have obliged on one or two occasions if it was urgent to get
in the harvest quickly.' 'I did, sir,' said Herse. 'They pulled
such sullen faces that I thought it would not harm the
blacks much. On the third morning I harnessed them and
brought in three loads of corn.' Kohlhaas, his heart beating,
cast his eyes to the ground and declared: 'Nothing of that
was mentioned to me, Herse!' Herse assured him that it
was true. 'My disobligingness,' he said, 'consisted of refusing
to yoke them up again when they had finished their mid-
day feed. Then the warden and the steward suggested that
I should accept free fodder in return and pocket the money
you had left behind for their keep, so I said that I would –
stick it somewhere else first, and turned on my heel and
left them.' 'But that was not reason enough for you to be
turned out of Tronka Castle,' replied Kohlhaas. 'God forbid!' exclaimed the groom, 'that was for a real heinous
crime. That evening the horses of two gentlemen visiting
the castle were brought to the stable and mine were tethered

to the door. When I took the blacks from the warden, who was stabling the other horses in person, and asked where the animals should now be kept, he pointed to a pig-sty built against the castle wall with boards and planks.' 'You mean,' interrupted Kohlhaas, 'it was such poor accommodation for horses that it was more like a pig-sty than a stable.' 'It *was* a pig-sty, sir,' replied Herse, 'really and truly a pigsty, with pigs running in and out and too low for me to stand up in.' 'Perhaps there was nowhere else for them to be kept,' replied Kohlhaas. 'In a way, the gentlemen's horses had priority.' 'It was a cramped place,' answered the groom, his voice dropping. 'All in all there were now seven gentlemen at the castle. If it had been you, you would have had the horses move up a little. I said that I wanted to go and rent a stable in the village, but the warden insisted that he had to keep an eye on the horses and that I was not to dare to take them out of the castle yard.' 'Hm!' said Kohlhaas, 'and what did you reply to that?' 'Because the steward said that the two guests were only staying one night and were riding on the next morning, I led the horses into the pig-sty. But the next day went by and nothing happened, and when the third day arrived, it was said that the gentlemen would be staying for some weeks at the castle yet.' 'But all in all it wasn't as bad in the pig-sty,' said Kohlhaas, 'as it seemed when you first put your nose in it.' 'Oh, to be sure,' replied the other. 'It was all right once I'd cleaned the place out a bit. I gave the maid a groschen to put the pigs somewhere else. And during the day I managed to get the horses standing upright by lifting off the roof boards as soon as it was morning, and putting them back on in the evening. So there they stood, poking their heads through the roof like geese and looking round for Kohlhaasenbrück or some other place where they'd get decent treatment.' 'Well then,' asked Kohlhaas, 'why in the world did they turn you out?' 'Sir, I'll tell you,' answered the groom. 'It was because they wanted to get rid of me.

Because as long as I was there, they couldn't ruin the horses. Everywhere I went, in the yard or in the servants' hall, they gave me filthy looks. And because I thought to myself: you can pull your faces till you choke to death, they picked on the first opportunity to throw me out of the castle.' 'But what was the cause?' cried Kohlhaas. 'They must have had some cause!' 'Oh, certainly,' answered Herse, 'and a very just one too. During the evening of the second day I had spent in the pig-sty I took the horses, which had got themselves covered in filth in there in spite of everything, and was going to ride them down to the pond. And just as I reached the castle gate and was turning off, I heard the warden and steward rushing out of the hall behind me, with servants and dogs and sticks, and shouting: "Stop thief! stop that scoundrel!" as if they were possessed. The guard blocked my way, and when I asked him and the raging mob that was running towards me what the matter was, the warden snatched my blacks' bridles and answered: "The matter! Where are you taking these horses?" and grabbed me by the shirt. "Where am I taking them? God Almighty!" said I, "I'm riding to the horse-pond. Do you suppose I'd –?" "To the pond!" shouted the warden, "I'll make you swim back to Kohlhaasenbrück, down the highroad, you rogue!" and, as the steward tugged at one of my legs, he hauled me off my horse with a vicious murderous wrench, throwing me full-length into the mud. "Hell and damnation!" I shouted. "There are the harnesses and blankets and a bundle of my washing still back there in the stable" – but he and the grooms set on me with their boots, whips and sticks until I collapsed half-dead outside the castle gate, while the steward took away the horses. And as I was muttering: "The thieving swine! Where are they taking my horses?" and struggling to my feet, the warden yelled "Get out of the courtyard!" And then "Get him, Caesar! get him, Hunter!" came the cry. "Get him, Spitz!" And a pack of over a dozen hounds came at me. Then I broke off a piece of fencing, a plank or something, and struck down three of the dogs dead beside me; but I'd been dreadfully mauled and was just having to fall back when a piercing whistle sounded, back went the dogs into the courtyard, the gates were slammed and bolted, and I collapsed unconscious on the road.' White in the face, but contriving to speak teasingly, Kohlhaas said: 'So you weren't really trying to escape, Herse?' And when Herse, flushing deeply, stared down at the ground, he went on, 'Admit it. You didn't like it in the pig-sty. You thought: it's more pleasant in the stables at Kohlhaasenbrück.' 'God damn it!' cried Herse, 'but I left the harnesses and blankets and a bundle of clothes in the sty! Wouldn't I have taken the three imperial florins with me that I'd hidden in a red silk kerchief behind the manger? Hell-fire and brimstone! When you speak like that, I wish I could light that match again that I threw away!' 'Come now,' said the horse-dealer, 'I meant nothing amiss! Look, I believe every word of what you have told me; and when the affair comes up I shall personally take the sacrament on it. I am sorry you have not fared better in my service; go, go to bed, Herse, have a bottle of wine brought to you and console yourself with the thought that you will get justice done you!' And thereupon he stood up, wrote a list of the articles his head groom had left behind in the pig-sty, entered their value, asked Herse how much he estimated his medical treatment would cost, and, after shaking his hand again, bade him leave the room.

He then recounted to Lisbeth, his wife, the whole course of the story in full explanatory detail, and declared that he was determined to seek redress in a public court of law. To his joy, he saw that she supported his intention whole-heartedly. She said that many other travellers would be passing the castle who might be less patient than he, that he would be doing God's work if he put a stop to abuses of this kind, and she would raise the sums needed to institute legal proceedings. Kohlhaas called her a loyal wife, spent that day and the next in the pleasure of her and the children's company, and as soon as his business permitted, set out for Dresden to take his grievance to court.

With the aid of a lawyer with whom he was acquainted, he drew up a statement in which he gave a detailed description of the outrage committed against him and his groom Herse by Junker Wenzel von Tronka. He demanded punishment of the Junker in accordance with the law, the restoration of the horses to their former condition, and compensation for what both he and his groom had suffered. The evidence in the case was clear. The fact that the horses had been retained unlawfully threw a decisive light on everything else, and even if it were assumed that the horses had only chanced to fall ill, the horse-dealer's demand that they should be returned to him in a healthy state would still stand. When Kohlhaas made investigations in the capital city, he found no lack of friends who promised to give his lawsuit active support. His widespread trade in horses had made him acquainted with the country's most important men, and the honesty with which he carried it out had earned him their goodwill. He dined several times very pleasantly with his advocate, who was himself a considerable personage; he deposited a sum of money with him to cover the costs of litigation, and after some weeks returned to Lisbeth, his wife, in Kohlhaasenbrück, completely confident of the outcome of his case. Yet months passed by, and the year had almost come to a close before he even received any communication from Saxony about the action he had brought there, let alone any decision on the case. After several times renewing his petition to the court, he asked his lawyer in a confidential letter what had caused such an excessive delay. It was then that he learnt that the Dresden court, in consequence of intervention from a higher level, had dismissed his case out of hand. When the astonished horse-dealer wrote back asking for an explanation of this, his lawyer informed him that Junker Wenzel von Tronka was related to two noblemen, Hinz and Kunz von Tronka, one of whom was Cupbearer to the sovereign and the other actually his Chamberlain. He advised him to attempt no further court proceedings, but take steps to recover possession of the horses, which were still at Tronka Castle. He gave him to understand that the Junker, who was at present in the capital, appeared to have instructed his servants to hand them over to him; and in conclusion he requested that Kohlhaas, if he were not content to let it rest there, should at least excuse him from acting further in the matter.

At this time Kohlhaas happened to be in Brandenburg, where the governor, Heinrich von Geusau, within whose jurisdiction Kohlhaasenbrück lay, was busy establishing a number of charitable institutions for the sick and poor from a very large fund which had become available to the city. He was concerned in particular with preparing for the use of invalids a mineral spring which was situated in one of the villages nearby and was credited with greater therapeutic powers than it subsequently turned out to possess. Geusau was acquainted with Kohlhaas, having done a certain amount of business with him during his period at the Electoral court, and he therefore allowed his groom Herse, who ever since that unhappy day at Tronka Castle had been suffering from pains in the chest when he breathed, to try the efficacy of this little spring, walled in and roofed over as it now was. The governor happened to be present, standing beside the bath in which Kohlhaas had laid Herse and giving some instructions, when a messenger brought the horse-dealer his Dresden lawyer's disheartening letter, which his wife had forwarded. While he was talking to the doctor, the governor noticed that Kohlhaas let fall a tear on the letter he had received and opened; whereupon he approached him in a cordial and friendly manner and asked what misfortune had befallen him. When the horse-dealer handed him the letter without a word, this worthy man, who knew about the abominable injustice committed against him at Tronka Castle, the consequences of which had impaired Herse's health possibly for the rest of his life, clapped him on the shoulder and told him not to lose courage; he would help him, he said, to obtain justice. That evening, when the horse-dealer had come at his bidding to the castle, he told him that he need only compose a petition to the Elector of Brandenburg accompanied by a brief account of the incident and his advocate's letter, and requesting his sovereign's protection against the injustices done to him on Saxon territory. He promised to place the petition, together with another package that was ready for dispatch, in the hands of the Elector, who would, if circumstances permitted, undoubtedly make representations on his behalf to the Elector of Saxony. Such a *démarche* would be all that was needed to obtain justice for Kohlhaas in the Dresden court, despite the machinations of the Junker and his family. Kohlhaas was delighted and thanked the governor most warmly for this fresh proof of his favour, saying he was sorry he had not raised the matter in Berlin immediately without taking any action in Dresden; and when he had been to the office of the local law-court, and composed an account of his grievances fully in accordance with what was required, and had given it to the governor, he returned to Kohlhaasenbrück, more reassured about the outcome of his case than ever before. But to his dismay, only a few weeks later, he was told by a court official who had gone to Potsdam on the governor's business that the Elector had passed the petition on to his Chancellor, Count Kallheim; and that the latter, instead of taking the appropriate course of applying direct to the Dresden court for investigation and punishment of the crime, had sought more detailed preliminary information from the Junker von Tronka. The official, who, sitting in his carriage in front of Kohlhaas's house, appeared to have been given the task of breaking this news to the horse-dealer, could not supply any satisfactory answer to his perplexed question why this procedure had been adopted. He merely added that the governor wished him to be patient, seemed anxious to continue his journey, and not until the end of their short conversation did Kohlhaas gather from a few chance words that Count Kallheim was related by marriage to the Tronka family.

Kohlhaas, who could now take no further pleasure in breeding horses, or in his home and farm, or scarcely even in his wife and children, waited through the next month with a feeling of despondency and foreboding. At the end of this period, just as he had expected, Herse, who had obtained some relief from the mineral bath, returned from Brandenburg with a lengthy rescript accompanied by a letter from the governor. It stated that he regretted he could do nothing about his lawsuit, that he was sending him a resolution from the State Chancellery which had been directed to him, that he advised Kohlhaas to take away the horses left behind at Tronka Castle and otherwise to let the affair rest. The resolution declared that Kohlhaas was, according to information received from the Dresden court, a vexatious litigant; that the Junker with whom he had left the horses was in no way trying to withhold them from him; that he should have them fetched from the castle, or at least inform the Junker where he should send them; that the State Chancellery wished in any event not to be troubled with any further contentions and complaints of this sort. Since for Kohlhaas the horses were not the issue – he would have been equally aggrieved had they been a couple of dogs – this letter made him foam with rage. A feeling of repugnance such as he had never experienced before filled his heart as he looked towards the gate whenever he heard a sound in the courtyard, expecting to see the Junker's men appear and, perhaps even with some excuse, hand the starved and emaciated horses back to him. Well schooled in the world's ways though he was, this would have been the one eventuality to which his feelings could have found no fitting response. Shortly afterwards, however, he heard, from a friend who had travelled that way, that the nags were as heretofore being used on the fields at Tronka Castle with the Junker's other horses. And in the midst of his grief at seeing the world in such monstrous disorder, an inward sense of contentment now flooded over him as he found harmony within his own heart.

He invited a neighbour to call on him, a local magistrate who had for a long time had the notion of extending his estate by purchasing land that bordered on it; and when this man had seated himself Kohlhaas asked him what price he would offer for his properties in Brandenburg and in Saxony, house and land, just as they stood, estate and chattels and all. At these words his wife Lisbeth paled. She turned away, picked up her youngest child who was playing behind her on the ground, and as the little boy toyed with her necklaces she stared in mortal anxiety past his red cheeks at her husband and at a document he held in his hand. The magistrate, looking at the horse-dealer in amazement, asked what had suddenly made him think of so strange a proposition. Kohlhaas, mustering as much cheerfulness as he could, replied that the idea of selling his farm on the banks of the Havel was not so new; they had both often discussed the matter before. By comparison the house on the outskirts of Dresden was a mere appendage of little importance, and, in short, if the magistrate would oblige him by taking over both properties, he was prepared to conclude the contract. He added, in a rather contrived jesting tone, that Kohlhaasenbrück was not the whole world; that there could be purposes compared with which his role as father and head of the household was subordinate and unworthy; in short, that he must tell him his mind was set on higher things, which might presently be heard of. The magistrate, reassured by these words, said jokingly to the horse-dealer's wife, who was kissing her child over and over again, that her husband would presumably not expect immediate payment, placed his hat and stick, which he had kept between his knees, on the table, and took the document from the horse-dealer's hands to read it. Moving closer to him, Kohlhaas explained that it was a contingent contract of sale which he had drawn up and which lapsed at the end of four weeks. He pointed out that nothing was missing except the signatures and the amount both of the purchase price and of the forfeit which he would agree to pay if, within four weeks, he should change his mind. And he good-humouredly called on his neighbour to make an offer, assuring him that he would not expect a high price and wanted a quick settlement. His wife was walking up and down the room, her bosom heaving in such agitation that the kerchief the little boy had been tugging at seemed about to slip right off her shoulders. The magistrate said that he could not possibly assess the value of the property in Dresden, whereupon Kohlhaas pushed across to him the letters that had been exchanged upon its purchase, and answered that he valued it at a hundred gold florins, although it was evident that he had paid almost half as much again. The magistrate re-read the contract and found that it particularly stipulated a right of withdrawal on his own part; he then said, with his mind already half made up, that he could not use the stud-horses in his stables. But when Kohlhaas replied that he did not in any case intend to sell the horses and that he also wanted to keep some weapons that were hanging in the armoury, he finally, after further and further hesitation, offered a sum which he had already mentioned to Kohlhaas once on a walk, partly as a joke, partly in earnest, and which bore no relation to the value of the property. Kohlhaas pushed pen and ink over to him to write with, and when the magistrate, who could not believe his senses, had again asked him if he were serious and the horse-dealer had rather testily retorted: 'Do you suppose I am merely making fun of you?'

he took the pen, though still looking very doubtful, and signed. He crossed out, however, the paragraph referring to a forfeit in the event of the vendor's changing his mind, undertook to make him a loan of a hundred gold florins on the security of the Dresden property which he had no wish actually to buy, and left him complete freedom to withdraw from the transaction within two months. The horse-dealer, touched by this behaviour, warmly shook him by the hand and when they had agreed, as one of the chief stipulations, that a quarter of the purchase price should without fail be paid immediately in cash and the rest credited to the vendor's bank account in Hamburg within three months, Kohlhaas called for wine to celebrate such a happy conclusion to the deal. He told the maid who brought in the bottles that Sternbald, the groom, was to saddle the sorrel for him, as he had to ride to the capital on some business. He hinted that before long, on his return, he would speak more candidly about matters which he must keep to himself for the present. Then, filling the glasses, he asked about Poland and Turkey, which at that time were engaged in hostilities with each other, and involved the magistrate in all sorts of political conjectures on this subject; finally he toasted the success of their transaction once more, and let him take his leave.

When the magistrate had left the room, Lisbeth fell on her knees before her husband. 'If you have any feeling for me and the children I have borne you,' she cried, 'if you have not already disowned us in advance for some reason which I cannot even guess, tell me what these terrible arrangements mean!' Kohlhaas said: 'Dearest wife, they mean nothing that should still worry you as things now stand. I have received a court decision informing me that my claim against Junker Wenzel von Tronka is a vexatious triviality. And because there must have been a misunderstanding, I have decided to present my case in person to our sovereign.' 'Why should you want to sell your house?' she cried, rising to her feet with a distraught gesture. The horse-dealer, drawing her gently to his bosom, replied: 'Because, dearest Lisbeth, I do not wish to remain in a country where I and my rights are not defended. If I am to be kicked, I would rather be a dog than a man! I am sure that you, as my wife, think the same in this respect as I.' 'How do you know,' she asked wildly, 'that you and your rights will not be defended? If you approach the Elector with your petition in all humility, as is proper, how do you know that it will be rejected or that he will refuse to listen to you?' 'Very well,' answered Kohlhaas, 'if my fear is groundless, my house will not yet have been sold. The Elector himself, I know, is just, and if only I can succeed in getting past the people who surround him and can reach him in person, I do not doubt I can obtain justice and joyfully return to you and my old business before the week is over. And then,' he added, kissing her, 'I shall have no wish but to stay with you until the end of my life! But,' he continued, 'it is advisable for me to be prepared for any eventuality, and so I want you to go away for a time, if possible, and take the children to your aunt in Schwerin, whom you have in any case not visited for a very long time.' 'What?' said his wife, 'I am to go to Schwerin? Across the border with the children to my aunt in Schwerin?' And she fell speechless with terror. 'Of course,' answered Kohlhaas, 'and if possible you must go at once, so that the steps I intend to take in my cause are not impeded by any secondary considerations.' 'Oh! I understand you!' she cried. 'Now you need nothing but weapons and horses; the rest can be taken by anyone who wants it!' And so saying she turned away, threw herself into an armchair and wept. Kohlhaas asked in perplexity: 'Dearest Lisbeth, what are you doing? God has blessed me with a wife, children and possessions: am I today, for the first time, to wish it were otherwise?' He sat down beside her affectionately, and she at these words blushed and embraced him. 'Tell me,' he said, stroking the curls back from her brow, 'what am I to do? Am I to abandon my case? Am I to go to Tronka Castle and beg the Junker to return my horses, then mount, and ride them home to you?' 'Yes, yes, yes!' Lisbeth wanted to say but did not dare; amid her tears she shook her head, hugged him closely and kissed his breast passionately again and again. 'Well, then!' cried Kohlhaas, 'if you feel that I must get justice if I am to go on practising my trade, then grant me the freedom I need in order to get it!' Thereupon he stood up, and told the groom who had come to say the sorrel was ready that the bays were to be harnessed the next day to take his wife to Schwerin. Lisbeth said that an idea had occurred to her. She rose to her feet, wiped the tears from her eyes, and asked her husband, who had sat down at a desk, whether he would give her the petition and let her, instead of him, go to Berlin and hand it to the Elector. Touched for more than one reason by this suggestion, Kohlhaas drew her down on his lap and said: 'Dearest wife, that is simply not possible! The Elector is heavily guarded and anyone approaching him is subjected to all sorts of unpleasantness.' Lisbeth replied that in very many cases such access was easier for a woman than for a man. 'Give me the petition,' she repeated, 'and if all you want is to be sure that it is in his hands, I will vouch for that: he shall get it!' Kohlhaas, who had ample evidence both of her courage and of her intelligence, asked how she planned to set about the task. Looking down in embarrassment, she replied that in the old days, when the castellan of the Electoral palace had held an appointment in Schwerin, he had courted her, and that he was now married, of course, with several children, but that he would not have forgotten her entirely; in short, that he was simply to leave it to her to take advantage of these and certain other circumstances which were too complex to describe. Kohlhaas kissed her joyfully, said that he accepted her proposal, and pointed out that she needed merely to stay with the castellan's wife in order to have access to the Elector in the palace itself. He gave her the petition, had the bays harnessed up, and sent her off, well wrapped up, with Sternbald, his trusty groom.

But of all the fruitless steps he had taken to further his cause, this journey was the most disastrous of all. For only a few days later Sternbald returned to the farm, slowly leading the carriage, in which his mistress lay prostrate, suffering from a dangerous contusion on the chest. Paling, Kohlhaas went up to the vehicle but could get no coherent account of what had caused the accident. According to the groom the castellan had not been at home, so they were forced to stay at an inn near the palace. The next morning Lisbeth had left the inn and instructed the groom to stay behind with the horses; she had not returned until evening, and was then in her present condition. It seemed that she had thrust herself forward too boldly towards the Elector, and through no fault of his, a rough and over-zealous member of his bodyguard had struck her a blow on the chest with the shaft of his lance. At least, that was what the people stated who brought her back to the hostelry towards nightfall in a state of unconsciousness: she was unable to say much herself on account of the blood welling up in her mouth. A courtier had taken the petition from her afterwards. Sternbald said he had wanted to mount a horse immediately and take his master the news of this unhappy event, but despite the objections of the surgeon who had been called, she had insisted on being brought back to her husband at Kohlhaasenbrück without sending any word of warning. She had been utterly worn out by the journey and Kohlhaas put her to bed, where she survived for a few more days, painfully struggling to draw breath. They tried vainly to restore her to consciousness in order to get some details of what had occurred. She lay there with a fixed, moribund stare and made no reply. Only very shortly before her death did her reason return. A minister of the Lutheran faith (which at that time was just beginning to flourish and which, following her husband's example, she had embraced) was standing beside her bed, reading a chapter from the Bible in loud pompous tones, when suddenly she looked up at him darkly, took the Bible out of his hand as if there were no need to read to her from it, and kept turning the pages as if she were searching for something. Then she turned to Kohlhaas, who was sitting on her bed, and pointed with her finger at the verse: 'Forgive your enemies; do good also unto them that hate you'; whereupon, pressing his hand, she gazed at him with deep emotion and expired. Kohlhaas thought to himself: 'May God never forgive me as I forgive the Junker!' Weeping profusely, he kissed her, closed her eyes and left the room. He took the hundred gold florins which the magistrate had already paid over for the stables in Dresden and ordered such a funeral as befitted a princess rather than his wife: an oak coffin banded with metal, silk cushions with gold and silver tassels and a grave eight ells deep lined with trimmed stones and mortar. He supervised the work personally from beside the grave, carrying his youngest child in his arms. On the day of the burial the corpse, as white as snow, was laid out in a hall which he had hung with black drapes. The pastor had just delivered a moving address from beside her bier when the Elector's reply to the petition which the dead woman had taken to him was delivered to Kohlhaas: it commanded him to fetch the horses from Tronka Castle and, upon pain of imprisonment, to make no further submissions concerning this matter. Kohlhaas put the letter in his pocket and ordered the coffin to be placed in the carriage. As soon as the grave mound had been raised, the cross planted on it, and the funeral guests dismissed, he threw himself down one last time by his wife's deserted bed, then immediately set about the work of his vengeance. He sat down and drew up an edict in which, 'by virtue of the authority inborn in him', he ordered Junker Wenzel von Tronka, within three days of sight of the document, to bring back to Kohlhaasenbrück the two black horses he had taken from him and worked to death on his fields, and fatten them in person in Kohlhaas's stables. He sent this edict by a mounted messenger whom he instructed to return to Kohlhaasenbrück immediately upon delivering it. When the three days had passed and the horses had not appeared, he summoned Herse, told him of the order he had issued to the Junker about fattening them, and asked him two questions: firstly, would he ride with him to Tronka Castle and fetch the Junker out, and would he secondly, when they had brought him back to Kohlhaasenbrück, take a whip to him in the stables if he should be behindhand in executing the terms of the edict? Herse had no sooner understood his master than he exultantly cried: 'Sir, this very day!' Tossing his cap in the air, he vowed he would have a scourge with ten knots made ready to teach the Junker how to curry a horse. Kohlhaas then sold his house, and packed his children off in a carriage across the border; at nightfall he gathered together his seven loyal grooms, armed them, gave them mounts, and set off for Tronka Castle.

As the third night was falling he assaulted the castle with this handful of men, riding down the toll-keeper and the guard who were standing in conversation in the gateway. They set fire to every outhouse in the curtilage, and as these burst into flames Kohlhaas rushed into the castle to find the Junker, while Herse dashed up the spiral staircase into the warden's tower and fell with cut and thrust upon him and the steward, who were sitting half undressed playing cards together. It was as if the avenging angel of heaven had descended on the place. The Junker, amid much laughter, was in the act of reading aloud to a gathering of young friends the edict issued to him by the horse-dealer: but no sooner had he heard the latter's voice in the courtyard than, turning as white as a sheet, he cried out to the company: 'Brothers, save yourselves!' and vanished. Kohlhaas entered the hall, seized Junker Hans von Tronka, as he came towards him, by the jerkin and hurled him into a corner, dashing out his brains against the stones. As his men overpowered and dispersed the other noblemen, who had drawn their swords, he demanded to know where Junker Wenzel von Tronka was; but in their dazed bewilderment none of them could tell him, and when, after kicking down the doors of two rooms that led into the wings of the castle, he had searched everywhere in the vast building but found no one, Kohlhaas went down into the courtyard, cursing, to see that the exits were guarded. In the meantime heavy smoke was billowing skywards from the castle, which with all its wings had caught fire from the burning outhouses, and while Sternbald and three grooms busied themselves dragging out everything that was movable, heaving it over the horses as legitimate plunder, Herse with triumphant shouts hurled the corpses of the warden, the steward and their wives and children out of the open windows of the tower. As Kohlhaas was coming downstairs from the castle the gouty old house-keeper who managed the Junker's household threw herself at his feet, and stopping on the stairs he asked her where Junker Wenzel von Tronka was. When she replied in a weak trembling voice that she thought he had taken refuge in the chapel, he called over two grooms with torches and, having no key, told them to break open the door with crowbars and axes; he overturned the altar and pews, but to his fury found no trace of the Junker. By chance, just as Kohlhaas was coming out of the chapel again, a young groom who served at Tronka Castle rushed up to take the Junker's chargers out of a large stone-built stable that was in danger of catching fire. At exactly that instant Kohlhaas espied his two blacks in a small thatched shed and asked the groom why he was not rescuing them. When the latter said that the shed was already on fire and put the key in the stable door, Kohlhaas violently snatched it out of the keyhole, threw it over the wall, and amid terrible laughter from his

men as they looked on, let fall a hail of blows on the boy
with the flat of his sword and drove him into the burning
shed to save the blacks. Yet when the groom emerged, white
with terror and holding the horses, only a few moments before the shed collapsed behind him, he could not find Kohlhaas. When he joined the other grooms in the courtyard and
asked the horse-dealer, who turned his back on him several
times, what he should now do with the animals, Kohlhaas
suddenly raised his foot to him in so terrifying a manner
that if he had delivered the kick it would have killed him.
Then, without a further word, he mounted his bay, rode to
the castle-gate and, while the grooms continued their plundering, he silently awaited daybreak.

When morning came the entire castle had been burnt
out, leaving nothing but walls and no one but Kohlhaas
and his seven men in it. He dismounted and again searched
every nook and cranny of the site, which was now bathed
in bright sunshine. Hard as it was for him, he had to admit
that the expedition to the castle had failed and so, with
his heart full of sorrow and anguish, he dispatched Herse
and some of the grooms to discover in which direction the
Junker had taken flight. He was especially perturbed at the
thought of a wealthy convent called Erlabrunn, situated
on the banks of the Mulde : its Abbess, Antonia von Tronka,
was known in the district as a pious, generous and saintly
woman, and to the luckless Kohlhaas it seemed only too
likely that the Junker, bereft of all necessities, had sought
refuge at this convent, since the Abbess was his own aunt
and had brought him up in early childhood. In the warden's
tower there was still a room fit to be lived in, and when
Kohlhaas had received this information he went up to it
and composed what he called a 'Declaration under the Writ
of Kohlhaas' in which he called upon the country to withhold all aid and comfort from Junker Wenzel von Tronka,
against whom he was engaged in a just war; instead he
required every inhabitant, not excepting his relatives and

friends, to surrender the Junker to Kohlhaas on pain of death and the certain destruction by fire of whatever they possessed. He had this declaration distributed throughout the region by travellers and strangers, and in particular he gave his groom Waldmann a copy with express instructions to deliver it personally to the lady Antonia, Abbess of Erlabrunn. Thereupon he spoke to a number of the servants at Tronka Castle who had been ill-satisfied with the Junker and, attracted by the thought of plunder, wanted to serve Kohlhaas instead. He armed them as infantrymen with cross-bows and short-swords, and instructed them how to ride behind the mounted grooms. And when he had sold off everything that the men had collected and distributed the money among them, he took in the castle gateway a few hours' rest from his grim labours.

Towards noon Herse returned and confirmed what his heart, always prepared for the worst turn of events, had already told him: the Junker was in the convent at Erlabrunn with the aged Lady Abbess Antonia von Tronka, his aunt. Apparently he had escaped through a door in the back wall of the castle that led out into the open and by a roofed-over stone stairway that took him down to some boats on the Elbe. Herse reported that at midnight he had reached a village on the river in an oarless and rudderless skiff, much to the astonishment of the inhabitants who had gathered at the sight of the fire at Tronka Castle; he had then left for Erlabrunn in a vehicle from the village. At this news Kohlhaas sighed deeply; he asked whether the horses had been fed and, when he was told that they had, he ordered his men to mount and reached Erlabrunn within three hours. Accompanied by the rumble of a thunderstorm on the distant horizon and with freshly lit torches, he and his troop rode into the courtyard of the convent. The groom Waldmann came to meet him and was just reporting that the writ had been properly handed over when the Abbess and the convent administrator appeared in the doorway, talking to each other in agitation. The administrator, an aged little man with snow-white hair, glared fiercely at Kohlhaas as his armour was strapped on, and boldly ordered the servants surrounding him to sound the alarm bell; meanwhile the Lady Abbess, as white as a sheet, with a silver crucifix in her hand, came down from the terrace and together with all her nuns threw herself on her knees before Kohlhaas's horse. While Herse and Sternbald overpowered the administrator, who had no sword, and led him off as their prisoner among the horses, Kohlhaas asked her where Junker Wenzel von Tronka was. Unfastening a great ring of keys from her girdle, she answered: 'In Wittenberg, worthy Kohlhaas!', and added in a quavering voice: 'Fear God and do no wrong!' At this Kohlhaas, hurled back into the hellish torment of unsatisfied revenge, turned his horse and was about to give the order to set the convent on fire, when a huge thunderbolt struck the ground close beside him. Wheeling his horse round to her again, he asked if she had received his writ. The lady answered in a weak and barely audible voice: 'Only this minute!' 'When?' 'Two hours, as God is my judge, after my nephew the Junker had already left!' And when the groom, Waldmann, to whom Kohlhaas turned with menacing looks, had stuttered a confirmation of this, explaining that flood-water from the Mulde had delayed his arrival until now, Kohlhaas regained his composure. A sudden terrible deluge of rain, beating down on the cobbles of the courtyard, extinguished the torches and relieved the anguish in his tormented heart. Briefly saluting the Abbess with his hat he turned his horse round, and shouting 'Follow me, brothers! The Junker is in Wittenberg!', he dug in his spurs and rode out of the convent.

As night fell, he stopped at an inn beside the highway, where he had to rest for a day because the horses were so exhausted. Well realizing that he could not challenge a town such as Wittenberg with a band of ten men (for that was his present strength) he composed a second writ. After a short account of what had befallen him in Saxony, he called on 'every good Christian', as he put it, 'to take up his cause against Junker von Tronka as the universal enemy of all Christians', and promised them 'pay and other perquisites of war'. In another declaration issued soon after, he styled himself 'a freeman of the Empire and the world, subject to God alone'. These expressions of his diseased and deluded fanaticism nonetheless brought him an influx of recruits from among riff-raff who, deprived of a living by the peace with Poland, were drawn by the sound of money and the prospect of plunder. So it was that he had thirty or more men with him when he returned along the right bank of the Elbe fully intending to burn Wittenberg to the ground. He camped with his horses and men under the roof of an old dilapidated brick shed in the solitude of a dark wood which in those days encircled the place. No sooner had he learnt from Sternbald, whom he had sent in disguise into the town with the writ, that it had already been made public there, than he and his band broke camp on Whitsun Eve. While the inhabitants were fast asleep he set fire to the town in several places at once, and as his men plundered the outskirts, he fastened up a notice on a church door, stating that he, Kohlhaas, had set fire to the town and that if the Junker were not handed over he would continue to raze it until, as he put it, 'he would not need to search behind any walls to find him'.

The inhabitants were terrified beyond words at this incredible outrage. Fortunately it was a fairly calm summer's night and the fire destroyed only nineteen buildings, though these did include a church; but as soon as the flames had been brought under some control towards daybreak, the aged governor, Otto von Gorgas, sent out a company of fifty men to capture the savage monster. The captain in command, however, Gerstenberg by name, adopted such poor tactics that the expedition, so far from defeating Kohlhaas, merely helped him to gain a most formidable military reputation; for when this officer split up his company into several detachments with the object, as he thought, of surrounding and so crushing Kohlhaas, the latter kept his force together, attacked at separate points and defeated his opponent piecemeal. Indeed by the evening of the following day, not one man of this entire troop on which the country had placed its hopes still stood in the field against him. Having lost some of his own men in this skirmish, Kohlhaas on the morning of the next day again set the town alight, and his deadly methods were so effective that a large number of houses and almost all the barns on the outskirts of the city were burnt to the ground. Once more he posted up the self-same writ, this time to the corners of the town hall itself, adding details of the fate of Captain von Gerstenberg whom the governor had sent out and whom he had routed. Outraged by his defiance, the governor set out with some cavalry at the head of a force one hundred and fifty strong. Upon Junker Wenzel von Tronka's written request, he gave him a bodyguard to protect him against any violence by the people of Wittenberg, who were determined that he should leave the town. After placing patrols in all the surrounding villages and leaving guards along the town walls to prevent any surprise attack, he himself rode out on St Gervaise's Day to capture the dragon who was devastating the land. The horse-dealer was cunning enough to evade this force; by skilful marching he lured the governor five leagues away from the town, and by various manoeuvres deluded him into thinking that in the face of numerical superiority he had fallen back into Brandenburg; then suddenly, as darkness fell on the third evening, he wheeled back at a gallop to Wittenberg and set it on fire for the third time. Herse, who had slipped into the town in disguise, carried out this dreadful feat, and the flames, fanned by a strong northerly wind, spread so fiercely and voraciously that within three hours they had reduced forty-two houses, two churches, several monasteries and schools and the Electoral governor's own residence to rubble and ashes. When the governor, who at dawn had believed his opponent to be in Brandenburg, was informed of what had happened, he returned in forced marches to find the town in general uproar. The people in their thousands were besieging the Junker's house, which had been barricaded with beams and posts, demanding with frenzied clamour his expulsion from the town. Two burgomasters, Jenkens and Otto by name, were standing in their official robes at the head of the entire council, vainly pointing out that they had no choice but to await the return of a courier sent to the President of the State Chancellery to obtain permission for the Junker's removal to Dresden, where he himself wished to go for a number of reasons. The unreasoning mob, armed with pikes and staves, paid no heed to these words, roughly handled some of the councillors who were calling for drastic measures, and were on the point of storming the house occupied by the Junker and levelling it to the ground when the governor, Otto von Gorgas, entered the town at the head of his cavalry. This worthy gentleman, who was accustomed to inspiring respect and obedience by his mere presence, had managed, as if by way of making amends for the failure of the expedition from which he was returning, to catch three stray members of the incendiary's band right in front of the city gates. As the prisoners were publicly put in chains, he assured the council in a shrewdly worded speech that he was confident of bringing in Kohlhaas himself the same way before long, for he was hot on his trail; and he thus succeeded, thanks to these various reassuring circumstances, in disarming the crowd's fears, and putting their minds to some extent at rest about the continued presence of the Junker until the courier returned from Dresden. Accompanied by some cavalrymen he dismounted and, when the pallisades and posts had been removed, entered the house; here he found the Junker repeatedly swooning, and attended by two doctors who were trying to revive him with essences and stimulants. Otto von Gorgas judged that this was not the moment to exchange words with him about his shameful behaviour, but merely told him with a look of silent contempt to get dressed and for his own safety to follow him to quarters reserved for prisoners of rank. When they had put a doublet on the Junker and a helmet on his head and he reappeared in the street, with his breast half exposed to ease his breathing and with the governor and his brother-in-law Count von Gerschau supporting him, a chorus of frightful curses and blasphemies rose to high heaven all round him. The people, whom the lansquenets could barely restrain, called him a blood-sucker, a wretched public menace and tormentor of mankind, the bane of Wittenberg and the ruin of Saxony; and after a pathetic procession through the wreckage of the town, during which his helmet several times fell off without his missing it, so that a knight following behind had to push it back on again, the prison was finally reached and the Junker disappeared into a tower under heavy guard.

Meanwhile the return of the courier with the Electoral resolution brought the town new cause for concern. The government, to which the citizens of Dresden had appealed directly in an urgent petition, was not prepared to grant the Junker permission to reside in the capital until the incendiary had been captured; on the contrary it required the governor to use what power he had at his disposal to protect the Junker where he now was, since he had to be somewhere; on the other hand, the worthy town of Wittenberg was to take comfort from the information that a force of five hundred men under the command of Prince Friedrich of Meissen was already on its way to shield it from further onslaught by Kohlhaas. But the governor well knew that a resolution in these terms could not possibly placate the townsfolk, not only because a number of minor victories scored by the horse-dealer at various points outside Wittenberg had started very ugly rumours about the strength to which his support had grown, but also because the kind of warfare he was waging, at dead of night, with men in disguise, using pitch, straw and sulphur, was new and without parallel and could have rendered ineffectual an even larger force than that brought by the Prince of Meissen. After brief reflection the governor therefore decided to suppress completely the resolution he had received. He simply had a letter in which the Prince of Meissen informed him of his impending arrival posted up all over the town. A covered carriage drove out of the prison-yard at dawn and took the road for Leipzig, accompanied by four heavily armed cavalrymen who intimated, in an equivocal manner, that their destination was the fortress of Pleissenburg. Having thus reassured the townsfolk as to the presence of the ill-starred Junker which had brought fire and the sword upon them, the governor himself set out with a troop of three hundred men to join forces with Prince Friedrich of Meissen. Meanwhile Kohlhaas, thanks to the peculiar role he had assumed in the world, had indeed grown in strength to a hundred and nine men. As he had also laid hands on an arsenal of weapons in Jassen and had armed his band to the teeth with them, he resolved to strike with lightning speed at the double storm he now knew to be approaching, before it could break over him. The very next night he accordingly attacked the Prince of Meissen after dark near Mühlberg. This fight, to his great grief, cost him the life of Herse, who fell at his side in the first exchange of shots; but in his bitter rage at this loss he inflicted, in an engagement lasting three hours, such damage on the Prince, who was unable to marshal his troops in the village, that by daybreak Meissen, badly wounded in several places and with his men in utter disarray, was forced to retreat towards Dresden. Emboldened to madness by this victory, Kohlhaas wheeled upon the governor before the latter could get wind of what had happened, engaging him in broad daylight and in open countryside near the village of Damerow. The battle raged until dusk and, though his losses were appalling, Kohlhaas gained even advantages. Indeed, the next morning he would undoubtedly with his remaining troops have renewed his attack on the governor, who had fallen back into the churchyard at Damerow, had von Gorgas not been informed of the Prince of Meissen's defeat at Mühlberg and considered it more prudent to retreat similarly to Wittenberg and await a more favourable opportunity. Five days after he had routed both these forces, Kohlhaas reached Leipzig and set three sides of the city on fire.

In the writ which he distributed on this occasion he styled himself 'an emissary of the Archangel Michael, who has come to punish with fire and sword all those who shall stand on the Junker's side in this quarrel, and to chastise in them the deceitfulness which now engulfs the whole world'. From the castle at Lützen, which he had captured and where he had entrenched himself, he appealed to the people to join him in establishing a better order of things; and the writ was signed, with a touch of madness, 'Given at the seat of our Provisional World Government, Lützen Castle'. It was fortunate for the inhabitants of Leipzig that steady rain kept the flames from spreading and that consequently, by speedy application of the existing fire-fighting arrangements, it was possible to confine the blaze to a few shops round the Pleissenburg. Nevertheless there was inexpressible panic in the city at the presence of the mad incendiary with his delusion that the Junker was in Leipzig; and when a troop of a hundred and eighty horse sent into the field against him returned in rout, the city council, not wishing to jeopardize the wealth of Leipzig, had no choice but to barricade all the gates and put the citizens on day and night guard outside the walls. It was in vain that the council had proclamations put up in the surrounding villages declaring categorically that the Junker was not in the Pleissenburg; the horse-dealer posted similar notices insisting that he was, and announcing that even if he were not in the fortress he, Kohlhaas, would continue to act as if he were until told where he really was. The Elector, informed by a courier of Leipzig's peril, declared that he was already assembling an army of two thousand men, which he would personally command, to capture Kohlhaas. He sternly rebuked Otto von Gorgas for the ambiguous and ill-considered subterfuge which he had used in order to get rid of the incendiary from the neighbourhood of Wittenberg; and there was indescribable confusion throughout Saxony and particularly in the capital when it was discovered that a notice addressed to Kohlhaas from an unknown person had been put up in the villages round Leipzig, stating: 'Junker Wenzel is with his cousins Hinz and Kunz in Dresden'.

Under these circumstances Dr Martin Luther, relying on the power of persuasive words and on the prestige which his position in the world had given him, undertook the task of inducing Kohlhaas to return within the confines of ordered human society; and in the belief that there was an element of integrity in the incendiary's heart, he had a proclamation in the following terms posted up in every town and village of the Electorate:

Kohlhaas, you claim to have been sent to wield the sword of justice, but what are you presuming to do in the insanity of your blind passion, you who from head to foot are the very embodiment of injustice? Because the sovereign whose subject you are denied you your rights, your rights in a dispute about some trivial possessions, you have monstrously rebelled with fire and sword, and like a wolf from the wilderness you invade the peaceful community of which he is the protector. You who seduce men with such lies and deceitful allegations, do you suppose they will avail a sinner like you before God on that Day on which the secrets of all hearts shall be revealed? How can you claim that you have been refused justice, when with your savage heart lusting for base personal vengeance you abandoned any attempt to obtain it after your first trifling efforts had failed? A benchful of court functionaries and bailiffs who suppress a letter presented to them or withhold a judgement they should deliver: are these your sovereign? And do I need to tell you, godless man, that your sovereign knows nothing about your case – indeed that the prince against whom you have revolted does not even know your name? When you stand before God's throne thinking to accuse him, he will be able to say serenely: Lord, I have done this man no wrong, for my soul is ignorant of his existence. Know that the sword which you bear is the sword of robbery and murder; you are a rebel and no warrior of the just God; your end on earth shall be the wheel and the gallows, and in the world hereafter the damnation that awaits all crime and ungodliness.

Wittenberg, etc.

Martin Luther

In the castle at Lützen Kohlhaas, who did not believe the notice that had gone up in the villages saying that Junker Wenzel was in Dresden (for it bore no signature at all, let alone that of the city council as he had demanded), was just turning over in his tormented heart a new plan for setting fire to Leipzig, when to their great dismay Sternbald and Waldmann saw Luther's proclamation, which had been nailed to the castle gate during the night. Not wanting to approach him about it themselves, they waited several days in vain for Kohlhaas to notice it. He was gloomy and turned in upon himself, and although he would appear in the evenings it was only to give brief instructions, and he saw nothing. So when, one morning, he was about to hang two men who had been out plundering in the district in violation of his orders, they resolved to draw his attention to it. He was just returning from the place of execution in the ceremonious manner which had become customary with him since he had issued his latest writ: a great archangelic sword on a red leather cushion, decorated with gold tassels, was borne in front of him, twelve men with burning torches followed, and the crowd timorously made way for him on either side. At that moment Sternbald and Waldmann, carrying their swords under their arms in a manner intended to attract his attention, stepped round the pillar to which the proclamation was nailed. As Kohlhaas came through the gateway, deep in thought and with his hands clasped behind his back, he raised his eyes and stopped short; the two men deferentially stood aside on seeing him, and he, glancing at them with a preoccupied air, strode quickly up to the pillar. But who shall describe the tumult of his mind when he saw the proclamation, its text accusing him of injustice, and its signature the dearest and most venerable name known to him, that of Martin Luther! His face flushed deep crimson and, removing his helmet, he read it through twice from beginning to end. Turning back to his men with a look of uncertainty on his face, he made as if to speak but said nothing; he removed the notice from the pillar, perused it yet again, then shouted: 'Waldmann! saddle my horse!' and 'Sternbald, come with me to the castle!' and vanished. Those few words had sufficed to disarm him in an instant, so low had he sunk. He quickly disguised himself as a Thuringian farmer, informed Sternbald that a matter of great importance obliged him to go to Wittenberg, entrusted him in the presence of some of his best men with the command of the forces he was to leave behind in Lützen, and assuring them that he would be back in three days, during which time there was no fear of an attack, he left for Wittenberg.

He put up at an inn under an assumed name and as soon as night fell, wearing a cloak and carrying a pair of pistols he had taken as booty from Tronka Castle, he entered Luther's room. Luther, who was sitting at his desk over papers and books when he saw this unknown and strange-looking man open the door and bolt it behind him, asked who he was and what he wanted. No sooner had the man, holding his hat respectfully in his hand and diffidently sensing the alarm he was about to cause, answered that he was Michael Kohlhaas, the horse-dealer, than Luther shouted: 'Leave this place!', adding, as he hastily rose from his desk to ring the bell, 'Your breath is pestilent and your presence perdition!' Without stirring from the spot Kohlhaas drew his pistol and said, 'Your Reverence, if you touch that bell this pistol will stretch me lifeless at your feet! Be seated and listen to me. You are as safe with me as with the angels whose psalms you write down.' Returning to his chair, Luther asked, 'What do you want?' Kohlhaas replied: 'To prove that you are wrong in thinking me an unjust man! In your proclamation you say that my sovereign knows nothing of my case: very well then, get me a safe conduct to Dresden and I shall go there and put my case before him.' 'You impious and terrible man!' cried Luther, whom these words had both bewildered and reassured, 'who gave you the right to attack Junker von Tronka in pursuance of decrees issued on no authority but your own, and when you could not find him in his castle to come down with fire and sword on the whole community that gave him shelter?' 'No one, your Reverence,' replied Kohlhaas, 'from this moment on! Information I received from Dresden deceived me and led me astray! The war I am waging against human society becomes a crime if this assurance you give me is true and society had not cast me out!' 'Cast you out!' cried Luther, staring at him. 'What mad idea has taken possession of you? Who do you say has cast you out from the community of the state in which you have lived? Has there ever, so long as states have existed, been a case of anyone, no matter who, becoming an outcast from society?' 'I call that man an outcast,' answered Kohlhaas, clenching his fist, 'who is denied the protection of the law! For I need that protection if my peaceful trade is to prosper; indeed it is for the sake of that protection that I take refuge, with all the goods I have acquired, in that community. Whoever withholds it from me drives me out into the wilderness among savages. It is he – how can you deny it? – who puts into my hands the club I am wielding to defend myself.' 'Who refused you the protection of the law?' cried Luther.

'Did I not write to you that the petition you delivered has not been seen by the sovereign to whom you delivered it? If state officials suppress lawsuits behind his back or make a mockery of his otherwise sacred name without his knowledge, who but God can call him to account for appointing such servants? Is a cursed wretch like you entitled to judge him for it?' 'Very well,' replied Kohlhaas, 'if my sovereign has not cast me out from the community he protects, then I will return to it. I say again, get me a safe conduct to Dresden and I will disperse the troops I have assembled at Lützen Castle; then I shall go to the Saxon High Court and reopen my case which it dismissed.' Luther, with an expression of annoyance, pushed papers to and fro on his desk and said nothing. He was angered by the defiant attitude this strange man adopted towards the state, and thinking of the writ which he had served on the Junker from Kohlhaasenbrück, he asked him what he expected of the Dresden court. Kohlhaas answered: 'Punishment of the Junker according to the law; the restoration of the horses to their former state; and damages for what I and my groom Herse, who fell at Mühlberg, suffered from the violence that was done to us.' 'Damages!' cried Luther. 'You have borrowed sums running into thousands, against bills and securities, from Jews and Christians alike, to pay for your savage personal revenge. Will you add them to your account as well when the reckoning is made?' 'God forbid!' retorted Kohlhaas, 'I do not ask for the return of my home and estate and the wealth I enjoyed, any more than the cost of my wife's funeral! Herse's old mother will claim the expenses of his medical treatment and produce an itemized statement of the property her son lost at Tronka Castle; and as for the loss I suffered through not selling the blacks, the government can have that valued by a qualified person.' 'You insane, incomprehensible, terrible man!' exclaimed Luther, staring at him. 'You have already taken with your sword the grimmest imaginable revenge on the Junker; what then still makes you insist on a court judgement against him which, even when it is finally pronounced, will only be of quite trivial severity?' With a tear rolling down his cheek Kohlhaas answered: 'Your Reverence, that judgement will have cost me my wife; Kohlhaas means to prove to the world that she did not die in an unjust cause. Let me have my will thus far and let the court deliver judgement; in all other points of dispute that may arise I will defer to you.'

'Well then,' said Luther, 'if the circumstances really are as public opinion has it, then what you demand is just. If you had succeeded in presenting your case to the sovereign for his decision before you arbitrarily took revenge into your own hands, I do not doubt that your demands would have been met point by point. But would you not, all things considered, have done better to forgive the Junker for your Redeemer's sake, and take the horses away, thin and scraggy as they were, and ride back with them to Kohlhaasenbrück for fattening in your stables?' 'Maybe,' said Kohlhaas, walking to the window, 'maybe, or maybe not! If I had known that it would take the heart's blood of my beloved wife to get them on their feet again, I might have done as your Reverence suggests, and not made a fuss of a bushel of oats! But now that they have come to cost me so dear, I think the matter should take its course. Let judgement be passed, as is my due, and let the Junker fatten my blacks for me.' With many thoughts passing through his mind, Luther picked up his papers again and told Kohlhaas that he would negotiate on his behalf with the Elector. In the meantime he should remain quietly in the castle at Lützen. If the sovereign granted him safe conduct he would be told of it by public proclamation. 'But,' he continued as Kohlhaas bent to kiss his hand, 'I do not know whether the Elector will show mercy. I have heard that he has assembled an army and is on the point of joining battle with you at Lützen Castle. However, as I have said, I shall spare no efforts.' With these words he stood up as if to dismiss him.

Kohlhaas remarked that he felt no apprehensions on that score with Luther as his advocate, whereupon the latter held out his hand; but the horse-dealer fell on one knee before him and said that he had another favour to beg. At Whitsun, when he usually received Communion, he had failed to go to church, owing to his military activities. Would Luther do him the kindness, without further preparation, of hearing his confession and in return granting him the benefit of the holy sacrament? Luther, after a moment of reflection, looked at him sharply and said: 'Yes, Kohlhaas, I will. But the Lord, of whose body you wish to partake, forgave his enemy.' And when Kohlhaas, taken aback, stared at him, he added: 'Will you likewise forgive the Junker who wronged you, go to Tronka Castle, mount your two blacks and ride them back to Kohlhaasenbrück for fattening?' 'Your Reverence,' said Kohlhaas, flushing and grasping his hand. 'Well?' '– even the Lord did not forgive all his enemies. Let me forgive the Electors, my two sovereigns, the warden and the steward, the lords Hinz and Kunz and whoever else has done me wrong in this affair; but, if it is possible, let the Junker be compelled to fatten my blacks for me again.' At these words Luther turned his back on him with a look of displeasure, and rang the bell. Kohlhaas stood up in confusion, wiping his eyes, as an assistant entered the anteroom with a lamp in response to this summons; and since Luther had sat down again to his papers and the assistant was trying vainly to open the bolted door, Kohlhaas opened it for him. Luther glanced across at the stranger and told his assistant to light him out; whereupon the man, somewhat disconcerted by the sight of the visitor, unhooked a house-key from the wall and, waiting for him to follow, moved back towards the half-open door of the room. Kohlhaas, holding his hat in both hands, said with some emotion: 'Then, your Reverence, am I not to have the comfort of making my peace, as I asked of you?' Luther replied curtly: 'With your Saviour, no; with your sovereign – that depends on the efforts I have promised you to make!' And with that he motioned to the assistant to carry out his duty without further delay. With a look of sorrow Kohlhaas crossed both his hands over his heart, followed the man who lighted him down the stair, and disappeared.

The next morning Luther sent off a letter to the Elector of Saxony. After a caustic passing allusion to the lords Hinz and Kunz von Tronka, the Chamberlain and Cupbearer who attended on His Highness's person and who, as was generally known, had suppressed Kohlhaas's lawsuit, he advised the Elector with characteristic candour that under such unfortunate circumstances there was no other course open but to accept the horse-dealer's proposal and grant him an amnesty for what had occurred so that he might reopen his case. Public opinion, he noted, was on the man's side in a highly dangerous degree, so that even in Wittenberg, which he had set on fire three times, there were those who spoke in his favour; and since if this present proposal were rejected he would undoubtedly, with malevolent animadversions, make it known to the people, the latter might easily be so far won over that the authority of the state would become powerless against him. He concluded that in so extraordinary a case any scruples about entering into negotiation with a subject who had taken up arms must be set aside; that the means used against him had in fact, in a certain sense, placed him outside society and its laws; and in short, that the situation would best be remedied if Kohlhaas were treated not so much as a rebel in revolt against the crown but rather as a foreign invading power, for which status, indeed, the fact that he was not a Saxon subject to some extent qualified him.

When the Elector received this letter there were present at the palace Prince Christiern of Meissen, the Imperial Marshal and an uncle of Prince Friedrich of Meissen who had been defeated at Mühlberg and was still laid up with his wounds; the Grand Chancellor of the High Court, Count Wrede; Count Kallheim, President of the State Chancellery; and the lords Hinz and Kunz von Tronka, respectively Cupbearer and Chamberlain, both of them childhood friends and intimates of the sovereign. The Chamberlain, Lord Kunz, who, in his capacity as a privy councillor looked after the Elector's privy correspondence and had authority to use his name and seal, was the first to speak. He explained at length that he would never have decided on his own responsibility to dismiss the case brought to the High Court by the horse-dealer against his cousin the Junker, had he not been deceived by false information into regarding it as a wholly groundless and idle piece of trouble-making. Coming to the present situation, he observed that no law either of God or of man authorized the horse-dealer to exact, as he was presuming to do, such monstrous personal vengeance for this judicial error. It would, he insisted, lend prestige to this accursed reprobate if they were to treat with him as with a lawful belligerent. The disgrace that would thereby be reflected upon the sacred person of the Elector was, he added in a burst of eloquence, so intolerable to him that he would rather bear the worst and see his cousin the Junker taken to Kohlhaasenbrück to fatten the blacks, in accordance with the mad rebel's decree, than have Dr Luther's proposal accepted. The Grand Chancellor of the High Court, Count Wrede, half turning to him, expressed his regret that the Chamberlain had not shown the same delicate solicitude for his sovereign's reputation when this unquestionably embarrassing matter first arose as he was now showing when it had become necessary to clear it up. He indicated to the Elector the reservations he felt about invoking the power of the state to enforce an obvious injustice. He alluded significantly to the horse-dealer's ever-increasing following in Saxony, pointed out that this thread of violence threatened to spin itself out indefinitely, and declared that there was no way to sever it and extricate the government from this ugly situation except plain fair dealing: they must immediately and without further scruple make good the wrong that had been done. When asked by the Elector what he thought of this, Prince Christiern of Meissen turned deferentially to the Chancellor and submitted that while the latter's attitude filled him with all due respect, his suggestion that Kohlhaas's wrongs should be righted left out of account the interests of Wittenberg and Leipzig and indeed the whole of the country ravaged by the horse-dealer, and prejudiced its just claim for compensation or at least for retribution. The order of the state had, he considered, been so disrupted on account of this man that it could hardly now be set to rights by principles of jurisprudence. He therefore supported the Chamberlain's view that they should employ the means appropriate in such cases, assemble an army of sufficient size, attack Kohlhaas in his entrenchment at Lützen and either capture or destroy him. The Chamberlain, bringing over two chairs from the wall and politely placing them in the room for the Prince and the Elector, said he was glad to find that a man of the Prince's integrity and perspicacity agreed with him on the question of how best to settle this perplexing affair. Holding the chair without sitting down, the Prince looked straight at him and said that he had no reason at all to be glad, since the proposed course of action inevitably entailed that as a preliminary measure he, Kunz von Tronka, should be arrested and put on trial for misuse of the sovereign's name. For although it might be necessary to draw a veil, before the seat of justice, over a whole series of crimes which had proliferated until they were simply too numerous to be called to account, this did not apply to the first of them, which had led to all the rest; and not until the Chamberlain was arraigned on this capital charge would the state be entitled to suppress the horse-dealer, whose grievances, as they well knew, were perfectly just; they themselves had put into his hand the sword he was now wielding. At these words the Junker looked in dismay at the Elector, who turned away, blushing deeply, and moved over to the window. After an embarrassed silence on all sides, Count Kallheim remarked that by such means they would never break out of the charmed circle in which they were caught. On such grounds it would be equally justifiable to put the Prince's nephew Friedrich on trial, for during the special expedition that he had led against Kohlhaas he had exceeded his instructions in a number of ways; thus if there was to be a reckoning with all those who had caused the present embarrassment, Prince Friedrich would also have to be included among them and called upon by the sovereign to answer for what had happened at Mühlberg. At this point, as the Elector crossed to his desk with a look of perplexity, the Cupbearer Hinz von Tronka spoke in his turn, saying that he could not understand how the decision that should be taken could have escaped men of such wisdom as were assembled here. As he understood it, the horse-dealer had undertaken to disband his men and cease his attacks in return merely for a safe-conduct to Dresden and a renewed examination of his case. But it did not follow that he would have to be granted an amnesty for his criminal acts of vengeance: there were two legal concepts which both Dr Luther and this council of state seemed to have confused. 'When,' he continued, placing his finger along his nose, 'the High Court in Dresden has passed judgement in the matter of the horses, then whichever way that judgement falls there is nothing to prevent us locking up Kohlhaas on charges of arson and robbery. This would be a politically expedient solution, combining the advantages of both the views expressed in our council, and it would I am sure commend itself both to present public opinion and to posterity.'

When neither the Prince nor the Grand Chancellor replied to this speech by Hinz the Cupbearer, but merely glanced at him, and the discussion thus seemed to be over, the Elector said that he would consider the various opinions put to them until the next meeting of the council. Although all was ready for the military campaign against Kohlhaas, it appeared that the preliminary step recommended by the Prince had greatly weakened the Elector's inclination to embark on it, for he was a man who felt the ties of friendship strongly. At any rate he asked the Grand Chancellor Count Wrede, whose view had seemed to him to be the most sensible one, to stay behind; and when Wrede showed him reports which indicated that the horse-dealer's strength had increased to four hundred men, indeed that owing to general dissatisfaction throughout the country caused by the Chamberlain's improper behaviour this number could be expected to double or treble in the near future, the Elector decided without further ado to accept Dr Luther's advice. He accordingly put Count Wrede in sole charge of the Kohlhaas affair, and only a few days later a proclamation appeared to the following effect:

We etc. etc. Elector of Saxony, having considered with especial favour the intercession addressed to Us by Doctor Martin Luther, do hereby grant to Michael Kohlhaas, horse-dealer from Brandenburg, safe-conduct to Dresden for the purpose of a renewed inquiry into his case, on the condition that within three days after sight of these presents he shall lay down the arms which he has taken up; it being understood on the one hand that if, as is not to be expected, the High Court at Dresden shall dismiss his complaint in the matter of the horses, he will be prosecuted with the full rigour of the law for presuming to seek redress for himself with his own hands; in the contrary event however, that tempering Our justice with mercy We shall grant to him and to all those under his command full amnesty in respect of the acts of violence which he has committed on Saxon territory.

No sooner had Kohlhaas received from Dr Luther a copy of this proclamation, which was displayed everywhere in the principality, than notwithstanding the conditional character of its undertakings he disbanded his men, sending them away with gifts, expressions of his gratitude and suitable admonitions. He surrendered all the money, arms and equipment he had taken as booty to the courts at Lützen as Electoral property; and when he had sent Waldmann to Kohlhaasenbrück with letters for the magistrate proposing the re-purchase of his farm if that was possible, and Sternbald to Schwerin to fetch his children whom he wanted to have with him again, he left the castle at Lützen and, taking what was left of his small fortune with him in the form of negotiable documents, made his way unrecognized to Dresden.

Day was just breaking and the whole city was still asleep when he knocked on the door of his small property in the suburb of Pirna which, thanks to the honesty of the magistrate, had remained in his possession. He told Thomas, the aged caretaker who opened the door to him in surprise and consternation, to inform the Prince of Meissen at the government headquarters that he, Kohlhaas the horse-dealer, had arrived. The Prince, on receiving this message, thought it advisable to see its sender at once and find out personally how matters stood between them. When he presently appeared with a retinue of knights and men he found an immense crowd already assembled in the streets leading to Kohlhaas's house. The news of the arrival of the avenging angel who was pursuing the oppressors of the people with fire and sword had roused the whole of Dresden, city and suburbs, from its slumbers; the front door had to be bolted to keep back the surging mob of curious onlookers, and boys climbed up to the windows to catch a glimpse of the incendiary having his breakfast inside. As soon as the Prince had succeeded in entering the house with the help of the guards who cleared a way for him, and had reached Kohlhaas's room, he asked the latter, who was standing only partly dressed by a table, whether he was Kohlhaas the horse-dealer; whereupon Kohlhaas, taking from his belt a wallet containing a number of documents relating to his affairs and respectfully handing it over, answered that he was. He added that, having disbanded his troops, he had come to Dresden under the safe-conduct granted to him by the Elector, in order to present in court his case against Junker Wenzel von Tronka concerning the horses. After quickly looking him over from head to foot, the Prince glanced through the papers in the wallet, asked him to explain the meaning of a certificate he found among them by which the court at Lützen acknowledged a deposit made in favour of the Electoral treasury, and then, in order to find out what kind of a man he was, put all sorts of questions to him about his children, his means, and the way of life he intended to adopt in the future. Judging from his answers that there were no grounds for misgivings on any score, he handed back the documents and said that nothing stood in the way of his proposed legal proceedings and that in order to initiate them he should apply directly to the Grand Chancellor of the High Court, Count Wrede. 'In the meantime,' said the Prince after a pause in which he went to the window and with a look of amazement surveyed the crowd gathered in front of the house, 'for the first few days you will have to accept a bodyguard to protect you both at home and in the streets!' Kohlhaas, disconcerted by this, looked down and made no reply. The Prince, coming away from the window, said: 'Very well, then, but if anything happens you will have only yourself to blame,' and turned towards the door to leave the house. Kohlhaas, having reconsidered the point, said to him: 'My lord, do as you please! If you give me your word that you will withdraw the guard as soon as I request it, I have no objection to the arrangement!' The Prince replied that that went without saying, and after he had instructed three lansquenets, who were presented to him for guard duty, that the man in whose house they were staying was free and that they were only to follow him when he went out in order to give him protection, he took leave of the horse-dealer with a condescending gesture and departed.

Towards noon, accompanied by his three bodyguards and followed by an immense crowd which had been warned by the police not to molest him in any way, Kohlhaas went to see the Grand Chancellor of the High Court, Count Wrede. The Count received him cordially and kindly in his anteroom, talked with him for fully two hours and, when he had listened to the entire sequence of events from start to finish, referred him to a famous Dresden lawyer appointed by the Court, who would draw up the statement of claim and submit it immediately. Without further delay Kohlhaas went to his residence and had a claim set out in terms exactly similar to those of the one originally rejected, calling for punishment of the Junker according to law, restoration of the horses to their previous condition, and damages both for himself and for his groom Herse who had been killed at Mühlberg, the latter to be paid to Herse's aged mother. When this was done he returned, accompanied by the still gaping crowd, to his house, resolving not to leave it again except on necessary business.

Meanwhile the Junker had been released from arrest in Wittenberg, and after recovering from a dangerous inflammation of the foot he had been summoned in peremptory fashion to present himself before the High Court in Dresden and answer the charges brought against him by the horse-dealer Kohlhaas concerning unlawful confiscation and gross ill-treatment of a pair of black horses. His cousins, the brothers Hinz and Kunz von Tronka, received him with great bitterness and contempt, calling him a worthless wretch who had brought shame and disgrace upon the entire family; they told him that he would now undoubtedly lose his case, and that he must make immediate arrangements to fetch the blacks, which, to the derision of all the world, he would be condemned to re-fatten. The Junker, in a weak and trembling voice, answered that he was more to be pitied than any man alive. He swore he had known almost nothing about this whole damnable affair which had plunged him into misfortune, and that the warden and the steward were to blame for it all, since quite without his knowledge and not even remotely on his instructions they had used the horses for harvesting and ruined them with excessive work, partly on their own fields. So saying, he sat down and implored his kinsmen not to wound and insult him and thus wilfully bring back the illness from which he had only just recovered. The next day the Chamberlain and the Cupbearer, who had property in the neighbourhood of the burnt-out Tronka Castle, wrote at their cousin Junker Wenzel's request, and since they had no choice but to do so, to their tenants and stewards there demanding information as to the whereabouts of the blacks, which had gone astray on that day of disaster and not been heard of since. Since, however, the castle had been totally destroyed and almost all its occupants slaughtered, nothing came to light except that a stable-boy, driven by blows from the flat of the incendiary's sword, had rescued them from the burning shed where they stood, but afterwards, on asking the raging monster where he was to take them and what he was to do with them, had got no answer but a kick. The Junker's gout-stricken old housekeeper, who had fled to Meissen, assured him in reply to his written inquiry that on the morning following that dreadful night the stable-boy had gone off with the horses towards the Brandenburg frontier; but all further investigations there proved fruitless, and the information must have been erroneous anyway, since the Junker had no stable-boy whose home was in Brandenburg or even on the Brandenburg road. Some men from Dresden who had been in Wilsdruf a few days after the fire at Tronka Castle reported that a groom had arrived there about that time leading two horses by the halter, which because they were in such a wretched condition and could go no further had been left in a cow-shed with a shepherd who had said he would feed them back to health. For a number of reasons it seemed very likely that these were the blacks in question, but according to people from Wilsdruf the shepherd there had sold them again, it was not known to whom; and a third rumour from an unidentified source even asserted that the horses had already departed this life and were buried in the Wilsdruf carrionpit. As may well be imagined, this turn of events was most welcome to the lords Hinz and Kunz, since it spared them the obligation to fatten the blacks in their stables for their cousin the Junker, who now had no stables of his own; for the sake of complete certainty, however, they sought verification of the report. Junker Wenzel von Tronka therefore, as liege lord of the demesne and lord justice, wrote formally to the court at Wilsdruf describing in detail the pair of horses which, he said, had been entrusted to his care but accidentally lost, and asking them to be so kind as to ascertain their present whereabouts and request and require the owner, whoever he might be, to deliver them to the stables of the Lord Kunz in Dresden, against generous reimbursement of all costs incurred. And accordingly, a few days later, the man who had purchased them from the shepherd in Wilsdruf actually appeared and led the skinny stumbling animals, tethered to his cart, into the city market-place; unluckily, however, for Junker Wenzel, and still more for honest Kohlhaas, this man turned out to be the knacker from Döbbeln.

Junker Wenzel was with his cousin the Chamberlain when the vague rumour reached him that a man had arrived in the city with two black horses which had survived the fire at Tronka Castle; at once, quickly rounding up a few servants from the house, they both went down to the palace square where the man was, intending, if these turned out to be Kohlhaas's animals, to pay his costs and take them from him and bring them home. But to their consternation the two gentlemen found that already, attracted by the spectacle, a crowd which increased from moment to moment had gathered round the two-wheeled cart to which the animals were fastened; and the people, amid uproarious laughter, were shouting to each other that here were the horses on whose account the state had been rocked to its very foundations – a pair of horses already in the hands of the knacker! The Junker, having walked all round the cart and stared at the wretched creatures, which seemed on the point of dropping down dead at any minute, said in embarrassment that they were not the horses he had taken from Kohlhaas. But Kunz the Chamberlain, after turning upon him a look of such speechless fury that if it had been made of iron it would have knocked him to pieces, flung open his cloak to reveal his orders and chain of office, and going up to the knacker asked him whether these were the blacks taken over by the shepherd at Wilsdruf, and sent for through the Wilsdruf courts by their owner Junker Wenzel von Tronka. The knacker, who was busy giving a fat, well-fed nag a bucket of water to drink, said, 'The blacks?' Putting the bucket down, he took the horse's bit from its mouth and added: 'The blacks tied to my cart were sold to me by the swineherd from Hainichen. Where he got them from and whether they came from the shepherd at Wilsdruf, I don't know.' He had been ordered, he said, picking up the bucket again and propping it between his knee and the shaft of the cart, by an officer of the Wilsdruf court to bring them to Dresden to the house of the Tronka family, but the Junker he was to see about it was called Kunz. With these words he turned round, took the pail with the water the horse had left in it and emptied it on to the cobblestones. The Chamberlain, surrounded by the stares of the mocking crowd and unable to engage the attention of the fellow, who busily and imperturbably went on with his work, said that he was the Chamberlain Kunz von Tronka, but that the blacks of which he was to take possession must be those belonging to the Junker his cousin. A groom who had managed to escape from the fire at Tronka Castle had given them to the shepherd at Wilsdruf and originally they had belonged to the horse-dealer, Kohlhaas. He asked the man, who was standing there with his legs apart and hitching up his breeches, if he knew nothing about this, and if he knew whether the swineherd from Hainichen had – for this was the vital point – perhaps acquired them from the Wilsdruf shepherd, or from a third person who, in his turn, had bought them from the shepherd. The knacker, after standing by his cart and passing water, said that he had been sent to Dresden with these blacks and was to get his money for them from the Tronka family. He did not understand what the gentleman was talking about, and whether the swineherd at Hainichen had got them from the shepherd at Wilsdruf or from Peter or Paul was all one to him, since they hadn't been stolen. And with that, putting his whip across his broad back, he strolled over to a tavern in the square to get himself some breakfast, since he was hungry. The Chamberlain, who had no idea what on God's earth to do with a pair of horses sold by the swineherd at Hainichen to the knacker at Döbbeln, unless they were indeed those same horses that the devil was riding through Saxony, asked the Junker for his views. But when the latter, with pale and quivering lips, replied that the most sensible course would be to buy the blacks whether they belonged to Kohlhaas or not, the Chamberlain, cursing the father and mother who had brought him into this world, flung his cloak round him again and walked away from the crowd, totally at a loss. Seeing Baron von Wenk, a friend of his, riding across the street, and calling him over, he asked him to stop at the house of the Grand Chancellor Count Wrede and with his assistance get Kohlhaas to come and examine the blacks; for he was determined not to leave the square just because the rabble were staring so mockingly at him and, with handkerchiefs pressed to their mouths, only seemed to be waiting for him to go before bursting into laughter. It happened that Kohlhaas, summoned by a court messenger to give certain explanations that were needed concerning the property deposited at Lützen, was in the Chancellor's room when the

Baron entered with his message. The Chancellor rose from his seat with an air of annoyance and left the horse-dealer, whom the Baron did not know, standing on one side with the papers in his hand; the Baron then told him of the embarrassing situation in which Kunz and Wenzel von Tronka found themselves. The knacker from Döbbeln, acting on inadequate instructions from the Wilsdruf courts, had turned up with a pair of horses in such a miserable condition that Junker Wenzel understandably hesitated to identify them as those belonging to Kohlhaas; for this reason, if they were to be taken from the knacker for the purpose of attempting to re-fatten them in the family's stables, ocular inspection by Kohlhaas would first be necessary to remove all doubt on the point. 'Would you therefore be kind enough,' he concluded, 'to have the horse-dealer fetched from his house and taken to the market-place where the horses are.' Removing his spectacles from his nose, the Grand Chancellor told the Baron that he was under two misapprehensions: firstly, if he though that the point in question could be settled only by ocular inspection on the part of Kohlhaas; and secondly, if he imagined that he, the Chancellor, was authorized to have Kohlhaas taken by a guard wherever the Junker wanted. He then introduced him to the horse-dealer who was standing behind him, and requested him, as he sat down and put on his spectacles again, to consult the horse-dealer himself in this matter. Kohlhaas, whose expression revealed nothing of what was passing through his mind, said that he was prepared to follow the Baron to the market-place and inspect the horses brought to the city by the knacker. As the Baron turned round in amazement towards him, he returned to the Grand Chancellor's desk and having given him, from the documents in his wallet, several pieces of information concerning the property deposited in Lützen, he took his leave. The Baron, who had blushed scarlet and crossed to the window, did likewise; whereupon, escorted by the three lansquenets acting on the Prince of Meissen's orders, and accompanied by a crowd of people, they walked to the palace square. Meanwhile Kunz the Chamberlain, defying the advice of several friends who had now joined him, was standing his ground among the people before the knacker from Döbbeln. As soon as the Baron appeared with the horse-dealer, he went up to the latter and asked him, holding his sword with pride and dignity under his arm, whether the horses standing behind the cart were his. Raising his hat respectfully to the gentleman who had asked him this question and whom he did not know, the horse-dealer, without replying, went across to the knacker's cart accompanied by all the noblemen present. He stopped at a distance of twelve paces from the animals, which were standing unsteadily with their heads bowed to the ground and not touching the hay put down for them by the knacker, glanced at them briefly, then turned back to the Chamberlain and said : 'My lord, the knacker is quite right; the horses tied to his cart belong to me.' With that he looked round at all the gentlemen, raised his hat again and, escorted by his bodyguard, left the square. As soon as the Chamberlain heard this he strode across to the knacker so quickly that the plume of his helmet shook, threw him a bag of money, and while the fellow, combing his hair back from his forehead with a lead comb, held the bag in his hand and stared at the money, he ordered a groom to untether the horses and lead them home. The groom, at his master's command, left a group of his friends and relatives who were in the crowd, and did in fact approach the horses, rather red in the face and stepping over a great pile of dung that had formed at their feet. But hardly had he taken hold of their halters to untether them when his cousin, Master Himboldt, seized his arm and shouting: 'Don't you touch those knacker's nags!' hurled him away from the cart. Then rather uncertainly stepping back across the pile of dung towards the Chamberlain, who had stood speechless at this incident, he told him he had better get himself a knacker's man if he wanted an order like that carried out. Foaming with rage, the Chamberlain glared for a moment at Himboldt, then turned round and shouted over the heads of the noblemen surrounding him, calling for the guards; and as soon as an officer with some Electoral guardsmen appeared from the palace at Baron von Wenk's behest, he gave him a brief account of the outrageous riot which the citizens of the town were presuming to instigate, and called on him to arrest the leader of the mob, Master Himboldt, whom he seized by the shirt, accusing him of having assaulted and thrust aside his groom who had been untying the blacks from the cart on his orders. Skilfully twisting himself free and pushing the Chamberlain back, Himboldt said: 'My lord! Telling a lad of twenty what he should and should not do is not inciting him to riot! Ask him if he's prepared to go against all custom and decency and touch the horses tied to that cart; if he'll do it after what I said, then let him! For all I care he can flay and skin them here and now!' At this the Chamberlain rounded on his groom and asked him if he took exception to carrying out his order to untether Kohlhaas's horses and take them home. When the young man, retreating into the crowd, diffidently answered that the horses would have to be made decent again before that could be expected of him, the Chamberlain pursued him, snatched off his hat which bore the family's coat of arms, stamped on it, drew his sword, and raining furious blows on him with the flat of the blade, instantly drove the groom out of the square and out of his service. Master Himboldt cried out: 'Down with the murderous tyrant!' and as the people, incensed by this scene, pressed together and forced the guard back, he threw the Chamberlain to the ground from behind, tore off his cloak and collar and helmet, wrenched his sword out of his hand and with a savage sweep of the arm hurled it away across the square. In vain Junker Wenzel cried out to the other noblemen to help his cousin, as he himself escaped from the riot; they had barely taken a step before the surging populace scattered them, and the Chamberlain, who had injured his head in falling, was abandoned to the full fury of the mob. His life was saved only by the appearance of a troop of cavalry-men who happened to be crossing the square and whom the officer commanding the Electoral guardsmen called to his assistance. When he had driven off the crowd, the officer arrested the raging Himboldt, and while he was being taken off to prison by some cavalrymen, two friends lifted the luckless, blood-bespattered Chamberlain from the ground and took him home. Such was the catastrophic outcome of this well-meant and honest attempt to give satisfaction to the horse-dealer in return for the wrongs that had been done to him. The knacker from Döbbeln, his business concluded, had no wish to delay any longer, and as the onlookers began to disperse he tied the horses to a lamp-post where they stood the whole day without anyone bothering about them, the laughing-stock of street-urchins and loiterers. Consequently, since they were deprived of all care and attention, the police had to take responsibility for them and instructed the Dresden knacker to keep them in his yard outside the city until further notice.

This incident, little as the horse-dealer was in fact to blame for it, nevertheless aroused throughout the land, even among the more moderate and well-disposed, a feeling that was highly prejudicial to the successful outcome of his case. The relationship now existing between him and the state seemed quite intolerable, and both privately and publicly people began to say that it would be better to do him an open wrong and dismiss the whole lawsuit again than to grant him justice in such a trivial affair, justice which he had extorted by violence, merely to satisfy his mad obstinacy. To complete the unfortunate Kohlhaas's ruin, it was the Grand Chancellor himself, with his excessive rectitude and resultant hatred of the Tronka family, who helped to intensify and spread this feeling. It was extremely improbable that the horses now in the hands of the Dresden knacker would ever be restored to the condition in which they had left the stables at Kohlhaasenbrück; yet even assuming that with skill and persistence they could be so nursed back, the disgrace that would thereby fall on the Junker's family in consequence of the present situation was so great, and their importance in Saxony as one of the foremost and noblest houses of the land was such, that the most proper and expedient course now seemed to be that the horse-dealer should be offered a sum of money in compensation. Some days later the President, Count Kallheim, made this proposal to the Grand Chancellor in the name of the Chamberlain who was still incapacitated by his injuries. But although the Chancellor wrote to Kohlhaas, advising him not to dismiss such an offer out of hand, he nevertheless requested the President in a curt and barely civil reply to spare him any further private interventions in this affair; the Chamberlain, he wrote, should approach the horse-dealer himself, whom Count Wrede described as a very reasonable and modest man. And the horse-dealer, whose determination had indeed been weakened by the incident in the market-place, was in accordance with the Chancellor's advice only waiting for an initiative from the Junker or his relatives, fully intending to accommodate them and to forgive everything that had happened. But to take such an initiative was precisely what these proud noblemen could not stomach, and greatly incensed by the reply they had received from the Grand Chancellor they showed it to the Elector, who had visited the Chamberlain on the following morning in the room where he was lying ill from his wounds. The sick Chamberlain asked him in a weak and pathetic voice whether, now that he had risked his life to comply with his sovereign's wishes in bringing this matter to a conclusion, he was also to expose his honour to public opprobrium by appearing with a plea for reconciliation and indulgence before a man who had heaped upon him and his family every imaginable ignominy and disgrace. When the Elector had read the letter he asked Count Kallheim with some embarrassment whether the High Court was not empowered to rely on the fact that the horses could not be restored to health and accordingly, without consulting Kohlhaas further, give judgement for mere monetary compensation, as if the horses were already dead. The Count replied: 'Your Highness, they *are* dead: in any legal sense they are dead because they have no value, and they will be physically dead too before they can be taken from the knacker's yard to their lordships' stables.' Thereupon the Elector, putting the letter in his pocket, said that he would speak to the Chancellor himself about it, and reassuring the Chamberlain, who had struggled half upright and gratefully seized his hand, he told him to look after his health, rose from his chair most graciously and left the room.

Thus matters stood in Dresden when another and more menacing storm approached from Lützen and gathered over poor Kohlhaas; and the crafty lords were clever enough to draw its lightning down upon his luckless head. A certain Johann Nagelschmidt, one of the men recruited by the horse-dealer and then dismissed after the proclamation of the Electoral amnesty, had seen fit a few weeks later to gather some of this rabble, capable as they were of any vileness, together again on the Bohemian border, and with them to pursue on his own account the trade to which Kohlhaas had introduced him. This scoundrel styled himself Kohlhaas's deputy, partly in order to intimidate the officers sent to arrest him and partly in order to entice the peasantry into participating in his outrages as before. With the ingenuity he had learnt from his master he spread rumours alleging that the amnesty had been violated in respect of many of the men who had peacefully returned to their homes, and indeed that Kohlhaas himself, with scandalous perfidy, had been arrested on his arrival in

Dresden and placed under guard. It thus became possible, in proclamations which closely resembled those of Kohlhaas, for him to represent his gang of incendiaries as an army recruited only for the glory of God and for the purpose of safeguarding the amnesty promised to them by the Elector; although, as already mentioned, all this was done not in the least for God's glory nor out of loyalty to Kohlhaas, for whose fate they cared not a straw, but in order to burn and plunder with the greater impunity and ease under the cover of such pretensions. When the first news of this reached Dresden, the noblemen could not conceal their delight at a turn of events which gave the whole affair so different a complexion. They recalled with sage dissatisfaction what a foolish step it had been, in defiance of their urgent and repeated warnings, to grant Kohlhaas an amnesty, thus deliberately giving, as it were, the signal for all kinds of riff-raff to follow in his footsteps. Not content with lending credence to Nagelschmidt's assertion that he had only resorted to arms in order to provide his oppressed master with support and security, they even expressed the definite opinion that his whole appearance on the scene was nothing but a plot hatched by Kohlhaas to alarm the government and force the court to give judgement for him all the sooner in a form which, point for point, would satisfy his lunatic stubbornness. Indeed, in front of some country gentlemen and courtiers gathered after dinner in the Elector's antechamber, the Cupbearer Hinz went so far as to suggest that the dispersal of his horde of brigands at Lützen had been nothing more than a damnable subterfuge; and with considerable irony at the expense of the Grand Chancellor's passion for justice, he cleverly linked some circumstantial evidence together to prove that the whole lot of them were still assembled in the forests of the principality and only waiting for a sign from the horse-dealer before bursting out again with fire and sword. Prince Christiern of Meissen, much disturbed by these latest developments which threatened to blacken his sovereign's reputation in the most injurious manner, immediately sought an audience with him at the palace; and clearly seeing that it was in the interests of the Tronka party to attempt to ruin Kohlhaas by bringing new charges, he asked the Elector's permission to have the horse-dealer interrogated without delay. Summoned by a court officer to the government headquarters, the horse-dealer appeared, in some astonishment, carrying his two little boys Heinrich and Leopold in his arms; for on the previous day Sternbald, the groom, had arrived with his five children from Mecklenburg where they had been staying, and various considerations too complex to expound here had decided him to pick up the boys and take them along with him to the hearing, as with a flood of childish tears they had begged him to do just as he was leaving them. After looking kindly at the children who had been set down beside their father, and good-naturedly asking them their ages and names, the Prince informed Kohlhaas of the liberties that were being taken in the valleys of the Erzgebirge by his former follower Nagelschmidt; and passing him the latter's so-called writs, he required him to say what he could in his own defence. Although in fact deeply alarmed by these shameful and treacherous documents, the horse-dealer nevertheless had little difficulty in satisfying a man of the Prince's integrity that the accusations made against him were groundless. He not only pointed out that, as things now stood, he needed no help from any third party to reach a favourable conclusion of his case, which was progressing to his entire satisfaction; but he was also able to demonstrate from some papers which he had with him and showed to the Prince the extreme improbability of any inclination on Nagelschmidt's part to lend him such assistance: for shortly before the disbanding of his force in Lützen he had been about to hang the fellow for rape and other outrages committed in the countryside, so that only the publication of the Electoral amnesty, which entirely

changed the situation, had saved him, and the following day
he and Kohlhaas had parted as mortal enemies.

Kohlhaas now, with the Prince's approval, sat down and
wrote an open letter to Nagelschmidt, in which he described
his claim to have taken up arms in order to uphold the
amnesty allegedly violated against him and his men as a
shameless and wicked fabrication. He stated that he had
neither been arrested on his arrival in Dresden nor put under
guard, and that his case was going forward just as he wished;
as to the acts of murder and arson committed in the Erzgebirge after publication of the amnesty, he gave Nagelschmidt over to the full vengeance of the law for these, as
a warning to the rabble he had collected around him. Extracts from the criminal trial which the horse-dealer had
conducted against him in Lützen Castle for the above-
mentioned crimes were appended to all this, for the enlightenment of the public concerning this ruffian who had been
intended for the gallows and was, as already stated, only
saved by the Elector's edict. The Prince accordingly reassured Kohlhaas about the suspicions which, under the
pressure of circumstances, it had been necessary to express
to him during this hearing. He promised that as long as *he*
was in Dresden the amnesty granted to him would in no
way be violated; then giving the two boys some fruit from
his table, he shook hands with them again, bade farewell
to Kohlhaas and let him go. The Grand Chancellor nevertheless recognized the danger hanging over the horse-dealer
and did his utmost to bring his case to a conclusion before
further events should complicate and confuse the issue; but
such confusion was exactly what the scheming Tronka
party desired and intended. Instead of tacitly, as hitherto,
admitting guilt and confining their efforts to the securing
of a mitigated judgement against the Junker, they now began
to raise crafty and quibbling arguments amounting to categorical denial of his guilt. Either they claimed that Kohlhaas's horses had only been detained at Tronka Castle by

the arbitrary action of the warden and steward, of which the Junker knew nothing or almost nothing; or they asserted that the animals had already been suffering from an acute and dangerous coughing sickness upon their arrival, and undertook to prove this by witnesses whom they would produce; and when extensive investigations and discussions had refuted these arguments, they even dragged up an Electoral edict twelve years old which in fact forbade the importation of horse stock from Brandenburg to Saxony on account of an outbreak of cattle disease: a crystal-clear proof not only of the Junker's right but of his duty to detain the horses brought by Kohlhaas across the border.

In the meantime, Kohlhaas had bought back his farm at Kohlhaasenbrück from the worthy magistrate, adding only a small sum to the price in compensation for losses incurred, and he wished to leave Dresden for a few days and return home, apparently in order to effect the legal settlement of this transaction. But his intention was, we do not doubt, connected less with this piece of business, urgent though it in fact was if the winter crop were to be sown, than with a desire to test his position under the present strange and obscure circumstances; and motives of another kind may also have been at work, which we may leave for all who know their own hearts to surmise. He therefore went to the Grand Chancellor, leaving his guard behind, and stated, showing him the magistrate's letters, that if his presence in court was not urgently required at this time, as appeared to be the case, he would like to leave the city and go to Brandenburg for a period of eight to twelve days, within which period he promised to be back. Casting down his eyes with an expression of concern and annoyance, the Chancellor said he had to confess that Kohlhaas's presence was now more necessary than ever in view of the crafty and hair-splitting defences that were being used by the other side and which meant that the court would need statements and explanations from him on a thousand and one unforeseen points. But when Kohlhaas referred him to his lawyer who was well informed on the case, and pressed his point modestly but persistently, promising to stay away for no more than a week, the Chancellor, after a pause, said briefly as he dismissed him that he hoped he would get himself a passport for this journey from Prince Christiern of Meissen.

Kohlhaas, who could read the Grand Chancellor's face well, was only strengthened in his resolve, and sitting down immediately he wrote to the Prince of Meissen, as chief government administrator, requesting a passport to Kohlhaasenbrück for one week, without giving any reason. In reply to this letter he received an official communication, signed by the commandant Baron Siegfried von Wenk, to the effect that his application for a passport to Kohlhaasenbrück would be submitted to His Serene Highness the Elector, and that as soon as the gracious consent were forthcoming the passport would be sent to him. When Kohlhaas inquired of his lawyer why this governmental communication was signed by a Baron Siegfried von Wenk and not by Prince Christiern von Meissen to whom he had applied, he was told that the Prince had gone to his estates three days ago and in his absence government business had been transferred to the commandant Baron Siegfried von Wenk, a cousin of the gentleman of the same name whom we mentioned earlier. Kohlhaas, whose heart began to beat uneasily at all these complications, waited for several days for a decision on his request which had been submitted with such surprising circumstantiality to the person of the sovereign. But a week or more went by, and still no decision reached him, nor did the High Court pass judgement although he had been definitely assured that it would do so; on the twelfth day he therefore sat down, firmly resolved to force the government's attitude to him into the open whatever it might be, and applied again, as a matter of urgency, for the desired passport. But to his consternation, on the evening of the following day which had likewise passed without the long-awaited reply, as he walked over to the window of his small back room, deep in thought about his present position and especially about the amnesty procured for him by Dr Luther, he glanced across to the small outbuilding in the yard which served as quarters for the bodyguard assigned to him by the Prince of Meissen on his arrival, and saw that the bodyguard was not there. When he summoned his old servant Thomas and asked him what this meant, the old man replied with a sigh : 'Sir, things are not quite as they should be. There are more soldiers today than usual and at nightfall they stationed themselves all round the house; two are standing with shields and pikes in the street in front of the main entrance, two are at the back door in the garden, and two more are lying in the front hall on some straw and say they are going to sleep there.'

Kohlhaas, his face paling, turned round and said : 'It's no matter, so long as they are there. Put out lamps when you go to the hall, so that they can see.' He then, on the pretext of emptying a pot, opened the front window shutters and convinced himself that what the old man had told him was true, for at that very moment the guard was even being silently changed, a procedure no one had thought of since the arrangement had begun. After observing this he went to bed, not indeed feeling much like sleep, but with his mind immediately made up about what to do the next day. For what he resented above all was that the government he was dealing with should keep up a pretence of justice when in fact they were violating his promised amnesty. If he was really a prisoner, of which there could be no more doubt, he intended to force them to declare clearly and unequivocally that this was so. Therefore, as soon as day broke, he ordered his groom Sternbald to harness his carriage and bring it to the front door, for the purpose, as he said, of driving to Lockewitz to see an old friend, the magistrate there who had met him a few days ago in Dresden and invited him and his children to visit him. The soldiers, whispering to each other when they saw all the active preparations for this being made in the house, surreptitiously sent one of their number into the city; within a few minutes a government officer arrived with some constables and went into the house opposite as if they had business there. Kohlhaas, who was busy getting his two little boys' clothes on, also observed what was happening and deliberately let the carriage wait longer than necessary outside the house. Then, as soon as he saw that the police preparations were complete, and affecting not to notice them, he walked out of the house with his children; telling the lansquenets on guard that they did not need to come with him, he lifted the boys into the carriage, and kissed and consoled his little girls who were weeping because he had arranged for them to stay behind with the old servant's daughter. Hardly had he himself stepped into the carriage when the officer and his constables emerged from the house opposite and asked where he was going. Kohlhaas replied that he wished to visit his friend the magistrate at Lockewitz, who had invited him a few days ago to come and see him with his two sons in the country. To this the officer answered that he would have to wait a few minutes in that case as, on the orders of the Prince of Meissen, some cavalrymen would be accompanying him. Looking down from the carriage, Kohlhaas asked with a smile whether it was thought that his life would be in danger in the home of a friend who had offered to entertain him at his table for a day. The officer answered with a good-humoured and friendly air that the danger was of course not great and added that the men were instructed not to incommode him in any way. Kohlhaas, now looking serious, pointed out that on his arrival in Dresden the Prince of Meissen had left it to his choice whether he would use the bodyguard or not; and when the officer showed surprise at this and referred in cautious terms to the arrangement that had been customary throughout his stay, the horse-dealer recounted to him the circumstances that had led to the guard being set up at his house. The officer assured him that the orders of the commandant Baron von Wenk, who was at present chief of police, made it his duty to give Kohlhaas uninterrupted protection against any risk, and that he must request him, if he did not wish to be escorted, to go to the government headquarters himself to clear up what must obviously be some misunderstanding. Kohlhaas, turning on the man a look that well expressed his feelings, but determined to force the issue, said he would do that. With his heart beating hard he got out of the carriage, told the servant to take the children back into the hall, and, leaving the groom and the carriage in front of his house, proceeded in the company of the officer and his guards to the government headquarters.

As it happened, the commandant Baron Wenk was just in the middle of inspecting a gang of Nagelschmidt's followers who had been captured the previous evening near Leipzig, and the noblemen with him were questioning these men about a number of points on which they wanted information, when the horse-dealer and his escort entered the hall. The interrogation was halted and in the sudden ensuing silence the Baron, as soon as he saw Kohlhaas, went over to him and asked him what he wanted. When the horse-dealer respectfully explained his intention of driving to Lockewitz to have lunch with the magistrate there, and said that he wished to leave his bodyguard of lansquenets behind since he did not need them, the Baron changed colour, seemed to swallow something else he was about to say, and advised Kohlhaas that he would do well to stay quietly at home and to postpone this meal with his friend at Lockewitz for the time being. With that he cut short the whole conversation, turned to the officer and told him that his orders concerning this man were to stand and he was not be be allowed to leave the city unless escorted by six mounted guards. Kohlhaas asked whether he was a prisoner, and whether he was to understand that the amnesty which had been solemnly vouchsafed to him before the eyes of all the world was now broken; whereupon the Baron suddenly wheeled round on him, his face flushing fiery red, and stepping close looked him straight in the eyes and exclaimed: 'Yes, yes, yes!' And with that he turned his back, left him standing and went back to Nagelschmidt's men. Kohlhaas left the room; and although he realized that his only way of saving himself, namely by flight, had now been made very much more difficult by what he had just done, he nevertheless did not regret it, for he now considered that he himself was no longer bound by any obligation to observe the terms of the amnesty. When he reached home he had the horses unharnessed and went to his room, deeply dejected and troubled, and still accompanied by the officer. The latter, to the horse-dealer's silent disgust, assured him that the whole thing was a misunderstanding which would shortly be cleared up, and meanwhile signalled to his constables to bolt all the doors leading from the house to the courtyard; but the front entrance, he hastened to point out, was still open, as always, for Kohlhaas to use as he pleased.

Meanwhile, in the forests of the Erzgebirge, Nagelschmidt had been so hard pressed on all sides by the police and the army that, since he wholly lacked the means to carry out the kind of role he had chosen, he hit upon the idea of really involving Kohlhaas in his venture. Having been fairly accurately informed by a passing traveller about how matters stood with the lawsuit in Dresden, he thought that despite the open hostility between them he could persuade the horse-dealer to enter into a new alliance with him. He therefore sent one of his men to him with a letter, written in barely legible German, which stated that if Kohlhaas were willing to come to Altenburg where the remnants of his disbanded force had got together again, and resume command of them, he for his part would help him with horses and men and money to escape from his arrest in Dresden; he also promised to be in future more obedient and generally more orderly and better behaved than in the past, and as proof of his loyalty and attachment undertook to come in person to the outskirts of Dresden and rescue Kohlhaas from his imprisonment. Now as ill-luck would have it, when the man carrying this letter reached a village just outside Dresden he fell into one of the violent fits to which he had been subject since childhood, and since he had the letter in the breast of his tunic, it was found by the people who came to his assistance; as soon as he had recovered, he was arrested and taken under guard, with a large crowd following, to the government headquarters. No sooner had the commandant, Baron von Wenk, read the letter than he went at once to the Elector at his palace where he found the lords Kunz and Hinz, the former now recovered from his injuries, and the President of the State Chancellery, Count Kallheim. These gentlemen were of the opinion that Kohlhaas should be arrested without delay and put on trial for secretly conspiring with Nagelschmidt; for they pointed out that such a letter could not have been written unless there had been previous communications from the horse-dealer's side and unless there had in general been a lawless and criminal association between the two men for the plotting of fresh atrocities. The Elector steadfastly refused to breach the safe-conduct granted to Kohlhaas on the basis of this letter alone; he thought indeed that from what Nagelschmidt had written it seemed more probable that there had been no previous alliance between the two of them. All he would consent to do in order to get to the bottom of the matter was, after long hesitation, to accept the President's suggestion that Nagelschmidt's messenger should be allowed to deliver the letter as if he had not been arrested; and they would then see whether Kohlhaas answered it. Next morning the man, who had been thrown into prison, was accordingly brought to government headquarters, where the commandant gave the letter back to him, and with the promise that he would be set free and excused whatever punishment he had incurred, ordered him to deliver it to the horse-dealer as if nothing had happened. The fellow unhesitatingly lent himself to this base deception, and with much pretence of secrecy he gained admission to Kohlhaas's room under the pretext that he had some crabs to sell (the police official having bought these for him at the market). Kohlhaas, who read the letter as his children played with the crabs, would in other circumstances have seized this ruffian by the scruff of the neck and handed him over to the guards at his door. But knowing that in the present atmosphere even this action might not be interpreted in a way that could make any difference, and feeling convinced that nothing in this world could rescue him from the affair in which he was enmeshed, he looked sadly at the fellow, whose face he knew well enough, asked him where he lived, and requested him to return in a few hours when he would tell him what decision to take to his master. He told Sternbald, who happened to come in, to buy some of the crabs from the man in the room, and when this purchase was concluded and the two men had left him without recognizing each other, he sat down and wrote a letter to Nagelschmidt to the following effect: first, that he accepted his proposal concerning the leadership of his followers in Altenburg, and that accordingly, to free him and his five children from their present state of quasi-arrest, Nagelschmidt should send him a carriage with two horses to Neustadt, near Dresden; that he would also, in order to make speedier progress, need a pair of relief horses on the highway to Wittenberg, that road being, though a detour, the only one by which he could reach him, for reasons too complicated to explain; that although he thought he could win over his guards by bribery, he would like to know that two stout-hearted, intelligent and well-armed men were at hand in Neustadt in case force were necessary; that he was sending him a roll of twenty gold crowns by his messenger to defray the costs of all these arrangements, the use of which sum he would reckon up with him after their completion; and further, that he declined as unnecessary Nagelschmidt's offer to take part personally in the rescuing of him from Dresden, in fact he expressly ordered him to remain in Altenburg as temporary commander of their men, who must not be left without a leader. When Nagelschmidt's man came back in the evening he gave him this letter, warning him to take good care of it and paying him generously. His intention was to go with his five children to Hamburg and there take a ship to the Levant or the East Indies or wherever else the sun shone down on people who were different from those he knew; for his heart was so burdened and broken with grief that he had already given up the idea of having his pair of blacks fattened again, even apart from the repugnance he felt at making common cause with Nagelschmidt for this purpose. Nagelschmidt's messenger had no sooner handed over the above letter to the Dresden commandant than the Grand Chancellor Wrede was relieved of his duties, the President Count Kallheim appointed head of the High Court in his place, and Kohlhaas, arrested on an order in council by the Elector, was taken heavily chained to the city dungeons. He was brought to trial on the evidence of the letter, copies of which were nailed up throughout the town; and since, when confronted with it at the bar of the court, he answered 'Yes' to the lawyer's question whether he recognized the handwriting as his own, but merely looked at the ground and answered 'No' when asked whether he had anything to say in his defence, he was sentenced to be tortured with red-hot tongs by knackers' men, then quartered, and his body burnt between the wheel and the gallows.

Thus matters stood for poor Kohlhaas in Dresden when the Elector of Brandenburg intervened to rescue him from the clutches of arbitrary despotic power and claimed him, in a note presented to the Saxon State Chancellery, as a subject of Brandenburg. For the worthy city governor Heinrich von Geusau, while walking with the Elector along the banks of the Spree, had acquainted him with the story of this strange and not utterly wicked man; and at the same time, pressingly questioned by his astonished sovereign, he could not avoid mentioning the discredit into which the latter's own person had been brought by the improper conduct of his High Chancellor, Siegfried von Kallheim. The Elector, much angered by this, called the High Chancellor to account, and finding that his kinship with the Tronka family was to blame for the whole thing, at once dismissed him from his post with indications of his severe displeasure, and appointed Heinrich von Geusau High Chancellor instead of him.

Now it happened at this time that the Kingdom of Poland, for reasons not known to us, was involved in a dispute with the House of Saxony, and was repeatedly and urgently pressing the Elector of Brandenburg to make common cause with the Poles against the Saxons. The High Chancellor, Herr von Geusau, being not unskilled in such matters, could therefore reasonably hope to satisfy his sovereign's desire to see justice done to Kohlhaas at all costs, without putting the peace of the whole realm at greater risk than consideration for a single individual warranted. Accordingly he not only demanded that Kohlhaas, in view of the altogether tyrannical procedures which had been used against him and which were offensive to both God and man, should be unconditionally and immediately handed over to be judged, if guilty, according to the laws of Brandenburg, on charges which the Electorate of Saxony might prefer against him through an attorney sent for this purpose to Berlin; but he also demanded a passport for an attorney whom his own Elector was minded to send to Dresden in order to ensure that Kohlhaas obtained redress against Junker Wenzel von Tronka in the matter of the black horses taken from him, and other flagrant and violent injuries done to him, on Saxon territory. The Chamberlain Kunz, who as a result of the changes of office in Dresden had been appointed President of the State Chancellery and who, for a number of reasons, was reluctant in his present straits to offend Brandenburg, replied in the name of his sovereign, who had been much disheartened by the note from Berlin, expressing astonishment at 'the unfriendly and inequitable manner in which it challenged the Elector of Saxony's right to try Kohlhaas according to his laws for crimes committed in his territories; it was, after all, general knowledge that the said Kohlhaas possessed a considerable property in Dresden, the capital city, and had himself never denied his Saxon citizenship'. But since Poland was already amassing an army of five thousand men on the Saxon frontier to press its claims by war, and since the High Chancellor von Geusau declared that Kohlhaasenbrück, the place from which the horse-dealer took his name, was situated in Brandenburg and that the execution of the death-sentence passed on him would be treated as a violation of international law, the Saxon Elector, on the advice of the Chamberlain Kunz himself who wanted to withdraw from the whole affair, summoned Prince Christiern von Meissen from his estates and decided, after a few words with this sensible man, to surrender Kohlhaas to the Berlin authorities in accordance with their demand. Although he was far from pleased by the improprieties that had occurred, the Prince had to take charge of the Kohlhaas affair at the wish of his hard-pressed sovereign and therefore asked him on what grounds he now wanted the horse-dealer charged in the High Court in Berlin. Since it was not possible to refer to the offending letter to Nagelschmidt owing to the ambiguous and obscure circumstances under which it had been written, and since the earlier plundering and incendiarism could not be mentioned either because of the proclamation pardoning them, the Elector decided to submit a report on Kohlhaas's armed invasion of Saxony to his Majesty the Emperor in Vienna, accusing Kohlhaas of breaking the public peace of the Empire and requesting his Majesty, on whom of course no amnesty was binding, to have Kohlhaas arraigned for this at the High Court in Berlin by an Imperial prosecutor. A week later the horse-dealer, still in irons, and his five children who had been retrieved from foundling homes and orphanages at his request, were put into a carriage and taken to Berlin by Friedrich von Malzahn, a lord whom the Elector of Brandenburg had sent to Dresden with an escort of six cavalrymen.

It happened that the Elector of Saxony had been invited by the Lord Sheriff, Count Aloysius von Kallheim, who at that time had a considerable estate on the Saxon border, to a great stag-hunt which had been arranged at Dahme for his diversion. He had travelled there in the company of Kunz the Chamberlain and his wife Heloise, daughter of the Lord Sheriff and sister of the President, and other distinguished lords and ladies, hunt-equerries and courtiers; and so it was that the whole company, still covered with dust from the chase, were sitting at table under the shelter of tents with streaming pennants which had been pitched on a hill right across the highway. Here they were being served by pages and noblemen's sons and listening to the merry strains of music from the foot of an oak-tree, when the horse-dealer and his mounted guard came riding slowly up the road from Dresden. For one of Kohlhaas's delicate young children had fallen ill, compelling his escort Herr von Malzahn to stop for three days at Herzberg, a precaution of which he did not feel it necessary to inform the government in Dresden since he was responsible only to his own sovereign. The Elector, with his tunic half open and wearing a plumed hat decorated with pine twigs in huntsman's fashion, was sitting next to the lady Heloise, who in his early youth had been his first love; and the gaiety of the colourful feast all round him having put him in high good humour, he said: 'Let's go and give this cup of wine to that poor fellow, whoever he is!' The lady Heloise, glancing at him affectionately, immediately rose up and, plundering the whole table, filled a silver dish handed to her by a page with fruits, cake and bread; the whole company had already swarmed out of the tent with refreshments of all kinds when Aloysius von Kallheim came up with an embarrassed expression and asked them to stay where they were. When the surprised Elector asked what had happened to upset him so, the Sheriff turned towards the Chamberlain and falteringly answered that Kohlhaas was in the carriage. At this incomprehensible news, for it was common knowledge that the horse-dealer had left six days ago, Kunz the Chamberlain took his cup of wine and, turning back towards the tent, emptied it into the sand. Flushing very red, the Elector set his down on a plate which a page, at a sign from the Chamberlain, held out for him; and as Friedrich von Malzahn, respectfully saluting the company, whom he did not know, slowly made his way among the tent-ropes that ran across the road and moved on towards Dahme, the guests, without giving the incident further thought, went back at the Lord Sheriff's request into the tent. As soon as the Elector had sat down, Kallheim secretly sent word to the authorities at Dahme asking them to see to it that the horse-dealer's journey continued without delay; but as Herr von Malzahn insisted, in view of the late hour, on staying the night in the place, they had to content themselves with his being accommodated quietly in a farmhouse belonging to the magistracy which lay off the road, hidden in woodland. Now it happened that in the evening when the guests, merry with wine and sated with rich desserts, had forgotten the whole affair, the Sheriff proposed that they should take up their hunting stations again, as a herd of deer had been sighted, and the whole company eagerly welcomed this suggestion. Armed with muskets, they hastened in pairs over hedges and ditches into the nearby forest; and so it was that the Elector and the lady Heloise, whom he was escorting as she wanted to watch the spectacle, were to their astonishment led by the guide assigned to them right through the yard of the farmhouse where Kohlhaas and the Brandenburg cavalrymen were lodged. When she heard this, the lady said: 'Come, your Highness!' and playfully taking the chain of office that hung round his neck and tucking it inside his silk tunic, she added: 'Let's slip into the farmhouse before the crowd catches us up and take a look at the extraordinary man who is spending the night there!' The Elector, flushing, caught her by the hand and said: 'Heloise! What can you be thinking of!' But looking at him in surprise, she answered that no one would recognize him in the huntsman's costume he was wearing; and, as she tried to draw him with her, a couple of hunt-equerries, who had already satisfied their curiosity, came out of the house and assured them that, thanks to the Sheriff's precautions, neither Malzahn nor the horse-dealer knew who was in this company gathered in the neighbourhood of Dahme. So the Elector pulled his hat down over his eyes with a smile and said: 'Folly, you rule the world, and your throne is a pretty woman's lips!'

It chanced that as his visitors entered the farmhouse Kohlhaas was sitting on a bale of straw with his back to the wall and was feeding some milk and a roll of bread to his child who had fallen sick in Herzberg; and when, to open the conversation, the lady asked who he was and what was wrong with the child, what crime he had committed and where he was being taken under escort, he saluted her with his leather cap and, continuing with his task, answered her sparingly but adequately. The Elector, standing behind the hunt-equerries, noticed a small leaden locket hanging by a silken thread from his neck and asked him, for want of anything better to talk about, what it signified and what was in it. Kohlhaas, taking it off, opening it and extracting a small piece of paper sealed with glue, replied: 'Ah yes, my lord, there is a strange story connected with this locket. It must have been seven months ago, the very day after my wife's funeral, when as you perhaps know I was setting out from Kohlhaasenbrück to capture Junker von Tronka, who had done me great injustice; and in order to carry out some negotiations, what they were about I don't know, the Elector of Saxony and the Elector of Brandenburg were meeting each other at the little market town of Jüterbock through which the route of my expedition took me. They had reached a satisfactory agreement by evening and were walking along the streets in friendly conversation, to watch the merrymaking at the fair which happened to be taking place in the town that day. There they came across a gypsy-woman who was sitting on a stool with an almanac telling the fortunes of people standing round her; and they asked her in jest if she didn't also have something to reveal to them that would be pleasant for them to hear. I had just stopped with my men at an inn, and was there in the market-place where all this happened, but as I was standing in the entrance to a church behind all the crowd I couldn't hear what the strange woman said to the gentlemen; so when the people laughingly whispered to one another that she was not one to let everyone into her secrets, and pressed forward to watch the scene that seemed about to take place, I got up on a bench behind me that was hewn out of the church entrance, not so much because I was really curious but to make more room for others who were. I had hardly reached this vantage-point, from which I had an uninterrupted view of the gentlemen and the woman, who was sitting on her stool in front of them and seemed to be scribbling something down, when she suddenly pulled herself up on her crutches, looked round at the people, and fastened her eyes on me, though I had never exchanged a word with her nor ever wanted to consult her skills; then she pushed her way across to me through the whole dense throng of onlookers and said: "There! if the gentleman wants to know, he will have to ask you about it!" And with those words, my lord, she stretched out her skinny, bony fingers and handed me this piece of paper. And when the whole crowd turned round to me and I asked her in astonishment: "What's this fine present you're making me, old lady?", she answered, after mumbling a lot of stuff in which all I could make out was, to my great amazement, my own name: "... an amulet, Kohlhaas the horse-dealer; keep it safely, one day it will save your life!" And with that she vanished. Well,' continued Kohlhaas good-humouredly, 'I must admit that although it was a close call in Dresden, I am still alive; and what will happen to me in Berlin, and whether I shall get by with it there too, only the future will tell.'

At these words the Elector sat down on a bench, and although when Heloise asked in dismay what was the matter with him he answered: 'Nothing, nothing at all!', he at once collapsed in a swoon to the floor before she had time to come to his assistance and catch him in her arms. Herr von Malzahn, who was entering the room on an errand at just that moment, exclaimed: 'God Almighty, what's wrong with the gentleman?' The lady called for water, the Elector's hunting companions lifted him up and carried him to a bed in the next room, and panic reached its height when the Chamberlain, fetched by a page, declared after several vain attempts to bring him to his senses that he showed every sign of having suffered a stroke. While the Cupbearer sent a mounted messenger to Luckau to fetch a doctor, he opened his eyes and the Lord Sheriff therefore had him put in a carriage and taken at walking pace to his hunting lodge not far away; but after his arrival there the strain of the journey caused him to faint twice more, and it was not until late the next morning, when the doctor had arrived from Luckau, that he recovered a little, though with distinct symptoms of an imminent brain fever. As soon as he was conscious, he half sat up in bed and immediately asked where Kohlhaas was. The Chamberlain, who misunderstood the question, took the Elector's hand and answered that he might set his mind at rest about that terrible man, for in accordance with instructions he himself had given after this latest strange and incomprehensible incident, he had remained behind in the farm at Dahme with his Brandenburg escort. He assured the Elector of his liveli-est sympathy and emphasized that he had most severely reproached his wife for the irresponsible and frivolous action that had brought his Highness into contact with the man: but what was it in the conversation that had so strangely and deeply affected him? The Elector said he must frankly confess that the mere sight of a trivial scrap of paper which the man carried on him in a lead locket had been responsible for the whole disagreeable occurrence. By way of explanation he added a lot more which the Chamber-lain found incomprehensible; then suddenly clasping the latter's hand between his own, he declared that it was of the utmost importance to him to obtain possession of the piece of paper, and asked him to take a horse without delay and ride to Dahme, where he was to buy the paper for him from Kohlhaas at any price. The Chamberlain, who could scarcely conceal his embarrassment, assured him that if this piece of paper was of value to him, nothing in the world was more important than to conceal this fact from the horse-dealer: for if a single indiscreet word once made him aware of it, all the riches the Elector possessed would not suffice to purchase it from that ferocious ruffian, whose vindictive-ness was insatiable. To reassure his master he added that they must think of some other means, and that it might be possible by subterfuge, using a third party who was quite uninvolved, to obtain the piece of paper to which he attached so much importance, as the scoundrel probably did not set much store by it for its own sake. Wiping the sweat off his brow, the Elector asked if they could immedi-ately send someone to Dahme for this purpose and mean-while halt the horse-dealer's journey until they had by hook or by crook got possession of the paper. The Cham-berlain, who could not believe his ears, replied that unfor-tunately, on any reckoning, the horse-dealer must already have left Dahme and crossed the border into Brandenburg

territory, where any attempt to hamper his further trans-
portation, let alone halt it, would lead to exceedingly disagreeable difficulties and complications, of a kind, indeed,
that might be quite insuperable. When the Elector fell back
on his pillow in silence with a gesture of utter despair, he
asked: 'What then is written on that piece of paper, and
by what strange and inexplicable chance does your Highness know that what is written on it concerns yourself?'
But the Elector looked askance at the Chamberlain, as if
he did not trust him to cooperate in this matter, and made
no reply; he lay there rigid, with his heart beating uneasily,
and stared at the lace of the handkerchief he was pensively
holding; then suddenly, under the pretext of having some
other business to discuss with him, he asked the Chamberlain
to send him the Junker vom Stein, an energetic and intelligent young man whom the Elector had often employed
before on secret missions.

After explaining the matter to him and impressing upon
him the importance of the piece of paper in Kohlhaas's
possession, he asked if he would earn his everlasting friendship by getting this paper for him before the horse-dealer
reached Berlin. When the Junker, as soon as he had to some
extent grasped the situation, strange though it was, assured
him that he would serve him to the utmost of his powers,
the Elector instructed him to ride after Kohlhaas, and since
money would probably not persuade him, speak carefully
to him in private and offer him his freedom and his life –
indeed immediately, if he insisted, though with all due
caution, help him with horses, men and money to escape
from the Brandenburg cavalrymen who were escorting him.
The Junker, after requesting a letter of authority in the
Elector's hand, at once set out with some men and, not
sparing the horses' wind, had the good fortune to overtake
Kohlhaas in a village on the border where he was eating a
midday meal with his five children and Herr von Malzahn
in the open air in front of a house. Herr vom Stein presented
himself as a stranger who was passing through and wished to

take a look at the remarkable man whom Herr von Malzahn was escorting, and the latter, introducing him to Kohlhaas, at once courteously invited him to take a seat at the table. As the cavalrymen were having their lunch at a table on the other side of the house, and Malzahn had to go to and fro to arrange details about their departure, the opportunity soon arose for the Junker to make known to the horse-dealer who he was and the special mission with which he had been entrusted. The horse-dealer already knew the rank and identity of the man who had fainted in the farmhouse at Dahme at the sight of the locket in question, and the excitement into which this discovery had thrown him needed only, for its culmination, that he should read the mysterious words on the paper, which for a number of reasons he was determined not to open out of mere curiosity. And so, remembering the ignoble and unprincely treatment meted out to him in Dresden despite his own unreserved willingness to make every possible sacrifice, he replied to Junker vom Stein that he was not prepared to hand over the paper. When the Junker asked him what prompted this strange refusal, considering that he was being offered nothing less than freedom and life for it, Kohlhaas answered: 'Noble sir! If your sovereign were to come and promise to destroy himself and the whole pack of those who help him wield the sceptre – destroy himself and them, do you understand? for that is indeed my soul's dearest wish – even then I would not give him this piece of paper which is more valuable to him than his life. I would say to him: you can send me to the scaffold, but I can make you suffer, and I mean to do so!' And so saying, his face deathly pale, he called over one of the cavalrymen and invited him to eat up the fair quantity of food that was still left in the dish; and for the remainder of the hour he spent in that village, with the Junker sitting at the table, he behaved to him as if he were not there, only turning to him again with a parting glance as he stepped into his carriage.

When the Elector heard this news, his condition deterior-

ated so gravely that for three fateful days the doctor feared
for his life, which was in danger from so many simultaneous
ills. Nevertheless, thanks to his naturally healthy constitu-
tion, after lying on a sick-bed for several painful weeks he
recovered at least sufficiently to be put in a carriage, well
tucked up with pillows and blankets, and taken back to
Dresden to his affairs of state. As soon as he arrived there
he summoned Prince Christiern von Meissen and asked him
how far advanced were the preparations for the departure
of the attorney Eibenmayer whom they had decided to send
to Vienna as their representative in the Kohlhaas affair, to
submit to his Imperial Majesty their complaint on the
violation by Kohlhaas of the peace of the Empire. The Prince
replied that in accordance with the Elector's order upon his
departure for Dahme, Eibenmayer had left for Vienna immediately upon the arrival of the jurist Zäuner, whom the
Elector of Brandenburg had sent as his advocate to Dresden
to present his charge against Junker Wenzel von Tronka
in the matter of the black horses. The Elector, flushing and
walking over to his desk, expressed surprise at this haste,
since to the best of his knowledge he had made it clear that
he wanted Eibenmayer's definitive departure delayed until
after a necessary consultation with Dr Luther, at whose
request Kohlhaas had been granted amnesty; he would then
have issued more precise and definite orders. So saying he
shuffled together some correspondence and documents lying
on his desk, with an air of suppressed anger. The Prince, after
a pause in which he stared at him in amazement, said that
he was sorry if he had incurred his displeasure in this matter;
he could, however, show him the written decision of the
State Council ordering him to dispatch the attorney at the
abovementioned time. He added that there had been no
word at the Council of any consultation with Dr Luther.
At an earlier stage it might have served some purpose to take
account of the views of this man of God, given his intervention on Kohlhaas's behalf; but this was no longer so,

now that the amnesty had been publicly violated and the horse-dealer arrested and handed over to the Brandenburg courts for judgement and execution. The Elector said that the mistake of sending off Eibenmayer was, he supposed, not very grave; but for the present, until he gave further orders himself, he did not want the attorney to open any proceedings against Kohlhaas in Vienna, and requested the Prince to send a dispatch-rider to him at once with instructions to that effect. The Prince replied that unfortunately this order came a day too late, since according to a report he had only just received Eibenmayer had already begun legal action and presented his complaint to the State Chancellery in Vienna. 'How,' asked the Elector in dismay, 'was this possible in so short a time?' The Prince answered that three weeks had already passed since Eibenmayer had left, and that his instructions had been that as soon as he reached Vienna he was to prosecute the affair with all possible speed; he added that any delay would, in this case, have been most improper, in view of the stubborn persistence with which the Brandenburg attorney Zäuner was pressing the charges against Junker Wenzel von Tronka – he had already applied to the court for an order that the black horses should be provisionally removed from the hands of the knacker with a view to their eventual restoration to health, and in spite of objections from the other side, the court had so ordered.

The Elector rang the bell, remarking that it did not matter and was of no consequence; then, after turning again to the Prince and questioning him on various indifferent matters, such as what else was going on in Dresden and what had happened during his absence, he motioned to him politely with his hand and dismissed him, though he was unable to conceal his innermost feelings. On the same day he asked him in writing for the whole Kohlhaas file on the pretext that he wished to work on the case personally owing to its political importance; and as he could not bear to contemplate the destruction of the one man from whom he could discover the mysterious message on the piece of paper, he wrote a letter in his own hand to the Emperor, imploring him with heartfelt urgency, for weighty reasons of which he hoped he might be able before long to give a clearer account, to grant him leave to withdraw provisionally, until a further decision could be reached, the charge brought by Eibenmayer against Kohlhaas. The Emperor, through his Chancellery of State, sent a note replying that he was extremely astonished by the apparent sudden change in the Elector's attitude; that the report submitted to him by Saxony had made the Kohlhaas affair a matter that concerned the entire Holy Roman Empire; that accordingly he, as supreme head thereof, saw it as his duty to appear as accuser in this case before the House of Brandenburg; and that since he had already sent Court Assessor Franz Müller to Berlin to act for him as prosecutor there and call Kohlhaas to account for breach of the public peace, there was no possible way of withdrawing the charge now, and the matter would have to take its course in accordance with the law.

This letter profoundly upset the Elector; and when, to his utmost distress, private reports presently began to reach him from Berlin indicating that the trial in the High Court had begun and forecasting that despite all the efforts of the advocate appointed for his defence Kohlhaas would probably end on the scaffold, the unhappy prince decided to make one more attempt, and wrote a personal letter to the Elector of Brandenburg begging him to spare the horse-dealer's life. He resorted to the argument that the amnesty which the man had been guaranteed made it improper to carry out a death sentence upon him; he assured the Elector that despite the apparent severity with which they had proceeded against Kohlhaas in Saxony it had never been his own intention to have him executed; and he described how inconsolable he personally would be if the protection which Berlin had claimed to be extending to the man turned out unexpectedly, in the event, to be to his greater disadvantage than if he had stayed in Dresden and his case had been decided according to Saxon law. The Elector of Brandenburg, to whom much in this account of the matter seemed ambiguous and obscure, answered that the zeal with which his Imperial Majesty's attorney was conducting the prosecution meant that any deviation from the absolute rigour of the law, such as the Elector of Saxony desired, was wholly out of the question. He remarked that the concern expressed to him by the Elector of Saxony was excessive, because although Kohlhaas stood arraigned in the Berlin High Court for crimes which the amnesty had pardoned, his accuser was not the Elector of Saxony, who had proclaimed that amnesty, but the supreme ruler of the Empire, who was not in any way bound by it. He also pointed out how necessary it was to make a deterrent example of Kohlhaas in view of the continuing outrages by Nagelschmidt, who with unprecedented audacity had already carried them into the territory of Brandenburg; and he requested the Elector of Saxony, if all these considerations carried no weight with him, to appeal to his Imperial Majesty himself, for if Kohlhaas was to be pardoned, this could only be done on the Emperor's initiative.

Grief and vexation at all these fruitless attempts plunged the Elector into a fresh illness; and when the Chamberlain visited him one morning, he showed him the letters he had sent to Vienna and to Berlin in his efforts to prolong Kohlhaas's life and so at least gain time in which to try to take possession of the piece of paper he carried. The Chamberlain fell to his knees before him and implored him by all that was sacred and dear to him to tell him what was written on the paper. The Elector asked him to bolt the door and to sit on his bed; then taking his hand and pressing it to his bosom with a sigh, he began the following narrative: 'I understand that your wife has already told you how the Elector of Brandenburg and I encountered a gypsy-woman on the third day of our meeting at Jüterbock. The Elector, being a man of lively disposition, decided to play a joke on this weird creature in public and so destroy her reputation for soothsaying, which had just been made the subject of some unseemly conversation at dinner; accordingly he went and stood with folded arms by the table where she was sitting, and demanded that if she was going to tell his fortune she should first give him a sign that could be verified on that same day, for otherwise, he said, he would not be able to believe what she told him even if she were the Roman Sibyl herself. After looking us quickly up and down the woman said that this would be the sign: the big horned roebuck which the gardener's boy was rearing in the park would come to meet us in this market-place before we had left it. Now you must understand that this roebuck, being intended for the Dresden court kitchens, was kept under lock and key in an enclosure, shaded by the oak-trees in the park and surrounded by a high wooden fence; furthermore, because it contained other smaller game and poultry, the whole park as well as the garden leading to it were kept carefully closed, and it was therefore quite impossible to imagine how this animal could come to us in the square where we were standing and thus fulfil the bizarre prophecy. Nevertheless, suspecting that some trick might be involved, the Elector briefly consulted me and, determined to carry out his jest and discredit once and for all anything she might subsequently say, he sent a message to the palace ordering that the roebuck should be slaughtered at once and prepared for the table on one of the following days. He then turned back to the woman, in front of whom all this had been said aloud, and asked: "Well now! What can you reveal about my future?" The woman, looking into his hand, replied: "Hail, my lord Elector! Your Highness will rule for many years, the house of your ancestors will flourish for many generations, and your descendants will become great and glorious and will achieve power above all the princes and lords of the world!" After a pause in which he looked pensively at the woman, the Elector stepped back to me and said in an undertone that he now almost regretted having sent off the messenger who would confute the prophecy; and while the noblemen in his retinue, with much rejoicing, showered money into the woman's lap, he asked her, giving her a gold coin from his own pocket as well, whether her greeting to me would have an equally sterling sound. After opening a box that stood by her and slowly and fussily sorting the money into it by denomination and quantity, the woman closed it again, held her hand up as if to shield her eyes from the sun, and looked at me. When I repeated the question and said jestingly to the Elector, as she examined my hand: "She does not seem to have anything pleasant to tell *me*!" she picked up her crutches, slowly pulled herself up with them from her stool, and with her hands held out mysteriously in front of her came up close to me and whispered plainly in my ear: "No!" – "Indeed!" I exclaimed in confusion, recoiling from her as she sank back on her stool with a cold lifeless stare as if her eyes were those of a figure of marble. "And from what quarter does danger threaten my house?" Taking some paper and charcoal and crossing her knees, the woman asked if I wanted her to write it down for me. And when I, being indeed in some embarrassment because the circumstances left me no choice, answered, "Yes, do that!" she said, "Very well! I shall write down three things for you: the name of the last ruler of your dynasty, the year in which he will lose his throne, and the name of the man who will seize it by force of arms." And having done so, in front of all the people, she rose to her feet, sealed the paper with some glue which she moistened between her withered lips, and pressed it with a lead signet-ring which she wore on her middle finger. But when I tried to take the paper from her, overcome with inexpressible curiosity as you may well imagine, she exclaimed: "Not so, your High-

ness!" and turned round and held up one of her crutches.
"That man over there with the plumed hat, who is standing behind the crowd on a bench in the church doorway,
will sell you this piece of paper, if you want it!" And with
that, before I had even rightly grasped what she said, she
left me standing there speechless with astonishment, clapped
her box shut behind her, slung it over her shoulder, and
mingled with the crowd around us; and I saw no more of her.
At that moment, to my deep relief I must say, the gentleman whom the Elector had sent to the palace reappeared
and informed him with great glee that the roebuck had been
slaughtered and dragged before his eyes by two huntsmen
into the kitchen. The Elector, in high good humour, put his
arm through mine to accompany me from the square and
said: "There we are, you see! The prophecy was just a
common swindle and not worth our time and money!" But
you can imagine our consternation when, even as he was
speaking, a cry went up round the whole square, and everyone turned and stared at a huge butcher's dog which was
trotting along towards us from the palace courtyard, its
teeth sunk in the neck of the roebuck which it had seized
as fair game in the kitchen; and with scullions and skivvies
in hot pursuit it dropped the animal on the ground just three
paces from us. And thus the woman's prophecy, the pledge
she had given for the truth of everything else she had
predicted, was fulfilled indeed, and the roebuck, dead though
it was, had come to meet us in the market square. A thunderbolt from the winter sky could not have struck me a more
deadly blow than this sight, and as soon as I was free of
the company I had been in, I immediately set about discovering the whereabouts of the man with the plumed hat
whom the woman had pointed out to me. But none of my
people, though I made them search without pause for three
days, could find the slightest trace of him. And now, my
dear friend Kunz, only a few weeks ago I saw him with my
own eyes in the farmhouse at Dahme!' And so saying he

dropped the Chamberlain's hand, wiped the sweat from his brow and fell back on to his bed.

The Chamberlain, who saw this incident in quite a different light but thought it would be wasted breath to try to persuade the Elector that his own view of it was mistaken, urged him to try yet again to find some means or other of getting possession of the piece of paper, and then to leave the fellow to his fate; but the Elector replied that no means whatsoever occurred to him, and that nevertheless the thought of not being able to get the paper, or indeed of even seeing all knowledge of its contents perish with the man who had it, tormented him to the point of despair. When his friend asked if attempts had been made to trace the gypsy-woman herself, the Elector answered that he had, under a fictitious pretext, ordered the government to search for the woman throughout the entire principality, which they were still vainly doing to this day, and that in any case, for reasons which he refused to go into, he doubted whether she could ever be traced in Saxony. Now it happened that the Chamberlain, on business connected with several large properties in Neumark inherited by his wife from the High Chancellor Count Kallheim, who had died soon after his dismissal from office, intended to travel to Berlin. And so, as he was genuinely fond of the Elector, he asked after brief reflection whether he would give him a free hand in the affair. When his master warmly grasped his hand and pressed it to his heart, saying: 'Be as myself in this matter, and get me that piece of paper!', the Chamberlain delegated his affairs of office, advanced his departure by several days and, leaving his wife behind, set off for Berlin accompanied only by a few servants.

In the meantime, as we have already mentioned, Kohlhaas had arrived in Berlin and on the Elector of Brandenburg's special instructions was lodged in a prison for persons of rank, where with his five children he had been made as comfortable as possible. Immediately upon the arrival of the Imperial Attorney from Vienna he had been put on trial before the High Court on the charge of breaking the peace of the Empire. Although he objected in his defence that he could not be indicted for the armed invasion of Saxony and the acts of violence which this had involved, since the Elector of Saxony had agreed at Lützen to pardon him on these counts, he was informed that His Imperial Majesty, whose representative was the prosecutor in this case, could not take that into consideration. When all this had been explained to him and he had been assured on the other hand that he would get full satisfaction in his case against Junker Wenzel von Tronka in Dresden, he soon accepted the situation without further demur. Thus it happened that on the very day of the Chamberlain's arrival, the law was pronounced upon Kohlhaas and condemned him to death by beheading; a sentence which, lenient though it was, no one believed would be carried out in view of the complications of the case – indeed the whole of Berlin, knowing how well-disposed the Elector was towards Kohlhaas, confidently hoped that he would exercise his prerogative and commute it to a mere term of imprisonment, though perhaps a long and severe one. The Chamberlain nevertheless realized that there might be no time to lose if the task assigned to him by his master was to be achieved, and set about it one morning by clearly and circumstantially showing himself, in his ordinary court dress, to Kohlhaas as the latter stood idly at his prison window watching the passers-by. From a sudden movement of the horse-dealer's head he concluded that he had noticed him, and he also noted with peculiar satisfaction that he involuntarily raised his hand to his breast as if to clasp the locket; surmising what had flashed through Kohlhaas's mind at that moment, he decided that this was sufficient preparation for the next step in his attempt to gain possession of the paper. He sent for an old woman, a rag-seller whom he had noticed hobbling about on crutches on the Berlin

streets among a crowd of other riff-raff plying the same
trade, and who seemed to him similar enough in age and
dress to the one described to him by the Elector; and assuming that the features of the old crone who had only briefly
appeared to hand him the piece of paper would not have
impressed themselves deeply on Kohlhaas's memory, he
decided to use this other one in her place and if possible get
her to impersonate the gypsy-woman to him. Accordingly,
in order to prepare her for the part she was to play, he told
her in detail of all that had occurred between the Elector
and the said gypsy-woman in Jüterbock, not forgetting to
stress particularly the three mysterious items on the paper,
since he did not know how much the gypsy had revealed
to Kohlhaas; and when he had explained to her that she
must mumble out an incoherent and unintelligible speech
conveying to him that some plan was afoot to get possession, by trickery or force, of this paper to which the Saxon
Court attached such extreme importance, he instructed her
to ask the horse-dealer, on the grounds that it was no longer
safe with him, to give it back to her for safe keeping for a
few crucial days. In return for a promise of substantial
remuneration, part of which she required the Chamberlain
to pay in advance, the old rag-seller immediately undertook
to carry out this task; and as she had for some months
known the mother of Herse, the groom killed at Mühlberg,
and this woman was allowed by the authorities to visit
Kohlhaas occasionally, she succeeded a few days later in
bribing the gaoler with a small sum and gaining access to
the horse-dealer.

But Kohlhaas, when he saw her enter his room and
noticed a signet-ring on her hand and a coral chain hanging
round her neck, thought he recognized the same old gypsy-
woman who had handed him the piece of paper in Jüterbock; and indeed (for probability and reality do not always
coincide) it chanced that something had happened here
which we must report, though anyone who so pleases is at

liberty to doubt it: the Chamberlain had committed the most appalling of blunders, for in the old rag-seller whom he had taken from the streets of Berlin to play the part of the gypsy-woman, he had picked upon the mysterious gypsy herself whose part he wanted to have played. At any rate this woman, as she leaned on her crutches and stroked the cheeks of the children who had shrunk back against their father at her strange appearance, told Kohlhaas that she had returned from Saxony to Brandenburg quite some time ago, and having heard an incautious question dropped by the Chamberlain in the streets of Berlin about the gypsy-woman who had been in Jüterbock in the spring of the previous year, she had at once pressed forward and offered, under a false name, to do the business he wanted done. The horse-dealer noticed a strange resemblance between her and his deceased wife Lisbeth, so much so that he almost asked her if she was her grandmother; for not only did her features and her hands, which though bony were still finely shaped, and especially the way she gestured with them as she spoke, remind him most vividly of his wife, but he also saw on her neck a mole just like one that Lisbeth had had on hers. With his thoughts in a turmoil he bade the old woman be seated and asked what on earth had brought her to him on an errand from the Chamberlain. With Kohlhaas's old dog sniffing round her knees and wagging his tail as she scratched his head, the woman replied that what the Chamberlain had commissioned her to do was to tell him to which three questions of importance to the Saxon Court the piece of paper contained a mysterious answer; to warn him of an emissary who had come to Berlin in order to get possession of the paper; and to ask it back from him under the pretext that it was no longer safe round his neck where he was carrying it. But her purpose in coming was to tell him that this threat of having the paper taken from him by trickery or force was no more than a crude and preposterous deception; he need not have the least fear for its safety under the protection of the Elector of Brandenburg in whose custody he was, indeed the piece of paper was much safer with him than with her, and he should take great care not to be parted from it by entrusting it to anyone under whatever pretext. Nevertheless, she concluded, she thought he would be wise to put it to the use for which she had given it to him at the fair in Jüterbock: namely, to heed the proposal conveyed to him by Junker vom Stein at the border, and surrender the paper to the Elector of Saxony in exchange for life and freedom. Kohlhaas, exulting in the power he thus possessed to strike a mortal wound at his enemy's heel just as it was grinding him into the dust, answered: 'Not for all the world, old lady, not for all the world!' and, squeezing the old woman's hand, merely asked her to tell him what answers the paper contained to those three momentous questions. The woman lifted his youngest child, who had been squatting at her feet, on to her lap and said: 'Not for all the world, horse-dealer Kohlhaas, but for this pretty fair-haired boy!' – and with that she laughed at the child, embraced and kissed him as he stared at her wide-eyed, and with her bony hands took an apple from her pocket and gave it to him. In confusion Kohlhaas said that when they were grown up the children themselves would praise his course of action, and that to keep the paper was the best thing he could do both for them and for their descendants. Besides, he asked, after the way he had been treated, who would guarantee him against being tricked again? Might he not end by having vainly sacrificed the piece of paper to the Elector, just as he had vainly sacrificed his army at Lützen? 'When a man has once broken his word to me,' he said, 'I will have no more dealings with him; and only at your own plain and unequivocal request, my good old woman, will I part with this piece of writing which in so miraculous a way gives me satisfaction for everything I have suffered.' Putting the child down, the woman said that in many ways he was right and that he could do whatever he pleased. Thereupon she picked up her crutches again and made as if to leave. Kohlhaas repeated his question concerning the contents of the mysterious message, and when she briefly replied that he could after all open it, though it would be mere curiosity to do so, he added that there were a thousand other things he would like to know before she left him: who she really was, how she came by the knowledge she possessed, why she had refused to give the paper to the Elector, for whom after all she had written the words on it, and why she had handed the magic message to him of all the thousands of others, to him who had never wanted her prophecies? Now it happened that at this very moment they heard the noise of some police officers coming up the stairs; the woman therefore, suddenly alarmed by the prospect of being found by them here, answered: 'Good-bye, Kohlhaas, good-bye! When we meet again, you will find out about all these things!' and made for the door. She called out to the children: 'Good-bye, little ones, good-bye!' and departed after kissing all of them in turn.

In the meantime the Elector of Saxony, a prey to his dismal thoughts, had summoned two astrologers, Oldenholm and Olearius, who enjoyed a high reputation in Saxony at that time, and consulted them about the contents of the mysterious piece of paper that was of such importance to himself and to all his descendants. And since the two men, after a profound investigation lasting for several days in the tower of the palace at Dresden, could not agree whether the prophecy referred to later centuries or to the present, alluding perhaps to the kingdom of Poland with which relations were still very hostile, their learned dispute quite failed to dispel the unhappy prince's uneasiness, indeed his despair, but rather increased and intensified it until he found it quite unendurable. And now in addition the Chamberlain sent word to his wife, who was about to follow him to Berlin, to break the news diplomatically to the Elector before she left that his attempt to get possession of the piece of paper held by Kohlhaas, with the help of an old woman who had not shown her face since, had failed, and that consequently their hopes of obtaining it were now very slender; for the sentence of death passed on the horse-dealer had now been signed by the Elector of Brandenburg, after he had meticulously scrutinized all the documents in the case, and the date of execution had already been fixed for the day following Palm Sunday. At this news the Elector of Saxony, consumed by anguish and regrets, shut himself up in his chamber like a lost soul; weary of life, he refused all food for two days, then on the third suddenly vanished from Dresden, after sending a brief message to the government that he was going to hunt with the Prince of Dessau. Where he really went and whether he travelled to Dessau we must leave in doubt, as the chronicles we have compared in order to compile this report are on this point strangely contradictory and incompatible. What is certain is that the Prince of Dessau was lying ill at this time in Brunswick at his uncle Duke Heinrich's house, quite unfit to go hunting, and that Kunz the Chamberlain's wife, the lady Heloise, arrived to stay with her husband in Berlin on the evening of the following day, accompanied by a certain Count von König-stein whom she introduced as her cousin.

Meanwhile the sentence of death was read out to Kohlhaas on the Elector of Brandenburg's orders, his chains were struck off and the documents taken from him in Dresden concerning his property and financial affairs were returned to him; and when the lawyer assigned to him by the High Court asked him how he wished to dispose of what he owned after his death, he drew up with a notary's assistance a will in favour of his children and appointed his trusty friend, the magistrate at Kohlhaasenbrück, as their guardian. His last days were accordingly spent in a peace and contentment which nothing could match; for soon after this, by special Electoral decree, the prison in which he was kept had also been opened and free access granted to all the many friends he possessed in the city. Indeed he even had the satisfaction of seeing the theologian Jakob Freising enter his prison as an emissary of Dr Luther, bringing him a letter in the latter's own hand – without doubt a very remarkable communication, all trace of which, however, has been lost; and from this minister, in the presence of two Brandenburg deacons who assisted, he received the sacrament of holy communion. And so the fateful Monday after Palm Sunday arrived, the day on which Kohlhaas was to make atonement to the world for his rash attempt to wrest justice from the world with his own hands; the whole city was astir, for the people even now had not abandoned hope of seeing him reprieved. He was just passing out of the gate of his prison under strong escort, carrying his two little sons (for he had expressly requested this favour at the bar of the court) and with the theologian Jakob Freising conducting him, while a mournful crowd of his friends shook hands with him in farewell, when the castellan of the Electoral palace pushed his way through to him with a distraught face and gave him a note which, he said, an old woman had handed in for him. Looking in astonishment at the man, whom he hardly knew, Kohlhaas opened the note, the fastening of which was impressed with a seal that immediately reminded him of the gypsy-woman. But to his indescribable astonishment he read the following message: 'Kohlhaas, the Elector of Saxony is in Berlin; he has gone ahead of you already to the place of execution and you may recognize him, if you care to, by a hat with blue and white plumes. I need not tell you the purpose that has brought him here: as soon as you are buried he intends to have the locket dug up and the paper inside it opened. – Your Elizabeth.' Utterly dumbfounded, Kohlhaas turned to the castellan and asked him whether he knew the strange woman who had handed him this message. But just as the castellan was answering: 'Kohlhaas, the woman ...', only to falter strangely in mid-speech, the horse-dealer was swept along in the procession which moved off again at that very moment, and could not catch what the man, who seemed to be trembling in every limb, was saying.

When he reached the place of execution, he found the Elector of Brandenburg with his retinue, including the High Chancellor Heinrich von Geusau, waiting on horseback surrounded by an immense crowd; on his right stood the Imperial Attorney, Franz Müller, with a copy of the death sentence in his hand; on his left, holding the Dresden High Court's verdict, was his own lawyer Dr Anton Zäuner; and in the middle of the semicircle which the crowd completed stood a herald with a bundle of possessions and the pair of black horses, now shining with health and pawing the ground with their hooves. For the High Chancellor von Geusau had won the case which he had brought in Dresden in his sovereign's name, and judgement had been given against Junker Wenzel von Tronka, point by point, without the least reservation; the horses, when they had been made honourable again by the waving of a flag over their heads and removed from the care of the knacker, had been fattened by the Junker's men and then handed over to the prosecuting attorney in the market square of Dresden, in the presence of a commission especially appointed to witness this fact. Accordingly, when Kohlhaas and his escort had come up the hill at the place of execution and stood before him, the Elector said: 'Well, Kohlhaas, the day has come on which justice will be done to you! Look: I here deliver to you everything of which you were deprived by force at Tronka Castle and which I, as your sovereign, was in duty bound to recover for you: your pair of blacks, the neckcloth, the imperial florins, the bundle of washing – everything, including the money for the medical treatment of your groom Herse who died at Mühlberg. Are you satisfied with me?' Kohlhaas took the court's verdict which was passed to him at a sign from the High Chancellor, and setting down beside him the two children he had been carrying, he read it through, his eyes wide and sparkling with triumph: then when he also found a clause condemning Junker Wenzel to two years' imprisonment, he knelt down at a distance before the Elector with his hands crossed over his breast, completely overwhelmed with emotion. Rising again and putting his hand to his bosom, he joyfully assured the High Chancellor that his dearest wish on earth had been fulfilled; then he stepped up to the horses, examined them, patted their plump necks, returned to the Chancellor and cheerfully declared that he bequeathed them to his two sons Heinrich and Leopold. The Chancellor Heinrich von Geusau looked kindly down at him from his horse, promised in the name of the Elector that his last wishes would be held sacred, and invited him to decide at his discretion on the disposal of the other items of property in the bundle. At this Kohlhaas, who had noticed Herse's aged mother in the crowd, called her over and handed her the things, saying: 'There, my good woman, these belong to you!' He also gave her the sum that had been added as his own damages to the money in the bundle, as a gift that would comfort and provide for her in her old age.

The Elector then called out: 'So, Kohlhaas the horse-dealer, you have thus been given satisfaction; prepare now to make satisfaction in your turn to His Imperial Majesty, whose representative stands here, for your violation of His Majesty's public peace!' Taking off his hat and throwing it to the ground, Kohlhaas said that he was prepared; after raising his children once more in his arms and embracing them, he handed them over to the magistrate from Kohlhaasenbrück and as the latter led them away from the scene with silent tears, he walked over to the block. He was just untying his neck-cloth and opening his tunic when he cast a quick glance round the circle of onlookers and caught sight, only a short distance away, of a figure he knew well: a man standing between two noblemen whose bodies half concealed him, and wearing a hat with blue and white plumes. With a sudden movement that caught his guards unawares, Kohlhaas strode up close to him, took the locket from round his neck, took out the piece of paper, unsealed it and read it; then, fixing his gaze steadily on the man with the blue and white plumes who was already beginning to harbour sweet hopes, he stuck it in his mouth and swallowed it. At this sight the man with the blue and white plumes swooned and collapsed in convulsions. But as his companions, in consternation, stooped over him and raised him from the ground, Kohlhaas turned back to the scaffold where his head fell beneath the executioner's axe. Here the story of Kohlhaas ends. Amid general lamentation from the public his corpse was laid in a coffin, and as the bearers lifted it to take him for decent burial in the cemetery on the outskirts of the city, the Elector sent for the dead man's sons and, declaring to the High Chancellor that they were to be educated in his school for pages, dubbed them knights forthwith. Soon after this the Elector of Saxony returned to Dresden physically and mentally a broken man, and for the sequel we refer our readers to history. But in Mecklenburg some hale and hearty descendants of Kohlhaas were still living in the century before this.

The Beggarwoman of Locarno

IN the foothills of the Alps, near Locarno in northern Italy, there used to stand an old castle belonging to an Italian marquis, which can now, when one comes from the direction of the St Gotthard Pass, be seen lying in ruins; a castle with high-ceilinged spacious rooms, in one of which the mistress of the house one day, having taken pity on an old sick woman who had turned up at the door begging, had allowed her to lie down on the floor on some straw they put there for her. The marquis, by chance, on his return from hunting, entered this room to place his gun there as usual, and angrily ordered the woman to get up from the corner in which she was lying and remove herself to behind the stove. As she rose, the woman's crutch slipped on the polished floor and she fell, dangerously injuring the lower part of her back; as a result, although she did manage with indescribable difficulty to get to her feet and to cross the room from one side to the other in the direction indicated, she collapsed moaning and gasping behind the stove and expired.

Several years later, when the marquis found himself in straitened financial circumstances owing to war and a series of bad harvests, he was visited by a Florentine knight, who wished to buy the castle from him because of its fine position. The marquis, who was eager to effect this transaction, told his wife to accommodate their guest in the above-mentioned room, which was standing empty and was very beautifully and sumptuously furnished. But in the middle of the night, to the consternation of the husband and wife, the gentleman came downstairs to them pale and distraught, assuring them on his solemn word that the room was haunted: for something that had been invisible to the eye had risen to its feet in the corner with a noise as if it had been lying on straw, and had then with audible steps, slowly and feebly, crossed the room from one side to the other and collapsed, moaning and gasping, behind the stove.

The marquis, filled with an alarm for which he himself could not account, dismissed his guest's fears with feigned laughter, and declared that to calm them he would at once get up and spend the remaining hours of darkness with him in his room, but the knight begged to be permitted to remain in the marquis's bedroom in an armchair, and when morning came he called for his carriage, took his leave, and departed.

This incident caused an extraordinary stir and, to the marquis's extreme vexation, deterred a number of purchasers; consequently, when his own servants began to repeat the strange and inexplicable rumour that a ghost was walking at midnight in that particular room, he resolved to take decisive steps to refute this report, by investigating the matter himself on the following night. Accordingly, when evening fell, he had his bed set up in the room in question and, without going to sleep, awaited midnight. But to his horror he did in fact, on the stroke of the witching hour, hear the inexplicable sounds: sounds as of someone rising from a bed of rustling straw, and crossing the room from one side to the other to collapse in moaning death-agony behind the stove. When he came down next morning the marquise asked him how his investigation had gone, whereupon he looked about him apprehensively and uncertainly, bolted the door, and assured her that the reports about the haunting were true. At this she was more terrified than ever before in her life, and begged him not to let the matter become generally known until he had once again, in cold blood, and in her presence, put it to the test. But sure enough, on the following night, both they and a loyal servant, whom they had asked to accompany them, heard the very same inexplicable, ghostly sounds; and it was only because of their urgent desire to get rid of the castle at all costs that they were able in their servant's presence to conceal the dread that seized them and to attribute the occurrence to some trivial and fortuitous cause which would no doubt come to light. When on the third evening the couple, determined to get to the bottom of the matter, again went upstairs with beating hearts to the guest-room, it chanced that the house dog, which had been unchained, met them at the door; whereupon, without any explicit discussion of why they did so, but perhaps instinctively desiring the company of some third living creature, they took the dog with them into the room. At about eleven o'clock they each sat down on a bed, two candles burning on the table, the marquise fully dressed, the marquis with a rapier and pistols, which he had taken out of the cupboard, laid in readiness beside him; and while they sat there trying as best they could to entertain each other with conversation, the dog lay down in the middle of the room with its head on its paws and went to sleep. Presently, at exactly midnight, the terrible sounds were to be heard again: someone visible to no human eye, someone on crutches rising and standing up in the corner of the room, the rustling of the straw, the tap, tap, of the advancing steps – and at the very first of these the dog, waking and starting to its feet with ears erect, began growling and barking exactly as if some person were walking towards it, and retreated backwards in the direction of the stove. At this sight the marquise, her hair standing on end, rushed from the room; and while her husband, snatching up his sword, shouted 'Who's there?', and on getting no answer lunged like a madman in all directions through the empty air, she called for her carriage, resolving to drive off at once to the town; but even before she had packed a few belongings together and gone clattering through the gate, she saw the whole castle burst into flames around her. The marquis, in a frenzy of horror, had seized a candle and, the house being panelled with wood throughout, had set fire to it at all four corners, weary of his life. In vain she sent in servants to rescue the unfortunate man; he had already perished miserably, and to this day his white bones, gathered together by the country people, still lie in that corner of the room in which he had ordered the beggarwoman of Locarno to rise from her bed.

St Cecilia

or

The Power of Music

(A legend)

TOWARDS the end of the sixteenth century, when iconoclasm was raging in the Netherlands, three brothers, young students from Wittenberg, met a fourth brother, who was a preacher in Antwerp, in the city of Aachen. Their purpose there was to claim an inheritance left to them by an elderly uncle whom none of them had known, and as they had no one in the place to turn to they took lodging at an inn. After a few days during which they had listened to the preacher's tales of the remarkable events in the Netherlands, it happened that the nuns of the convent of St Cecilia, which at that time stood just outside the gates of Aachen, were due to celebrate the Feast of Corpus Christi; and in consequence the four brothers, inflamed by misguided enthusiasm, youth, and the example of the Dutch Protestants, decided to provide this city, too, with the spectacle of an iconoclastic riot. The preacher, who had already more than once been the ringleader in similar enterprises, took steps on the previous evening to collect together a number of young men devoted to the new doctrine, students and the sons of merchants, and they spent the night in the inn wining and dining and cursing popery; then, when day dawned over the city's battlements, they provided themselves with axes and all kinds of instruments of destruction in order to set about their wanton task. They gleefully agreed on a signal at which they would begin to smash the windows, which were of stained glass depicting biblical scenes; and certain that they would have a large following among the people, they set out towards the cathedral when the bells began to ring, determined to leave not one stone standing on another. The Abbess, who at daybreak had already been warned by a friend of the imminent danger, vainly sent repeated messages to the Imperial officer commanding the city, requesting a guard to protect the convent; the officer, who was himself an enemy of popery and as such, covertly at least, an adherent of the new doctrine, found a politic pretext for refusing her the desired protection, on the grounds that it was all a figment of her imagination and her convent was not threatened in the slightest. In the meantime the hour of the feast approached and the nuns, with much fear and prayer and despondent apprehension of what would happen, prepared to celebrate Mass. They had no one to protect them but a seventy-year-old convent administrator, who stationed himself with a few armed servants at the entrance to the church. In convents, as is well known, the sisters are practised players of all kinds of instruments and perform their music themselves, often with a precision, intelligence and depth of feeling which (perhaps on account of the feminine nature of that mysterious art) are not to be found in male orchestras. Now it happened, and this made the crisis all the more acute, that the nun who normally conducted the orchestra, Sister Antonia, had fallen violently ill of a nervous fever a few days before; consequently the convent was in the most painful embarrassment not only on account of the four impious brothers, who were already to be seen standing muffled up in cloaks among the columns of the church, but also because of the problem of finding a suitable piece of music to perform. The Abbess had on the previous evening ordered the performance of an extremely old Italian setting of the Mass by an unknown master which the orchestra had already played several times with most impressive effect, for this composition had a special sanctity and splendour; and now, more than ever determined to adhere to this choice, she sent once more to Sister Antonia to inquire how she was. But the nun who took her message returned with the news that Sister Antonia was lying in a state of complete unconsciousness, and that there was absolutely no question of her being able to conduct the piece of music proposed. In the meantime some ugly scenes had already taken place in the cathedral, where gradually more than a hundred miscreants had gathered, of all ages and of high and low estate, armed with axes and crowbars: the armed servants posted at the entrance had been subjected to ribald mockery, and the rioters had not scrupled to shout the most impudent and shameless insults at the sisters, one or other of whom from time to time entered the nave or transepts on some pious business; so much so that the administrator came to the sacristy and implored the Abbess on his knees to cancel the celebration and take refuge with the city commandant. But the Abbess resolutely insisted that this festival, ordained for the glory of the Most High God, must take place; she reminded the administrator of his duty to defend with life and limb the service and the solemn procession to be held in the cathedral; and as the bell was already tolling she ordered the nuns, who were standing round her trembling with fear, to select any oratorio they pleased, no matter what its quality, and begin the performance of it at once.

The nuns, proceeding to the organ gallery, were about to do so – distributing the parts of a piece of music which they had already frequently performed, and testing and tuning the violins, oboes and bass viols – when suddenly Sister Antonia, fresh and well though a trifle pale, appeared at the top of the steps carrying under her arm the score of the ancient Italian Mass on the performance of which the Abbess had so urgently insisted. When the nuns asked her in amazement where she had come from and how she had recovered so suddenly, she replied: 'Never mind that, sisters, it is of no consequence!' Whereupon she distributed the parts which she had brought with her, and herself sat down at the organ, glowing with enthusiasm, to begin conducting the wonderful piece of music. And so it came about that something like a miraculous, heavenly consolation entered the hearts of the pious women; they immediately sat down at their musicstands with their instruments; indeed, the very anxiety they were in helped to raise their souls as if on wings through all the heavens of harmony; the music was played with supreme and splendid brilliance; during the whole performance not a breath stirred from where the congregation stood and sat; especially at the *Salve regina* and even more at the *Gloria in excelsis* it was as if the entire assembly in the church had been struck dead. In short, despite the four accursed brothers and their followers, not even a particle of dust on the floor was blown out of place, and the convent continued to flourish right until the end of the Thirty Years War, when by virtue of an article in the Treaty of Westphalia it was nevertheless secularized.

Six years later, long after this incident had been forgotten, the mother of the four young men arrived from the Hague and, tearfully declaring to the civic authorities at Aachen that they had vanished without trace, put legal inquiries in hand in the hope of discovering where they had gone. She stated that the last news heard of them in the Netherlands, where in fact their home was, had been a letter written at the time in question, on the eve of the Feast of Corpus Christi, by the preacher to a friend of his, a schoolteacher in Antwerp; in four closely-written pages he gave a high-spirited and indeed boisterous advance report of a proposed enterprise against the convent of St Cecilia, about which, however, his mother declined to enter into further details. After a number of vain attempts to trace the persons for whom the unhappy woman was searching, someone finally remembered that quite a few years earlier, approximately at the time she stated, four young men of unknown nationality and origin had been admitted to the city lunatic asylum, for the foundation of which the Emperor had recently provided, and were still confined there. As, however, their illness consisted in a kind of religious obsession, and their behaviour, to the best of the court's knowledge, was said to be extremely gloomy and melancholy, the mother could not set much store by this report, since it bore little relation to the temperament of her sons which she knew only too well, and more especially because it rather seemed to indicate that the persons in question were Catholics. Nevertheless, curiously struck by a number of details in the description she was given of them, she went one day to the asylum in the company of a court official and asked the warders if they would be kind enough to give her permission to see the four unfortunate deluded men who were in their charge. But how shall we describe the horror of the poor woman when, on entering the room, she immediately, at first glance, recognized her sons! Wearing long black robes, they were sitting round a table on which a crucifix stood, and this they seemed to be worshipping, with their folded hands silently resting on the table-top. The woman, sinking down half fainting on to a chair, asked what they were doing, to which the warders replied that they were merely adoring the Saviour, 'for' (they added) 'they claim to understand better than anyone else that He is the true Son of the One God. These young men,' they said, 'have been leading this ghostly existence for six years now; they hardly sleep and hardly eat and never utter a word; only once, at midnight, they rise from their chairs, and they then chant the *Gloria in excelsis* in voices fit to shatter the windows of the house.' The warders ended by assuring her that nevertheless the young men were physically in perfectly good health; that they even undeniably possessed a certain tranquillity of mind, although of a very grave and solemn sort; that when told they were mad they would pityingly shrug their shoulders, and that they had already several times declared that if the good city of Aachen only knew what they knew, it too would lay aside all its activities and gather, as they had done, round the crucified Lord to sing the *Gloria*.

The woman could not bear the terrible sight of her unfortunate sons and almost immediately asked to be taken home, hardly able to walk; and on the following morning she went to visit Herr Veit Gotthelf, a well-known cloth-merchant in the city, hoping to get some information from him about the cause of this appalling event, for he was a man mentioned in the preacher's letter, from which it appeared that he had himself been a zealous participant in the plan to destroy St Cecilia's convent on the day of Corpus Christi. Veit Gotthelf the cloth-merchant, who in the meantime had married, had several children, and had taken over his father's prosperous business, welcomed the stranger very kindly; and on hearing the request that brought her to him he bolted the door, made her sit down on a chair, and spoke as follows: 'My good lady! I was indeed closely associated with your sons six years ago, and if you will promise not to involve me in any legal inquiry in this connection, I will frankly and unreservedly confess to you that we did, indeed, have the purpose which this letter mentions. And since the execution of the deed was planned to the very last detail with truly godless ingenuity, it remains incomprehensible to me why it came to nothing; Heaven itself seems to have granted its holy protection to the convent of those pious women. For you must know that your sons had already permitted themselves to disturb the celebration of Mass with a certain amount of boisterous levity, intended as a prelude to more decisive action; more than three hundred ruffians from this city, misguided as it was then, were standing ready with axes and torches of pitch, simply waiting for the preacher to give the prearranged signal at which they would have razed the cathedral to the ground. But instead, as soon as the music began, your sons surprised us by suddenly, with a simultaneous movement, taking off their hats; slowly, as if with inexpressibly deep

and ever greater emotion, they pressed their hands to their
bowed faces, and no sooner had a few moments of moving
silence passed than the preacher suddenly turned round and
called to us all in a loud and terrible voice to bare our heads
as he had done! Some of our companions vainly whispered
to him and frivolously nudged him, urging him to give
the agreed signal for the riot: instead of answering, the
preacher crossed his hands on his breast and sank down on
his knees, whereupon he and his brothers, with their fore-
heads fervently pressed into the dust, recited in a murmur
the entire series of the prayers he had mocked only a few
moments earlier. Thrown into utter confusion of mind by
this sight, the pack of miserable fanatics, bereft of their
ringleaders, stood irresolute and inactive until the end of the
Mass, the wonderful music of which went on pouring down
from the organ gallery; and then, since at that moment
several arrests were made on the commandant's orders and
some of the offenders who had behaved in a disorderly
fashion were seized by a guard and led away, there was
nothing left for the wretched rabble to do but to leave the
sacred building as quickly as possible, mingling for protection with the crowd as it thronged out of the doorway. In
the evening, after vainly inquiring several times for your
sons at the inn, I went out again to the convent with some
friends, full of the direst foreboding, to seek information
about them from the men at the door who had given valuable assistance to the Imperial guard. But how, worthy
madam, shall I describe to you my consternation when
I beheld those four men still lying, with folded hands, kissing the ground with their breasts and brows, prostrated
in ardent adoration before the altar, as if they had been
turned to stone! The administrator of the convent, arriving
at this moment, vainly plucked them by their cloaks and
shook them by their arms, bidding them leave the cathedral, telling them that it was already growing quite dark and
there was no one left in it: raising themselves half erect as

if in a trance, they paid no attention to him until he made his followers grasp them under the arms and lead them out of the main entrance, whereupon they finally followed us to the city, though often sighing and looking back in heart-rending fashion towards the cathedral, which was gleaming and glowing behind us in the last rays of the sun. On the way back, my friends and I repeatedly and with much tender concern asked them what in all the world had happened to them that was so terrible and had been able to cause such a revolution in their very souls; they looked kindly at us, pressed our hands, gazed pensively at the ground and, from time to time, alas! wiped tears from their eyes with an expression which it still breaks my heart to remember. Then, on reaching their lodgings, they cleverly and neatly tied birch twigs together to make themselves a cross, and this they set up on the large table in the middle of the room, pressing it into a little mound of wax, between two candles which the maid brought; and while their friends, arriving in increasing numbers as the time passed, stood aside wringing their hands or gathered in small groups, speechless with distress, to watch their silent spectral doings, they sat down round the table, apparently impervious to everything else that was going on about them, and quietly began to worship with folded hands. When a servant brought the meal which had been ordered that morning for the entertainment of their friends they would have none of it, nor did they later, as night fell, want the bed which, since they seemed so weary, she had made up in the next room; in order not to annoy the landlord, who was much put out by this behaviour, their friends had to sit down on one side at a lavishly laid dinner table and consume the food that had been prepared for a large party, seasoning it with the salt of their bitter tears. Then, suddenly, it struck midnight; your four sons, after listening intently for a moment to the bell's dull tolling, suddenly rose with a simultaneous movement from their seats; and as we stared across at them, laying down our napkins and wondering anxiously what so strange and disconcerting an action might portend, they began, in voices that filled us with horror and dread, to intone the *Gloria in excelsis*. It was a sound something like that of leopards and wolves howling at the sky in icy winter; I assure you, the pillars of the house trembled, and the windows, smitten by the visible breath of their lungs, rattled and seemed about to disintegrate, as if handfuls of heavy sand were being hurled against the panes. At this appalling spectacle we scattered in panic, our hair standing on end; leaving our cloaks and hats behind, we dispersed in all directions through the surrounding streets, which in no time were filled by more than a hundred people startled out of their sleep; the crowd forced its way through the door of the inn and upstairs to the dining-room, seeking the source of this ghastly and hideous ululation which rose, as if from the lips of sinners damned eternally in the utter-most depths of burning hell, to God's ears and implored his mercy. Finally, as the clock struck one, having heeded neither the incensed landlord nor the shocked exclamations of the numerous bystanders, they fell silent; with a cloth they wiped from their brows the sweat that trickled down in great beads to their chins and breasts; and spreading out their cloaks they lay down on the floor to rest for an hour from the torment of their task. The landlord, letting them have their way, made the sign of the cross over them as soon as he saw they were asleep; and glad of a momentary respite from the trouble, he persuaded the crowd of on-lookers, who were furtively whispering to each other, to leave the room, assuring them that in the morning things would change for the better. But alas! at very first cock-crow the unhappy brothers rose to their feet again, and turning to the cross on the table they resumed the dismal, spectral, monkish routine which only exhaustion had forced them briefly to interrupt. They heeded neither admonition nor assistance from the landlord, who was overcome by

distress at this pitiable sight; they requested that the numerous friends who normally came to visit them every morning
should be courteously denied admittance; they asked him
for nothing more than bread and water, and if possible
some straw to lie on at night, so that in the end the inn-
keeper, who was accustomed to doing a fine trade from
their high-spirited carousals, was obliged to report the whole
incident to the authorities and ask them to have these four
men removed from his house since it was evident that they
were possessed by the devil. Accordingly they were medic-
ally examined by order of the magistrates, and being found
insane they were, as you know, lodged in a room in the
madhouse which the late Emperor in his generosity had
founded within the walls of our city for the benefit of such
unfortunates.' All this Veit Gotthelf, the cloth-merchant,
told the woman, together with various other things which,
however, we prefer not to mention, for we think we have
said enough to make the essentials of the matter clear; and
he once again urged her not to implicate him in any way if
there should be a judicial investigation concerning these
events.

Three days later the woman, profoundly shaken by his
narrative and with a friend supporting her, made her way
out to the convent, since it happened to be a fine day for
a walk and she had formed the sad intention of taking a
look at the terrible place in which God had struck down
her sons, blasting them as if with invisible lightning; but as
building was in progress at the cathedral the entrance was
boarded up, and when they stood on tiptoe to peer with
difficulty through the chinks between the boards the two
women could see nothing of the interior except the splendid
rose window at the far end of the church. On an intricate
structure of slender scaffolding many hundreds of workmen,
singing merrily, were busy raising the height of the spires
by a third at least, and decorating their hitherto only slate-
covered roofs and pinnacles with strong bright copper that

glittered in the sun. And behind the building a thunderstorm lowered, a deep black cloud with gilded edges; it had spent itself already over Aachen and the surrounding district, and after hurling a few more powerless flashes of lightning in the direction of the cathedral, it dissolved and subsided in the east with surly mutterings. It so happened that as the women, lost in thought, watched this double spectacle from the steps of the great convent building, a passing nun happened to learn who the woman standing by the entrance was, whereupon the Abbess, who had heard that she carried with her a letter concerning the Corpus Christi incident, immediately sent the sister down with a message requesting the woman from the Netherlands to come up and see her. The latter, although alarmed for a moment by this summons, nevertheless respectfully set about obeying it, and while her friend, at the nun's invitation, went to wait in a side room just by the entry, the stranger was led upstairs and the double doors of a beautiful upper chamber were opened to admit her to the presence of the Abbess herself. The latter was a noble lady of serene and regal appearance, seated on an armchair with a footstool resting on dragon's claws; on a desk at her side lay the score of a piece of music. The Abbess, after having a chair brought for her visitor, told her that she had already been informed by the burgomaster of her arrival in the city; she inquired in a kindly manner how her unhappy sons were, and pointed out that since this was something for which there was no remedy she should accept it with as much composure as possible. Having said this, she expressed her wish to see the letter which the preacher had written to his friend, the schoolmaster in Antwerp. The woman was for a moment greatly embarrassed by this request, for she had enough knowledge of the world to realize what might be the consequences of her acceding to it; but the Abbess's venerable countenance inspired absolute trust, and it seemed quite unthinkable that she should intend to make any public use of the letter's contents. After a few moments of hesitation she therefore took it from her bosom and handed it over to the princely lady, pressing a fervent kiss on her hand as she did so. While the Abbess was reading through the letter, her visitor now cast a glance at the score which lay, casually opened, on the music-desk; and as it had occurred to her, on hearing the cloth-merchant's report, that it might well have been the power of the music that had so shattered and confounded the minds of her poor sons on that dreadful day, she turned to the nun who was standing behind her chair and shyly asked her whether this had been the piece of music performed in the cathedral on that strange Corpus Christi morning six years ago. The young sister said that she remembered, indeed, having heard this was so, and that ever since then it had been the custom for the work, when not actually being used, to be kept in the Reverend Mother's room; whereupon the woman, in deep emotion and with many thoughts rushing through her mind, rose and stood in front of the music-desk. She gazed at the unknown magical signs, with which some terrible spirit seemed to be marking out its mysterious sphere; and the earth seemed to give way beneath her when she noticed that the score happened to be standing open at the *Gloria in excelsis*. She felt as if the whole dreadful power of the art of sound, which had destroyed her sons, were raging over her head; she thought the mere sight of the notes would make her fall senseless, and after quickly pressing the sheet to her lips in an impulse of infinite humility and submission to Divine Omnipotence, she sat down again on her chair. Meanwhile the Abbess had finished reading the letter, and said as she folded it up, 'God Himself, on that wonderful day, protected the convent against the presumption of your grievously erring sons. The means He used in doing so will no doubt, since you are a Protestant, be a matter of indifference to you; moreover, you would scarcely understand what I might say to you on this subject. For let me tell you that absolutely nobody knows who it really was who, in the stress of that terrible hour, when the forces of iconoclasm were about to burst in upon us, sat calmly at the organ and conducted the work which there lies open before you. It has been proved by evidence given on the following morning in the presence of the administrator and of several other men, and recorded in the archives, that Sister Antonia, the only one of us who was able to conduct that work, was for the whole of the time during which it was being performed lying in a corner of her cell, sick, unconscious, and totally paralysed; one of the sisters, who because she was her kinswoman had been directed to look after her during her illness, did not leave her bedside during the whole of that morning on which the Feast of Corpus Christi was celebrated in the cathedral. Indeed, Sister Antonia herself would undoubtedly have testified and confirmed the fact that it had not been her who had appeared so strangely and surprisingly in the organ gallery, if her utterly senseless condition had permitted us to question her about it and if she had not, on the evening of that very same day, died of the nervous fever from which she was suffering and from which we had previously thought her life to be in no danger. Moreover, the Archbishop of Trier, to whom this incident was reported, has already made the only comment that can explain it : namely that Saint Cecilia herself performed this miracle which was both so terrible and so glorious; and I have only just received a Papal brief confirming this.' So saying she handed the letter, which she had asked to see only to learn further details of what she already knew, back to the woman, promising her as she did so that she would make no use of it; she inquired further whether there was any hope of her sons recovering their wits and whether she could perhaps in this respect, by money or any means, be of assistance to her. But the woman, weeping and kissing the hem of the Abbess's robe, answered no to both questions, whereupon the Abbess dismissed her with a kindly gesture.

And here this legend ends. The woman, realizing that

her presence in Aachen served no purpose, left behind her a small capital sum to be held in trust by the courts for the benefit of her poor sons, and returned to the Hague, so deeply moved by the whole incident that a year later she was received back into the bosom of the Catholic Church; her sons, for their part, lived to an advanced age and died happily and peacefully, after once more, as was their custom, performing the *Gloria in excelsis*.

The Betrothal in Santo Domingo

ON Monsieur Guillaume de Villeneuve's plantation at Port-au-Prince in the French sector of the island of Santo Domingo there lived at the beginning of this century, at the time when the blacks were murdering the whites, a terrible old negro called Congo Hoango. This man, who came originally from the Gold Coast of Africa, had seemed in his youth to be of a loyal and honest disposition, and having once saved his master's life when they were sailing across to Cuba, he had been rewarded by the latter with innumerable favours and kindnesses. Not only did Monsieur de Villeneuve at once grant him his freedom, and on returning to Santo Domingo make him the gift of a house and home; a few years later, although this was contrary to local custom, he even appointed him as manager of his considerable estate, and since he did not want to re-marry provided him, in lieu of a wife, with an old mulatto woman called Babekan, who lived on the plantation and to whom through his first wife Congo Hoango was distantly related. Moreover, when the negro had reached the age of sixty he retired him on handsome pay and as a crowning act of generosity even made him a legatee under his will; and yet all these proofs of gratitude failed to protect Monsieur de Villeneuve from the fury of this ferocious man. In the general frenzy of vindictive rage that flared up in all those plantations as a result of the reckless actions of the National Convention, Congo Hoango had been one of the first to seize his gun and, remembering only the tyranny that had snatched him from his native land, blew his master's brains out. He set fire to the house in which Madame de Villeneuve had taken refuge with her three children and all the other white people in the settlement, laid waste the whole plantation to which the heirs, who lived in Port-au-Prince, could have made claim, and when every single building on the estate had been razed to the ground he assembled an armed band of negroes and began scouring the whole neighbourhood, to help his blood-brothers in their struggle against the whites. Sometimes he would ambush travellers who were making their way in armed groups across country; sometimes he would attack in broad daylight the settlements in which the planters had barricaded themselves, and would put every human being he found inside to the sword. Such indeed was his inhuman thirst for revenge that he even insisted on the elderly Babekan and her young daughter, a fifteen-year-old mestiza called Toni, taking part in this ferocious war by which he himself was feeling altogether rejuvenated: the main building of the plantation, in which he was now living, stood in an isolated spot by the road, and since it often happened during his absences that white or creole refugees came there seeking food or shelter, he instructed the two women to offer assistance and favours to these white dogs, as he called them, and thus delay them in the house until his return. Babekan, who suffered from consumption as a result of a cruel flogging that had been inflicted on her when she was a girl, used on these occasions to dress up her young daughter in her best clothes, for Toni's yellowish complexion made her very useful for the purpose of this hideous deception; she urged her to refuse the strangers no caresses short of the final intimacy, which was forbidden her on pain of death; and when Congo Hoango returned with his negro troop from his expeditions in the surrounding district, immediate death would be the fate of the wretches who had allowed themselves to be beguiled by these stratagems.

Now in the year 1803, as the world knows, when General Dessalines was advancing against Port-au-Prince at the head of thirty thousand negroes, everyone whose skin was white retreated to this stronghold to defend it. For it was the last outpost of French power on this island, and if it fell no white person on Santo Domingo had any chance of escape. And thus it happened that just when old Hoango was not there, having set out with his black followers to take a consignment of powder and lead right through the French lines to General Dessalines, on a dark and stormy and rainy night someone knocked at the back door of his house. Old Babekan, who was already in bed, got up, merely throwing a skirt round her waist, opened the window and asked who was there. 'By the Blessed Virgin and all the saints,' said the stranger in a low voice, placing himself under the window, 'before I tell you, answer me one question!' And reaching out through the darkness of the night to grasp the old woman's hand, he asked: 'Are you a negress?' Babekan said: 'Well, you must surely be a white man, since you would rather look this pitch-black night in the face than a negress! Come in,' she added, 'there's nothing to fear; I am a mulatto woman, and the only person except myself who lives in this house is my daughter, a mestiza!' and so saying she closed the window, as if intending to come down and open the door to him; but instead, on the pretext that she could not at once lay hands on the key, she snatched some clothes out of the cupboard, crept upstairs to her daughter's bedroom and woke her. 'Toni!' she said, 'Toni!' 'What is it, mother?' 'Quick!' said Babekan. 'Get up at once and dress! Here are clothes, clean white linen and stockings! A white man on the run is at the door and wants to be let in!' 'A white man?' asked Toni, half sitting up in bed. She took the clothes which the old woman handed to her and said: 'But mother, is he alone? and will it be safe for us to let him in?' 'Of course, of course!' replied the old woman, striking a light, 'he is unarmed and alone and trembling in every limb for fear of being attacked by us!' And so saying, as Toni got up and put on her skirt and stockings, she lit the big lantern which stood in the corner of the room, quickly tied the girl's hair up on top of her head in the fashion of the country, laced up her bodice and put on her hat, gave her the lantern and ordered her to go down to the courtyard and fetch the stranger in.

Meanwhile the barking of some dogs in the yard had wakened a small boy called Nanky, an illegitimate son of Hoango's by a negress, who slept in the outhouses with his brother Seppy; and seeing in the moonlight a man standing by himself on the steps at the back door, he at once, as he was instructed to do in such cases, rushed to the main gate through which the man had entered, and locked it. The stranger was puzzled by this and asked the boy, whom to his horror he recognized at close quarters as a negro: 'Who lives in this settlement?' And on hearing his answer that since Monsieur de Villeneuve's death the property had been taken over by the negro Hoango, he was just about to hurl the boy to the ground, snatch the key to the main gate from his hand and escape into the open, when Toni, holding the lantern, came out of the house. 'Quick!' she said, seizing his hand and drawing him towards the door, 'come in here!' As she spoke she was careful to hold the lantern in such a way that its beam would fall full on her face. 'Who are you?' exclaimed the stranger, struggling to free himself and gazing, surprised for more reasons than one, at her lovely young figure. 'Who lives in this house in which you tell me I shall find refuge?' 'No one, I swear by the heavens above us, but my mother and myself!' said the girl. And she renewed with great eagerness her efforts to draw him in after her. 'What, no one!' cried the stranger, snatching his hand from hers and taking a step backwards. 'Did this boy not tell me just now that a negro called Hoango is living here?' 'No, I tell you!' said the girl, stamping her foot with an air of vexation, 'and although the house belongs to a monster of that name, he is absent just now and ten miles away!' And so saying she dragged him into the house with both hands, ordered the boy to tell no one who had arrived, seized the stranger by the hand as they passed through the door, and led him upstairs to her mother's room.

'Well,' said the old woman, who had been listening to the whole conversation from the window and had noticed by the lamplight that their visitor was an officer, 'what's the meaning of that sword you're wearing under your arm all ready to draw?' And she added, putting on her spectacles: 'We have risked our own lives by granting you refuge in our house; have you come in here to reward this kindness with treachery, as is customary among your fellow countrymen?' 'God forbid!' replied the stranger, who was now standing right in front of her chair. He seized the old woman's hand, pressed it to his heart, cast a few diffident glances round the room and then unbuckled his sword, saying: 'You see before you the most wretched of men, but not an ungrateful villain!' 'Who are you?' asked the old woman, pushing up a chair for him with her foot and telling the girl to go into the kitchen and prepare as good a supper for him as she could manage in a hurry. The stranger replied: 'I am an officer in the French army, but as you may already have guessed, not myself a Frenchman; my native country is Switzerland and my name is Gustav von der Ried. How I wish I had never left home for this accursed island! I have come from Fort Dauphin, where as you know all the whites have been murdered, and my purpose is to reach Port-au-Prince before General Dessalines succeeds in surrounding and besieging it with the troops under his command.' 'From Fort Dauphin!' exclaimed the old woman. 'So you actually succeeded, with your white face, in travelling all that way right through a nigger country in revolt?' 'God and all the saints protected me!' replied the stranger. 'Nor am I alone, my good old woman; I have left some companions behind me, including a venerable old man who is my uncle, with his wife and five children, not to mention several servants and maids who belong to the family; a company of twelve souls, with only two wretched mules to help us, and I have to escort them in indescribably laborious night marches, for we dare not let ourselves be seen by daylight on the highway.' 'Why, heaven save us!' exclaimed the old woman, shaking her head compassionately and taking a pinch of snuff. 'And where are your travelling companions at this moment?' The stranger hesitated for a moment and then replied: 'You are someone I can trust; in your face, like a gleam of light, there is a tinge of my own complexion. I will tell you that my family is hidden a mile from here, by the seagull pond, in the thick woods that cover the hills round it; hunger and thirst forced us the day before yesterday to take refuge there. We sent our servants out last night to try to buy a little bread from the country people, but in vain; for fear of being caught and killed they made no effective attempt to do so, and consequently I myself, at mortal risk, had to leave our hiding-place tonight to try my luck. If I am not much deceived,' he continued, pressing the old woman's hand, 'heaven has led me to compassionate people who do not share the cruel and outrageous resentment that has seized all the inhabitants of this island. Please be kind enough – I will pay you very well for it – to let me have a few baskets full of food and refreshments; we are only five more days' journey from Port-au-Prince, and if you would provide us with the means to reach that town, we shall forever afterwards think of you both as the saviours of our lives.' 'Indeed, indeed, this frenzy of resentment,' said the old woman hypocritically. 'Is it not as if the hands of one and the same body or the teeth of one and the same mouth raged against each other simply because they were differently made? Am I, whose father came from Santiago in Cuba, responsible for the faint gleam that appears on my face during the day? And is my daughter, who was conceived and born in Europe, responsible for the fact that the full bright light of that part of the world is reflected in her complexion?' 'What!' exclaimed the stranger, 'do you mean to say that you yourself, who as the whole cast of your features shows are a mulatto and therefore of African origin, that both you and this charming mestiza who opened the door of the house to me, are condemned to the same fate as us Europeans?' 'By heaven!' replied the old woman, taking her glasses from her nose, 'do you suppose that this little property, which through years of toil and suffering we acquired by the work of our hands, does not provoke the rapacity of that horde of ferocious plundering devils? If we did not manage to protect ourselves from their persecution by means of the only defence available to the weak, namely cunning and every imaginable dissimulation, then let me assure you that that shadow of kinship with them which lies on our faces would not save us!' 'It's not possible!' cried the stranger. 'Who on this island is persecuting you?' 'The owner of this house,' answered the old woman, 'the negro Congo Hoango! Since the death of Monsieur de Ville-neuve, the previous owner of this plantation, whom he savagely murdered at the outbreak of the revolt, we who, as his relatives, keep house for him are subject in every way to his whims and brutalities. Every time we offer, as an act of humanity, a piece of bread or a drink to one or other of the white refugees who sometimes pass this way, he repays us for it with insults and ill-treatment; and it is his dearest wish to inflame the vengeance of the blacks against us white and creole half-dogs, as he calls us, partly in order to get rid of us altogether because we reproach him for his savagery against the whites, and partly in order to gain possession of the little property that we would leave behind us.' 'Poor creatures!' said the stranger, 'poor pitiable wretches! And where is this monster now?' 'With General Dessalines' army,' answered the old woman. 'He set out with the other blacks from this plantation to take him a consignment of powder and lead which the General needed. We are expecting him back in ten or twelve days, unless he has to go off on other business; and if on his return he should discover, which God forbid, that we have given pro-tection and shelter to a white man on his way to Port-au-Prince while he has been devoting all his efforts to the extermination of the entire white race on the island – then believe me, the lives of all of us would be forfeit.' 'God, who loves humanity and compassion,' replied the stranger, 'will protect you in your kindness to a victim of misfortune! And since in that case,' he added, moving closer to the old woman, 'you have incurred the negro's resentment anyway, so much so that even if you were to go back to obeying him it would no longer do you any good, could you perhaps see your way, for any reward you like to name, to giving shelter for a day or two to my uncle and his family, who are utterly exhausted by our journey, and could here recover their strength a little?' 'Young man!' said the old woman, in amazement, 'what are you asking of me? How could we possibly lodge a party of travellers as big as yours in a house standing right by the roadway without the fact becoming known to the whole neighbourhood?' 'Why not,' urged the stranger, 'if I myself were to go out at once to the pond and lead my party back to this settlement before daybreak? If we were to lodge them all, masters and servants alike, in one and the same room in this house, and perhaps even take the precaution, in case of the worst, of carefully shutting up the doors and windows there?' The old woman, after considering the suggestion for a little, replied that if he were to attempt to fetch his companions from the mountain ravine and bring them to the settlement that night, he would undoubtedly encounter a troop of armed negroes who were expected to be advancing along the military highway, as some forward patrols had already reported. 'Very well,' replied the stranger, 'then for the present let us content ourselves with sending the poor wretches a basket of food, and postpone till tomorrow night the operation of conducting them to the settlement. Are you willing to do that, my good woman?' 'Well,' said the old woman, as the stranger showered kisses on her bony hand, 'for the sake of the European who was my daughter's father I will do this kindness for you, as his fellow countrymen

in distress. At daybreak tomorrow sit down and write a
letter to your friends inviting them to come here to me in
this settlement; the boy you saw in the yard can take them
the letter together with some provisions, stay overnight
with them in the mountains to make sure they are safe,
and at dawn the following day, if they accept the invitation,
act as guide to bring the party here.'

In the meantime Toni had returned with the meal she had
prepared in the kitchen, and as she laid the table she asked
the old woman, throwing a roguish glance at the stranger:
'Well, tell me, mother! Has the gentleman recovered from
the fright he was in at our door? Is he now convinced that
there is no one lying in wait for him with poison and
dagger, and the negro Hoango is not at home?' Her mother
said with a sigh: 'My child, as the proverb says, once burnt
twice shy of the fire. The gentleman would have acted fool-
ishly if he had ventured into this house without making sure
to what race the people living here belonged.' The girl, standing in front of her mother, told her how she had held the
lantern in such a way that its full beam had fallen on her
face. 'But,' she said, 'his imagination was obsessed with
blackamoors and negroes, and if a lady from Paris or Marseilles had opened the door to him, he would have taken
her for a negress.' The stranger, putting his arm round her
gently, said in some embarrassment that the hat she had
been wearing had prevented him from seeing her face. 'If
I had been able,' he continued, pressing her ardently to
his breast, 'to look into your eyes as I am doing now, then
even if everything else about you had been black, I should
have been willing to drink with you from a poisoned cup.'
He had flushed red as he said these words, and the girl's
mother now urged him to sit down, whereupon Toni seated
herself beside him at the table and, propping her head in
her hands, gazed at the stranger as he ate. The latter asked
her how old she was and what was her native town; her
mother spoke for her and told him that when she had been

accompanying her former employer, Madame de Villeneuve she had conceived Toni in Paris and that that was where, fifteen years ago, she had been born. She added that the negro Komar, whom she had afterwards married, had in fact adopted the child, but that her real father had been a rich merchant from Marseilles called Bertrand, and that consequently her name was Toni Bertrand. Toni asked him whether he knew a gentleman of that name in France; the stranger answered he did not, that it was a big country, and that during the short time he had spent there before embarking for the West Indies he had met no one called Bertrand. The old woman added that in any case, according to fairly reliable reports she had received, Toni's father was no longer living in France. She said that his ambitious and enterprising temperament found no satisfaction within the restrictions of bourgeois life; at the outbreak of the Revolution he had involved himself in public affairs and in 1795 had joined a French diplomatic mission to the Ottoman court; from there, so far as she knew, he had never returned. The stranger, smiling at Toni, took her hand and said: 'Why, in that case you are a nobly born and rich girl!' He urged her to make use of these advantages, saying that she might well expect, with her father's assistance, to rise again to a social position more distinguished than her present one. 'That can hardly be so,' replied the old woman, restraining her evident resentment at this remark. 'During my pregnancy in Paris, Monsieur Bertrand, feeling ashamed of me because he wanted to marry a rich young lady, went before a court and formally repudiated the paternity. I shall never forget the brazen perjury he committed to my face; the consequence was that I fell into a bilious fever, and soon after that Monsieur de Villeneuve ordered me to be given sixty lashes too, as a result of which I have suffered from consumption to this day.' Toni, resting her head pensively on her hand, asked the stranger who he was, where he had come from and where he was going; to which he replied, after a short pause of embarrassment at the old woman's embittered speech, that he was accompanying his uncle Herr Strömli's family from Fort Dauphin and had left them behind him at the seagull pond on the wooded mountainside under the protection of two young cousins. At the girl's request he gave some details of the outbreak of the rebellion in Fort Dauphin. He told how at midnight, when everyone was asleep, a treacherous signal had been given for the blacks to start massacring the whites; how the leader of the negroes, a sergeant in the French pioneer corps, had had the malevolence to set fire at once to every ship in the harbour in order to cut off the whites' retreat to Europe; how their family had only just had time to escape from the town with a few possessions and how, the revolt having flared up everywhere simultaneously all along the coast, they had no choice but to set out, with two mules they had managed to find, heading straight across the island for Porte-au-Prince, which being defended by a strong French army was now the only place still holding out against the increasing power of the negroes. Toni asked how it was that the whites had come to incur such hatred in this place. The stranger, a little disconcerted, replied that the cause lay in the general relationship which as masters of the island they had had with the blacks. 'And to tell you the truth,' he added, 'I will not attempt to defend that situation, but it is one which has lasted for many centuries. The mad lust for freedom which has seized all these plantations has driven the negroes and creoles to break the chains that oppressed them, and to take their revenge on the whites for much reprehensible ill-treatment they have had to suffer at the hands of some of us who do our race no credit.' After a short pause he continued: 'I was particularly struck and horrified by the action of one young girl, a negress, who was lying sick with yellow fever just at the time when the revolt broke out, for the plight of Fort Dauphin had been greatly worsened by an epidemic of this disease. Three years earlier she had been the slave of a white planter, who because she would not let him have his way with her had vented his spite on her by harsh treatment and later sold her to a creole planter. On the day of the general uprising the girl heard that her former master, pursued by the furious negroes, had taken refuge in a woodshed nearby; remembering his ill-treatment of her, she therefore sent her brother to him as evening fell, inviting him to stay the night with her. The wretched man, who knew neither that the girl was sick nor what disease she was suffering from, came to her room full of gratitude, thinking himself saved, and took her in his arms; but he had scarcely been half an hour in her bed caressing her and fondling her when she suddenly sat up with an expression of cold, savage fury and said: "I whom you have been kissing am infected with pestilence and dying of it: go now and give the yellow fever to all your kind!" ' And as the old woman loudly proclaimed her abhorrence of such a deed, the officer asked Toni: 'Could you ever do a thing like that?' 'No!' said Toni, casting her eyes down in confusion. The stranger, laying his napkin on the table, declared that it was his deep inner conviction that no tyranny the whites had ever practised could justify a treachery of such abominable vileness. 'Heaven's vengeance is disarmed by it,' he exclaimed, rising passionately from his seat, 'and the angels themselves, filled with revulsion by this overturning of all human and divine order, will take sides with those who are in the wrong and will support their cause!' So saying, he walked across for a moment to the window and stared out at the night sky, where stormy clouds were drifting past the moon and the stars; then, as he had the impression that the mother and daughter were looking at each other, although he could see no sign of any communication between them, an unpleasant feeling of annoyance came over him; and turning to them he asked to be shown the room where he could sleep.

Toni's mother, looking at the clock on the wall, observed that in any case it was nearly midnight; and taking a candle she asked the stranger to follow her. She led him to the room assigned to him, at the end of a long corridor; Toni brought his coat and various other things he had discarded; her mother showed him the very comfortably made-up bed where he would sleep, and after telling Toni to get a footbath ready for the gentleman, she wished him good night and took her leave. The stranger put his sword in a corner of the room and laid on the table a pair of pistols he carried at his waist. As Toni pushed the bed forward and spread a white sheet over it he looked round the room. He very soon concluded from the luxury and taste with which it was furnished that this must have been the bedroom of the plantation's former owner; a feeling of apprehension seized his heart like the beak and talons of a bird of prey, and he began to wish himself back with his friends in the woods, hungry and thirsty as when he had come here. Meanwhile, from the kitchen nearby, the girl had fetched a basinful of hot water, spiced with aromatic herbs, and invited the officer, who was leaning against the window, to refresh himself with it. The officer, silently removing his neckcloth and his waistcoat, sat down on a chair; he began baring his feet, and as the girl, crouching before him on her knees, continued the little preparations that were needed for his bath, he gazed at her attractive figure. Her hair, in its abundance of dark curls, had rolled over her young breasts when she knelt down; there was something extraordinarily graceful about her limbs and about the long lashes that drooped over her lowered eyes; but for her complexion, which repelled him, he could have sworn that he had never seen anything more beautiful. He was also struck by a remote resemblance, he did not himself yet rightly know to whom, which he had noticed as soon as he entered the house and which drew his whole heart towards her. When she rose after completing her tasks he caught hold of her hand, and knowing that there was only one way of finding out whether the girl had sincere feelings or not he drew her down on to his knees and asked her whether she was already engaged to be married. 'No!' she murmured, lowering her great black eyes with a sweet air of modesty; and without stirring on his lap she added that a young negro called Konelly who lived in that neighbourhood had proposed to her three months earlier, but that she had refused him because she was too young. The stranger, embracing her narrow waist with his two hands, replied that in his country there was a proverb that a girl of fourteen years and seven weeks was old enough to marry. As she gazed at the small golden cross he wore around his neck, he asked her how old she was. 'Fifteen,' replied Toni. 'Well then!' said the stranger. 'Has he not got enough money to set up house with you in the way you would like?' Toni, without raising her eyes to him, answered: 'Oh no! On the contrary,' she added, letting go of the cross which she was holding in her hand, 'Konelly has become a rich man as a result of the things that have happened recently; his father has gained possession of the whole settlement that used to belong to his master the planter.' 'Then why did you refuse his offer?' asked the stranger. He tenderly stroked the hair back from her forehead and said: 'Perhaps he didn't attract you?' The girl shook her head briefly and laughed; and when the stranger, whispering playfully into her ear, asked whether it was necessary to be a white man in order to gain her favour, she suddenly, after a fleeting pensive pause, and with a most charming blush spreading suddenly over her sunburnt face, sank against his breast. The stranger, moved by her sweetness and grace, called her his darling girl and clasped her in his arms, feeling that the hand of God had swept away all his anxieties. He could not possibly believe that all these signs of emotion she showed him were merely the wretched antics of cold-hearted, hideous treachery. The thoughts that had preyed on his mind were dispersed like a host of ominous birds; he reproached himself for having failed even for a moment to appreciate her true feelings, and as he rocked her on his knees and drank in the sweet breath that rose from her lips towards him, he pressed a kiss on her forehead, as if in token of reconciliation and forgiveness. Meanwhile the girl had sat upright with a strange startled suddenness, as if listening for steps in the passage approaching the door; in a kind of pensive reverie she readjusted the clothing over her breast which had become disarranged; and only when she realized that her alarm had been mistaken did she turn again to the stranger with a mischievous smile, reminding him that if he did not use the hot water soon it would get cold. 'Well?' she asked in some surprise, as the stranger said nothing but went on gazing at her thoughtfully, 'why are you examining me so closely?' She tried to conceal the embarrassment that had overcome her by busying herself with lacing up her bodice, then exclaimed laughingly: 'You strange gentleman, whatever do you find so remarkable in my appearance?' The stranger had passed his hand across his brow; he suppressed a sigh, lifted her from his lap and replied: 'An extraordinary resemblance between you and a friend of mine!' Toni, obviously noticing that his happy mood had left him, took him kindly and sympathetically by the hand and asked: 'Who is she?' Whereupon, after reflecting for a moment or two, he made the following answer: 'Her name was Marianne Congreve and she came from Strasbourg. Her father was a merchant in that city, I had met her there shortly before the outbreak of the Revolution and had been lucky enough to obtain her consent to marry me, as well as her mother's approval. Oh, she was the most loving, the most faithful creature on earth; and when I look at you, the terrible and moving circumstances in which I lost her come back so vividly to my mind and fill me with such sorrow that I cannot restrain my tears.' 'What?' asked Toni, pressing herself tenderly and lovingly against him, 'she is no longer alive?' 'She died,' answered the stranger, 'and it was her death alone that taught me the very essence of all goodness and nobility. God knows,' he continued, bowing his head in grief upon her shoulder, 'how I allowed myself to be so utterly reckless as to make certain remarks one evening in a public place about the terrible Revolutionary Tribunal which had just been set up. I was denounced, my arrest was sought; and since I had been fortunate enough to escape to the outskirts of the city, the bloodthirsty band of my pursuers, failing to find me but insisting on some victim or other, even rushed to my fiancée's house; and so infuriated were they by her truthful declaration that she did not know where I was, that with outrageous cynicism, on the pretext that she was my accomplice, they dragged her instead of me to the scaffold. No sooner had this appalling news been conveyed to me than I emerged from the hiding-place into which I had fled, and hastened, pushing my way through the crowd, to the place of execution, where I shouted at the top of my voice: "Here I am, you inhuman monsters!" But she, already standing on the platform beside the guillotine, on being questioned by some of the judges who as ill-fortune would have it did not know me by sight, gave me one look which is indelibly imprinted on my soul, and then turned away, saying: "I have no idea who that man is!" And a few moments later, amid a roll of drums and a roar of voices, at the behest of those impatient butchers, the iron blade dropped and severed her head from her body. How I was saved I have no idea; a quarter of an hour later I was in a friend's house, swooning and recovering consciousness by turns, and towards evening, half bereft of my senses, I was lifted into a carriage and conveyed across the Rhine.' With these words the stranger, letting go of the girl, returned to the window, where she saw him, in deep emotion, bury his face in a handkerchief; at this, for more than one reason, she was overcome by a sense of human compassion, and impulsively followed him, throwing her arms round his neck and mingling her tears with his.

There is no need to report what happened next, for it will be clear to anyone who has followed the narrative thus far. When the stranger regained possession of himself and realized what he had done, he had no idea what its consequences might be; but for the time being at least he understood that he was saved, and that in this house he had entered there was nothing for him to fear from the girl. Seeing her sitting on the bed, with her arms folded across her and weeping, he did everything he could to console her. He took from his breast the little golden cross which was a present from his dead fiancée, the faithful Marianne, and leaning over Toni and caressing her with the utmost tenderness he hung it round her neck, saying that it was his bridal gift to her. As she went on weeping and did not listen to him, he sat down on the edge of the bed, and told her, stroking and kissing her hand, that he would tomorrow morning seek her mother's permission to marry her. He described to her the little estate he possessed on the banks of the Aar; a house sufficiently comfortable and spacious to accommodate her and her mother as well, if the latter's age would permit her to make the journey; he described his fields, gardens, meadows and vineyards, and his venerable aged father who would welcome her there with gratitude and love for having saved his son's life. As her tears continued and poured down over the pillow he embraced her passionately, almost weeping himself, and begged her to tell him how he had wronged her and whether she could not forgive him. He swore that the love he felt for her would never fade from his heart and that it had only been the turmoil and confusion of his senses, the strange mixture of desire and fear she had aroused in him, that had led him to do such a deed. In the end he reminded her that the morning stars were glistening in the sky and that if she stayed in this bed any longer her mother would come and surprise her there; he urged her, for the sake of her health, to get up and rest for a few hours in her own bed; filled with the direst alarm by her condition, he asked her if she would perhaps like him to lift her in his arms and carry her to her room. But since she made no answer to anything he said and simply lay there motionless among the scattered pillows, cradling her head in her arms and sobbing quietly, and since daylight was already gleaming through both the windows, he had no choice but to pick her up without further ado; he carried her, hanging over his shoulder like a lifeless thing, up the stairs to her bedroom, and after laying her on her bed and with many tender caresses repeating to her again everything he had said already, he once more called her his beloved bride and kissed her on both cheeks, then hurried back to his room.

As soon as day had fully dawned, old Babekan went upstairs to her daughter, sat down by her bed and told her the plan she had decided upon for dealing with the stranger and his travelling companions. Since the negro Congo Hoango would not be back for two days it was all-important, she thought, to delay the stranger in the house for that period without admitting his family of kinsmen, whose presence might be dangerous on account of their numbers. The scheme she had thought of for this purpose, she said, was to pretend to the stranger that according to a report just received General Dessalines and his army were about to march through this district, and that it would therefore be much too dangerous to accommodate the family in the house, as was their wish, until he had passed by in three days' time. Finally, she said, the party must be provided with food so that they would not move on, and otherwise delayed in the delusion that they would find refuge in the house, so that they might all be overpowered later on. She added that this was an important matter, since the family were probably carrying property of considerable value with them; and she told her daughter that she relied on her full cooperation in the project she had just outlined to her. Toni, sitting up in her bed and flushing with anger, replied that it was shameful and contemptible to violate the laws of hospitality in this way against people whom one had lured into one's house. She said that a man who was being pursued and had entrusted himself to their protection ought to be doubly safe with them, and declared that if her mother did not abandon the bloodthirsty scheme she had proposed, she would at once go and tell the stranger that the house in which he had thought he had reached safety was a den of murderers. 'Toni!' exclaimed her mother, pressing her hands against her sides and staring wide-eyed at the girl. 'Yes, indeed!' replied Toni, lowering her voice. 'What harm has this young man done to us? He is not even a Frenchman by birth, but a Swiss, as we have learned; so why should we fall on him like bandits and kill him and rob him? Do such grievances as we may have against the planters here exist in the part of the island from which he comes? Is it not, rather, quite obvious that he is an entirely noble-minded and honourable man who has in no way participated in the injustices committed by his race against the blacks?' The old woman, observing the remarkable vehemence with which the girl spoke, merely stammered her astonishment. She asked her what wrong the young Portuguese had done whom they had recently clubbed to death at the gateway; she asked what crime the two Dutchmen had committed whom the negroes had shot in the yard three weeks ago; she demanded to know what accusation could be brought against the three Frenchmen and against so many other individual fugitives of the white race who since the revolt had been executed in this house with muskets, pikes and daggers. 'By the heavens above us,' replied her daughter, rising wildly to her feet, 'you are very wrong to remind me of these atrocities! The inhuman deeds in which you all forced me to take part have for a long time sickened me to the very soul; and in order to satisfy the vengeance of God upon me for all that has happened, I swear to you that I would rather die ten times over than allow a hair of that young man's head to be touched as long as he is in our house.' 'Very well,' said the old woman, suddenly adopting a conciliatory tone. 'Then the stranger can go on his way! But,' she added, rising to leave the room, 'when Congo Hoango returns and finds out that a white man has spent the night in our house, then you may give an account to him of the compassionate feelings that moved you, in defiance of his express orders, to let such a visitor go again once he had been let in.'

On hearing this remark, which despite its apparent mildness barely concealed the old woman's malice, Toni sat on in her room in a state of some consternation. She knew her mother's hatred for the whites too well to be able to believe that Babekan would let an opportunity for gratifying it pass by unused. Alarmed by the thought that she might immediately send out to the neighbouring plantations for negroes to come and overpower the stranger, she got dressed and followed her mother without delay to the living-room downstairs. Babekan appeared to be doing something at the cupboard where the food was kept, but as Toni entered it she left it with an air of confusion and sat down at the spinning-wheel; the girl stood gazing at the proclamation fixed to the door, which on pain of death forbade all blacks to give accommodation and shelter to whites; then, as if frightened into an understanding of the wrong she had committed, she suddenly turned and fell at the feet of her mother, who as she well knew had been watching her from behind. Embracing the old woman's knees, she begged her to forgive the wild things she had said in defence of the stranger, excused herself as having been only half awake when the proposals for outwitting him had been unexpectedly put to her while she was still in bed, and declared herself willing to surrender him utterly to the vengeance of the existing laws of the land, since these had decreed his destruction. The old woman, after a pause during which she looked the girl straight in the face, said: 'By heaven, this speech of yours has saved his life, for today at least! For since you were threatening to protect him, I had already poisoned his food, and that would have delivered him, dead at any rate, into the hands of Congo Hoango, in accordance with his orders.' So saying she rose, took a pan of milk that was standing on the table, and poured its contents out of the window. Toni, scarcely believing her senses, stared at her mother in horror. The old woman sat down again by the girl, who was still on her knees on the floor, raised her to her feet, and asked her what could have happened in the course of a single night to change her attitude so suddenly. Had she spent any length of time with the stranger yesterday evening after preparing his bath? And had she had much conversation with him? But Toni, whose heart was beating fast, made no answer, or no definite answer, to these questions; she stood with downcast eyes, pressing her hands to her head, and said that she had had a dream; but one look at her unhappy mother's breast, she added, stooping down quickly to kiss the old woman's hand, had recalled to her mind all the inhumanity of the race to which this stranger belonged. Turning and pressing her face into her apron she assured Babekan that as soon as the negro Hoango arrived she would see what sort of daughter she had.

Babekan was still sitting there pensively, wondering what might be the cause of the girl's strange impassioned mood, when the officer entered the room with a note which he had written in his bedroom, inviting his family to spend a few days in the negro Hoango's plantation. Evidently in the best of spirits, he greeted the mother and daughter very affably, and giving the note to the former, asked her to send someone to the woods with it immediately, at the same time providing for the needs of the party as she had promised. Babekan got up with an air of agitation, putting the note away in the cupboard and saying: 'Sir, we must ask you to go back to your bedroom at once. The road is full of negro patrols passing one after another, and they report to us that General Dessalines is about to march through this district with his army. The door of this house is open to all, and you will not be safe in it unless you hide in your bedroom which looks out on the main courtyard, and lock its doors very carefully as well as fastening the window shutters.' 'What?' said the stranger, surprised, 'General Dessalines –' but the old woman interrupted him, knocking three times on the floor with a stick. 'Ask no questions!' she said. 'I will follow you to your room and explain it all to you there.' As she thrust him out of the living-room with anxious gestures, he turned round again at the door and exclaimed to her: 'But my people are waiting for me and surely you will at least have to send a messenger to them who –' 'That will all be attended to,' broke in the old woman and at that moment the bastard negro boy of whom we have already spoken entered the room, summoned by the tapping of her stick. Then Babekan told Toni, who was looking into the mirror with her back turned to the stranger, to pick up a basket containing food which stood in the corner of the room; and the mother, the daughter, the stranger and the boy went upstairs to the bedroom.

Here the old woman, settling herself comfortably into an armchair, explained that the campfires of General Dessalines' army had been seen flickering all through the night on the hills that cut off the horizon – this was in fact the case, although until the moment of speaking not a single negro from among his troops, who were advancing southwestwards towards Port-au-Prince, had yet been observed in this area. She thus succeeded in plunging the stranger into a turmoil of anxiety which, however, she was later able to calm, assuring him that she would do everything in her power to save him, even if the worst came to the worst and the troops were billeted on her. When he repeatedly and urgently reminded her that in these circumstances she must at least assist his family with provisions, she took the basket from her daughter's hand, gave it to the boy and told him to go out to the seagull pond in the nearby wood on the hillside and deliver it to the foreign officer's kinsmen whom he would find there. She added that he must inform them that the officer himself was well; he was to say that friends of the white people, who for taking sides with them had themselves to suffer a great deal from the blacks, had taken him into their house out of compassion. Finally, she said, he must tell them that as soon as the highway was clear of the expected negro troops, steps would at once be taken to offer shelter in the house to the family as well. 'Do you understand?' she asked when she had finished speaking. The boy, putting the basket on his head, replied that he knew very well the seagull pond which she had described to him, having sometimes gone there with his friends to fish, and that on finding the foreign gentleman's family who had camped there he would convey to them exactly the message that he had been given. When the old woman asked the stranger whether he had anything to add he pulled a ring from his finger and handed it to the boy, telling him to deliver it to the head of the family, Herr Strömli, as a token that the information he was bringing was correct. Babekan then made various arrangements designed, as she said, to ensure the stranger's safety; she ordered Toni to close the shutters, and in order to dispel the resulting darkness in the room she herself lit a candle, using a tinder box which she took from the mantelshelf and which gave her some trouble as at first it would not kindle a light. The stranger took advantage of this moment to put his arm gently round Toni's waist and asked her, whispering in her ear, how she slept and whether he ought to inform her mother of what had happened; but Toni made no reply to the first question and to the second, freeing herself from his arm, she answered: 'No, not a word, if you

love me!' She concealed the anxiety which all these deceitful preparations by her mother aroused in her, and on the
pretext that she must make some breakfast for the stranger,
she rushed downstairs to the living-room.

From her mother's cupboard she took the letter in which
the stranger in his innocence had invited his family to follow the boy back to the settlement, and taking a chance on
whether her mother would miss it, she hurried after the boy
who was already on his way along the road. She was resolved, if the worst should happen, to perish with the young
officer whom she now regarded, in her heart and before
God, no longer as a mere guest to whom she had given protection and shelter, but as her betrothed husband; and she
had decided, as soon as he was strongly enough supported in
the house by his followers, to declare this to her mother
who would in these circumstances, as she reckoned, be
thrown into confusion. Hastening breathlessly along the
road she overtook the negro boy. 'Nanky,' she said, 'my
mother has changed her plan about Herr Strömli's family.
Take this letter! It is to Herr Strömli, the old man who
is the head of the family, and it invites him to spend a
few days in our settlement with his whole party. Be a
clever boy and do everything you possibly can to persuade
him to accept this arrangement; the negro Congo Hoango
will reward you for your help when he comes back!'
'Very well, Cousin Toni,' answered the boy, carefully folding up the letter and putting it in his pocket. 'And am I,'
he asked, 'to act as guide to bring the party back here?'
'Of course,' replied Toni. 'That is obvious, because they
don't know the district. But it is possible that there may
be troops marching along the highway, so you must not set
out before midnight; after that, however, you must be as
quick as you can to get them back here before dawn. Can we
rely on you?' she asked. 'You can rely on Nanky!' answered
the boy. 'I know why you are enticing these white fugitives
into the plantation, and I shall serve the negro Hoango
well!'

Toni then took the stranger his breakfast, and after it had been cleared away the mother and daughter went back into the living-room at the front of the house to go on with their domestic tasks. After some time, inevitably, the old woman went to the cupboard and naturally enough missed the letter. She pressed her hand for a moment against her head, not trusting her memory, and asked Toni where she could have put the note that the stranger had given her. Toni, after remaining silent for a moment with downcast eyes, answered that to her knowledge the stranger himself had put it back in his pocket and then torn it up, in the presence of both of them, upstairs in his room. Her mother stared at the girl wide-eyed, saying she was sure she could remember him handing it to her and that she had put it in the cupboard; but since after much vain searching she failed to find it and since a number of similar incidents had made her regard her memory as unreliable, she finally had no choice but to accept her daughter's account of the matter. She could not, however, conceal her extreme vexation at this occurrence, pointing out that the letter would have been of the greatest importance to the negro Hoango as a means of luring the family to the plantation. At midday and in the evening, as Toni was serving food to the stranger and she sat at the corner of the table to talk to him, she several times took the opportunity of asking him about the letter; but Toni, whenever this dangerous point was approached, cleverly changed the subject or confused the conversation, so that her mother was never able to make any sense of what the stranger said about the letter or discover what had really become of it. Thus the day passed; after the evening meal Babekan locked the stranger's room, for his own safety, as she said; and after some further discussion with Toni about what trick she might use to get possession of a similar letter on the following day, she went to bed and ordered her daughter to do the same.

As soon as Toni, who had longingly waited for this moment, reached her bedroom and had convinced herself that her mother was asleep, she took the picture of the Holy Virgin from where it hung by her bed, placed it on a chair, and knelt down before it with clasped hands. She besought the Saviour, the divine Son of Our Lady, in a prayer of infinite fervour, to grant her enough courage and constancy to confess to the young man to whom she had surrendered herself the crimes that burdened her young soul. She vowed at all costs, whatever pain it might bring to her heart, to conceal nothing from him, not even the pitiless and terrible intention with which she had enticed him into the house on the previous day; yet she hoped that for the sake of what she had already done towards securing his rescue he would forgive her, and take her back with him to Europe as his faithful wife. Wonderfully strengthened by this prayer, she rose and took the master key that opened all the rooms in the house, and with it crept carefully, not lighting a candle, along the narrow passage that ran across the building, to the door of the stranger's bedroom. She opened it softly and approached his bed, where he was lying in a deep sleep. The moonlight shone on his fresh, youthful face, and the night breeze, blowing through the open windows, ruffled the hair on his brow. She leaned gently over him, breathing in his sweet breath, and called him by name; but he was immersed in a deep dream, which seemed to be about her: at all events she repeatedly heard him, with trembling lips, ardently whisper the syllables 'Toni!' She was overcome by a feeling of indescribable sadness, and could not bring herself to drag him down from the heights of enchanting fantasy into the depths of base and miserable reality; and sure in any case that he would wake of his own accord, she knelt down by his bed and covered his dear hand with kisses.

But what words can describe the horror that seized her a few moments later when suddenly, from inside the courtyard, she heard the noise of men and horses and weapons, and could quite clearly recognize the voice of the negro

Congo Hoango, who with the whole band of his followers had unexpectedly returned from General Dessalines' camp. She rushed to hide behind the window curtains, carefully avoiding the moonlight which might have betrayed her presence, and sure enough she could at once hear her mother delivering a report to the negro of everything that had happened during his absence, including the European refugee's arrival in the house. The negro, lowering his voice, commanded silence among his troops in the courtyard, and asked the old woman where the stranger was at that moment; whereupon she pointed out the room to him and at the same time took occasion to inform him of the strange and remarkable conversation she had had with her daughter about the fugitive. She assured the negro that the girl was betraying them and that the entire project of overpowering the stranger was therefore at risk. At all events, she said, she had well noted that the treacherous slut had crept secretly to his bed at nightfall, and there she would be still taking her ease at this very moment; she would even now, if indeed the stranger had not got away already, be warning him and devising with him some means of effecting his escape. The negro, who had had proof in the past of the girl's loyalty in similar cases, exclaimed in reply: 'Surely what you tell me is impossible!' Then in a fury he shouted: 'Kelly! Omra! Bring your guns!' And thereupon, without another word, he climbed the stairs with all his negroes following him, and entered the stranger's room.

Toni, who in the course of just a few minutes had witnessed this whole scene, stood as if thunderstruck, numbed into immobility. For a moment she considered waking the stranger, but for one thing she knew that because of the troops in the courtyard he could not possibly escape, and in addition she foresaw that he would seize his weapons and thus, with the negroes outnumbering him as they did, be struck down and killed at once. Indeed, the most terrible thought of all those that occurred to her was that the unfortunate man, finding her standing beside his bed at such a time, would assume that she had betrayed him and, driven to despair by so disastrous an illusion, would ignore her advice and senselessly rush into the negro Hoango's arms. At this moment of unspeakable anguish her eyes fell upon a piece of rope which, by some unaccountable chance, was hanging from a hook on the wall. God himself, she thought, as she snatched it down, had put it there to save her and her lover. In a trice she wound it round the young man's hands and feet, knotting it firmly and ignoring his stirrings and resistance; then, when she had pulled the ends tight and tied them fast to the bedstead, she pressed a kiss on his lips and, delighted to have regained control of the situation for a moment, rushed out to meet Hoango who was already clattering up the stairs.

When the negro, still incredulous of the old woman's report about Toni, saw her emerging from the room which had been pointed out to him, he stopped in amazement and confusion and stood still in the corridor at the head of his troop of torchbearers and armed men. 'Disloyal traitress!' he cried out, and turning to Babekan, who had advanced a few steps towards the stranger's door, he asked: 'Has the stranger escaped?' Babekan, who had found the door open but not looked through it, returned to him with a face of fury, exclaiming: 'The deceitful hussy! She has let him get away. Be quick and set guards on every exit, before he reaches open country!' 'What's the matter?' asked Toni, staring with an air of astonishment at the old man and the negroes who stood round him. 'The matter?' retorted Hoango, and so saying he seized her by her bodice and dragged her to the bedroom. 'Are you all crazy?' cried Toni, repulsing the old negro, who stood rooted to the spot at the sight that met his eyes. 'There lies your stranger, tied up in his bed by me; and by heaven, this is not the worst deed I have done in my lifetime!' So saying she turned her back on him and sat down at a table, apparently in tears. The old man turned to her mother, who was standing on one side in confusion, and said: 'Oh, Babekan, what tale is this you have been deceiving me with?' 'Thank heavens!' replied the old woman, examining in some embarrassment the rope that held the stranger captive, 'he is here, although I don't understand how all this came about.' The negro, sheathing his sword, went to the bed and asked the stranger who he was, where he had come from, and where he was going. But since the prisoner merely struggled convulsively to free himself and could utter no words except an anguished moan of 'Oh, Toni! Oh, Toni!', Babekan spoke for him and told Hoango that he was a Swiss called Gustav von der Ried, and that he was on his way from the harbour town Fort Dauphin with a whole family of European dogs who were at this moment hiding in the mountain caves by the seagull pond. Hoango, seeing the girl sitting there disconsolately with her head propped on her hands, went over to her, called her his dear girl, patted her on the cheeks and asked her to forgive him for the over-hasty suspicion of her that he had expressed. The old woman, who had also gone up to her daughter, stood with her hands on her hips, shaking her head. 'But why,' she asked her, 'did you rope the stranger to the bed, when he had no idea of the danger he was in?' Toni, actually weeping with distress and rage, turned suddenly to her mother and answered: 'Because you are blind and deaf! Because he knew perfectly well the danger that was hanging over him! Because he was trying to get away; because he had asked me to help him escape; because he was plotting against your own life, and would quite certainly have carried out his intention before daybreak if I had not tied him up while he was asleep.' The old negro caressed and comforted the girl and ordered Babekan to say no more on the subject. He ordered two of his musketeers to come forward with their guns and execute immediately upon the stranger the law to which his life had fallen forfeit; but Babekan whispered secretly to him: 'No, for heaven's sake, Hoango!' She took him aside and pointed out to him that the stranger, before they executed him, must write a letter asking his family to join him, so that by this means the family could be enticed into the plantation, whereas it would be in many respects dangerous to attack them in the forest. Hoango, taking into account the probability that the family would not be unarmed, approved this suggestion; since it was now too late to have the agreed letter written, he detailed two of his men to guard the white fugitive, and after taking the further precaution of examining the ropes and even, since he found them too loosely tied, summoning two or three of his followers to tighten them, he left the room with his whole troop, and before very long the whole household had retired to bed.

But Toni had only been acting a part when the old man had grasped her again by the hand and she had said good night to him and retired to her room; as soon as all was quiet in the house she got up again, slipped through a back door and out into the open country, and with the wildest despair in her heart ran along the road that intersected the main highway, towards the place from which Herr Strömli's family would be coming. For the glances full of contempt which the stranger had cast at her from his bed had pierced her heart like knife wounds; a burning feeling of bitterness now mingled with her love for him, and she exulted in the prospect of dying in this enterprise designed to save his life. Fearing to miss the family, she stood waiting under a pine tree past which they would all have to come if they had accepted the invitation; and sure enough, as agreed, the first ray of dawn had scarcely appeared on the horizon when the voice of the boy Nanky, who was acting as their guide, could be heard from some way off among the trees.

The procession consisted of Herr Strömli and his wife, the latter riding on a mule; his five children, two of whom, Adelbert and Gottfried, young men of eighteen and seventeen, were walking beside the mule, three servants and two maids, one of whom was riding the other mule with an infant at her breast; twelve persons in all. They advanced slowly along the path, which was criss-crossed with tree-roots, and reached the trunk of the pine; whereupon Toni, very quietly in order not to give alarm, stepped out from the shadow of the tree and called to the procession to stop. The boy at once recognized her, and when she asked where Herr Strömli was he eagerly introduced her to the elderly head of the family, while men and women and children surrounded her. She addressed Herr Strömli in resolute tones, interrupting his words of greeting. 'Noble sir!' she said, 'the negro Hoango has quite unexpectedly returned to the settlement with his whole troop of followers. You cannot enter it now without exposing your lives to the utmost danger; indeed your cousin, who was unfortunate enough to be admitted to the house, is doomed unless you take your weapons and follow me to the plantation, where the negro Hoango is holding him prisoner!' 'Merciful heavens!' exclaimed the whole family in alarm; and the mother, who was ill and exhausted from the journey, fainted and fell from her mule to the ground. While the maidservants, called by Herr Strömli, ran up to help their mistress, Toni was besieged with questions by the young men, and fearing the boy Nanky she took Herr Strömli and the other men aside. Not withholding her tears of shame and remorse, she told them all that had happened: how matters had stood at the moment of the young man's arrival at the house, and how her private conversations with him had quite incomprehensibly changed everything; what she had done, almost mad with fear, when the negro had come back, and how she was resolved to risk her life to free him again from the trap in which she herself had caught him. 'My weapons!' cried Herr Strömli, hastening to his wife's mule and taking down his musket. And as his stalwart sons Adelbert and Gottfried and the three sturdy servants were also arming themselves, he said: 'Cousin Gustav has saved the life of more than one of us: now it is our turn to do him the same service.' Thereupon he lifted his wife, who had recovered herself, back on to the mule, took care to have the boy Nanky's hands tied so that he would be a kind of hostage, and sent all his womenfolk and children back to the seagull pond guarded only by his thirteen-year-old son Ferdinand who was also armed. Then he questioned Toni, who had taken a helmet and a pike for her own use, about the numerical strength of the negroes and how they were positioned in the courtyard, and after promising her to do his utmost in this enterprise to spare both Hoango and her mother, courageously placed himself, trusting in God, at the head of his small company and began, with Toni as guide, to advance towards the settlement.

As soon as they had all crept in by the back gate, Toni pointed out to Herr Strömli the room in which Hoango and Babekan lay asleep; and while he and his men silently entered the unlocked house and took possession of all the negroes' firearms, she slipped off round to the stable in which Nanky's five-year-old half-brother Seppy was sleeping. For Nanky and Seppy, Hoango's bastard children, were very dear to the old negro, especially the latter, whose mother had recently died; and even if they were to succeed in liberating her captured lover, it would clearly still be very difficult for them to get back to the seagull pond and from there to Port-au-Prince, where she intended to escape with them. She therefore rightly concluded that it would be very advantageous for the company of fugitives to be in possession of both the little boys, as a form of guarantee for their safety should they be pursued by the negroes. She succeeded, without being seen, in lifting the boy out of his bed and carrying him in her arms, half asleep and half awake, over into the main building. Meanwhile Herr Strömli and his men, as stealthily as possible, had entered Hoango's bedroom: but Hoango and Babekan, instead of being in bed as he expected to find them, had been wakened by the noise and were both standing in the middle of the room, although half naked and helpless. Herr Strömli, musket in hand, shouted to them to surrender or he would kill them; but Hoango, instead of replying, snatched a pistol from the wall and fired a wild shot at the company, grazing Herr Strömli's head. This was the sign for the latter's followers to attack him furiously; after Hoango had fired a second shot which went through the shoulder of one of the servants, a blow from a cutlass wounded him in the hand, and both he and Babekan were overpowered and lashed with ropes to the frame of a large table. In the meantime Hoango's negroes, twenty or more in number and sleeping in the outbuildings, had been wakened by the shots, and hearing old Babekan screaming in the house, had rushed out and were furiously trying to force their way into it to regain their weapons. In vain Herr Strömli, whose wound was insignificant, stationed his men at the windows and tried with musket fire to check the advance of the negro rabble; heedless of the fact that two of them already lay dead in the courtyard, they were about to fetch axes and crowbars in order to break down the door of the house which Herr Strömli had bolted, when Toni, trembling with apprehension and carrying the boy Seppy in her arms, entered Hoango's room. Herr Strömli, greatly relieved to see her, snatched the boy from her and, drawing his hunting knife, turned to Hoango and vowed that he would instantly kill his son if he did not call out to his negroes and order them to withdraw. Hoango, whose strength was broken by the sword-wound in three fingers of his hand, and whose own life would have been in danger if he had refused, consented after a moment's consideration to do this, and asked them to lift him from the ground. Led by Herr Strömli, he stood at the window and taking a handkerchief in his left hand he waved it and shouted to his negroes in the yard, telling them that he had no need of their help to save his life, and that they were to leave the door untouched and get back into their outhouses. This brought about a lull in the fighting; at Herr Strömli's insistence, Hoango sent a negro who had been taken prisoner in the house out into the yard to repeat his order to some of his men who were still standing there discussing what to do; and since the blacks, although they could make neither head nor tail of the matter, could not disregard this official communication, they abandoned their enterprise, for which everything was already prepared, and gradually, although grumbling and cursing, retired to their sleeping-quarters. Herr Strömli had the boy Seppy's hands tied up in front of Hoango and told the latter that his intention was simply and solely to free the officer, his cousin, from his imprisonment on the plantation, and that if no obstacles were put in the way of their escape to Port-au-Prince, then neither his, Hoango's, life nor those of his children would be in any danger and the two boys would be returned to him. Toni approached Babekan and, full of an emotion which she could not suppress, tried to give her her hand in farewell, but the old woman vehemently repulsed her. She called her a contemptible traitress and, bound as she was to the legs of the table, twisted herself round and predicted that God's vengeance would strike her even before she could enjoy the fruits of her vile deed. Toni replied: 'I have not betrayed you; I am a white girl and betrothed to this young man whom you are holding prisoner; I belong to the race of those with whom you are openly at war and I will be answerable before God for having taken their side.' Herr Strömli then set a guard on the negro Hoango, having again as a precaution had the ropes secured round him and firmly fixed to the doorposts; he had the servant who was lying unconscious on the ground with a shattered shoulder-blade lifted and carried away; and after finally telling Hoango that in a few days' time he would have both children, Nanky as well as Seppy, fetched back from Sainte Luce, where the first French outposts were stationed, he took Toni by the hand; overcome by a variety of emotions she could not forbear weeping as, with Babekan and old Hoango hurling curses after them, he led her from the bedroom.

In the meantime, as soon as the first main fighting at the windows was over, Herr Strömli's sons Adelbert and Gottfried had on their father's instructions hurried to their cousin Gustav's room, and had been fortunate enough to overcome, after a stubborn resistance, the two blacks who were guarding him. One of them lay dead in the room; the other, shot and severely wounded, had dragged himself out into the corridor. The brothers, the elder of whom had himself been wounded, though only slightly, in the thigh, untied their dear beloved cousin from the bed: they embraced and kissed him, gave him firearms and other weapons, and joyfully invited him to accompany them to the front room where, since victory was now assured, Herr Strömli would no doubt be already making all the arrangements for their withdrawal. But their cousin Gustav, half sitting up in the bed, merely pressed their hands warmly; he was silent and distracted, and instead of taking the pistols they offered him, raised his right hand to his forehead and passed it across it in a gesture of inexpressible sorrow. The young men had sat down beside him and asked what was wrong; he put his arms round them and laid his head on the younger brother's shoulder without saying a word; and just as Adelbert, thinking he was going to faint, was about to rise and fetch him a glass of water, the door opened and Toni entered carrying the boy Seppy and holding Herr Strömli by the hand. At this sight Gustav changed colour: he stood up, clinging to his friends for support as if he were on the verge of collapsing, and before the two youths could tell what he intended to do with the pistol he now snatched from them, he had, gritting his teeth with rage, fired a shot straight at Toni. It went right through her breast; with a stifled cry of pain she staggered another

265

few steps towards him and then, handing the little boy to Herr Strömli, sank down at his feet; but he hurled the pistol over her to the ground, kicked her away from him, calling her a whore, and threw himself down on the bed. 'Why, you monster!' cried Herr Strömli and his two sons. The latter rushed to the girl, raised her in their arms and shouted for one of the old servants who during their march had given medical assistance in many similar desperate cases; but the girl, convulsively pressing her hand against the wound, pushed her friends back, and pointing to the man who had shot her gasped brokenly with her last breath: 'Tell him –!', and again, 'tell him –!' 'What are we to tell him?' asked Herr Strömli, for death was robbing her of speech. Adelbert and Gottfried rose to their feet and cried out to the perpetrator of this appalling and senseless murder: 'Do you not know that this girl saved your life, that she loves you and that it was her intention to escape to Port-au-Prince with you, to whom she has sacrificed everything, her parents, and all she had?' They shouted into his ears: 'Gustav! can't you hear us?', and shook him and pulled him by the hair, for he was lying on the bed heedless of them and of everything. Gustav sat up. He glanced at the girl where she lay writhing in her blood, and the fury which had impelled him to the deed gave way not unnaturally to a feeling of common compassion. Herr Strömli, weeping hot tears and with his handkerchief to his eyes, asked him: 'Wretched man, why did you do that?' Cousin Gustav, who had risen from the bed and was standing looking down at the girl and wiping the sweat from his brow, answered that she had with infamous treachery tied him up in the night and handed him over to Hoango the negro. 'Oh!' cried Toni, reaching out her hand towards him with a look no words can describe, 'dearest friend, I tied you up, because –!' but she could not speak, nor even reach him with her hand; her strength suddenly failed her and she fell back on to Herr Strömli's lap. 'Why?' asked Gustav, turning pale and kneeling down beside her. Herr Strömli, after a long pause during which they waited in vain for an answer from Toni, the silence broken only by her dying gasps, replied for her and said: 'Because, unhappy man, there was no other way to save you after Hoango's arrival; because she wanted to prevent the fight you would undoubtedly have started, and to gain time until we reached you, for thanks to her we were already hurrying here to rescue you by force of arms.' Gustav buried his face in his hands. 'Oh!' he cried without looking up, and the earth seemed to give way under his feet, 'is this true, what you are telling me?' He put his arm round her and gazed into her face, his heart rent with anguish. 'Oh', cried Toni, and these were her last words, 'you should not have mistrusted me!' And so saying, the noble-hearted girl expired. Gustav tore his hair. 'It's true!' he exclaimed, as his cousins dragged him away from the corpse, 'I should not have mistrusted you, for you were betrothed to me by a vow, although we had not put it into words!' Herr Strömli, lamenting, undid the girl's bodice and urged the servant, who was standing by with a few crude instruments, to try to extract the bullet which he thought must have lodged in her breast-bone; but all their efforts, as we have said, were in vain, the shot had pierced right through her and her soul had already departed to a better world. During this, Gustav had gone over to the window; and while Herr Strömli and his sons, weeping silently, were discussing what was to be done with the body, and whether the girl's mother should be called to the scene, he took up the other, still loaded pistol, and blew his brains out with it. This new deed of horror threw his kinsmen into utter consternation. He it was whom they now tried to help; but the wretched man's skull was completely shattered, parts of it indeed adhering to the surrounding walls, for he had thrust the pistol into his mouth. Herr Strömli was the first to regain his composure, for already bright daylight was shining through the windows and the negroes were reported to be stirring again in the courtyard; there was therefore no choice but to begin the company's immediate withdrawal from the settlement. Not wishing to abandon the two dead bodies to the wanton violence of the negroes, they laid them on a board, and the party with muskets reloaded set out in sorrowful procession towards the seagull pond. Herr Strömli, carrying the boy Seppy, walked first; next came the two strongest servants bearing the dead bodies on their shoulders; behind them the wounded man limped along with the help of a stick; and Adelbert and Gottfried escorted the slowly advancing cortège, one at each side, with their guns cocked. The negroes, seeing the group so weakly defended, emerged from their quarters with pikes and pitchforks and seemed to be about to launch an attack; but Hoango, whose captors had prudently released him, came out of the house on to the steps and signalled to his men to leave them alone. 'At Sainte Luce!' he called out to Herr Strömli, who had already reached the gateway with the dead bodies. 'At Sainte Luce,' Herr Strömli called back; whereupon the procession, without being pursued, passed out into the open country and reached the forest. At the seagull pond, where they found the remainder of the family, a grave was dug for the dead and many tears shed for them; and when the rings that Toni and Gustav both wore had been exchanged as a final gesture, the two lovers were lowered, amid silent prayers, into the place of their eternal rest. Five days later Herr Strömli was fortunate enough to reach Sainte Luce with his wife and his children, and there, as he had promised, he left the two negro boys behind. Entering Port-au-Prince shortly before the beginning of the siege, he fought on its ramparts for the cause of the whites; and when the city after stubborn resistance had fallen to General Dessalines, he and the French army escaped aboard ships of the British fleet; the family sailed to Europe, where without further mishap they reached their native Switzerland. There Herr Strömli settled, using the rest of his small fortune to buy a house near the Rigi; and in the year 1807, among the bushes of his garden, one could still see the monument he had erected to the memory of his cousin Gustav, and to the faithful Toni, Gustav's bride.

The Foundling

ANTONIO PIACHI, a wealthy Roman dealer in property, was sometimes obliged to make long journeys on business. He would then usually leave his young wife Elvira behind in Rome in the care of her relatives. On one of these occasions he travelled with his eleven-year-old son Paolo, the child of an earlier marriage, to Ragusa. It so happened that a plague-like disease had here recently broken out and was spreading panic through the city and the surrounding districts. Piachi, who had not heard this news till he was on his way, stopped on the outskirts to inquire about it. But when he was told that the epidemic was growing daily more serious and that the authorities were talking about closing the town, anxiety on his son's behalf made him abandon all his business plans, and taking horses he set off again the way he had come.

When he was in the open he noticed beside his carriage a young boy who held out his hand towards him beseechingly and appeared to be in great distress. Piachi told the driver to stop, and the boy on being asked what he wanted replied in his innocence that he had caught the plague; that the sheriff's officers were pursuing him to take him to the hospital where his father and mother had already died; and he begged Piachi in the name of all the saints to let him come with him and not leave him behind to perish in the town. As he spoke he clasped the old man's hand, pressed it and kissed it and covered it with tears. Piachi, in his first impulse of horror, was about to push the boy violently away, but the latter at that very moment turned pale and fell fainting to the ground. The good old man's pity was stirred; with his son he got out of his carriage, lifted the boy into it, and drove off, though he had not the least idea what to do with him.

At his first stop he was still negotiating with the people at the inn how he might best get rid of him again when on the orders of the police, who had got wind of the affair, he was arrested; and he and his son and the sick boy, whose name was Nicolo, were transported under guard back to Ragusa. All Piachi's remonstrances against the cruelty of this procedure were in vain; arriving at Ragusa, all three of them were taken in a bailiff's charge to the hospital; and here, although he himself remained well and the boy Nicolo recovered his health, Piachi's son, the eleven-year-old Paolo, became infected and died three days later.

The city gates were now reopened, and Piachi, having buried his son, obtained permission from the police to leave. Grief-stricken, he stepped into his carriage, and at the sight of the now empty seat beside him he took out his hand-kerchief to weep freely: at that moment Nicolo, cap in hand, stepped up to the carriage and wished him a good journey. Piachi leaned out, and in a voice broken by convulsive sobbing asked the boy whether he would like to travel with him. The latter had no sooner understood the old man than he nodded and answered, 'Oh yes, indeed I should!' The hospital authorities, on being asked by the property dealer whether Nicolo might be allowed to accompany him, smiled and assured him that the boy was an orphan and would be missed by nobody. He therefore, greatly moved, lifted him into the carriage and took him back to Rome in place of his son.

On the highway outside the gates Piachi had his first good look at the boy. He was handsome in a strangely statuesque way; his black hair hung down from his forehead in simple points, overshadowing a serious, wise-looking face which never changed its expression. The old man asked him several questions, but he answered them only briefly; he sat there in the corner, uncommunicative and absorbed in himself, with his hands in his trouser pockets, looking pensively and diffidently out of the windows of the carriage as it sped along. From time to time, with a noiseless movement, he took out a handful of nuts he was carrying with him, and while Piachi wept and wiped his eyes, the boy cracked the shells open between his teeth.

In Rome Piachi introduced him to his excellent young wife Elvira with a brief explanation of what had happened. She could not withhold bitter tears at the thought of her young stepson Paolo, whom she had loved dearly; but she embraced Nicolo, stranger though he was and stiffly as he stood before her, showed him to the bed in which Paolo had slept and gave him all the latter's clothes to wear. Piachi sent him to school where he learnt to read and write and do arithmetic. He had very understandably become all the fonder of the boy for having had to pay so high a price for him; and after only a few weeks, with the consent of the kind-hearted Elvira who had no prospects of bearing her elderly husband any other children, he adopted him as his son. Later, having dismissed from his office a clerk with whom he was for various reasons dissatisfied, he appointed Nicolo in his place, and was delighted with the active and useful assistance which the latter gave him in his complicated business affairs. The only fault that the old man, who was a sworn enemy of all bigotry, had to find with him was the company he kept with the monks of the Carmelite monastery, who were paying very friendly attentions to the boy on account of the large fortune he would one day inherit from his adoptive father; and Elvira's only criticism of Nicolo was that he seemed to have a precocious propensity for the fair sex. For at the age of fifteen he had already, while visiting these monks, succumbed to the wiles of a certain Xaviera Tartini, a concubine of the bishop's; and although on Piachi's stern insistence he broke off this liaison, Elvira had reason to believe that in these delicate matters Nicolo was not a model of self-denial. When, however, at the age of twenty he married Elvira's niece, Constanza Parquet, an attractive young Genoese lady who had been educated in Rome under her aunt's supervision, this particular trouble at least seemed to have been cured at its source. Both his foster-parents were equally pleased with him, and to give him proof of this they drew up a splendid marriage settlement, making over to him a considerable part of their large and beautiful house. And in short, when Piachi reached the age of sixty he took for Nicolo the final step that a benefactor could take: he gave him legal possession of the entire fortune on which his property business rested, retaining only a small capital for himself, and withdrew with his faithful, virtuous Elvira, whose worldly wishes were few, into retirement.

There was in Elvira's nature an element of silent melancholy, originating in a touching episode that had occurred during her childhood. Her father, Filippo Parquet, was a well-to-do Genoese dyer, and the back of his house, designed for the exercise of his trade, stood right at the sea's edge on a massive stone embankment; huge beams, built into the gable, projected for several yards over the water and were used for hanging out the dyed material. On one ill-fated night fire broke out in the house and at once blazed up in all the rooms simultaneously as if the place were built of pitch and sulphur. The thirteen-year-old Elvira, surrounded on all sides by terrifying flames, fled from staircase to staircase and found herself, she scarcely knew how, standing on one of these beams. The poor child, hanging between heaven and earth, had no idea how to save herself: behind her the fire from the burning gable, fanned by the wind, was already eating into the beam, and beneath her was the wide, desolate, terrible sea. She was just about to commend herself to all the saints, choose the lesser of two evils, and jump down into the water, when suddenly a young Genoese of patrician family appeared in the doorway, threw his cloak over the beam, took her in his arms and with great courage and skill, by clinging to one of the damp cloths that hung down from it, lowered himself into the sea with her. Here they were picked up by the gondolas afloat in the harbour, and carried ashore amid much acclamation from the bystanders. But it turned out that on his way through the house the gallant young man had been severely wounded on the head by a stone falling from the cornice, and it was not long before he lost consciousness and collapsed. He was carried to the house of his father, the marquis, and the latter, when he found that he was taking a long time to recover, summoned doctors from all over Italy who trepanned his son's skull repeatedly and extracted several pieces of bone; but by a mysterious dispensation of Providence all their skill was in vain. Only seldom did he show some signs of life in the presence of Elvira, who had come to nurse him at his mother's request; and after three years of very painful illness, during which the girl did not leave his bedside, he clasped her hand for one last time and expired.

Piachi, who had business connections with this young nobleman's family and made the acquaintance of Elvira in the marquis's house while she was nursing his son, married her two years later; he was particularly careful never to mention the young man's name or otherwise re-call him to her, as he knew that her delicate and sensitive mind was deeply disturbed by the memory. The slightest circumstance that even remotely reminded her of the time when this youth had suffered and died for her sake always moved her to tears, and on such occasions there was no comforting or quieting her. She would at once leave what-ever company she was in, and no one would follow her, for they knew by experience that the only effective remedy was to let her weep quietly by herself till her grief was stilled. No one except Piachi knew the cause of these strange and frequent fits of emotion, for never in her life had she uttered one word alluding to the episode. They were usually explained as a nervous disorder, the aftermath of a violent fever which she had contracted just after her marriage, and this account served to forestall any further inquiry into their origin.

Nicolo, who despite his father's orders had never wholly severed his connection with the above-mentioned Xaviera Tartini, had on one occasion secretly met her at the carnival, without his wife's knowledge, pretending to have been invited to a friend's house; and late that night, when everyone was asleep, he returned home in the costume of a Genoese cavalier which he chanced to have chosen. It so happened that during the night the elderly Piachi felt unwell and Elvira, since the maids were not to hand, had got out of bed to assist him and had gone to fetch a bottle of vinegar from the dining-room. She had just opened the cupboard in the corner and was standing on a chair to search among the glasses and carafes, when Nicolo softly opened the door and stepped into the dining-room in his plumed hat, with cloak and sword, carrying a candle which he had lighted in the hall. Unsuspectingly, without seeing Elvira, he crossed to his bedroom door and had just made the disconcerting discovery that it was locked, when Elvira, standing on her chair behind him with bottles and glasses in her hand, caught sight of him and immediately, as if stricken by some unseen horror, fell to the floor in a dead faint. Nicolo turned round, pale and startled, and was just about to rush to her assistance when he reflected that the noise she had made would certainly bring Piachi to the scene; being anxious to avoid the old man's reproaches at all costs, he snatched with panic haste at a bunch of keys which Elvira carried at her side, and having found one which opened his door he threw the keys back into the dining-room and vanished. Piachi, ill as he was, had jumped out of bed; he lifted up his unhappy wife and rang for the servants, who appeared with lights, and presently Nicolo too came out in his dressing-gown and asked what had happened. But Elvira, her tongue numbed by horror, could not speak, and since Nicolo was the only other person who could have cast any light on the matter, it remained an unexplained mystery. Elvira, trembling in every limb, was carried to her bed, where she lay ill for several days with an acute fever;

nevertheless she had enough natural good health to recover tolerably well, and apart from a strange depression with which it left her the incident was without consequence.

A year had thus passed when Constanza, Nicolo's wife, died in childbirth together with her first child. The loss of this virtuous and well-educated young woman was an event not only regrettable in itself but doubly so in that it gave fresh occasion for the indulgence of Nicolo's two vices; his bigotry and his passion for women. Once again he began to linger for days on end in the cells of the Carmelite monks, on the pretext of seeking consolation, although it was known that while his wife was alive he had shown her very little love or fidelity. Indeed, before Constanza had even been buried, Elvira, in the course of making arrangements for the funeral, entered Nicolo's room one evening and found him there with a girl whom, with her painted face and her fripperies, she recognized only too well as Xaviera Tartini's chambermaid. On seeing her, Elvira lowered her eyes and turned and left the room without a word to Nicolo. She said nothing to Piachi or to anyone else about this, and contented herself with kneeling down sadly by Constanza's body and weeping, for the latter had loved Nicolo passionately. But it so happened that Piachi, who had been out in the town, met the girl as he was entering the house; and well realizing what her business here had been, he accosted her sternly and induced her, half by subterfuge and half by force, to give him the letter she was carrying. He went to his room to read it and found that it was, as he had guessed, an urgent message from Nicolo to Xaviera, telling her that he longed for a meeting and asking her to appoint a time and place. Piachi sat down and, disguising his handwriting, replied in Xaviera's name: 'Presently, before dark, at the Church of Santa Maria Maddalena'. He sealed the note with a borrowed crest and had it handed in to Nicolo's room as if it had just been delivered from the lady. The ruse was entirely successful: Nicolo immediately took his cloak and left the house, without a thought for Constanza who was laid out in her coffin. Thereupon Piachi, in deep indignation, cancelled the solemn funeral which had been arranged for the following day, and summoned a few bearers to take up the laid-out corpse just as it was and carry it quietly, with only himself and Elvira and a few relatives as mourners, to the vault of Santa Maria Maddalena where it was to be buried. Nicolo, waiting wrapped in his cloak at the portico of the church, was astonished by the approach of a funeral procession composed of persons well known to him, and he asked Piachi, who was walking behind the coffin, what this meant and whom they were burying. But the old man, without looking up from the prayer book in his hand, merely answered: 'Xaviera Tartini'; whereupon the mourners, entirely ignoring Nicolo's presence, once more uncovered the body and blessed it, and then lowered it into the tomb to be sealed away.

As a result of this deeply humiliating episode, Nicolo was filled with a burning hatred for Elvira, whom he believed to be responsible for the public disgrace which her husband had inflicted on him. For several days Piachi did not speak to him; and since Nicolo nevertheless stood in need of his favour and goodwill in connection with Constanza's estate, he was constrained to seize his adoptive father's hand one evening with every appearance of remorse and swear to give up Xaviera once and for all. He had, however, no intention of keeping this promise; on the contrary, in the face of opposition he merely became more defiant and more cunning in the art of evading the good old man's vigilance. At the same time he thought he had never seen Elvira look more beautiful than at the moment when, to his consternation, she had opened his door and closed it again at the sight of the maid. A soft flush of indignation had lent infinite charm to her gentle face which only seldom showed any emotion; and he thought it incredible that she, with so many attractions, should not herself occasionally walk the primrose path of that indulgence for which she had just punished him so shamefully. He burned with the desire, should this turn out to be the case, to repay her in kind by informing her husband; and all he needed and sought was an opportunity for carrying out this plan.

On one occasion, when Piachi happened to be out of the house, he was passing Elvira's door when he heard, to his surprise, the sound of someone talking in her room. A malicious hope at once flashed through his mind; he stooped down to look and listen through the keyhole and there, great heavens! what should he see but Elvira lying. in an attitude of swooning ecstasy, at someone's feet. He could not make out who it was, but he quite clearly heard her as, in the very accents of passionate love, she whispered the name 'Colino'. With beating heart he went to the window in the passage and there took up a position from which he could watch her bedroom door without seeming to do so; and presently he heard the latch being quietly raised. Here at last, he told himself, was the exquisite moment for his unmasking of this spurious saint: but instead of the ex- pected stranger it was Elvira herself who emerged from the room, casting a completely unperturbed and indifferent glance at him as she did so. She had a piece of handwoven cloth under her arm, and after locking her room with one of the keys which she carried with her, she walked quite calmly downstairs with her hand on the bannister. To Nicolo this hypocritical display of composure seemed the very height of cynical cunning; she was scarcely out of sight when he rushed to fetch a master key, and after look- ing cautiously about him he stealthily opened the bedroom door. But to his amazement the room was quite empty, and though he searched every nook and cranny he could find no trace of a man, except for a life-sized portrait of a young cavalier which stood in an alcove behind a red silk curtain, lit by a special lamp. Nicolo was startled, though without knowing why, and as the painted figure stared at him with its wide-open eyes a host of thoughts rushed through his mind. But before he could collect and compose them he began to be apprehensive that Elvira would discover him and punish him in some way; he closed the bedroom door again in some confusion and withdrew.

The more he thought about this remarkable incident, the more convinced he became of the importance of the picture he had discovered, and the more acute and urgent grew his curiosity to know whose portrait it was. For he had clearly seen Elvira's posture: she had been kneeling, and it was quite certain that she had been doing so in front of the young nobleman on the canvas. In the uneasiness of mind that possessed him he went to Xaviera Tartini and told her of his strange experience. Xaviera was just as anxious as Nicolo to discredit Elvira, whom she blamed for all the difficulties that were being put in the way of their liaison; and she declared that she would like to see the portrait in the bedroom. For she could boast an extensive acquaintance among the Italian nobility, and if the young man in question had at any time been in Rome and was a person of the least consequence, the chances were that she would know him. Sure enough it happened before long that Piachi and his wife went into the country one Sunday to visit a relative; and no sooner was the coast thus clear than Nicolo hastened to Xaviera, brought her to the house accompanied by a small daughter whom she had had by the Cardinal, and introduced her into Elvira's room on the pretext that she was a lady wishing to see the paintings and embroideries. But no sooner had he drawn back the curtain than the child, whose name was Clara, utterly confounded him by exclaiming: 'Why, God bless us, Signor Nicolo! but that's a picture of you!' Xaviera fell silent. The portrait did indeed, the longer she looked at it, bear a singular resemblance to him, especially when she remembered, as well she might, the Genoese costume he had worn a few months ago for their clandestine visit to the carnival.

Nicolo tried to laugh off the sudden flush of embarrassment which came over him; he kissed the little girl and said: 'Indeed, my dear Clara, it's about as much like me as you are like the man who thinks he is your father!' But Xaviera, in whom the bitter pangs of jealousy were stirring, merely looked at him; and after stepping in front of the mirror and remarking that after all the identity of the person was a matter of indifference, she took her leave of him rather coldly and left the room.

As soon as Xaviera had gone, Nicolo fell into a great state of excitement over this scene. He remembered with delight the strange and violent turmoil into which Elvira had been thrown by his fanciful appearance on the night of the carnival; and the thought of having inspired a passion in this walking model of womanly virtue was almost as sweet to him as that of taking his revenge on her. Having now the prospect of gratifying both desires at one and the same time, he waited impatiently for Elvira's return and for the moment when he would look into her eyes and crown his still hesitant hopes with certainty. In this elation the one thing that gave him pause was the distinct recollection that when he had spied on her through the keyhole, the name which the kneeling Elvira had addressed to the picture had been 'Colino'. And yet there was something about the sound of this name – a rather unusual one in Italy – that filled him with sweet reveries, though he could not tell why; and faced with the choice of disbelieving one of two senses, his eyes or his ears, he naturally inclined to the evidence that was more flattering to his desires.

Meanwhile several days passed before Elvira returned from the country, where she had been staying with a cousin; from his house she brought back with her a young kinswoman who wanted to see Rome, and being occupied with polite attentions to this young lady, she cast only a fleeting and insignificant glance at Nicolo as with the most amiable courtesy he helped her out of her carriage. For several weeks, which were devoted to the entertainment of her guest, the house was in an unwonted turmoil; visits were made to places in and outside the city which would be likely to appeal to a young and lively girl; and Nicolo, busy in his office and therefore not invited on any of these expeditions, began again to harbour keen resentment against Elvira. Bitter feelings rankled in him as he thought of the unknown man she so devoutly adored in secret; and the torment of his depraved heart reached its height on the evening after the young kinswoman's departure, an evening for which he had waited with longing, but on which Elvira, instead of speaking to him, sat in silence for an hour at the dining-room table, busy with a piece of needlework. It so happened that Piachi, a few days earlier, had been inquiring after the whereabouts of a box of little ivory letters with which Nicolo had been taught to read as a boy; for since no one needed them now, it had occurred to him to make a present of them to a small child in the neighbourhood. But the maidservant who had been told to look for them among various other discarded objects had only been able to find the six letters that formed the name Nicolo; no doubt because the others, having less relevance to the boy himself, had attracted his interest less, and had at one time or another been thrown away. These six letters had now been lying in the dining-room for several days, and Nicolo, as he sat gloomily brooding at the table with his head propped on his arm, picked them up and toyed with them; and as he did so he discovered – purely by chance, for he had never in his life been so astonished – the combination of the letters that spelt the name 'Colino'. Nicolo, who had been quite unaware of this anagrammatic aspect of his name, was once again seized by the wildest hopes, and cast a hesitant anxious glance at Elvira who was sitting beside him. The correspondence between the two words struck him as more than merely fortuitous; with secret delight he pondered the implications of his strange discovery, and taking his hands from the table he waited with beating heart for the moment when Elvira would look up and see the name lying there plainly visible. His expectations were not disappointed; for no sooner had she, in an idle moment, noticed this display of the letters and unsuspectingly leaned forward (for she was a little short-sighted) to read them, than she fixed a sudden strange look of anguish on Nicolo's face as he sat gazing down at them with affected indifference. She resumed her work with an indescribable expression of sadness; thinking herself unobserved she wept quietly, and a soft flush covered her cheeks. These signs of emotion did not escape Nicolo, who was unobtrusively watching her, and he no longer had any doubt that she had merely been disguising his own name by this transposed spelling. He saw her put out her hand and gently disarrange the letters, and his wild hopes reached their height as she rose, laid aside her sewing and disappeared into her bedroom. He was just about to leave his seat and follow her when Piachi entered and, on inquiring for Elvira was told by one of the maïdservants that she had felt unwell and gone to lie down. Piachi, without seeming particularly alarmed, turned and went to her room to see how she was; and when he returned a quarter of an hour later, announced that she would not appear for dinner, and then did not mention the matter again, Nicolo remembered the many mysterious scenes of this kind that he had witnessed, and felt convinced that he now held the clue to their meaning.

The following morning, as he sat gloating over his new discovery and considering how he might best exploit it, he received a note from Xaviera in which she asked him to come and see her, as she had some interesting news for him about Elvira. Xaviera, as the Bishop's protégée, enjoyed the intimate acquaintance of the Carmelite monks; and since it was to the Carmelite monastery that Nicolo's adoptive mother went to confession, he had no doubt that Xaviera must have succeeded in eliciting some information about the secret history of her feelings which would prove favourable to his unnatural desires. There was, however, an un-

pleasant surprise in store for him; for Xaviera, after greeting him with an oddly roguish air and drawing him down
beside her on to the divan where she was sitting, declared
that what she had to tell him was simply that the object of
Elvira's love was a man who had already been dead and
buried for twelve years. The original of the portrait he had
found in her bedroom in the alcove behind the red silk curtain was Aloysius, Marquis of Montferrat; an uncle in Paris
in whose house he had been educated had called him
Collin, this being later changed in Italy to the nickname
Colino; and he was the young Genoese nobleman who had
so heroically rescued her from the fire when she was a child
and been mortally injured in doing so. Xaviera added that
she must ask Nicolo not to make any use of this secret,
as it had been entrusted to her in the Carmelite monastery,
under the seal of absolute discretion, by someone who himself had no right to it. Nicolo, flushing and turning pale by
turns, assured her that she could set her mind at rest; and
being quite unable to conceal from her mischievous glances
the embarrassment into which this disclosure had flung
him, he excused himself on the pretext of having some
business and took his hat, his upper lip twitching un-
pleasantly as he left her.

Humiliation, lust and the desire for revenge now con-
spired in his mind to engender a deed of unutterable vileness. He well knew that deception would be the only access
to Elvira's pure soul; and at the first opportunity Piachi
gave him by going for a few days into the country, he prepared to execute the satanic plan on which he had decided.
He procured again the very same costume in which he had
appeared to Elvira a few months earlier as he was secretly
returning late at night from the carnival; and putting on the
cloak and doublet and feathered hat of Genoese cut, exactly
as the figure in the portrait wore them, he stealthily entered
her room just before bedtime. He hung a black cloth over
the picture in the alcove, and with a staff in his hand, in the

precise posture of the young nobleman on the canvas, awaited Elvira's adoring homage. And his reckoning, sharpened by shameful passion, had been entirely correct; for she presently entered, undressed quietly and calmly, and had no sooner drawn back as usual the silk curtain of the alcove and set eyes on him, than with a cry of 'Colino! my beloved!' she fell senseless to the floor. Nicolo stepped out of the alcove; he stood for a moment absorbed in contemplation of her charms and gazed at her delicate figure now suddenly paling in the embrace of death; but presently, since there was no time to be lost, he took her up in his arms, snatched the black cloth from the portrait, and carried her to the bed in the corner of the room. Having done this he went to bolt the door, but found it already locked; and confident that even after recovering her disordered senses she would offer no resistance to the fantastic and supernatural apparition for which she must take him, he now returned to the bed and set about reviving her with burning kisses on her lips and breasts. But the Nemesis that dogs the heels of crime had decreed that Piachi, who was to have been absent, as the wretched Nicolo supposed, for another few days, should chance to return to his house unexpectedly at that very moment. Thinking Elvira would already be asleep, he crept softly along the corridor; and as he always carried the keys with him, he was able to open the door without making a sound and stepped suddenly into the room. Nicolo stood speechless; and as there was no possibility of dissembling his disgraceful intentions, he threw himself at the old man's feet and implored his forgiveness, vowing never to cast eyes upon his wife again. And Piachi did, indeed, feel inclined to deal with the matter discreetly. Bereft of words by something which Elvira whispered to him as she revived in his arms and gazed with horror at her assailant, he merely closed the curtains of her bed, took a whip from the wall, opened the door and pointed to it, indicating thereby to Nicolo in what direction he must now immediately betake himself. But the latter, seeing that nothing was to be gained by his show of penitence, behaved at this point in a manner worthy of Tartuffe himself: he suddenly stood up and declared that it was for Piachi to leave the house, for he, Nicolo, was now its owner by deed of gift and he would defend his title to it against all comers. Piachi could scarcely believe his ears; disarmed by this inconceivable piece of effrontery, he put down the whip, took his hat and stick and ran to the house of his old friend, the lawyer Dr Valerio. He rang the bell until a maid opened the door, and on reaching his friend's room collapsed unconscious beside his bed before he could utter a word. The lawyer took him, and later Elvira as well, into his house for the night, and set off in haste next morning to procure the arrest of the abominable Nicolo. But the infernal scoundrel's legal position was strong; and while Piachi vainly sought ways and means to dispossess him of the property over which he had already given him full rights, he had at once gone hotfoot with his deed of settlement to the Carmelite monks and appealed to them for protection against, as he said, the old fool who was now trying to evict him. In the end, after he had consented to marry Xaviera, whom the Bishop wanted taken off his hands, wickedness prevailed, and this prince of the Church was able to induce the authorities to issue a decree confirming Nicolo's title to the property and enjoining Piachi to leave him in possession without further interference.

Only the previous day Piachi had buried the unhappy Elvira, who as a result of the recent episode had fallen into a burning fever and died. Maddened by this double blow he went into the house with the injunction in his pocket, and with rage lending him strength he felled Nicolo, who was of weaker build, to the floor, and crushed out his brains against the wall. No one else in the house noticed his presence until the deed was already done; by the time they found him he was holding Nicolo between his knees and stuffing the injunction into his mouth. Having done so he stood up, surrendered all his weapons, and was then imprisoned, tried, and condemned to death by hanging.

In the Papal State there is a law by which no criminal may be led to his death before he has received absolution. This Piachi, when his life had been declared forfeit, stubbornly refused to do. After all the arguments of religion had been vainly adduced to convince him of the heinousness of his behaviour, he was led out to the gallows in the hope that the sight of the death that awaited him might frighten him into penitence. On one side stood a priest who in a voice like the last trump described to him all the terrors of hell into which his soul was about to be plunged; opposite stood another, holding in his hand the Body of Christ, the sacred means of redemption, and spoke to him of the glorious abodes of eternal peace. 'Will you accept the blessed gift of salvation?' they both asked him. 'Will you receive the sacrament?' 'No,' replied Piachi. 'Why not?' 'I do not want to be saved, I want to go down into the deepest pit of hell, I want to find Nicolo again – for he will not be in heaven – and continue my vengeance on him which I could not finish here to my full satisfaction.' And so saying he ascended the ladder and called upon the hangman to perform his duty. In the end the execution had to be stayed and the wretched man taken back to prison, for the law protected him. On three successive days similar attempts were made and every time without avail. On the third day, forced once more to come down from the ladder unhanged, he raised his fists in a gesture of bitter rage and cursed the inhuman law that forbade him to go to hell. He called upon the whole legion of devils to come and fetch him, swore he had no other wish but to be doomed and damned, and vowed he would throttle the first priest who came to hand if by so doing he might get to hell and lay hold of Nicolo again! When this was reported to the Pope, he ordered that Piachi should be executed without absolution; and unaccompanied by any priest, he was strung up very quietly in the Piazza del Popolo.

The Duel

TOWARDS the end of the fourteenth century, just as the night of St Remigius was falling, Duke Wilhelm of Breysach, who ever since his clandestine marriage to Countess Katharina von Heersbruck, a lady of the family of Alt-Hüningen and regarded as his inferior in rank, had lived in a state of of feud with his half-brother Count Jakob Rotbart,* was returning home from a meeting with the German Emperor at Worms. In consideration of the death of all his legitimate children he had succeeded in obtaining from the Emperor a decree legitimizing his natural son Count Philipp von Hüningen, to whom his wife had given birth before their marriage. Looking forward to the future more hopefully than at any time since his succession to the dukedom, he had already reached the park behind his castle when suddenly, from among the bushes, an arrow sped out of the darkness and transfixed his body just below the breast bone. His chamberlain Herr Friedrich von Trota, amazed and appalled by this event, managed with the help of some other knights to carry him into the castle, where his distraught wife, having hastily summoned a council of the vassals of the realm, held him in her arms as with his last remaining strength he read aloud the imperial deed of legitimation; and when, despite some lively opposition, for by law the crown should have passed to his half-brother Count Rotbart, the vassals had complied with his last express wish and, subject to the Emperor's approval, had recognized Count Philipp as successor to the throne under the guardianship and regency of his mother in view of his minority, the Duke lay back and died.

The Duchess now ascended the throne without further

* Literally 'Count Jakob (the) Redbeard'.

formality, merely dispatching a deputation to her brother-in-law Count Jakob Rotbart to notify him of the fact; and the consequence of this was, or at least outwardly seemed to be, exactly what had been predicted by a number of gentlemen at the court who claimed to know the Count's secretive temperament: Jakob Rotbart, shrewdly judging how matters now stood, accepted with a good grace the injustice his brother had done him; at all events he made no attempt whatsoever to set aside the dispositions of the late Duke, and heartily congratulated his young nephew on his accession. In the most friendly and affable way he invited the envoys to dine with him, and described to them the free and independent life he had led in his castle since the death of his wife, who had left him a princely fortune; he told them how much he enjoyed the society of the wives of his noble neighbours, the wine from his own estates, and hunting with boon companions. He added that a crusade to the Holy Land, to expiate the sins of his impetuous youth, which he ruefully confessed were growing yet more grievous with age, was the sole enterprise he still had in mind for his declining years. His two sons, who had been brought up in definite hopes of succeeding to the ducal throne, bitterly but vainly protested against the heartless indifference with which he thus so surprisingly acquiesced in the irrevocable invalidation of their claims. He curtly and contemptuously ordered them to hold their tongues, beardless youths as they were; on the day of the former Duke's solemn funeral he made them follow him to the town and there duly assist him in laying their uncle to rest; and after paying homage to his nephew the young prince in the throne-room of the ducal palace, with the rest of the court nobility and in the presence of the Regent, he declined all her offers of positions and dignities and returned to his castle accompanied by the blessings of the people, whose admiration he earned in double measure by such magnanimity and restraint.

The Duchess, after this unexpectedly happy solution to her first problem, now turned her attention to her second duty as Regent, namely the search for her husband's assassins, a whole band of whom was reported to have been seen in the park; and to this end she and her Chancellor, Herr Godwin von Herrthal, examined the arrow that had killed him. It yielded, however, no clue to the identity of its owner, except perhaps for the remarkable fact of its very fine and rich workmanship. Strong, crisp, gleaming feathers had been set in a slender and powerful shaft of dark walnut, finely turned; the head was coated with shining brass and only the very tip, sharp as a fish-bone, was of steel. The arrow must have been intended for the armoury of some rich nobleman who either had many enemies or was devoted to the chase; and since a date engraved on the upper end of it indicated that it had been manufactured not long ago, the Chancellor advised the Duchess to have it sent round, under her crown seal, to every workshop in Germany, in the hope of discovering the master craftsman who had made it and from him, if he could be traced, the name of the client who had ordered it.

Five months later the Chancellor, Herr Godwin, to whom the Duchess had entrusted the whole inquiry, received an affidavit from an arrowsmith in Strassburg, declaring that he had, three years ago, made some three score of such arrows, and a quiver to match, for Count Jakob Rotbart. The Chancellor, dumbfounded by this statement, kept it secretly locked away for several weeks, partly because, despite the Count's wild and dissolute life, he knew or believed him to be too noble-minded ever to be capable of so foul a deed as the murder of his brother; partly also because, despite the Regent's many other excellent qualities, he did not sufficiently trust her sense of justice in a matter concerning the life of her bitterest enemy, and he therefore felt bound to proceed with the utmost caution. In the meantime he followed up this strange clue with further discreet inves-

tigations, and when by chance it came to light, on evidence
from the town prefecture, that the Count, who normally
never or very seldom left his castle, had been absent from
it on the night of the Duke's assassination, he considered it
his duty to disclose his findings; and accordingly at one of
the next meetings of the Council of State, he acquainted
the Duchess in detail with the extraordinary and disturbing
suspicion which, on these two counts, fell upon Jakob
Rotbart, her brother-in-law.

The Duchess, however, had of late been congratulating
herself on her friendly relations with the Count and was
particularly anxious not to give offence to him by any ill-
considered action; consequently, to the Chancellor's dismay, she showed no pleasure at all on receiving this dubious
information. On the contrary, after twice reading the papers
through attentively she expressed considerable annoyance
that so uncertain and delicate a matter should have been
publicly raised at the Council of State; she was of the
opinion that the allegation must be based on some error
or calumny, and absolutely forbade it to be taken to the
courts. Indeed, in view of the extraordinary popular esteem,
amounting almost to adoration, which the Count for under-
standable reasons had enjoyed since his exclusion from
the throne, she thought even this mere mention of the
matter in the Council of State extremely dangerous; and
foreseeing that there would be rumours about it in the town
which would reach his ears she had the two points of indictment, together with the alleged evidence, delivered to him
at his castle with a most magnanimous covering letter in
which she declared that it must all be the result of some
strange misunderstanding, assured him that she was convinced in advance of his innocence, and earnestly requested
him not to embarrass her by troubling to refute them.

The Count, who was at table with a party of friends when
the knight bearing the Duchess's message arrived, rose courteously to his feet and took the letter over to a window

embrasure to read it while his friends stared at the ceremonious messenger, who had declined to be seated; but
no sooner had their host finished reading than he changed
colour and handed them the papers, saying: 'Look at this,
my friends! A shameful charge has been trumped up against
me – I am accused of murdering my brother!' As they
crowded round him in alarm he took the arrow from the
knight with an angry glare and added, concealing his profound consternation, that the missile did indeed belong to
him, and that it was also true that on the night of St Remigius he had been absent from his castle. His friends denounced this malicious and contemptible imposture, cast
the suspicion of the murder back upon the shameless
accusers themselves, and were about to heap insults on the
Duchess's envoy as he began to speak in defence of his
mistress, when the Count, after re-reading the documents,
suddenly interposed himself, exclaiming: 'Calm yourselves,
my friends!' Thereupon he took his sword from where
it was standing in a corner of the room, and handed it over
to the knight with the words: 'I am your prisoner!' When
the latter asked in amazement whether he had heard him
aright, and whether he in fact acknowledged the two
charges drawn up by the Chancellor, the Count answered:
'Yes! yes! yes!', adding however that he hoped he would
not be expected to offer any proof of his innocence except
at the bar of a court formally convened by the Duchess. His
own knights, highly dissatisfied with this announcement,
tried vainly to convince him that he was not in this case
accountable to anyone but the Emperor; the Count, persist-
ing in his strange change of attitude and his reliance on the
Regent's justice, declared his determination to appear before
the High Court of the Duchy. Wrenching himself free from
them, he was already calling out of the window for his
horses, saying that he was willing to leave at once with
the messenger and submit himself to the confinement befitting his rank, when his companions forcibly intervened

and offered a proposal which they finally prevailed upon him to accept. A letter signed by all of them was written to the Duchess, demanding a safe conduct for the Count, as was the right of every nobleman in such circumstances, and offering, as surety that he would appear before the court of her appointment and accept whatever verdict it might pass on him, the sum of twenty thousand marks in silver.

The Duchess, to whom this communication was as inexplicable as it was unexpected, and who knew that very unpleasant rumours about why the charges had been brought were already popularly current, thought it advisable to withdraw herself completely from the proceedings and to submit the whole dispute to the Emperor. On the Chancellor's advice she sent him all the documents in the case and asked him, in his capacity as supreme overlord, to relieve her of the investigation of a matter in which she was herself an interested party. The Emperor, who happened to be in Basle at that time, negotiating with the Swiss Confederation, agreed to this request; he set up then and there a tribunal consisting of three counts, twelve knights, and two assistant judges; and after granting Count Jakob Rotbart, against a bail of twenty thousand silver marks, the safe conduct for which his friends had applied, he called upon him to appear before the aforesaid tribunal and give answer on the two points, namely: how the arrow which he confessed was his property had come to be in the murderer's hands, and secondly, where he had been on the night of St Remigius.

On the Monday after Trinity, Count Jakob Rotbart, with a splendid escort of knights, presented himself in Basle at the bar of the court before which he had been summoned, and after passing over the first question, which he declared to be a complete mystery to him, he came to the second, which was decisive for the judgement of the case, and made the following statement, resting his hands on the railing as he spoke and gazing at the assembly with his little eyes

glinting under their red lashes: 'My lords and gentlemen!'
he said, 'you accuse me, despite my amply demonstrated
indifference to the acquisition of a crown and sceptre, of
having committed the vilest conceivable deed, the murder
of my brother, who was, it is true, not very well disposed
towards me, but no less dear to me for that; and as part of
the evidence for your indictment, you adduce the fact that
on the night of St Remigius when the crime was committed
I was, contrary to the custom I have observed for many
years, absent from my castle. Now I very well know the
obligations of a gentleman with regard to any ladies whose
favour he privily enjoys and I assure you that if it had not
pleased heaven to visit me, like a bolt from the blue, with
this strange and fateful conjunction of circumstances, the
secret which I carry silently in my heart would have died
with me and perished in dust, not to rise again until the
angel should sound the last trump which will burst open
our graves and call me to stand before God. But His Majesty
the Emperor, speaking through you, puts to my conscience
a question which, as you will yourselves realize, must over-
ride all such considerations and scruples; therefore, since you
wish to know why it is neither probable nor even possible
that I was involved in the murder of my brother either
personally or indirectly, I must tell you that on the night
of St Remigius, that is at the time when the deed was perpetrated, I was secretly visiting the beautiful daughter of the
Lord Sheriff Winfried von Breda, the widowed lady Littegarde von Auerstein, whose love I had won.'

Now the reader should know that the widowed Littegarde
von Auerstein was not only the most beautiful lady in the
country but had also, until the utterance of this scandalous
slur, enjoyed the purest and most blameless of reputations.
Since the loss of her husband, the Commandant von Auerstein, who had died of an infectious fever a few months
after their marriage, she had lived a quiet and withdrawn
life in her father's castle; and it was only at the latter's

request, for in his old age he would have been glad to see her married again, that she consented to appear now and then at the hunts and banquets organized by the gentlemen of the surrounding neighbourhood, particularly by Herr Jakob Rotbart. On these occasions many lords from the richest and noblest families of the land pressed their attentions upon her, and among them the dearest to her heart was the Chamberlain Herr Friedrich von Trota, who had once during a hunt gallantly saved her life from a charging wounded boar; but fearing to displease her two brothers, who counted on inheriting her fortune, she had been unable, despite all her father's exhortations, to make up her mind to accept his hand in marriage. And indeed, when her elder brother Rudolf married a rich young lady from that part of the country, and when, after remaining childless for three years, they had to the family's great joy been blessed with a male heir, so much pressure was put upon her by plain speech and insinuation that she formally bade farewell, in a letter which cost her many tears, to her friend Herr Friedrich, and to preserve unity within the family she accepted her brother's suggestion that she should become the Abbess of a convent on the Rhine not far from her ancestral home.

It was just at the time when this plan, upon representations made to the Archbishop of Strassburg, was about to be put into execution, that the Lord Sheriff Winfried von Breda received from the court appointed by the Emperor the scandalous notification concerning his daughter Littegarde, together with an order to bring her to Basle to answer the charge raised against her by Count Jakob. The letter indicated the exact time and place at which the Count, in his evidence, claimed to have paid his secret visit to the lady Littegarde, and the court even sent with it a ring which had belonged to her dead husband and which he declared he had received from her hands, on his departure, as a souvenir of the night they had spent together. Now it happened that Herr Winfried, on the day this letter arrived, was suffering from a serious and painful ailment of old age; supported by his daughter, he was tottering round the room in a state of extreme agitation, already contemplating the mortality to which all that lives is subject; and so it was that upon reading the court's terrible communication he was immediately seized by apoplexy, and dropping the letter, collapsed on the floor, paralysed in every limb. The horrified brothers, who were present, lifted him and summoned a doctor, who lived within the precincts of the castle in order to be near at hand to attend him; but all efforts to restore him to life were vain. He expired as the lady Littegarde still lay senseless in the arms of her waiting-women, and when she came to herself she lacked even the bittersweet consolation of having been able to speak, in defence of her honour, a single word that he might take with him into eternity. The consternation of the two brothers at this appalling event was beyond description, as was their fury at its cause, the imputed shameful misconduct of their sister, which unfortunately seemed only too credible. For they knew all too well that Count Jakob Rotbart had persistently paid court to her throughout the whole previous summer; he had held a number of tournaments and banquets solely in her honour, and had on each of these occasions distinguished her from all the other ladies of the company by attentions which had seemed highly improper even then. Indeed, they remembered that Littegarde, at just about the time of the St Remigius' Day in question, had claimed to have lost during a walk this very ring, a present from her husband, which had now turned up so strangely in the hands of Count Jakob; and so they did not doubt for one moment the truth of the statement which the Count had made against her in court. In vain, as their father's corpse was carried off amid the lamentations of the household, she clung to the knees of her brothers and begged them to hear her for only one moment. Rudolf, aflame with indignation, turned on her and demanded to know whether she could produce a witness to disprove the accusation; but she tremblingly replied that she could invoke no testimony save that of her irreproachable way of life, since it happened that her chambermaid had been absent on a visit to her parents, and therefore not in attendance on her in her bedroom, on the night in question; whereupon Rudolf spurned her with his foot, snatched a sword from the wall and unsheathed it, shouted in a passion of hideous anger for the dogs and servants, and ordered her to leave the house and castle forthwith. Littegarde stood up, pale as death, and silently evading the blows he aimed at her, asked him at least, since he insisted on her leaving, to give her time to make the necessary preparations; but in reply Rudolf, foaming with rage, merely shouted at her to get out of the house; and since he even ignored the pleas of his own wife, who intervened to urge upon him more forbearance and humanity, furiously thrusting her aside and striking her with his sword-hilt so that it drew blood, the unfortunate Littegarde, more dead than alive, had no choice but to leave the room. She staggered across the courtyard, where the common people stood round staring at her, to the gate of the castle; here Rudolf had a bundle of linen handed to her, into which he had put some money, and he himself shut and locked the gate behind her with curses and execrations.

This sudden fall from the heights of serene and almost untroubled happiness to the depth of incalculable and quite helpless misery was more than the poor woman could endure. Clinging to the fence by the rocky path she stumbled down it, not knowing where to go, yet hoping at least to find some lodging for that night; but before she had even reached the entrance to the little straggling village in the valley she collapsed on the ground, her strength already utterly exhausted. Oblivious of all the troubles of this world, she lay there for perhaps an hour, and the whole

place was already plunged in darkness when she regained
consciousness to find herself surrounded by a number of
sympathetic villagers. For a boy playing on the cliffside had
noticed her there and reported this strange and surprising
discovery to his parents; whereupon the latter, to whom
Littegarde had often given bountiful assistance and who
were extremely dismayed to learn of her wretched plight,
immediately set out to do whatever might be in their
power to help her. Thanks to their attentions she soon recovered herself, and looking back at the castle which stood
closed behind her, she also regained her balance of mind;
but declining the offer of two women to take her up to
the castle again, she merely asked the villagers if they would
be kind enough to provide her at once with a guide who
would help her to continue her journey. The good people
vainly sought to persuade her she was in no fit state to
travel; Littegarde insisted, on the grounds that her life would
be in danger if she remained one moment longer within
the boundaries of the castle domain; and as the crowd
round her increased and still stood nonplussed, she even
attempted to force her way through it and to set out alone,
despite the darkness of the night which had now fallen.
Accordingly the villagers, fearing to be held responsible by
their masters at the castle if she should come to any harm,
felt compelled to do as she wished and fetched her a vehicle
in which, after they had repeatedly asked her where she
wanted to go, she was driven off in the direction of Basle.

But scarcely were they outside the village when, after
considering the situation more carefully, she changed her
mind and told her driver to turn round and take her to
Trota Castle, which was only a few leagues away. For she
was well aware that without someone to help and support
her, she could not hope to prevail in the court at Basle
against an adversary such as Count Jakob Rotbart; and she
could think of no one more worthy to be entrusted with the
task of defending her honour than her gallant friend, the

noble-hearted Chamberlain Friedrich von Trota, who as she well knew still devotedly loved her. It was perhaps about midnight, and the lights in the castle were still glimmering when she drove up, utterly worn out by her journey. A servant of the house came to meet her and she sent him ·to announce her arrival to the family; but even before he had done his errand the ladies Bertha and Kunigunde, Herr Friedrich's sisters, appeared from the front door, having, as it chanced, been downstairs in the anteroom on some household business. They knew Littegarde very well and greeted their friend joyfully as they helped her down from her carriage: then, though not without some trepidation, they took her upstairs to their brother, who was sitting at a desk immersed in the papers concerning a lawsuit in which he was involved. With indescribable amazement Herr Friedrich, hearing sounds behind him, turned round and saw the lady Littegarde, white and distraught, the very image of despair, falling upon her knees before him. 'My dearest Littegarde!' he exclaimed, rising and lifting her to her feet: 'What has happened to you?' Littegarde sank into a chair and told him the whole story: how Count Jakob Rotbart, to clear himself of the suspicion of murdering the Duke, had made a vile statement about her to the court at Basle; how at the news of this her old father, ailing as he was at the time, had at once had a stroke and died of it a few moments later in the arms of his sons; and how the latter in furious indignation, without heeding anything she might say in her defence, had treated her with dreadful cruelty and finally turned her out of doors like a criminal. She begged Herr Friedrich to see her suitably escorted to Basle and put in touch with an advocate there, who would wisely and prudently counsel her and take her part when she appeared before the Emperor's court of inquiry to answer that shameful allegation. She assured him that if it had been uttered by a Parthian or a Persian on whom she had never set eyes it could not have surprised her more than it did coming from Count Jakob Rotbart, whom she had always deeply abhorred for his ugly reputation as well as for his looks; and she had, she said, always rejected with the utmost coldness and contempt the compliments he had sometimes taken the liberty of paying her on festive occasions during the previous summer. 'Say no more, my dearest Littegarde!' cried Herr Friedrich, seizing her hand with noble ardour and pressing it to his lips. 'Waste no words defending your innocence and justifying yourself. There is a voice that speaks for you in my heart, and it carries a far livelier conviction than any assurances, indeed than all the evidence and proofs which the combination of events and circumstances may well enable you to bring in your favour before the court at Basle. Your unjust and ungenerous brothers have abandoned you: therefore accept me as your friend and brother, and grant me the honour of being your advocate in this case; I will restore your shining and untarnished reputation before the court at Basle and in the eyes of all the world!' Thereupon he took Littegarde, whose eyes were streaming with tears of gratitude and emotion at his magnanimous words, upstairs to his mother Frau Helena, who had already withdrawn to her bedroom; he explained to this dignified old lady, who was particularly fond of Littegarde, that the latter was a guest who had decided to stay for a time in his castle in consequence of a quarrel that had broken out in her family. That very night a whole wing of the spacious castle was put at her disposal, the cupboards in the rooms were abundantly stocked for her with clothing and linen supplied by the two sisters from their stores, and she was also provided suitably, indeed lavishly, with servants, quite befitting her rank. On the third day Herr Friedrich von Trota, accompanied by many mounted knights and squires, was already on his way to Basle, without having given any indication of how he proposed to set about proving the case in court.

In the meantime the court at Basle had received from

Littegarde's two brothers at Breda Castle a letter concerning the recent incident there, in which, either because they really believed her to be guilty or because they had other reasons for desiring to ruin her, they declared their unfortunate sister to be a proven criminal meriting the full rigours of the law. At all events they were so ungenerous and untruthful as to represent her expulsion from the castle as a voluntary departure; they described how, upon some expressions of indignation on their part, she had left immediately, unable to utter a word in defence of her innocence; and alleged that as they had vainly tried to discover her whereabouts, they could only suppose that she was now crowning her disgrace by wandering at large in the company of some further adventurer. At the same time, to restore the honour of the House of Breda which she had besmirched, they applied to the court to have her name struck off the family tree; they also demanded, adducing complicated legal arguments, that as a punishment for her unspeakable misdeeds she should be deemed to have forfeited all claims on the inheritance of their noble father, whose death her disgrace had precipitated. Now the judges at Basle were by no means disposed to comply with these requests, which in any case were a matter not within their competence; but since in the meantime Count Jakob, on hearing the news from Breda, gave clear and unmistakable evidence of his concern for Littegarde's fate and was known to have secretly sent out riders in search of her in order to offer her refuge in his castle, the court decided that there was no longer any ground for doubting the truth of his evidence, and that the charge of assassination of the Duke, which was still pending against him, should at once be withdrawn. In fact, this concern which he showed for the unhappy woman in the hour of her need even swung public opinion very much in his favour, strongly divided as it was for and against him; whereas his exposure to general scorn of a lady whose amorous favours he had enjoyed had hitherto been sharply criticized, the extraordinary and sinister circumstances in which nothing less than his life and honour had been at stake were now held to excuse it, and to have left him with no alternative but to reveal without further scruple his adventure on the night of St Remigius. Accordingly, on the Emperor's express command, Count Jakob Rotbart was again summoned before the court to be solemnly and publicly acquitted of the suspicion of complicity in the murder of the Duke. The herald, in the great hall of the court, had just read aloud the letter from Rudolf von Breda and his brother, and the judges, with the accused man standing beside them, were about to give effect to the imperial decree and proceed formally to his honourable discharge, when Herr Friedrich von Trota advanced to the bar and, invoking the right of any impartial spectator, requested permission to look at the letter for a moment. Consent was given, and the eyes of the whole assembly were turned on him; but scarcely had the paper been handed to him by the herald than Herr Friedrich, after a fleeting glance at it, tore it from top to bottom and hurled the pieces, with his glove wrapped round them, into Count Jakob Rotbart's face, declaring him to be a vile and contemptible slanderer and vowing to prove before all the world, in a life and death ordeal by combat, the lady Littegarde's innocence of the offence of which he had accused her. Count Jakob Rotbart, turning pale and taking up the glove, said: 'As surely as God judges righteously in an ordeal by arms, even so surely shall I prove to you, in honourable knightly combat, the truth of what I was forced to disclose about the lady Littegarde!' And turning to the judges he added: 'Noble sirs, pray inform His Imperial Majesty of Herr Friedrich's intervention, and request him to name the time and place at which we may meet each other, sword in hand, to decide this dispute!' Accordingly the court adjourned and the judges sent a deputation to the Emperor reporting what had happened; whereupon the latter, somewhat shaken in his belief in the Count's innocence by the appearance of Herr Friedrich as Littegarde's champion, summoned her to Basle to witness the duel, as the code of honour required, and appointed St Margaret's Day as the time, and the castle square at Basle as the place, for the armed encounter, in the lady Littegarde's presence, between Herr Friedrich von Trota and Count Jakob Rotbart, to clear up the strange mystery surrounding this affair.

Accordingly, at noon on St Margaret's Day the sun had just reached its zenith over the towers of the city of Basle, and an immense crowd of people, for whom benches and platforms had been put up, had filled the castle square, when the herald, standing in front of the balcony on which the judges of the duel had taken their places, sounded his threefold summons, and Herr Friedrich and Count Jakob, both armed from head to foot in gleaming bronze, advanced into the lists to decide their cause by combat. Almost all the knights of Swabia and Switzerland were present on the sloping terrace of the castle just behind the square; and on the castle balcony, surrounded by his courtiers, sat the Emperor himself, together with his consort and the princes and princesses, his sons and daughters. Shortly before the beginning of the fight, as the judges were assigning to each combatant his due share of light and shade, Frau Helena and her two daughters Bertha and Kunigunde, who had accompanied Littegarde to Basle, again appeared at the entrance to the square and asked the guards standing there for leave to enter and speak a few words with the lady Littegarde, who in accordance with ancient custom was seated on a stage inside the lists. For although this lady's way of life appeared to justify complete respect for her and the most absolute reliance on the truth of her assurances, nevertheless the evidence of the ring which Count Jakob possessed, and still more the fact that, upon the night of St Remigius, Littegarde had given leave of absence to her chambermaid, the only person who might have borne witness for her, filled their minds with acute misgivings; they resolved to test once more whether even under the stress of this decisive moment she was sustained against the accusation by a perfectly clear conscience, and to try to convince her that if any burden of guilt did indeed lie on her soul it would be vain and indeed blasphemous to attempt to cleanse herself of it by appealing to the sacred verdict of arms, which would infallibly bring the truth to light. And indeed Littegarde had very good reason to reflect carefully on the action Herr Friedrich was now taking on her behalf: the stake awaited both her and her friend Herr von Trota if God, in this iron ordeal, should decide not for him but for Count Jakob Rotbart and for the truth of the testimony against her to which he had sworn. Seeing Herr Friedrich's mother and sisters approaching from the side entrance Littegarde rose from her seat with that air of dignity which was natural to her and which the sorrow now afflicting her so deeply made still more moving, and, going to meet them, inquired what brought them to her at so fateful a moment. 'My dearest daughter,' said Frau Helena, taking her aside, 'will you not spare a mother, who has nothing but her son to comfort her in her desolate old age, the grief of mourning at his graveside? Before this duel begins, will you not take a carriage and accept from us a large gift of money and of whatever else you need, and go to one of our properties on the other side of the Rhine, where you will be suitably and kindly welcomed, and which we will also make over to you as a gift?' Littegarde stared at her for a moment, the colour leaving her face, and as soon as she had taken in the full meaning of these words she went down on one knee before her and said: 'Most honoured and noble madam! In this decisive hour God is to give his verdict on the innocence of my heart: does your apprehension that he will pass judgement against me originate in the mind of your noble son?' 'Why do you ask that?' replied Frau Helena. 'Because in that case I implore him, if he wields his sword with any lack of confidence, rather not to draw it, and to surrender the lists to his adversary on whatever fitting pretext he can find; and since I can accept nothing from his compassion, to waste none on me but to abandon me to my fate, which I commit to the mercy of God!' 'No!' said Frau Helena in confusion, 'my son knows nothing of this! He pledged his word to the court to champion your cause, and it would ill befit him to act as you suggest now that the hour of trial has come. As you can see, he stands confronting your adversary the Count, already armed for the fight and firmly believing in your innocence; it was I and my daughters who thought of this proposal in the stress of the moment, when we considered what advantages might be gained and how much misfortune might be avoided.' 'Then,' said Littegarde, ardently kissing the old lady's hand and wetting it with her tears, 'then let him do what he has promised to do! No guilt stains my conscience; and even if he were to fight this duel without helmet or armour, God and all his angels will protect him!' So saying she stood up and led Frau Helena and her daughters to some chairs that had been placed on the same platform behind her own, which was draped in scarlet and on which she now sat down.

At a nod from the Emperor the herald then sounded the signal for the fight to begin, and the two knights advanced upon each other with sword and shield. Herr Friedrich wounded the Count with his very first blow; the point of his not particularly long sword slashed him on the wrist just where the joints of the armour overlapped. But the Count, leaping back in alarm as he felt the pain and examining the wound, found that although it bled quite copiously the skin was only superficially grazed; consequently, as a murmur of disapproval at this unseemly behaviour arose from the assembled knights on the terrace, he advanced again and resumed the fight with renewed energy as if he had not been hurt at all. Now the struggle raged between the two combatants like a conflict of two tempestuous winds, or as when two high-piled storm clouds meet and hover about each other without mingling, while darts of lightning are hurled between them amid the crash of repeated thunder. Herr Friedrich, his shield and sword outheld, stood as firm as if he were taking root in the ground, for the flagstones had been removed and the soil deliberately loosened, and so he dug himself in up to his spurs, indeed to his ankles and calves, fending off from his breast and head the cunning thrusts of the small and nimble Count, who seemed to be attacking him from all sides at once. The fight, counting the intervals in which both adversaries had to pause and take breath, had already lasted nearly an hour when the spectators on the benches began murmuring again. This time their dissatisfaction seemed to be not with Count Jakob, who was showing himself eager enough to bring the struggle to an end, but with Herr Friedrich's policy of remaining planted like a post on one and the same spot and his strange, seemingly timid or at least obstinate refusal to attack in his turn. Although there may have been reasons for his tactics, Herr Friedrich was nevertheless too sensitive not to abandon them immediately in response to the wishes of those who at this moment were sitting in judgement over his honour; he stepped boldly forth from the spot initially chosen, on which he had built up a kind of natural fortification round his feet, and smashed down several fresh and doughty blows aimed at the head of his opponent, who already seemed to be weakening, though with skilful side-stepping he still managed to parry them with his shield. Yet not more than a few moments after the fight had thus changed its character, Herr Friedrich suffered a mishap, which scarcely seemed to indicate the presence of higher powers presiding over the issue: catching his foot in his spurs, he stumbled, fell forward, and as he knelt there in the dust supporting himself with one hand, his body weighed down by his helmet and armour, Count Jakob Rotbart seized a rather ignoble and unchivalrous advantage and thrust his sword into his exposed side. With a momentary cry of pain, Herr Friedrich leapt to his feet. Indeed, closing his visor and swiftly turning to face his opponent, he prepared to resume the fight: but as he leant on his sword, bent double with pain and with darkness swimming before his eyes, the Count struck again with his two-handed sword, twice thrusting it home into his breast, just under the heart, whereupon Herr Friedrich crashed with a clatter of armour to the ground, dropping his sword and shield beside him. The Count, after tossing his weapons aside, and as the trumpets sounded a threefold flourish, set his foot on the fallen knight's breast. The Emperor himself and all the spectators rose from their seats with muted exclamations of dismay and compassion, while Frau Helena, following her two daughters, rushed to the side of her beloved son where he lay in the dust, weltering in blood. 'Oh, my dear Friedrich!' she cried, kneeling down by his head in anguish, while the lady Littegarde, who had swooned and was lying senseless on the floor of the platform, was lifted by two constables and carried off to prison. 'Oh vile brazen wretch that she is,' added Frau Helena, 'to come here knowing herself guilty and to dare to arm her most faithful and chivalrous friend for an ordeal by duel, and seek God's judgement on her behalf in an unrighteous combat!' So saying she raised her dear son from the ground, while her daughters took off his armour, and with loud lamentations tried to stanch the blood that flowed from his noble heart. But on the Emperor's orders constables approached and took him into their charge, as having also incurred the penalties of the law; with the help of some doctors he was put on a stretcher and, with a large crowd following, likewise committed to prison: Frau Helena and her daughters, however, were given permission to stay with him there until his death, which no one doubted would occur before long.

Yet it presently became evident that Herr Friedrich's wounds, although dangerously affecting vital parts, were by some strange providence not mortal; on the contrary not many days passed before the doctors who had been assigned to him were able to assure his family with certainty not only that his life would be saved but also that given his natural strength he would make a complete recovery within a few weeks without any permanent injury to his body. As soon as he regained consciousness, of which pain had deprived him for a long time, he repeatedly asked his mother what had become of Littegarde. He could not help weeping when he heard that she was in a dismal prison and a prey to the most terrible despair, and, caressing his sisters' faces, begged them to visit her and comfort her. Frau Helena, amazed at his words, urged him to forget so shameless and contemptible a woman; in her view the crime which Count Jakob had mentioned to the court, and which the outcome of the duel had now fully brought to light, was pardonable, but not the ruthless cynicism of appealing to the sacred judgement of God as if she were innocent, although knowing herself to be guilty, and without any consideration for the noble-hearted friend whom she thereby brought to ruin. 'Oh, mother,' said the Chamberlain, 'what mortal man, even if he were possessed of the wisdom of the ages, could presume to interpret the mysterious verdict that God has given in this duel?' 'What!' cried Frau Helena, 'is the meaning of this divine judgement not clear to you? Were you not defeated in the fight by the sword of your adversary, in a manner all too plain and unequivocal?' 'Perhaps so!' replied Herr Friedrich. 'For a moment he had the advantage of me; but did the Count really defeat me? Am I not alive? Have I not returned miraculously to flourishing health, as if God had breathed new life into me? Perhaps in no more than a few days I shall have strength enough again, indeed be doubly and triply strengthened, to continue the fight which a trifling accident obliged me to interrupt.' 'Foolish man!' cried his mother, 'do you not know that according to the law a duel which has been declared by the judges to be concluded cannot be resumed in order to invoke the divine verdict a second time in one and the same case?' 'That is of no consequence!' retorted the Chamberlain. 'What do I care for these arbitrary human laws? Can a fight that has not been continued until the death of one of the two opponents be held to have been concluded, if one considers the matter at all rationally? If I were permitted to resume it, have I not cause for hope that I should make good the mishap that befell me, and win from God with my sword a verdict quite contrary to that which, on a limited and short-sighted view, He is at present assumed to have delivered?' 'Nevertheless,' replied his mother with misgivings, 'these laws which you claim to disregard are the established and prevailing laws; whether rational or not, they have the authority of divine command-ments, and by them you and she, as a pair of abominable criminals, are consigned to the utmost rigour of penal juris-diction!' 'Alas!' cried Herr Friedrich, 'wretch that I am, that is the very thing that plunges me into despair! She is judged to be guilty and her life is forfeit; and I, who sought to prove her virtue and innocence to the world, I myself have brought this misery upon her, because for one fatal moment I tripped in the fastenings of my spurs. Perhaps God intended, quite independently of her cause, to punish the sins of my own heart – and now her lovely limbs must be given to the flames and her memory be ignominious for ever!' At these words bitter tears of manly grief rose to his eyes; seizing his handkerchief he turned to the wall, and Frau Helena and her daughters knelt at his bed in silent emotion, mingling their tears with his and kissing his hand. Meanwhile the gaoler had entered the room with food for him and his family, and Herr Friedrich, on asking him how the lady Littegarde was faring, gathered from his curt and indifferent replies that she was lying on a bundle of straw and had not yet spoken a word since the day of her im-prisonment. This news filled Herr Friedrich with the utmost alarm; he commissioned the gaoler to tell the lady, for her reassurance, that by a strange dispensation of Providence he was making a complete recovery, and that he begged leave, as soon as his health should be restored and with the permission of the castle warden, to visit her in her prison. But according to the gaoler's report – and he said he had had to shake her several times by the arm, for she was lying on the straw like a madwoman neither hearing nor seeing anything – her reply was a refusal : for the rest of her days on earth she desired to see no one. It was even learnt that on the very same day she had written to the warden in her own hand bidding him admit no one to her presence, whoever it might be, and Chamberlain von Trota least of all. In consequence, Herr Friedrich, impelled by the most acute anxiety as to her state of mind, chose a day on which he felt an exceptional revival of his strength, and with the warden's permission went with his mother and sisters to the room in which she was confined, unannounced yet sure that she would forgive him.

But it was with indescribable horror that the wretched Littegarde, hearing the noise at the door and rising from the scattered straw on which she lay, with her breast half exposed and her hair all undone, saw instead of the expected gaoler her noble and excellent friend the Chamberlain, entering with the assistance of Bertha and Kunigunde; a sad and moving spectacle, for he bore many signs of the sufferings he had endured. 'Leave me !' she cried, falling back on her couch with an expression of despair and covering her face with her hands : 'leave me, if there is any pity in your heart !' 'Dearest Littegarde, what does this mean ?' answered Herr Friedrich. Supported by his mother he stood at her side and stooped down with inexpressible emotion to take her hand. 'Let me alone !' she cried, crawling on her knees over the straw until she had retreated several paces from him. 'Do not touch me or I shall go mad! You fill me with horror; the crackling of flames is less terrible to me than the

sight of you!' 'I fill you with horror?' answered Herr
Friedrich in amazement. 'Sweet, generous Littegarde, I am
Friedrich, your friend: how have I deserved such a reception from you?' As he spoke, his mother motioned to Kunigunde to place a chair for him and make him sit down
on it, weak as he was. 'Oh God!' cried Littegarde, throwing
herself at his feet and burying her face in the ground in
the most terrible anguish, 'oh my beloved, leave this room
and leave me to myself! I clasp your knees with all the
ardour of my heart, I wash your feet with my tears, I
writhe before you like a worm in the dust and beg you
for one act of mercy: oh my lord and master, leave the
room, leave it at once and leave me to my fate!' Herr
Friedrich stood there before her in utter consternation. 'Is
it so painful for you to see me, Littegarde?' he asked,
looking gravely down at her. 'It is horrifying, it is unbear-
able, it breaks my heart!' answered Littegarde, leaning on
her outstretched hands and desperately hiding her face between the very soles of his feet. 'Hell with all its ghastly
terrors is sweeter to me, and I can better bear to contemplate it than to see your face turned towards me in grace
and love and shining on me like the spring!' 'Oh God in
heaven!' cried the Chamberlain, 'why is your soul in such
contrition? What am I to think? Unhappy woman, did the
ordeal speak true, and are you guilty of that crime of which
the Count accused you before the court, are you guilty of
it?' 'Guilty, convicted and cast out, judged and condemned
in time and for eternity!' cried Littegarde, frenziedly beating her breast. 'God speaks the truth and is infallible; go, I
am at my wits' end, I have no strength left. Leave me alone
with my grief and my despair!' At these words Herr Friedrich fainted; and as Littegarde, covering her head with a
veil, lay back on her pallet as if to take final leave of the
world, Bertha and Kunigunde rushed weeping to the side
of their senseless brother to try to revive him. 'Oh, may
God's curse be upon you!' cried Frau Helena, as the Chamberlain opened his eyes again. 'May you be cursed to ever-

lasting remorse on this side of the grave and beyond it to everlasting damnation, not for the sin which you now confess but for your merciless inhumanity in not confessing it until you had dragged my innocent son down with you into destruction! Fool that I am!' she continued, turning her back on Littegarde in contempt, 'if only I had believed what I was told just before the duel began by the Prior of the Augustinian monastery here! He told me in confidence that the Count had made his confession to him, in pious preparation for the decisive hour that awaited him, and had sworn to him on the sacred Host that the statement he made to the court about this wretched woman was the truth! He told the Prior about the garden gate at which, as they had agreed, she waited for him at nightfall and let him in; he described to him the room, a remote one in the uninhabited castle tower, to which she led him, unnoticed by the guards; and the bed, piled high with comfortable and luxurious cushions under a canopy, in which she secretly lay with him in shameless debauchery! An oath taken at such a moment cannot be a lie; and had I, blind as I was, reported this to my son, even as the duel was just about to begin, it would have opened his eyes, and he would have shrunk back from the edge of the abyss by which he stood. But come!' Frau Helena exclaimed, gently embracing Friedrich and kissing his brow. 'Indignation that deigns to speak to her does her too much honour; let her see our backs turned on her, and be crushed by the reproaches we refrain from uttering, and so may she despair!' 'The infamous wretch!' retorted Littegarde, stung by these words and sitting upright. She bowed her head to her knees in misery, and, weeping hot tears into her handkerchief, she continued: 'I remember that my brothers and I, three days before that night of St Remigius, were at his castle; he was giving a feast in my honour as he often did, and my father, who liked to see homage paid to my youthful charms, had persuaded me to accept his invitation, accompanied by my brothers. Late that evening, when the dance was over and I went to my bedroom, I found on my table there a note, in unknown handwriting and unsigned, which contained a declaration of love in clear terms. As it happened, both my brothers were in my room to discuss arrangements for our departure, which we had agreed should be on the following day; and since I was not accustomed to having any kind of secrets from them I showed them the strange find I had just made and about which I was speechless with astonishment. They at once recognized the Count's handwriting and were wild with fury, indeed my elder brother wanted to take the paper and go at once to the Count's room; but my younger brother persuaded him that this would be unwise, since the Count had prudently not signed the note; and so, deeply outraged by his insulting behaviour, they both left with me in the carriage that very same night and returned home, vowing never again to honour his castle with their presence. And this,' she added, 'is the one and only association I have ever had with that vicious and contemptible man!' 'What?' said the Chamberlain, turning his tear-stained face towards her. 'These words were music to my ears! – speak them again!' he went on after a pause, kneeling down in front of her and folding his hands. 'Did you then not betray me for that scoundrel, and are you pure of the sin with which he charged you before the court?' 'Beloved!' whispered Littegarde, pressing his hand to her lips. 'Are you?' cried the Chamberlain, 'are you?' 'As pure as the heart of a newborn child, as the conscience of an absolved penitent, as the body of a nun who has died in the sacristy while taking the veil!' 'Oh almighty God!' cried Herr Friedrich, clasping her knees, 'thank you for saying that! Your words restore me to life, death holds no further terrors for me, and eternity, which only just now I saw extending before me like an ocean of limitless misery, rises again in my sight like a realm filled with a thousand radiant suns!' 'Unhappy man,' said Littegarde, drawing back from him,

'how can you have any faith in my words?' 'Why not?'
asked Herr Friedrich ardently. 'You are mad, you are deluded!' exclaimed Littegarde. 'Did God not give his judgement against me in the sacred ordeal? Were you not
defeated by the Count in that fateful duel, and did he not
prove by combat the truth of what he alleged against me to
the court?' 'Oh my dearest Littegarde,' cried the Chamberlain, 'preserve your senses from despair! Build up, firm as a
rock, the feeling that lives in your heart – hold fast to it and
do not waver, even if earth and heaven should perish
under your feet and over your head! Between two thoughts
that confuse our senses, let us choose the more intelligible,
the more comprehensible one, and before you believe yourself guilty, rather believe that I won the duel I fought for
you! – Oh God, lord of my life,' he added, burying his face
in his hands, 'save my soul too from confusion! As surely
as I hope to be saved, I believe that the sword of my adversary did not defeat me, for though he cast me down in the
dust and trod me under foot, I have risen to life again.
When in faith we invoke the supreme wisdom of God, what
obligation lies upon Him to reveal and pronounce the truth
at that very same instant? Oh Littegarde,' he concluded,
pressing her hand between his, 'in life let us look ahead to
death, and in death to eternity, and hold fast and un-
shakeably to the conviction that your innocence will be
brought to light; by means of the duel I fought for you it
will be brought to the bright radiant light of the sun!' As
he said this the castle warden entered, and reminded Frau
Helena, who sat weeping at a table, that so much emotion
could be harmful to her son; Herr Friedrich therefore let
himself be persuaded by his family to return to his prison,
but he carried with him the sense of having given and received some comfort.

In the meantime, before the tribunal which the Emperor
had set up in Basle, the charge of sinful invocation of divine
judgement by ordeal had been brought against both Herr

Friedrich von Trota and his friend the lady Littegarde von Auerstein, and in accordance with the existing law they had been condemned to an ignominious death by fire at the place where the duel itself had been fought. A deputation of officials was sent to announce this sentence to the prisoners, and it would have been carried out at once, as soon as the Chamberlain was restored to health, if it had not been the Emperor's secret intention that Count Jakob Rotbart, against whom he could not suppress a certain feeling of mistrust, should be present at the execution. But the strange and remarkable fact was that Count Jakob still lay sick of the small and apparently insignificant wound which Herr Friedrich had inflicted on him at the beginning of the duel; an extremely corrupted condition of his bodily humours prevented its healing from day to day and from week to week, and all the skill of the doctors who were gradually called in from the whole of Swabia and Switzerland could not avail to close it. Indeed, a corrosive discharge, of a kind quite unknown to the medical science of those days, began to spread through the whole structure of his hand, eating it away like a cancer right down to the bone; in consequence, to the horror of all his friends, it had become necessary to amputate the entire diseased hand, and later, since even that did not put an end to the purulent corrosion, his entire arm. But this too, although commended as a radical cure, merely had the effect, as could easily have been foreseen nowadays, of increasing the malady instead of relieving it; his whole body gradually began to rot and fester, until the doctors declared that he was past saving and would even die within a week. The Prior of the Augustinian monastery, believing that the terrible hand of God was at work in this unexpected turn of events, vainly urged him to confess the truth concerning his dispute with the Duchess-Regent; the Count, shaken and appalled, once more took the holy sacrament on the truth of his testimony, and with every sign of the utmost terror committed his soul to eternal damnation if he had falsely slandered the lady Littegarde. Now in spite of the viciousness of the Count's habits there were two reasons for believing that this assurance was essentially given in good faith : firstly because the sick man did indeed have a certain piety of disposition which seemed to preclude the swearing of a false oath at such a time, and secondly because the watchmen at Breda Castle, whom he claimed to have bribed to let him in secretly, had been interrogated and had definitely stated that this was correct, and that the Count had in fact been inside Breda Castle on the night of St Remigius. The Prior was therefore almost bound to conclude that the Count himself had been deceived by some unknown third party; and the wretched man, to whom this terrible thought had also occurred when he had heard of the miraculous recovery of the Chamberlain, had not yet reached the point of death when, to his utter despair, the new supposition was fully confirmed. For the reader should know that before the Count had begun to turn lustful eyes on the lady Littegarde he had already for a long time been conducting an improper liaison with Rosalie, her maid-in-waiting; almost every time her mistress paid a visit to him he used to entice this girl, who was a wanton and loose-living creature, into his room at night. Now on the occasion of Littegarde's last stay at his castle with her brothers she had received, as already mentioned, an amorous letter from him declaring his passion for her, and this had aroused the resentment and jealousy of the maid, whom the Count had already neglected for several months. She had had to accompany Littegarde on her immediate departure, but had left behind her a note to the Count in her mistress's name, in which she informed him that the indignation of her brothers at his behaviour made it impossible for them to meet now, but that she invited him to visit her, for the purpose he had in mind, on the night of St Remigius, in the apartments of her father's castle. The Count, delighted at the success of his enterprise, at once wrote a second letter to Littegarde assuring her that he would duly arrive on the night in question, but asking her, in order to avoid any mischance, to send a trustworthy guide to meet him who would lead him to her rooms; and since the chambermaid, who was practised in all sorts of intrigue, had been expecting such a reply, she succeeded in intercepting it, and in another forged letter wrote to him that she would wait for him herself at the garden gate. Then, on the evening before the appointed night, on the pretext that her sister in the country was ill and that she wanted to visit her, she asked Littegarde for leave of absence, and having obtained her consent she in fact, in the late afternoon, left the castle carrying a bundle of belongings and set out in the direction of her home, making sure that everyone saw her do so. But instead of completing this journey she reappeared at the castle at nightfall, on the pretence that a storm was blowing up; and in order, as she said, not to disturb her mistress, as she wanted to start off again early the next morning, she managed to get herself accommodated for the night in one of the empty rooms in the tower, a part of the castle which was neglected and little used. The Count, who was able to get into the castle by bribing the keeper and was admitted at the garden gate at midnight, as agreed, by a veiled woman, suspected nothing, as one may well imagine, of the trick that was being played on him; the girl pressed a fleeting kiss on his lips and led him by way of various stairs and passages in the disused side wing to a room which was one of the finest in the castle itself, and in which she had already carefully shuttered the windows. Here she had taken his hand and made a tour of the doors, listening at each of them with a great air of mystery, and had warned him in a whisper, on the pretext that her brother's bedroom was close by, not to speak a word; whereupon she sank down with him on the bed that stood ready beside them. The Count, mistaking her shape and figure, was intoxicated with delight at having made such a conquest at his age; and when she dismissed him at the first light of

dawn, placing on his finger, as a souvenir of the night that
had passed, a ring which Littegarde had received as a present from her husband and which the maid had stolen
on the previous evening for this very purpose, he promised
her to requite this gift, as soon as he got home, with another
ring which his late wife had presented to him on their
wedding day. And three days later he kept his word, secretly
sending this ring to the castle, where Rosalie was again
skilful enough to intercept it; but being perhaps apprehensive that this adventure might lead him too far, he sent
no further word and found various pretexts for avoiding a
second meeting. Later on, the girl was dismissed on account
of a theft, the suspicion of which rested fairly clearly on
her, and sent back to her parents' home on the Rhine, where
in the course of nine months the consequences of her immoral life became visible; and on being very strictly questioned by her mother she named Count Jakob Rotbart as
the father of her child and disclosed the whole story of her
secret intrigue with him. As to the ring which the Count
had sent her, she had fortunately only been able to offer it
very cautiously for sale, fearing to be taken for a thief,
and in fact its value was so high that she had not found
anyone willing to buy it from her; consequently there could
be no doubt that what she had said was true, and her
parents, relying on this obvious piece of evidence, went to
the courts and brought an action against Count Jakob for
maintenance of the child. The courts, to which the strange
story of the legal proceedings in Basle was already known,
hastened to communicate this discovery to the imperial
tribunal as being of the greatest importance for the outcome
of the case before it; and since an official happened to be
leaving just then for Basle on public business, they gave
him a letter for Count Jakob Rotbart, enclosing the girl's
sworn statement and the ring, in the hope of thus clearing
up the terrible mystery which had become the chief topic
of conversation in the whole of Swabia and Switzerland.

On the very day appointed for the execution of Herr Friedrich and Littegarde, which the Emperor, unaware of the doubts that had arisen in the mind of the Count himself, considered it impossible to postpone any longer, the official with this letter entered the room of the sick man, who was writhing to and fro on his bed in anguish and despair. 'Enough!' cried the Count when he had read the letter and been given the ring, 'I am weary of seeing the light of day! Get me a stretcher,' he added, turning to the Prior, 'and take me out to the place of execution, wretch that I am : my strength is sinking into the dust, but I do not want to die without having performed one just deed!' The Prior, very much moved by this, at once did as he wished and had him lifted by four servants on to a litter; and just as an immense crowd, at the tolling of the bell, were gathering round the stake to which Herr Friedrich and Littegarde had already been bound, he and the wretched Count, who was clutching a crucifix, arrived at the spot. 'Stop!' cried the Prior, as he had the litter set down in front of the Emperor's balcony. 'Before you light that fire, listen to the words of this sinner, for he has something to tell you!' 'What!' cried the Emperor, rising pale as death from his seat, 'has God by his sacred verdict not declared the justice of his cause? And after what has happened how can you dare for one moment to suppose that Littegarde is innocent of the offence with which he charged her?' So saying, he descended from the balcony in amazement; and more than a thousand knights, whom the whole crowd followed down over the benches and barriers, thronged round the sick man's couch. 'Innocent,' replied the Count, half raising himself from it with the Prior's support, 'innocent as the almighty God declared her to be on that fateful day, in the sight of all the assembled citizens of Basle! For he was smitten with three wounds, each one of them mortal, and yet, as you can see, he is flourishing with vitality and strength; whereas one stroke from his hand, which scarcely seemed to touch the outermost surface of my life, has worked its

slow, terrible way through to the very core of it, and has
cut me down in my strength as a storm fells an oak tree.
But in case any doubter should still be unconvinced, here is
the proof: it was her chambermaid Rosalie who received
me on that night of St Remigius, whereas in the delusion
of my senses I, wretch that I am, thought I held in my
arms the lady herself, who has always spurned my advances
with contempt!' The Emperor, hearing these words, stood
as if petrified. Then turning towards the stake he dispatched
a knight, ordering him to ascend the ladder himself and
release the Chamberlain as well as the lady, who had
already swooned in her mother's arms, and to bring them
both before him. 'Well, there is an angel keeping watch over
every hair of your head!' he exclaimed when Littegarde,
with her bosom half bared and her hair dishevelled, approached him with her friend Herr Friedrich, who was himself so moved by this miraculous deliverance that his knees
almost gave way as he led her by the hand through the
crowd of people who made way for them in wonder and
awe. They knelt down before the Emperor, who kissed them
both on the brow; and after asking the Empress for her
ermine cloak and putting it round Littegarde's shoulders,
he took the latter's arm, with all the assembled nobility
looking on, intending to conduct her himself to the apartments of his imperial palace. And as the Chamberlain, too,
was being clad in a plumed hat and knightly robe instead
of the condemned criminal's smock he had been wearing,
the Emperor turned to the Count where he lay wretchedly
tossing to and fro on his litter, and moved by a feeling of
pity, for after all it could not be said that Count Jakob had
entered sinfully or blasphemously into the duel that had
destroyed him, he asked the doctor who stood there whether
there was any chance of saving the unhappy man's life.
'There is none!' answered Jakob Rotbart, shaken by terrible
convulsions and with his head supported on his doctor's
lap, 'and I have deserved the death I now die. For I confess
now, since the arm of earthly justice will no longer reach

me, that I am the murderer of my brother, the noble Duke Wilhelm of Breysach: the villain who shot him down with an arrow from my armoury had been hired by me six weeks earlier to do this deed, by which I hoped to gain the crown!' And upon this declaration the black-hearted reprobate collapsed on to the litter and expired. 'Oh, then it was as my husband the Duke himself suspected!' cried the Regent, who was standing beside the Emperor, for she too had followed the Empress down from the palace balcony to the square. 'He said so to me at the very moment of his death but with broken words which I then scarcely understood!' The Emperor replied in indignation: 'Then the arm of justice shall at least reach your dead body! Take him,' he cried, turning round to the constables, 'and hand him over to the executioners, judged and condemned as he is; to brand his memory with shame let him burn at that same stake where we were about to sacrifice two innocent lives on his behalf!' And thereupon, as the corpse of the wretch burst into crackling red flames and the blast of the north wind scattered and blew it away in all directions, he led the lady Littegarde into the castle, with all his knights following. By an imperial decree he restored to her the inheritance of her father, of which her ungenerous and avaricious brothers had already taken possession; and only three weeks later the wedding of the brave and virtuous lovers took place in the palace at Breysach. The Duchess-Regent, delighted by the whole course the affair had taken, gave a large part of the Count's possessions, which had fallen forfeit to the law, as a bridal present to Littegarde. But the Emperor, after the marriage, awarded a golden chain of honour to Herr Friedrich; and as soon as he returned to Worms after the conclusion of his business in Switzerland, he gave orders that in the statutes governing sacred ordeal by combat, at all points where they assume that such a trial immediately brings guilt to light, the words 'if it be God's will' were to be inserted.

Chronology

1777 *18 October*: Bernd Wilhelm Heinrich von Kleist is born in Frankfurt-an-der-Oder. He is the eldest son of the military officer (Captain) Joachim Friedrich von Kleist and his second wife Juliane Ulrike von Kleist, née von Pannwitz. Heinrich has four siblings: Friederike, Auguste, Leopold and Juliane; he also has two half-sisters, Wilhelmine and Ulrike, from his father's first marriage. Ulrike (1774–1849) would remain close to him throughout most of his life.

The young Kleist is taught by his private tutor Christian Ernst Martini, who recognizes Kleist's curiosity and intellectual drive. He later describes Heinrich as a 'nicht zu dämpfenden Feuergeist' (an undampable mind of fire).

1788 *18 June*: Death of his father. Heinrich is sent to Berlin, where he is educated together with his cousins Wilhelm von Pannwitz and Ernst von Schönfeld by the Huguenot preacher Samuel Heinrich Catel.

1792 *1 June*: Kleist joins the Guard Regiment at Potsdam as a lance-corporal (Gefreiter-Korporal).

1793 *3 February*: Death of his mother.

1793–5 Kleist takes part in the Prussian Rhine campaign against Napoleon. In a military camp at Mainz he reads Christoph Martin Wieland's *Sympathies*, a philosophical work which conveys an optimistic Enlightenment world view. Kleist later describes in a letter how he had read Wieland's work with great enthusiasm and that it had had a formative influence on his own idealistic thinking as a young man. Poem: *The Higher Peace*.

1797 *7 March*: Promotion to the rank of lieutenant.

1798 Kleist's first piece of philosophical writing, *Essay*

*concerning the Sure Way to Find Happiness and Enjoy It without
Blemish, Even Amid Life's Gravest Tribulations* (for his friend
Otto August Rühle von Lilienstern).

1799 After having repeatedly expressed his dissatisfaction
with the career of an army officer (cf. his letter to Martini,
18 and 19 March 1799) Kleist voluntarily resigns his
commission.

10 April: Matriculation at the University of Frankfurt-
an-der-Oder. Until July 1800 Kleist attends lectures on
natural law, mathematics, physics, cultural history and Latin.

1800 Engagement to Wilhelmine von Zenge.

August–October: Journey to Würzburg with his friend Ludwig
Brockes. In his letters Kleist makes oblique references to
the purpose of this journey, which continues to be a matter
of considerable debate among Kleist scholars. For some,
Kleist's remarks suggest that he was suffering from phimosis
and intended to undergo specialist treatment at Würzburg;
others have seen evidence of Kleist's involvement in indus-
trial espionage; others still have supposed that Kleist was
seeking contact with the freemasons in an attempt to find
support for his further education.

November 1800–March 1801: Kleist resides in Berlin and
takes part in the session of the Technical Deputation, a
state-run Prussian institution responsible for overseeing
factories and the development of new technology.

1801 'Kant-Krise' (Kant crisis): In a letter to Wilhelmine
von Zenge dated 22 March Kleist expresses a feeling of
disillusionment after his encounter with the 'new so-
called Kantian philosophy' (*neuere sogenannte Kantische
Philosophie*). He describes himself as having lost his belief
in the value of education and knowledge and as suffering
from a crisis of uncertainty. Kleist abandons his studies
and travels with Ulrike via Dresden to Paris.

July–November: Ulrike and Kleist stay in Paris. A vivid
description of his experiences in Paris can be found in his
letter to Luise von Zenge (16 August 1801).

End of November: Journey to Frankfurt-am-Main, where Kleist and Ulrike part. Kleist continues his journey to Basel and Bern.

1802 Switzerland: From April onwards Kleist lives on the small island of Delosea at Thun in the hope of leading a quiet country life. Wilhelmine cannot be persuaded to join him. Kleist works on his first drama, *The Ghonorez Family* (an early version of *The Schroffenstein Family*). Beginnings of *Guiscard* and *The Broken Jug*.

May: Kleist breaks off the engagement to Wilhelmine.

July to August: Stay in Bern. Illness.

October: Journey to Jena and Weimar together with Ulrike and Ludwig Wieland, the son of Christoph Martin Wieland.

November: First edition of *The Schroffenstein Family* (anonymously published by Geßner in Bern).

Christmas with the Wieland family in Ossmannstedt.

1803 *January–March*: Stay with the Wielands in Ossmannstedt. Work on *Robert Guiscard*, *Amphitryon* and *The Broken Jug*. Wieland's daughter Luise feels strongly attracted to Kleist.

March–April: Stay in Leipzig.

April–July: Stay in Dresden.

July–October: Journey with Ernst von Pfuel to Bern, Thun, Milan, Geneva and Paris. After a long struggle with his work on *Guiscard* Kleist makes a final attempt to finish the drama in September. He burns the manuscript at the end of October.

Journey from Paris to St Omer on the northern coast of France, where Kleist tries to join the French army as it is about to invade England. Physical and psychological breakdown. Kleist is sent back to Prussia by the Prussian envoy Lucchesini.

1804 *9 January*: Debut performance of *The Schroffenstein Family* at Graz. Kleist stays for about four months with Dr Georg Wedekind at Mainz in order to recover from his breakdown. In the meantime, several sojourns in Paris.

June: Returns to Berlin. Kleist is threatened with a charge of high treason on account of his application for foreign military service. In his defence he refers to temporal mental instability, but nonetheless requests employment in the civil service.

1805 *January*: Employment at the ministry of finance.

May: Kleist moves to Königsberg in order to pursue his studies further. He works for the administrative services (*Domänenkammer*) and attends lectures at the university on economics and political science (*Finanz- und Staatswissenschaften*) given by Christian Jakob Kraus. The essay *On the Gradual Formation of Ideas in Speech* probably dates from this period. Begins his work on the first version of *Michael Kohlhaas*.

1806 Work on *The Broken Jug* and, during the summer, on *Penthesilea*.

August: Kleist is ill again and suffers bouts of depression.

Mid August: Leave of absence for medical reasons. Final leave from civil service.

October: Defeat of the Prussian army at Jena and Auerstedt; collapse of the Prussian state.

Kleist finishes his drama *Amphitryon* and the novella *Jeronimo and Josephe* (which is later published as *The Earthquake in Chili*).

1807 With two other former officers Kleist travels from Königsberg through the French occupied areas to Berlin, where he is arrested by the French on suspicion of spying. As a prisoner of war he is brought to the camp Fort de Joux and later to Châlons sur Marne, where he works on *Penthesilea* and *The Marquise of O—*.

May: *Amphitryon* is published by C. Arnold in Dresden.

July: Kleist returns to Dresden after his release from captivity. He associates with the city's intellectual and artistic circles and makes the acquaintance of the romantic philosopher and conservative political thinker Adam Müller, with whom he publishes *Phöbus*, a journal for the arts.

Work on *Käthchen of Heilbronn*.

First publication of *Jeronimo and Josephe*.

1808 *January*: Kleist sends his recently finished *Penthesilea* to Goethe and receives a critical response.

Parts of Kleist's works are published in the *Phöbus* (a fragment of *Penthesilea*, *The Marquise of O*——, parts of *The Broken Jug*, the *Guiscard* fragment, extracts from *Kätchen of Heilbronn* and the beginning of *Michael Kohlhaas*).

March: The first staging of *The Broken Jug* by Goethe at Weimar is a failure. Kleist strongly resents Goethe for having distorted his play and allegedly even expresses the wish to challenge him in a duel.

July: The full-length *Penthesilea* is published by Cotta in Tübingen. The Phöbus project gets into financial difficulties.

Kleist works on his political play *Die Herrmannsschlacht*, which he finishes in December. He hopes that it will stimulate national feelings against foreign (French) rule.

1809 *First half of the year*: Kleist writes patriotic poems and political essays.

March: Last issue of the *Phöbus*.

April: Kleist travels with the historian Friedrich Christoph Dahlmann to Prague and Znaim. In Prague he approaches the Austrian resistance party and plans the edition of an anti-Napoleonic journal (*Germania*). Political essay supporting the Austrian resistance, *On the salvation of Austria* (*Über die Rettung von Österreich*).

1810 *End of January*: Journey to Berlin after a short stay at Frankfurt-am-Main.

March: Four stagings of *Kätchen of Heilbronn* in Vienna.

In the course of this year Kleist finishes an early version of *The Prince of Homburg* and works on a second, extended version of *Michael Kohlhaas*.

September: The first volume of the Tales (*Michael Kohlhaas*, *The Marquise of O*——, *The Earthquake in Chili*) is published by Reimer in Berlin and is presented at the Leipzig book convention.

October–April: Kleist edits Berlin's first popular daily newspaper, *Berliner Abendblätter*.

1811 *February*: Publication of *The Broken Jug* by Reimer in Berlin.

March: Last issue of the *Abendblätter*.

May/June: After the failure of the *Abendblätter* project Kleist's financial situation becomes increasingly desperate. He appeals to the king for a regular pension, but in vain.

June: Suggests that Reimer publish *The Prince of Homburg*. Reimer refuses.

August: Publication of the second volume of the Tales (*The Betrothal in Santo Domingo*, *The Beggarwoman of Locarno*, *The Foundling*, *St Cecilia or the Power of Music*, *The Duel*).

October: Kleist's family at Frankfurt-an-der-Oder refuses to lend him further financial support.

November: Kleist and Henriette Vogel, who is suffering from incurable cancer, plan to commit joint suicide.

21 November: On a small hill overlooking the Wannsee, a lake close to Potsdam, Kleist first shoots Henriette Vogel, then turns the gun upon himself.

Further Reading

Editions

Heinrich von Kleist, *Brandenburger* (1988–1991: *Berliner*) *Ausgabe*, ed. Roland Reuß, Peter Staengle (Basel, Frankfurt-am-Main, 1988–).

Heinrich von Kleist, *Sämtliche Werke*, ed. Helmut Sembdner, 2 vols., 9th edn (Munich, 1993).

Heinrich von Kleist, *Sämtliche Werke und Briefe*, 4 vols., (Frankfurt-am-Main, 1987–97).

General

Brown, Hilda Meldrum, *Heinrich von Kleist: The Ambiguity of Art and the Necessity of Form* (Oxford, 1998).

Ellis, John, *Heinrich von Kleist: Studies in the Character and Meaning of his Writings* (Chapel Hill, NC, 1979).

Graham, Ilse, *Heinrich von Kleist: Word into Flesh: A Poet's Quest for the Symbol* (Berlin and New York, 1977).

Nobile, Nancy, *The School of Days: Heinrich von Kleist and the Traumas of Education* (Detroit, MI, 1999).

Schmidt, Jochen, *Heinrich von Kleist: Die Dramen und Erzählungen in ihrer Epoche* (Darmstadt, 2003).

Stephens, Anthony, *Heinrich von Kleist: The Dramas and Stories* (Oxford and Providence, RI, 1994).

On the Stories

Allan, Séan, *The Stories of Heinrich von Kleist: Fictions of Security* (Rochester, 2001).

Dietrick, Linda, *Prisons and Idylls: Studies in Heinrich von Kleist's Fictional World* (Frankfurt-am-Main, 1985).

Dyer, Denys, *The Stories of Kleist* (London, 1977).

Fischer, Bernd, *Ironische Metaphysik: Die Erzählungen Heinrich von Kleists* (Munich, 1988).

Hinderer, Walter (ed.), *Kleists Erzählungen: Interpretationen* (Stuttgart, 1998).

Marx, Stefanie, *Beispiele des Beispiellosen: Heinrich von Kleists Erzählungen ohne Moral* (Würzburg, 1994).

Michael Kohlhaas

Allen, Seán, "'Der Herr aber, dessen Leib du begehrst, vergab seinem Feind": The Problem of Revenge in Kleist's *Michael Kohlhaas*', *Modern Languages Review*, 92 (1997), 630–42.

Bogdal, Klaus-Michael, *Heinrich von Kleist: Michael Kohlhaas* (Munich, 1981).

Grathoff, Dirk, 'Michael Kohlhaas', in *Kleists Erzählungen: Interpretationen*, ed. Walter Hinderer (Stuttgart, 1998), 43–66.

The Duel

Demeritt, Linda, 'The Role of Reason in Kleist's "Der Zweikampf"', *Colloquia Germanica*, 20 (1987), 38–52.

Neumann, Gerhard, 'Der Zweikampf: Kleist's "einrückendes" Erzählen', in *Kleists Erzählungen: Interpretationen*, ed. Walter Hinderer (Stuttgart, 1998), 216–46.

The Earthquake in Chili

Hamacher, Werner, 'Das Beben der Darstellung', in *Positionen der Literaturwissenschaft*, ed. David Wellbery (Munich, 1985), 149–73.

Oellers, Nobert, 'Das Erdbeben in Chili', in *Kleists Erzählungen:*

Interpretationen, ed. Walter Hinderer (Stuttgart, 1998), 85–110.

St Cecilia or the Power of Music

Haase, Donald P., and Freudenberg, Rachel, 'Power, Truth and Interpretation: The Hermeneutic Act and Kleists "Die Heilige Cäcilie"', *Deutsche Vierteljahrsschrift*, 60 (1986), 88–103.

Laurs, Axel, 'Narrative Strategy in Kleist's "Die Heilige Cäcilie"', *Australasian Universities Modern Languages Association* (1983), 220–33.

The Betrothal in Santo Domingo

Brittnacher, Hans, 'Das Opfer der Anmut: Die schöne Seele und das Erhabene in Kleists *Die Verlobung in St. Domingo*', *Aurora*, 54 (1994), 167–89.

Werlen, Hansjakob, 'Seduction and Betrayal: Race and Gender in Kleist's *Verlobung in St. Domingo*', *Monatshefte für deutschen Unterricht, deutsche Sprache und Literatur*, 84 (1992), 459–71.

The Foundling

Newman, Gail M., 'Family Violence in Heinrich von Kleist's *Der Findling*', *Colloquia Germanica*, 29 (1996), 287–302.

Ryder, Frank G., 'Kleist's "Findling": Oedipus manqué?', *Modern Languages Notes*, 92 (1977), 509–25.

Schröder, Jürgen, 'Kleists Novelle "Der Findling": Ein Plädoyer für Nicolo', *Kleistjahrbuch* (1985), 109–27.

The Marquise of O—

Cohn, Dorrit, 'Kleist's "Marquise von O." and the Problem of Knowledge', *Monatshefte*, 67 (1975), 129–44.

Swales, Erika, 'The Beleaguered Citadel: A Study of Kleist's Die Marquise von O . . .', *Deutsche Vierteljahrsschrift für Literaturwissenschaft und Geistesgeschichte*, 51 (1977), 129–47.

Weiss, Hermann F., 'Precarious Idylls: The Relationship between Father and Daughter in Heinrich von Kleist's Die Marquise von O.', *Modern Languages Notes*, 91 (1976), 538–42.

THE STORY OF PENGUIN CLASSICS

Before 1946 ...'Classics' are mainly the domain of academics and students, without readable editions for everyone else. This all changes when a little-known classicist, E. V. Rieu, presents Penguin founder Allen Lane with the translation of Homer's *Odyssey* that he has been working on and reading to his wife Nelly in his spare time.

1946 *The Odyssey* becomes the first Penguin Classic published, and promptly sells three million copies. Suddenly, classic books are no longer for the privileged few.

1950s Rieu, now series editor, turns to professional writers for the best modern, readable translations, including Dorothy L. Sayers's *Inferno* and Robert Graves's *The Twelve Caesars*, which revives the salacious original.

1960s The Classics are given the distinctive black jackets that have remained a constant throughout the series's various looks. Rieu retires in 1964, hailing the Penguin Classics list as 'the greatest educative force of the 20th century'.

1970s A new generation of translators arrives to swell the Penguin Classics ranks, and the list grows to encompass more philosophy, religion, science, history and politics.

1980s The Penguin American Library joins the Classics stable, with titles such as *The Last of the Mohicans* safeguarded. Penguin Classics now offers the most comprehensive library of world literature available.

1990s The launch of Penguin Audiobooks brings the classics to a listening audience for the first time, and in 1999 the launch of the Penguin Classics website takes them online to a larger global readership than ever before.

The 21st Century Penguin Classics are rejacketed for the first time in nearly twenty years. This world famous series now consists of more than 1300 titles, making the widest range of the best books ever written available to millions – and constantly redefining the meaning of what makes a 'classic'.

The Odyssey continues ...

The best books ever written

PENGUIN (🐧) CLASSICS

SINCE 1946

Find out more at www.penguinclassics.com